THE ITALIAN

T L SWAN

For my Family

GRATITUDE

The quality of being thankful;

Readiness to show appreciation for and to return kindness.

Trust in the universe.
It always delivers.

1

Olivia

I STARE up at the sign above the door, and I smile.

When in Rome

That's me, in Rome, loving myself sick.

The weather is warm, the scenery is breathtaking, and Rome is everything I dreamt it would be.

I'm in week two of a five-week Italian vacation. I've been to Venice and I've been to Tuscany. I may also be in the middle of a small midlife crisis, but whatever. It's forced me out of my comfort zone and into this Heaven, so I'll take it.

I push open the dark, heavy, timber door, and I walk into the bar and restaurant. It's dusk outside, and the restaurant is large with a huge back garden area. Fairy lights are lighting up the space, and it has a party feel to it with jovial laughter echoing loudly around me. A three-piece band are playing at the front, and the place is a hive of activity. One man is singing, while two others play guitar. I can't understand what they're saying but I don't need to. It sounds so good—*so Italian.*

I take a seat at a table for two outside in the courtyard.

"Buona sera." The waiter grins as he approaches.

I smile nervously. "Do you speak English?"

"Ah, yes, Madame. How can I help you?"

I quickly peruse the menu. "May I have a Prosecco, please?"

"Ottimo." He nods and takes off in the direction of the bar, leaving me to look around in wonder at the gorgeous surroundings.

Everything is exaggerated in Italy. The hand gestures, the laughing, the story telling.

The beauty of the language. I could sit and listen to people speak Italian all day, and I have done so for fourteen days straight now.

It's been the best trip. I thought I would have been nervous traveling on my own, but I've found an inner bravery I didn't know I had. I've eaten out every night by myself, and I haven't once felt self-conscious or unsafe. The people are all so lovely and friendly that I feel totally at home.

I glance around the crowded bar and see people drinking, laughing, and having the time of their lives. I find myself smiling as I watch them talk with their friends.

The waiter comes back with an entire bottle of Prosecco, and my face falls. Oh jeez,

I meant a glass, not the whole damn bottle. I'm going to have to pace myself.

I watch on as he pours me a glass. "Grazie." I smile.

He nods as he gestures to the food menu. "I back soon, okay?"

"Yes, okay." I open my menu and look down at the choices as he runs off to tend to other customers.

Everything is written in Italian. Some choices I can make out, and others I have no idea about. I look at the people at the tables around me to see what they are eating.

There's pizza, pasta, something in a hot pot. Everything does look delicious, though. I look up to the bar and stare straight into the eyes of a man. I didn't notice him before. He's standing with a group of men. He's huge, towering above the others around him. His black hair has a little length to it, with a curl, and his eyes are dark. Those eyes are unmistakably locked on me, and he doesn't look away. Instead, he dips his head and gives me a slow, sexy smile.

My stomach flips—his gaze is intense… hungry.

Is he doing that to me, or is his girlfriend behind me?

I sip my drink and casually look at the surrounding tables. I drag my eyes back to my menu and scan back through the choices. He has me flustered from just one look. From my peripheral vision, I feel him still watching me, and I glance back over.

Our eyes meet and he smiles again, prompting me to give him a reaction. I have no idea if he's smiling at me or not, but I decide to play along with the fantasy that is him.

I give a weak smile, and then in slow motion his lips curl into the sexiest damn smile I've ever seen. How can a smile be so fucking sexy?

He's absolutely drop dead gorgeous—tall, dark, exotic. He's everything I'm not.

I look back down at my menu.

Focus fool.

Abbacchio alla Cacciatora

Abbacchio Brodettato
Bistecca Fiorentina
Braciole
Braciolone
Bresaola
Brodo
Cacciatore

I frown as I look down at the choices, and I turn the page. A million delicious things on the menu, and I'm about to no doubt order something crap that I'll hate.

I glance back up to the Italian Stallion and he's gone. My heart drops.

"Looking for me?" I hear a deep voice say from behind me.

I jump and turn and see him standing behind me. "W-what?" I stammer as I stare up at the god.

His eyes hold mine. "I asked if you were looking for me."

I stare at him, electricity zaps through the air between us. I'm unable to think because of his close proximity. He's even more delicious up close, if that's even possible.

"Ahh." I pick up my drink and take a big gulp. "No, actually."

He chuckles, the sound deep and raspy. It does things to my insides.

He holds out his hand for me to take. "My name is Enrico Ferrara."

I place my hand into his. Its big, warm, and holy hell, is this happening?

Enrico sounds *so exotic.*

"I've been watching you from the bar," he says with a heavy accent.

"You have?"

"Do you need some help?"

Help with what? Kissing? Undressing? Unzipping your trousers?

Stop it.

He smirks to himself as if knowing exactly what I was thinking. "Help with the menu." He gestures to the menu in my hand. "I saw you frowning while reading it."

"Oh, of course." I giggle nervously and drain my glass. *Idiot.* "Yes, that would be great, thank you."

He sits down opposite me and steeples his hands under his chin. His eyes are assessing me. "Come ti chiami?"

I don't know what he just said, but fuck, it sounded good. "I don't speak Italian, I'm sorry."

"What is your name?" he repeats in English.

"Oh." I shake my head, flustered. Honestly, this guy needs to go away, I'm embarrassing myself here. "Olivia Reynolds."

He picks up my hand across the table and slowly kisses the backs of my fingers, leaving me to watch on. "Olivia," he purrs. "What a beautiful name."

Oh jeez. "Thank you."

We stare at each other, and my heart is beating hard in my chest from the feeling of his lips. A trace of a smile crosses his mouth, and he's clearly amused by my physical reaction to him.

Annoyed with myself, I snatch my hand away and open my menu. Unexpectedly, he does the same.

"What would you like to eat, bella?"

You. I would like to eat you. "What would you suggest?" I ask casually as I pretend to read through the choices. I can't see a thing. I have double vision from the smell of his aftershave. Why does he smell so good?

He raises his brow at me. "You like meat?"

I swallow the lump in my throat. "Yes."

His eyes drop to my lips, and I feel my insides clench.

Okay...what the actual hell is going on here? This guy is insanely sexual.

"When was your last meal?"

I look up into his stare...what are we talking about here? Food? Sex? It's been twelve hours since food and twelve months since sex.

I'm basically fucking starving in all areas. "Too long."

Arousal flares in his eyes, and I know in that very second that we *are* talking about sex.

He sits back and steeples his hands under his chin again. "You're beautiful. Where are you from?"

"Australia."

"Where is your man?"

I frown. "I haven't met him yet."

Our eyes lock as tension bounces between us. I've never encountered a sexual attraction to someone like this before. You read about it, but it's never actually happened to me.

I break the silence. "Where is your... other half?"

"I don't have one."

"Oh." I pretend to read the menu once more.

"What are you doing in Rome?" he asks.

"I'm on vacation."

"Alone?"

"No. My girlfriends are back at the hotel," I lie. Rule 101: never tell anyone you are travelling alone. See, Mom, I do remember some rules.

"Why are you here alone... in this bar?"

"You're very nosey." He frowns as if not understanding the term. "Inquisitive," I add.

"I don't understand."

"You want to know everything."

He breaks out into a broad beautiful smile. "I do." He reaches over and picks up a piece of my shoulder length, honey-blonde hair. "So fair," he says. "Is your hair fair like this everywhere?"

I swallow the lump in my throat as my heart has an epileptic fit.

He smiles as if fascinated and takes my face in his hands. "Blue eyes."

"The opposite to you," I breathe.

"Opposites attract." His eyes drop to my lips again.

Okay, what the actual fuck is going on here?

I pull out of his grip and open the menu in a fluster. "The food," I remind him.

He sits back, clearly annoyed that I pulled away from him. "I already know what you are eating tonight."

"You do?"

His eyes hold mine. "And so do you."

I begin to hear my heartbeat pounding in my ears. Is he thinking what I'm thinking? "What's that?"

"Pasta."

"Pasta?" I frown.

"Yes, of course. What did you think I meant?"

I giggle and refill my glass.

"What were you thinking, Olivia?"

"I don't know. You have me all flustered."

He frowns. "Flustered?" I can see him trying to translate the word. "Like a chicken? You mean plucked?"

I laugh. "Yes, plucked like a chicken."

He smiles and holds his glass up to clink it with mine. "I hope to pluck you many more times tonight, Olivia."

The word play between P and F has never been so high. I

smile goofily as we stare at each other, electricity buzzes between us, our glasses touch.

I need to change the subject. "What do you do for work, Enrico?"

"Poliziotto."

"Huh?"

"Policeman?"

"Ah." I smile. "Law enforcer."

"Yes."

I feel myself relax a little. If he's a policeman, I'm safe.

A man approaches the table and says something in Italian. Enrico answers him, and then turns to me.

"Olivia, meet my brother Andrea."

"Hello." I smile as we shake hands.

"Hello, nice to meet you." He smiles. He's slightly younger than Enrico, but with the same gorgeous bloodline: dark hair, olive skin, and big brown eyes. He, too, is deliciously handsome, though in a completely different way to his brother. He seems softer but the family resemblance is strong.

"Andrea is a doctor here in Rome," Enrico says proudly.

"Oh, wow, that's amazing." I begin to feel at ease. He's a cop and his brother is a doctor. Maybe Enrico isn't a serial killer after all.

"Thank you. Are you English?" Andrea asks.

"Australian."

"Ah, I see." He smiles and turns to his brother. "Are you coming with me, Rico, or are you staying? I have to go now. I have work in the morning."

Rico. They call him Rico. *I like that.*

Enrico's eyes come back to me. "No, I'm going to eat pasta with Olivia, and then show her why I'm the best dancer in all of Italy."

Andrea rolls his eyes, and I smile into my drink.

Sounds so fun.

"All right then, good luck, Miss Olivia." Andrea bends to kiss my cheeks. "You will need it. It was nice to meet you."

"Goodbye, Andrea."

He disappears, and Enrico turns back to me with a satisfied smile. "What am I feeding you, bella? You need energy for dancing."

I giggle and open my menu, this is the best night of my life. "Pasta," I remind him.

"Ah, yes." His eyes dance with delight. "That's right. Pasta it is."

"So, tell me about yourself." He drops his chin onto his hand as his elbow rests on the table. "What is the Olivia Reynolds story?"

We've eaten, drank two bottles of wine, and now we're sitting in the darkened courtyard, fairy lights are lighting up the space and the music now soft and romantic. I'm feeling very tipsy indeed.

"Well." I sip my wine. "I'm here on a holiday... I guess to try and find myself."

"Are you lost?"

"Perhaps." I smile bashfully across the table at him.

"Why?"

"I don't know." I contemplate his question. "I feel like I'm searching for something, but I don't know what it is yet. I'm here to try and figure that out."

He gives me a slow sexy smile. "Maybe it's me. Maybe you're looking for an Enrico Ferrara?"

"Oh yes, that's the logical answer, how many of you are there?" I giggle.

"Just one." He smiles. "One is enough."

"How long have you lived in Rome?"

"About ten years. I moved here when I joined the police force. Where do you live in Australia?"

"Sydney. Have you ever been?"

"No, it's on my list, though. I don't travel far."

"Really, why not? I love to travel."

"I prefer Italy. I travel around Europe regularly, but Australia is a long way from here. How long does it take to travel there by plane?"

"Twenty-one hours."

"Twenty-one hours," he scoffs. "On a plane? You must be crazy, woman."

I giggle at his horror. "We're used to it. Australia is on the opposite side of the world from everywhere. If we want to travel, it's a twenty-four-hour plane trip to most places. That, combined with the terrible jetlag from time zones, it turns a lot of people off."

He frowns and sips his drink. "Do you work at home?"

"Yes, I'm a fashion designer."

He smiles, as if surprised. "Really?"

"Uh-huh."

"What do you design?"

I shrug, embarrassed. "Well, I'm designing pyjamas at the moment for Kmart."

"Kmart?" He frowns.

"It's a department store."

"What pyjamas would you put me in?" he asks. I watch his tongue dart out as he sips his drink, and my sex clenches in appreciation.

"I don't think pyjamas would do you justice. I imagine your birthday suit is enough."

His eyes have a tender glow to them as he watches me, and my heart constricts in my chest. He really is a beautiful man.

Embarrassed by my forwardness, I change the subject. "But it's only temporary. I would love to work in fashion one day. That's the ultimate dream."

"Who's your favorite designer?"

"Umm, let's see." I narrow my eyes. "Valentino or Dolce and Gabbana."

"And you've applied to both of those houses?"

"Yes. Nothing back from them yet, though."

"One day," he replies.

I smile. "One day."

"Finish your drink, bella. I'm taking you dancing."

"Bella?" I frown. God, he doesn't even remember my name.

He takes my hand over the table and lifts it to his mouth. "Bella means beautiful."

He kisses my fingertips. "And you really are very beautiful, Olivia. I can't take my eyes off of you."

Oh, I like him.

"To be honest, I'm having a hard time staying on my side of the table. I want us to dance so I can have you in my arms," he says softly.

Nerves dance in my stomach. "Then take me dancing, Mr. Ferrara," I whisper.

He smiles darkly, tips his head back, and he drains his glass. "Let's go."

Three hours later and the room is spinning to the sound of my laughter. Enrico and I are dancing and he's throwing me around like a rag doll. He is holding me by the hand and is spinning me around and around.

We've drunk way too much, and now it's late—3:00 a.m., to be precise—and we've come to our third bar of the night. I don't remember the last time I laughed so much. He's funny, smart, and seriously gorgeous. He's also making me feel like the most beautiful woman in the world.

I couldn't tell you if anyone else is here, because all I can see is him.

He's the epitome of tall, dark, and handsome, with his square jaw, dark, wavy hair, and the biggest brown eyes I have ever seen. His lips are pouty and a beautiful shade of red. He has this joyfulness that seeps out of him, as if he doesn't have a care in the world. His laugh is loud, echoing, and his voice has a deep huskiness that speaks to something deep inside of me.

A slow song comes on. Enrico pulls me close and wraps his arms around me. "Finally," he whispers as he kisses my temple.

"Finally?" I smile, liking the way his lips feel on me.

"Finally, a slow song that allows me to hold you close."

He towers above me. He's so tall that I only come up to his shoulder. One of my hands is in his, while he holds me by the waist with his other. The air between us is electric. My heart is pumping hard and fast.

What would it be like to have sex with a virile, intense man like this?

Imagine fucking him.

A deep ache begins to grow inside of me. I can feel myself getting wet as my need for his body grows. Enrico slowly dips his head, and his lips softly dust mine, his tongue gently asking for permission to enter my mouth. I grant him access. His kiss is slow and erotic, and it does things to me as I get a visual of him on top of me. Naked. Fucking me hard—so hard. Our bodies wet with perspiration. I'm aching for him to touch me.

His hand tightens around my waist, pulling me closer as we kiss. I lose control and my hands go to his hair, bringing him closer to me.

For fifteen minutes, we stand on the dancefloor, kissing like we are the only people in the room. I can feel his hard cock up against my stomach. His eyes have darkened to nearly black, and I can feel the want in his vice-like grip.

He's different to any man I've ever met. It could be the whole Italian thing, of course, but I feel like it's more than that. There's more to him than meets the eye. Perhaps that's just my inexperience with gorgeous men speaking. Maybe all players make women feel like this. Maybe it's a spell that only a few men know how to cast.

A special kind of black magic.

Suddenly, achingly aware that I'm dripping wet and acting like a horny ho, I whisper, "I should get going."

His eyes hold mine, and some kind of silent acknowledgement runs between us. He bends and kisses me softly, a promise of more.

After a beat, he replies, "I'll walk you home."

Half an hour later, we arrive at my hotel, hand in hand. "This is me," I say nervously.

He turns toward me, takes my face in his hands, and he kisses me again, waiting for an invitation to come in. Our lips dance as my mind runs at a million miles a minute. Visions of us naked together play like a perfect porno in my mind.

But... I can't. I can't do it. As much as I want to, I can't sleep with a stranger. It's not who I am.

Damn you, conscience.

"It was nice meeting you," I say.

His face falls as he stares at me, his chest rising and falling as he battles his arousal.

"I'm sorry," I whisper. "I…" I hesitate, because damn, saying it out loud seems so lame. "I'm not the type of girl who sleeps around."

Tenderness crosses his face but he remains silent.

"You make me wish I was." I smile bashfully.

We kiss, and then he holds our foreheads together as we both try to come down from our high.

"Can I see you tomorrow?" he asks. "I have the weekend off. I can take you sightseeing."

"Really?"

He takes a step back from me, creating distance, and I know he's trying to calm his throbbing body down.

"Okay." I smile.

"I'll pick you up at ten?"

I look at my watch. "That's only six hours away."

His eyes dance with mischief. "I know. It seems stupid to go all the way home. I can just stay here until then."

I giggle. "Nice try. Go home, Ricki."

He chuckles, and with one last lingering kiss, he opens the front door of my hotel. I walk in, trying to act cool and hide the over the top smile on my face.

I turn back to him through the glass. He has his hands tucked in his pockets as he watches me. I give him a wave, and he blows me a kiss. I get into the elevator with my heart jumping all over the place. I smile broadly at my reflection in the elevator mirrored wall.

Holy shit…. what the hell just happened?

2

Olivia

THERE'S KNOCKING at the door. It grows louder.

Knock, knock, knock.

Huh?

I lift my heavy head from my pillow. What's that?

The knocking continues. What the hell? Who's at the fucking door at this ungodly hour. I roll over to retrieve my phone.

8:30 a.m

I wince in disgust.

The knocking is getting harder now—more urgent.

Shit, what if the buildings on fire? I sit up with a start.

"Coming!" I call.

I walk to the door and peek through the tiny hole to see Enrico standing in the hall.

What the heck?

I keep the chain on, open the door, and peer through the crack.

"Good morning, Olivia." He smiles proudly.

"What...?" I pause and drag my hand through my hair self-consciously. I must look appalling. "What are you doing here?"

"I'm here for our date."

"I thought you said ten?" I frown.

"I couldn't wait."

I stare at him, looking all perky and like he's had a million hours sleep, while I look like roadkill. "I'm not ready. I just woke up."

"That's fine." He smirks and bounces on his toes. "I can wait."

I glance around my messy room. "Give me a moment."

I slam the door shut in his face and run like a mad woman, stuffing all of my things back into my suitcase. I glance down at myself wearing only panties and a singlet. This won't do. I throw on a dress, and I run into the bathroom to brush my teeth, while trying my hardest to wipe the mascara from under my eyes.

He couldn't wait.

A thrill runs through me, and I smile as I brush my teeth with vigor. I rush back out and see a pair of panties that have fallen out of my suitcase. I pick them up and quickly stuff them under my pillow.

Right.

I drop my shoulders as I try to calm myself down before I open the door, acting completely calm.

Rico smiles knowingly. "Hello."

"Hi." I smirk. God, he really is delicious. "Please, come in."

He walks past me and looks around my room.

"You do know it's 8:34, right?" I mutter dryly.

"I do." He stands, not knowing where to sit. He's wearing blue jeans that fit snug to his thighs and a white T-shirt. His dark hair is messed up, and his big red lips are completely kissable. He's basically sex on legs.

"We only went to bed five hours ago. Why are you looking all perky?" I gesture to his gorgeousness.

He drops his hands to his hips. "Perky? What is that word?"

I scratch my nest-hair. "Eager."

His eyes dance with mischief. "I am eager. I thought we could have breakfast together."

I stare at him, unsure if a date with someone who has this much energy this early is really a wise thing. "I have to shower first. Do you want to go and get a coffee or something? I'll be about twenty minutes."

"No. I'll wait." He drops to sit on my bed.

I stare at him. I need to dig through my suitcase to try and find the perfect outfit, and I have no idea how to do that while he's sitting there watching me.

"Umm." I glance over at my suitcase.

"I'll wait out on the balcony, shall I?"

"Yes," I say, relieved. "Do that." I open the door, and he walks out. He sits down at the small table overlooking the street. "Play with your phone or something," I tell him.

Delight dances in his eyes as he watches me. "Okay."

I walk back into the room and unzip my suitcase, what I really want to do is do a handstand on my bed or something.

Holy shit, is this really happening?

I rustle through my clothes—all crumpled and messy. Why don't I have something ironed, for fuck's sake? What will I wear?

"What are we doing today?" I call.

"Everything!" he calls back.

Everything. I poke my head around the corner. "Define everything."

He looks up and our eyes meet. My breath catches. I think he's the most beautiful man I have ever laid eyes on.

"Swimming," he eventually says.

I frown. "Swimming?"

"Among other things. I thought we could do some sight-seeing on my motorbike, and then go for a drive down to the beach this afternoon."

My eyes widen. "You have a motorbike?"

"I do. Do you like motorbikes."

"I *love* motorbikes."

"Me, too."

"This sounds fun," I beam.

"That's me." He throws me a cheeky wink. "Mr. Fun."

I giggle because we both know that's an appalling lie, he's Mr. Intense, not Mr. Fun.

"If you say so," I tease. I walk back inside and do another little jig to myself. This is the best day of my frigging life.

I grab my things and head into the shower, trying to be as quick as I can because I know he's waiting.

He's waiting… *for me.*

Ten minutes later, I come back out into the room in denim shorts and a pale pink T-shirt to find my bed made and my panties laid out. I stare at them, mortified. They're the ones I stuffed under my pillow when he arrived.

I turn to him. "You made my bed?"

"Yes."

"Why?"

His eyes hold mine, dark and dangerous. "I wanted to."

I swallow the lump in my throat.

"I found these under your pillow." He picks them up and twirls them around on his finger. "Did you take them off last night when you were alone in bed?"

I open my mouth to say something but no words come out.

He steps forward, closer to me. "Did you touch yourself last night when you got back from our date?"

I frown. I have two options here. One, go along with his notion that I'm a sexy ho...or two, shatter his dreams and tell him I'm a slob who left my panties on the floor. "Did you?" I fire back, unable to push a lie past my lips.

He steps forward again. "I did."

The air crackles between us.

"And?" I whisper.

"I blew three times." His dark eyes hold mine. "Seems that you're quite the aphrodisiac, Miss Olivia Reynolds."

The air leaves my lungs as I imagine him alone in the dark, pleasuring himself.

Dear God.

He runs his fingertips down my cheek, and I stare up at him. His gaze drops to my lips, and my sex clenches.

Kiss me.

Enrico cups my face and grabs a handful of my hair.

Kiss me.

He places his thumb under my bottom lip and opens my mouth slightly as if imagining something. A frown mars his face as he stares at my open mouth.

Kiss me, goddamn it.

He seems to suddenly refocus and then blinks once. "We should get going. Breakfast is waiting." He steps back from me.

Wait, what? Where's my kiss?

"Okay, sure." I grab my purse and supplies, and I turn to him in a fluster. "I'm ready, are you?"

He smirks, knowing full well that I was waiting for him to kiss me. "Oh, I'm ready. Let's go Olivia."

———

"Table for two, please," Enrico asks the waiter.

"This way, please," the Italian waiter replies.

We follow him through the restaurant and out of a door that opens up to a courtyard. The ground is made of cobblestones, and colorful flowers light up the area in large pots. Its quaint and cute.

The waiter pulls out my chair. "Thank you." Rico sits down opposite me.

"Can I get you something to drink?" the waiter asks.

Rico looks over at me. "Would you like an espresso, Olivia?"

I scan the menu quickly. I don't think my poor hungover stomach can handle a strong coffee this morning. "I'll have an English breakfast tea, please."

The waiter smiles and scribbles down my order.

"I'll have an espresso with an extra shot of coffee," Rico says.

"Thank you."

The waiter leaves us alone, and nerves bubble in my stomach again.

Rico pours us both a glass of water. "You look beautiful today."

I smile. "Liar." I rearrange the napkin on my lap. "I'm feeling very secondhand."

He frowns, not understanding what I mean.

"I feel hungover from last night. I feel a little sick," I clarify.

"Oh." He smiles. "I see." He opens the menu and peruses the choices, and I do the same. "What are you having?"

In order to feel better, I need full fat and double of everything. But then in order to get Rico to kiss me, I need to appear less pig-like.

"Maybe fruit?" I lie, testing the water. I'm so not getting fruit but I'll ease into the conversation with that.

He frowns as he reads. "You should eat something hearty. It will make you feel better."

"Okay." Well, that plan worked fabulously. "If you insist." I look over the choices. "What are you having?"

"Granola and fruit."

"You know, I make a wonderful granola," I say proudly. "I roast it myself." I don't make much, but I do make that.

"Do you?" He raises his brow. "Well, I hope that one day you will make it for me."

I shrug casually, as if super-hot guys ask for my granola every day. "I'll see what I can do."

He chuckles, and his eyes linger on my face. Nerves dance in my stomach under his gaze. I've never spent time with a man who's this good looking before. Enrico simply oozes sex appeal, and it's not missionary style sex appeal, either. I'm talking bone-shattering, wet with perspiration, fuck you into oblivion kind of sex. The stuff you see on cable and think about for weeks.

"Can I take your order?" the waiter asks.

Rico gestures to me. Such a gentleman. "I will have the avocado and eggs, please." I frown because I want something sweet, too.

The waiter looks to Rico. "And you, sir?"

"She's not finished," he mutters, unimpressed with the waiter dismissing me.

“Oh, apologies.” The waiter turns back to me. “Will that be all?”

I’m flustered that they’re both watching me. “I was just going to get something sweet, but it doesn’t matter.”

“Get the...” Rico quickly scans the menu. “The Maritozzo.”

I shrug. “Sure. Sounds good.”

“I’ll have the granola with a bowl of fruit on the side.” He folds the menus and gives them back to the waiter, and we watch as he disappears out of sight.

Rico sits back and rubs his pointer over his lips as he watches me. It’s as if he’s assessing me.

“What?” I smile.

“Nothing.” He sips his water. “Just admiring the scenery.”

I feel my cheeks flush with embarrassment, and I really want to ask him what he was imagining last night when he was pulling his dick. Of course, I won’t.

“Do you come here often?” I ask.

“First time. My apartment is on the other side of town. Old Rome.”

“It’s a beautiful city, isn’t it?”

“I love it here.”

“Do you live alone?”

“I do now. My brother Andrea and I used to live together but we haven’t for five or six years. He lives near the hospital now.”

“You have just the one brother?”

“No, I have another brother, Matteo. He lives in France at the moment. He’s a scientist and is working with a pharmaceutical company doing research.”

“Wow.” I smile. “A doctor, a scientist, and a policeman. Your parents must be proud.”

"I have a sister, too. Francesca. She's only fifteen." He smiles wistfully, and I can tell he has a soft spot for her.

"Three big brothers to protect her." I widen my eyes. "Lucky girl."

He chuckles as our drinks arrive. "Thank you," Rico says to the waiter before he turns back to me. "Francesca doesn't think so. Apparently, we're the bane of her existence."

I giggle, imagining being on the wrong side of Enrico. What a nightmare that would be.

"What about you? Where do you live?" he asks.

"I live in Sydney."

"Who with?"

"Alone."

His face falls. "You live alone?"

"Yes."

"How old are you?"

"Twenty-seven. How old are you?"

"I'm thirty-two."

"Old," I say.

He chuckles and his eyes linger on my face again. "So, you..." He stops himself.

"Go ahead. Ask whatever you wanted to."

"You have just come out of a relationship?"

I shrug. "Yes and no."

"What does that mean?"

"I broke up with my childhood sweetheart when I was twenty-four, and then..." I pause, embarrassed. "Then I met my next boyfriend and I was with him for a couple of years. We broke up over a year ago."

Our breakfast arrives. It looks amazing as the waiter puts it down in front of us. "Grazie." I smile before we are left alone again.

Rico looks back up at me. “Why did you break up with the last boyfriend?”

“He wasn’t the one.”

“Who broke it off?”

“I did.”

He picks up his coffee and sips it, seemingly mollified.

“Why are you still single, Rico?”

“I haven’t had a serious girlfriend in years.”

“Why not?”

“I guess I wasn’t ready to settle down.” He pauses and then shrugs. “I don’t know.”

Alarm bells start to go off. *Player.*

Feeling brave, I blurt out, “Do you sleep around?”

He holds his cutlery mid-air, clearly surprised by my question. “Would it matter if I did?”

“Not really, but it would give me an indication as to who you are.”

“Do you think that the number of people you sleep with determines what kind of person you are?”

“Maybe.”

“In that case, how many men have you had sex with?”

“Two.”

He stares at me, and then blinks. Whether that’s in shock, horror, or awe, I can’t work out.

“Two?” he gasps.

I bite my bottom lip to stop myself from laughing. “Does that scare you?”

He picks up his coffee and takes a huge gulp before he finally responds. “Should it?’

“Not at all. I’m just super fussy. I have impossibly high ideals when it comes to men.” I bat my eyelashes to try and be cute.

He smirks as if pleased with my answer.

"You didn't answer my question, Rico," I tease as I cut into my toast.

"That's because I'm choosing to avoid it."

I giggle. "You just answered it anyway."

He smiles broadly and gives me a cheeky wink.

The energy between us suddenly becomes playful and light. He's a player. I'm a good girl. The boundaries are set. No false pretenses.

"So, where are you taking me on the back of your bike today, Mr. Ferrara?"

He gives me the best come fuck me look I've ever seen. "Somewhere you've never been before."

The air crackles between us, and I get the feeling my good girl image just became his ultimate challenge. Nervous butterflies dance in my stomach.

He takes a spoonful of granola. "When in Rome, Olivia."

"Do as the Romans do?"

"Or." He shrugs casually. "Just do the Romans."

"Oh, that's witty." I giggle.

He chuckles. "You like that?"

"You're such a romantic."

"It comes naturally." He raises his coffee cup to me, and I laugh out loud.

"Lucky me."

We've been to the Ostia Antica ruins, The Coliseum, and around the eclectic streets of Rome. The roar of the engine echoes as Rico's motorbike pulls to a slow stop at the parking lot of the beach. It's around 3:00 p.m. in the afternoon and the sun is high in the sky. I cling to his broad back. My legs are tucked around him, and the day has been dreamy.

We've laughed, talked, and I have to admit that Enrico Ferrara is one hell of a tour guide. Although, half of the time as he spoke about the attractions, I was just staring at his lips, imagining them on me. Imagining being the key word because, well, he hasn't fucking touched me all day. Not once.

He hasn't held my hand, grazed my arm with his, or anything. I've clung to his back on this motorbike like the groupie that I am, sure, but other than that... nothing. There has been no kissing at all. Not even a peck.

What the hell is going on?

Last night we kissed all night, he was all over me. Couldn't get enough, today.... nothing. Maybe he doesn't like me anymore.

Maybe I blurted out too much information about myself this morning. Damn it, why did I tell him my pathetic number of lovers? He probably thinks I'm a dud.

And he would be right. Who has two fucking lovers? Losers, that's who.

I am getting sick of being the good girl all the damn time. What I wouldn't give to be wild and free for once.

Rico pulls the motorbike to a stop, and I slowly climb off the back and step onto the road. He turns to me and takes my helmet off. I hold my breath, and he smiles down at me. Does he know what I'm thinking?

"The bathrooms are over there if you want to get changed." He gestures to the restroom.

"Okay, thanks." I make my way to the bathroom and into the cubicle to put on my white string bikini. My hands shake nervously. I try and stretch the fabric over my behind, but this bikini feels so freaking small now that I have to go out there in it. I put my face into my hands. I'm a ball of nervous energy. He has me tied in knots.

I take out my phone and text my best friend Natalie. She'll probably be at work but this is the first time I've had a moment alone to text her about last night… and today. Holy crap, there's a lot to tell her.

Hi, I'm at the beach in a bikini.
Been on the back of a god's motorbike all day, sight-seeing.
I'm totally loving Rome xoxoxox

I hit send.

"Okay, let's do this," I whisper out loud to myself. I exhale heavily and fake confidence before I walk out to the beach.

Rico is waiting for me, wearing black shorts… only shorts. He's super tall and has a broad chest with a scattering of black hair covering it. His tanned, olive skin is rippled with muscle. I count his six pack of abs. I stop still on the spot as my breath catches.

Holy fuckballs.

Rico's eyes drop down my nearly naked body and he bites his bottom lip to hide his smile. "Hello," he purrs.

"Hi," I breathe as the air leaves my lungs.

"Nice swimsuit." He raises a brow.

I adjust the top to try and cover more of my boob. "Thanks. It felt bigger in the store."

He drops his head, as if stopping himself from saying something he shouldn't. "Shall we go over here?"

"Uh-huh."

He gestures for me to walk in front of him, and I die a little. Oh, God, he wants to watch my behind as I walk. It's going to be jiggling to hell.

"No, after you, I insist," I say.

He smirks, and we walk side-by-side over to the beach. "Do you want to get a deck chair?"

"I'm happy to lie on the sand."

He stares at me for a beat. "On your back on the sand it is."

That statement sounded so sexual that it's just ridiculous.

We find a spot, and he lays out the two towels before he lies down on one. I sit beside him. He closes his eyes and puts his face up to the sun. "Sol has been good to us."

I slide down beside him. "Who?"

"Sol, the god of the sun."

I smile dreamily as I close my eyes. "How do you know so much about your country's history? You've rattled off everything today like a professional tour guide."

"It interests me."

"Thank you for today. It's been amazing. I appreciate you taking the time to show me around."

"The day is not over yet, bella," he murmurs with his eyes closed.

I stare at him for a moment. Why hasn't he touched me?

"Can I ask you something?"

"Anything."

"Is there something wrong?"

"No, why?"

"You haven't touched me today," I whisper.

His eyes come over to me, and he rolls on his side to face me. "Why do you think I'm lying here with my eyes closed?" He picks up my hand and kisses my fingertips. "I haven't touched you today because I know that if I did, I may not be able to stop. My attraction to you, Olivia, is stronger than I am."

I smile softly.

"I dragged myself from your side last night, and then when I got home…" His eyes darken and drop to my lips. "I jerked off for two hours trying to get my cock to go down. He wanted you *so fucking bad*."

My brows rise. "How did that go?" I whisper.

"My hand definitely wasn't you, and my cock definitely isn't satisfied."

"Jesus, Rico," I whisper. "Don't mince your words, will you?"

"Why would I?"

I stare at him as the air swirls between us. I want him. I want every hard inch of this gorgeous man. To hell with being a good girl. I've never had a one-night stand, and damn it, I deserve one. This can be a hall pass from my annoying conscience. I know I'm never going to see him again, and that's okay. I want him, and screw this, I'm having him. He can always be that beautiful man I met in Italy—the one from another world.

I grab my sunscreen and hand Rico the bottle. "Can you put sunscreen on me, please?" I ask.

He licks his lips. "You're playing with fire."

Our eyes are locked.

"When in Rome, right?" I raise my brow, and then I roll onto my stomach as excitement begins to tear through my system. I'm really doing this. I can almost hear my lady parts all cheering in a mosh pit somewhere from deep inside. After a beat, I hear the sunscreen bottle being squeezed, and I close my eyes. It's an oil-based sunscreen. My heart is beating so hard. I hear his hands rub together, and then I feel him straddle my behind. The weight of his body on top of mine pushes me into the sand and wakes up a demon inside of me. He's heavy, broad, and… oh, fuck…

He unfastens my bikini top, and I scrunch my eyes shut against the towel. Shit!

His hands slide up my back in a strong, slow motion, and

my sex clenches with appreciation. His fingers drift up and over my shoulders, and then down my sides, skimming the sides of my breasts. Goosebumps scatter across my skin.

I can't breathe.

He nudges forward and I feel his erection up against my behind. My heart freefalls from my chest. Oh, fuck yeah. God, he feels good.

Calm down, calm down, calm down, I repeat over and over in my head.

I can't calm the fuck down, though, because a god has his hands on me and I'm about to have an oily orgasm in public.

It's been way too long.

I close my eyes as his hands explore every inch of my back and legs.

"Roll over, baby."

Baby! That sounds good.

I hold my bikini top to my breasts and roll onto my back. His eyes are dark and filled with desire. He reapplies sunscreen to his hand and leans on his elbow beside me before he begins to run more oil into my body. I scrunch my eyes shut.

Filled with nerves, I can't watch his face as he studies me this way for the first time. He rubs his palms over my stomach, down over my hipbones, and my inner thighs.

I have to concentrate hard on not spreading my legs like every instinct is screaming at me to do.

"Olivia," he whispers. "Creamy, white, perfect skin." His voice is almost a purr and it does things to my insides. "These curves." He hisses in approval, and his hand slides under my bikini top as he cups my breast, momentarily losing focus.

"The sun doesn't reach there." I smile.

"Ah." He pulls his hand out. "That's right, sorry. I got carried away."

I giggle, and I hear the oil being poured out again.

"Don't I have enough on?" I ask.

"No, I'll probably have to do this all day." His hand falls back to my stomach, moving in circles.

I laugh and feel myself begin to relax..... *oh, I really like him.* I know I could go into this weekend being shy and mousy with a stranger—which is what I would normally do—but it always ends the same way with every guy. We meet, go along happily, but when push comes to shove, I block him out and push him away. I've had many opportunities over the years to sleep around. I've just never felt the need before. This time feels different, and perhaps I could go into this weekend pretending that I already know Rico better than I really do.

I love sex. I love making love. I love everything about the beautiful male body. Damn, I've missed it. I may have only been with two men, but they spoilt me sexually. They were the best teachers a girl could have ever asked for. I was sexually compatible with both of them, and it broke my heart that neither of them could hold me mentally. I loved both for different reasons, but I never felt complete, not even when I was safely in their arms. Something has always been missing in my life; an invisible barrier, holding me back from moving forward. I don't know if it's my career, lack of travel or experience. Perhaps it's what my best friend Natalie thinks, and I really do have a hang up I have from my childhood after living through a divorce.

Maybe I'll never get over my disappointment from my parents' divorce. I don't know. It was a case of *it's me, not you* with both of them.

They were perfect... just not perfect for me.

I'm brought back to the moment as Rico's hand skims my hip bone, and he inhales sharply. I can feel his arousal through his hands, he's on the edge.

Why does it feel so good driving a man wild with need for my body?

The power is like a drug to my system, and screw it, I'm going to make it my mission to make him insane. I may just be another notch on his Italian bedpost, but I'm going to make sure he remembers me. I'm going to get an axe and chop his fucking bedpost down. I arch my back and spread my legs a little.

"It's been so long since I've been touched," I whisper.

Rico's eyes darken and his lips slowly part. I know he's imagining touching me there. "How long?" he breathes.

"Over twelve months."

He frowns, as if puzzled by the notion. "How the fuck do you go without sex for twelve months, Olivia?"

I love the way he says my name. With his accent, he says it with four syllables.

Ol-liv-i-a.

I arch my back again. "With great difficulty," I whisper as I stare up at him. I can feel my sex as it throbs. Aching...

"You're making it very hard for me to behave," he mutters as his hand slides underneath my bikini top once more. My nipple peaks with excitement, and he rolls it between his fingertips.

"Maybe I don't want you to," I whisper.

"Maybe I need to take you home."

"Maybe you do."

He leans down and his lips take mine. His tongue slowly slides through my mouth with just the right amount of pressure.

Fuck.

I could come. Just from his kiss, I could come.

We kiss again, this time with more urgency, and he leans over so I can feel his erection against my hip.

I want to drive him wild. I want to drive him wild in public.

Game on.

"Let's go swimming," I breathe. I stand and pull him to his feet with one hand. The tip of his cock is peeking over the top of his shorts. It's pink, broad, and holy fucking shit, I've never seen anything so perfect. Unable to help it, I smile and kiss him as I tuck him back in. My libido hits fever pitch. She begins to warm up, knowing that a marathon is on its way.

Enrico and I walk down to the water. The beach is nearly empty with only a few people swimming down the other end. We wade in up to our necks. The water is fresh and salty, and Rico takes me into his arms and wraps my legs around his waist. My hands roam up and over his broad shoulders as we float. I can feel every muscle on his cut body. We kiss softly, enjoying the feel of each other's bodies.

I'm like a feather in his arms.

Our kiss turns desperate as he grinds my sex onto his swollen cock.

I can't hear, I can't see. I can only feel him and his magical body beneath my hands.

Unable to help it, I reach down and slide the front of his shorts down. I want to feel him. I want to feel what I'm about to have.

He's large. My hand hardly fits around him, and I can feel every vein on his engorged length. My insides clench, and I whimper in appreciation.

He falls still, and we stare at each other as I slowly stroke him.

"Don't come until I say so," I breathe.

He smiles darkly as if amused by my request. "You trying to top from the bottom, baby."

I pull him hard, and his eyes close as he almost loses his

footing. "From where I'm standing Rico, it's you that's trying to top from the bottom."

He chuckles and pumps my hand hard. His eyes flicker with a level of arousal that I've never seen in a man before. "I'll come when I'm fucking ready," he growls.

My insides begin to liquefy. Holy fucking fuck. He's off-the-hook hot.

We get into a rhythm; I pull, he pumps. Our lips are locked, and I don't know if anyone is watching us or what we look like from land, but I don't care.

I want this. I want to blow Rico Ferrara's mind in the Mediterranean Sea.

His eyes are closed, and his hands fall limp on my hips. I know he's close. He can't function. His breathing is ragged, and he keeps pumping in an orgasm-induced stupor. I smile against his lips, proud of myself. Who knew I was capable of being this wild and spontaneous? I reach down with my other hand to cups his balls. I bring them up as I tighten my grip on his cock.

He shudders with a moan. I stroke him hard again, and his eyes flicker.

I put my mouth to his ear. "You can come now, Rici," I whisper. "You have my permission."

He grabs my hair at the nape and drags my face to his. "This isn't how it works, Olivia. I'm in control of the orgasms here."

"But are you?" I laugh. I pump him hard, and he tips his head back as he loses control and jerks forward to come in a rush. I continue to stroke him as I empty him. His breathing is labored now. His eyes are rolling back in his head.

And I am triumphant.

Take *that* on your bedpost.

His kiss is tender and soft, and he holds his forehead to mine as he comes back to Earth.

"Jesus fucking Christ, Olivia," he pants.

I kiss him and push back to swim away on my back. I spread my arms out and float beneath the sun. I feel euphoric—on cloud nine.

Enrico stands still, watching me. He seems shocked… or perhaps confused. I can't read him but it's a look I haven't seen before. He swims over to me and scoops me up into his arms to kiss me tenderly. "Let's go home." His touch is gentle, tame for the moment.

I smile against his lips as I brush the hair back from his forehead. "No, I want to drink margaritas and lie in the sun. Let's enjoy each other's company for a while longer."

He inhales sharply as he stares at me. "What kind of goddess are you, Olivia Reynolds?"

"The Ferrara Goddess," I tease.

He laughs out loud. It's deep and permeating and it echoes through the air. Rico grabs my behind and pulls me closer. "Never a truer word has been spoken."

The air swirls between us, "You called me Rici."

"Felt right."

He smiles darkly, "Yes… yes, it did."

Five hours later, we arrive at my hotel room.

We sprawled out beneath the sun until it went down. We drank margaritas and had a beautiful seafood dinner. The day is already perfect. Rico has been itching to get me home. It's eating him that he was the first to come and that I haven't… yet.

I eventually open the door with his lips pressed to the back of my neck. Like a pair of teenagers, we can't stop kissing. He's like this perfect version of the male species—one that I can't get enough of.

We walk into my room and the atmosphere instantly changes between us.

Carefree laughter falls serious, and our kiss intensifies. Nothing stands between us now. Without hesitation, he reaches down and lifts my sundress over my head. He stands and steps back, his eyes dropping down my body as I stand here in my bikini. He slowly circles me, and his eyes drink in every inch. I close my eyes.

What if he doesn't like what he sees?

I drop my head and stare at the floor. The intensity of this situation is too much to bear.

"La donna più bella che abbia mai visto." He pauses for a moment and then as if realizing that I can't understand him says. "Olivia, look at me."

I drag my eyes up to meet his.

He cups my face in his hand. "You are the most beautiful woman I have ever seen. Every inch is pale and perfect."

I swallow the lump in my throat.

With his eyes following his movements, he runs his hand over my collarbone. He unfastens my bikini top and throws it to the side. His hand cups my breast.

He slowly bends, kisses each one, and then takes my nipple in his mouth. My breasts are more than a handful for him. He hisses in appreciation. "Magnificent."

Magnificent.

My breath quivers as I try to hold it together.

He kisses lower, over my stomach before moving down.

I close my eyes again.

Jesus Christ, I did not think this is how a one-night stand

was going to feel. I thought it was all *wham bam* fucking in the dark.

He leans lower and drops his head to my sex, and there, he inhales deeply. His eyes close, his face filled with pleasure.

"Dolce Madre di Dio, sto per leccarti." He looks up at me while on his knees. I have no idea what he just said, but by the look in his eye, I know it was filthy. And it sounded fucking good.

He stands to kiss me. It's deep, long, and hard. Rico walks me backward across the room, and he guides me down onto my side on top of the mattress. My legs are hanging over the side.

I frown in question, and he picks up my foot to kiss it. "Relax, bella."

My insides melt as I watch him.

There's no mistaking who's in charge this time. He may have momentarily lost his head at the beach, but we both know he likes to be in control.

He stands between my legs and slowly removes my bikini bottoms. He smiles darkly as he sees the small patch of fair hair there.

"You weren't lying to me. You are blonde everywhere."

He dusts the backs of his fingertips through my short hair. With dark eyes, he pushes one leg to the side, and then puts my other foot onto his shoulder.

Dear God, I'm wide open for him. He's hardly touched me and I'm about to come.

"Hai mai avuto un grande uomo prima?"

"Speak English so I can understand," I whisper.

He pauses for a moment as if contemplating translating what he just said to me. "I need to watch your face when I do this." He runs his hand down the back of my thigh that is on his shoulder, and he circles his fingertips through the lips of my sex. Our eyes are locked, and he slowly slides two thick fingers inside me.

I clench as my back arches off the bed. Rico hisses his approval. He lets out a low guttural moan, slowly takes his fingers out, and then slides them back in.

The sound of my arousal fills the room.

"Oh God," I whisper. This is ridiculous. I'm completely open and he's still fully dressed. "Take your clothes off."

He keeps pumping me with his fingers, completely distracted by his task.

"Rici," I demand. "Clothes off. Now."

He takes his shirt off over his head and my breath catches. I know I spent the day staring at him, but I've never seen a man like this. Rippled with muscle, his chest is broad with dark hair. There's olive skin, a six pack of abs, and that distinct V that disappears into his shorts. Still looking at me, he slides his shorts down, and my eyes widen as I swallow a lump of fear.

He chuckles at my reaction.

"I... I..." Holy shit, I have no words for that dick.

"You'll be fine," he whispers darkly.

Will I? Will I really, though? Or will they read about me in some kind of travel no-no brochure in years to come. Pasty white Aussie girl gets fucked by Italian stallion and dies on the stake... literally.

Rico begins to work me, first with two fingers, and then with three. I see stars as I lose all my inhibitions. My legs hang limp for him, granting him an all access pass.

I grab the blanket in my hands beneath me, and within a few pumps, I shudder as I begin to feel the oncoming freight train.

Not yet... not yet.

Hold it.

Please hold it.

Fuck you, sex deprivation. I can't be this uncool and come in four minutes flat.

But I do, and I see stars. I cry out to the sound of his voice whispering things in Italian. After that, it all becomes a blur.

I hear a packet tear open, and I watch him roll on the condom. He lifts my other leg to his chest and slowly feeds himself into me. His eyes are locked on the place that we meet. My mouth hangs open at his claiming, and he smiles down at me.

"Ouch," I whimper. I begin to thrash beneath him as the pressure become too much. "Rici."

"Sei nata per cavalcare questo cazzo. Prendilo." I frown in question. "It's okay, it's okay." He leans down and kisses me. "I'm being careful. I'll let you get used to me first. I won't hurt you." I wince. "Olivia."

I close my eyes as the burn of his possession becomes almost too much.

"Look at me," he whispers.

I drag my eyes up to his.

"Open up and let me in. I need you." His voice is hushed and calming.

As if my body only bows to his command, she opens a little, and he pushes forward.

"Kiss me," I plead, reaching for him.

He falls down over me and stares at me for a moment as he brushes the hair back from my forehead. An unexpected tenderness runs between us, and his lips softly take mine in his as he pushes all the way in.

We stay still, my heart racing at his possession. Our kiss turns frantic. Oh God, I need him, too.

"Sono rovinato," he whispers.

"What?" I pant.

He smiles against my lips. "I'm ruined, Olivia."

I lift my pelvis. "I haven't started ruining you yet, Mr. Ferrara."

He chuckles and pumps me hard. "Oh, yes, you fucking have." He lifts me, and pulls out slowly before he pushes back in slowly. The sting of his large cock stretching me wide open is almost unbearable. We go slow for a while, staring at each other in awe. I've never had sex like this before. I've never been completely owned like this.

He begins to ride me with hard, punishing hits. The bed is hitting the wall, his teeth are on my neck, his hands are holding my legs back… his large cock is deep inside of me, stroking me —stretching me. He's taking what he needs from my body.

Some men make love but Enrico Ferrara fucks.

He's strong and hard… so hard.

The sound of my arousal sucking him in is loud. Our skin slapping together echoes around the room.

I'm tight and he's big, but somehow it works between us. We're like animals as we fuck. Nothing could stop us from taking what we need from each other.

"Fuck, fuck, fuck," he moans. "No not yet," he pants. I smile, knowing he's trying to hold off his orgasm and can't.

I love that he can't.

"Fuck me," I pant against his lips. "Harder."

He lifts my hips and holds himself deep. He jerks hard as he comes in a rush, his throbbing cock sending shockwaves through my body as I clench around him.

We both cry out and come together.

And then he kisses me. It's soft, loving, and tender. It causes my heart to freefall from my chest.

He's got things the wrong way around.

It's me who's now ruined.

The sun peeks through the side of the drapes, and I frown as I wake.

I feel the warmth of a large hand on my stomach and look over in surprise.

Rici is on his side, facing me, fast asleep, looking like an Adonis. His dark curls and olive skin are a stark contrast to the white bedlinen.

I move my leg and wince. Oh fuck, I'm sore. Sorer than sore.

He may have been gentle with me the first time, the other three times, not so much.

He fucked me till I was raw.

The man is an animal *and* a god.

I go to the bathroom, throw a long shirt on, and then I hop back into bed while the room is still darkened. Enrico slowly wakes and then as if acting on instinct, grabs me and pulls my body to his. He kisses me softly with his big bee-stung lips. "Good morning, my Olivia." His voice is husky.

Now *that's* a wake-up hello. "Good morning."

He holds me tight and runs his lips over my temple. "What a night, hey?"

I smile, embarrassed at how crazy he got me. I turned into an animal. I kiss his chest. "Sex with you is incredible... and different."

He pulls back to look at me. "Different? How is it different?"

"Well." I pause as I try to articulate my thoughts. "I've only ever had sex with someone I have been in love with before."

He smirks, amused by my statement. His hand trails up over

my shoulder, and he tames my hair down. "This was *better* different, then?"

"I wouldn't say better. Just different."

"I beg to differ. No sex could be better than what we had last night. That was the gold medal of sex." He bites my neck and scooches down lower in the bed to snuggle into my chest.

I laugh and kiss his forehead. It's weird how comfortable we are with each other. This isn't how I imagined a one-night stand to be at all. I thought it would be cold and clinical.

His eyes dance with mischief as he leans his head on my breast. "Explain this in-love sex thing to me."

I run my fingers through his hair. "Well, there's a feeling that runs between the two of you."

"Boredom?" he mutters dryly.

I laugh out loud. "No."

"Oh, let me guess," he teases. "So, you love him, and he loves you. You feel like you can't live without the other, and you call each other ten times a day to talk about boring shit. You only have sex with each other, always missionary style, and everything is planned beforehand. Oh, I can't even talk about it without falling asleep." He bites my nipple hard. I flinch as I giggle at his answer.

"No, that's not it."

"What, then?"

I brush the hair black back from his forehead. His big brown eyes look up at me as they wait for my answer. "It's having someone love you and all your faults, even when you forget to love yourself."

He stares at me and I smile softly. "Well, that's obviously why I never fell in love before."

"What is?"

"I don't have any faults, and nobody could love me better

than I already love myself." He bites my nipple hard, and then drops down to nip my hip bones. I squeal with laughter.

I fight to pull his head up. "You idiot. I could totally make you fall in love with me if I wanted to."

He laughs against my stomach as he trails his teeth lower. "If you say so."

"I'm not joking." I squeal as I try escape his onslaught. He bites my inner thigh and I struggle. He pulls my sex apart with his fingers and we both fall silent as the mood suddenly changes from playful to intense.

"There's one part of you that I really do love," he whispers before kissing me there with an open mouth. My sex clenches.

Oh.... he's just so.

His tongue swipes through my open flesh, and I close my eyes as I run my fingers through his curly hair. He lifts my legs and puts them over his shoulders. He licks me again and I feel his breath on my most private parts. Goosebumps scatter up my legs.

"I should warn you... if you do that to me you will never be the same. I will ruin you for all other women."

"Undoubtedly." He laughs, and I smile up at the ceiling.

He licks me again, this time deeper and with the flat of his thick tongue. My toes curl. My hands cling to his muscular shoulders.

Wow.

I fucking love Rome.

An hour later, I lean up against the tiles in the shower as Rico rubs his soapy hands all over as he washes me. I'm sleepy, sated, and damn if I haven't just had the best night of my life. He takes care of me and washes my legs, my sex, my behind, and then moves around behind me to wash my back.

I smile dreamily with my eyes closed. "Can you move to Australia and become my slave?"

He moves my hair to one side and kisses my neck tenderly. "Now, there's an idea."

His soapy hands roam over my breasts and stomach. He has explored every inch of my body, as if memorizing it. "What are your plans?" he asks.

"What do you mean?"

"When do you leave?"

"Monday morning. I'm meeting my friend Natalie in Sorrento and we're travelling through the Amalfi Coast for two weeks. After that, I come back to Rome for a few days before flying home."

"You know... one night really isn't enough to get the full Roman experience."

I smile. "Oh really?"

His lips slide to my neck again. "You should probably come back to my house for the weekend."

I bite my lip to hide my smile. "And why would I do that?"

"To clean my bathroom."

I burst out laughing and spin back to him. Suddenly, we fall serious. "You want me to stay with you?" He nods, and I run my fingers through his two-day stubble.

"I should warn you," I begin.

"I know. If you clean my bathroom I will be ruined for other women."

I laugh out loud. I wasn't going to say that at all. "Precisely."

3

Olivia

I STARE at the exotic building in front of us. It has cream-colored rendering with a beautiful terracotta tiled roof.

"You live here?" I frown.

"Uh-huh," Rico says as he pays the driver. They begin to speak to each other in Italian.

We had to catch an Uber here to bring my suitcase. We'll pick up his motorbike later.

He takes my hand and helps me out of the car.

"Grazie," he calls.

The building is swanky with a big garden and a circular driveway. I look around in shock. This is not where I would have expected him to live at all.

He leads me through the fancy metal gates and up toward the huge double doors. "Who do you live here with?" I ask.

"By myself."

"So, this is an apartment?"

"I guess."

"You guess?"

We arrive at a set of huge, black double doors. The round, brass door knocker is about the size of my head.

"In Italy, we call it a penthouse." He pushes the door open and a large, sweeping staircase comes into view. There's an elevator to the side of the foyer. "I live on the second floor."

I stare at him, confused. "So, other people live here, too?"

"No, the other two apartments are empty." He leads me into the elevator by the hand. "My grandfather owns this building. The other penthouses are for when he and my father are in town."

I look around at the marble floors and smoke-mirrored walls. Jeez, he must come from money. "They don't live here in Rome?" I ask.

"They live on country estates."

"Together?" I ask as we walk up the stairs.

"No, they have separate properties that they live in with their wives, my mother, and my grandmother."

"That's nice." I smile as we continue up the steps. "Your family are all still together?"

He turns, surprised by my statement. "What do you mean?"

"I mean, your parents and grandparents are all still married?"

"Of course," he scoffs. "Ferrara's marry for life. Family is everything to us."

I shake my head, embarrassed that I just sounded so blasé about divorce. My parents divorced when I was a small child, and both have since divorced again. That's my normality. We get to the first floor and he takes his keys out. "My parents are divorced," I announce.

He frowns as he stares at me. "And you think this is a good thing?"

"No, but it is what it is." I shrug. "I can't change it."

He raises his eyebrows as he stares at me and I have no idea what he's thinking. He opens the door and my eyes widen at what I see. Holy shit.

"Are you serious?" I whisper as my eyes fly around the space.

This isn't money. This is over the fucking top luxury. It's like a palace, only way better. Above us are gilded gold and hand painted ceilings. The floors are covered in huge Persian rugs, contrasting with gorgeous, dark wood antique furniture. The colors are rich and exotic—almost historical.

It looks like the Vatican or some shit. "You live here?" I squeak.

He smiles at my reaction and walks in. He carelessly chucks his keys onto the counter, as if it's just a normal side table and not some two-thousand-year-old artefact.

"Yes." He puts his hands onto his hips as he looks around, unimpressed.

"Jeez." I feel the blood drain from my face.

"I don't notice it. I've grown up in homes like this, so it has no..." He pauses for a moment. "It's my normal. It's just a house. I would prefer modern furnishings, but this is a family property, so I make do."

"Make do?" I scoff. "Enrico, this is not making do. This is—"

"What?"

I stop myself before I say something insulting. *Spoilt brat* comes to mind. "Your grandfather owns this?"

He takes my hand and leads me through the apartment. "Yes."

"What does he do?"

"He owns multiple businesses—my father, too."

"Oh." I frown as I look around.

There's a huge living area that looks like something out of a movie. It's filled with deep red velvet couches, and there are antiques everywhere. The artwork alone is incredible. It's all very stuffy. We pass through a formal dining room, and I count the chairs at the huge table. Twenty! There are twenty fucking chairs at the table.

"What kind of businesses?" I ask. Does he own Amazon or some shit?

"He manufactures sports cars. He owns a football team. He owns a lot of properties. He has many different avenues of income."

The kitchen is made of black marble with a huge island counter in the middle. We walk down the hall and into another living room. It's a little less formal but still out of this world. We pass a gymnasium, five bedrooms, and I've lost count of all the bathrooms.

I feel ill.

Thank God he isn't coming to my shitty one-bedroom apartment in Sydney. If only he knew what a pauper he was sleeping with, he'd probably run for the hills. It took me a year just to save for this trip. I really *should* be cleaning his fucking bathroom.

"And this is my bedroom." He opens a door at the end of the hall, and I smile in relief.

This is more like it.

It's modern in here. There's a large king-sized bed covered with white linen. Bright abstract artwork sits on the walls, and there's an airy sitting room to the right with a brown leather couch and television. Huge palms in terracotta pots are dotted throughout the space. An all-white bathroom is to the left, which has a huge stone bath and a double shower inside it. The place is homey, and so much more like what I expected from him.

"I live mostly in here," he says.

"You don't like the rest of the apartment?"

"I do. I wouldn't have it like that if it were mine, but I can't change it. This building and the furnishings have been in our family for centuries."

"How long have you lived here alone?" I ask as I walk around his room looking at things.

"Ten years." He takes me into his arms. "Where do you want to go today?"

"Anywhere with you."

The wind in my face makes me smile. Rico's hand is protectively on my thigh as he drives. I kiss his shoulder, and I'm filled with happiness.

I've had the best day ever.

We've been driving around on his motorcycle. We went out for lunch and had a lazy afternoon sightseeing around Rome.

He is the tour guide of all tour guides. We've laughed and talked, and I think he may just be the most beautiful man I've ever met.

He's gorgeous, that goes without saying, but there's more to him than meets the eye. Sure, he's an Italian stallion, and yes, he has a fuckable package, but I actually like talking to him. He's interesting, intelligent, funny, and sexy as all hell. I imagine every woman he meets falls madly in love with him.

I can see why.

Not that I'll ever tell him that. He has enough confidence for all of Rome. I don't need to add to his ego.

But even I have to admit, every minute with this man is a gift.

A twinge of regret kicks in. Why, oh why does he have to live in fucking Italy?

I just have to make the most of it.

The memory of Rici Ferrara will be my ultimate souvenir.

He's someone I'll always remember.

The candlelight flickers across our faces, and I smile at the man sitting opposite me. Ironically, we are in an Italian restaurant having dinner. We spent the early evening in bed. Determined to make every second of our weekend count, he dragged me out to dinner. I was happy being naked in bed. Toast would have been fine for dinner if it were up to me.

"Tell me again what you do for work? I forget, I was blinded by your beauty the other night," he says. "I know you said design, but for what?"

I smile. "I design pyjamas," I remind him.

"You have your own shop?"

"No. I design for Kmart."

"Kmart?"

"It's an Australian department store."

"Oh." He raises his brows. "How did you train for this job?"

"I went to design school. I never imagined that this is the job I would end up with."

"Why not?"

"I always wanted to design for a fashion label like Gucci, Hermes, or Chanel."

He swirls his wine around in his glass. "Why don't you?"

"I don't know." I exhale heavily. "I have tried but I know jobs are ridiculously hard to get with that kind of label. I mean, it's not that I don't love my job, because I do. It's just not what I imagined. You know?"

He nods. "I never thought I would end up being a policeman."

"Really?" I ask, surprised. "Isn't that the kind of job kids want to do all their lives?"

He chuckles. "I guess."

"Your bruschetta," the waiter says as he puts our entrees onto the table in front of us.

"Grazie."

Rico dishes out my serve and then his. He likes to be in control. Not that I mind at all. It's nice having him fuss over me.

"Why did you become a policeman then?" I ask. "It's not something that you fall into by accident."

"My father wanted me to do it."

"Really?"

"Yes, he wanted me to get some life experience. He got me an interview through one of his friends. I didn't have my heart set on anything else, so I humored him and thought that I could always leave later if I didn't like it."

"What did you want to do?"

"I only ever wanted to be happy. A job won't do that for me."

What a wonderful thing to aspire for. I lean onto my hand and smile goofily across the table at him.

"What?" He smirks.

"You know, for a fuck boy, you really are quite endearing."

He laughs in surprise. "A fuck boy?" He puts his hand on his stomach and really laughs, and I find myself laughing too. Other people in the restaurant look over at our table.

"What?" I ask.

"I have never been called that before. Even when I was a boy, I was never called that." His eyes dance with delight. "You really are quite the surprise package, Olivia."

I lift his hand to my lips and kiss his fingertips, his eyes have a tender glow to them as he watches me.

"Wait until you see me clean your bathroom." I smile.

He chuckles again. "I look forward to it."

"I have a surprise for you tonight," Rico says as he lies down beside me on his bed.

I sit up onto my elbow.

"What?"

It's Sunday morning, and he has been on the phone organizing something. He's been speaking Italian, though, so I have no idea what is going on.

He grins. "Let's just say that I think you'll be pleased with me."

We stare at each other as something runs between us. It's been there since last night when we made love—a tenderness. A feeling of closeness. It's unexpected and disarming.

Does he feel it, too?

I'm being completely myself and he likes me as I am. I feel cherished. I feel cared for and desired, and damn it, why the fuck does he live in Italy?

"What's the surprise?" I ask to change the direction of my thoughts.

"It happens at 11:00 p.m."

"I'm intrigued. Why that time?"

"That's the time that the gods choose." He rolls me over onto my back and smiles down at me.

"Are you going to fuck me at 11:11," I tease. "Is that what the gods want?"

He laughs out loud and it's a beautiful sound. "No, I'm going to fuck you at 12:11. 11:11 is for something else—something better."

I giggle as his lips touch mine. "Nothing could be that good."

It's 11:00 p.m. and I'm standing at the side door of the Pantheon.

Enrico is behind me, and I am encased by his protective arms. We've had another amazing day and this is his surprise for me.

"Rici," I whisper up at him.

"Yes?"

"I love this surprise already."

He gently kisses my lips.

I have no idea what it is. The Pantheon isn't even open, but it's cool just being here in this greatness.

The door opens and a man comes into view. He's wearing a suit and seems important. He bows his head. "Enrico, my child, come in."

I bite my lip. "What the hell?" I whisper as we follow the man.

The Pantheon is lit up with candles and spotlights. It's perfect.

It's like something out of a movie.

Rico turns to me and takes my hands in his. "Tonight, Olivia, we get to speak to the gods."

"What?"

"Through centuries, this has been my family's tradition. We each have a turn. It wasn't my year, but I swapped with someone so you could experience this, too."

"Rici," I whisper in wonder. My eyes roam around the huge round space, at the marble columns and the beautiful flooring.

"Pantheon means honor of gods, and it is the best preserved Roman monument," he says. "It's over two thousand years old and still has the original flooring and marble."

My eyes follow his voice as he points to the marble statues that stand around as if guarding the magnificence.

"It is the tomb to many of our great Italians. Vittorio Emmanuelle II. Umberto and his queen Margherita. Rafael and his lover."

He looks down at me and I rise up onto my toes to kiss him. "Thank you for bringing me here."

"The Oculus." He points to the ceiling. I look up and my mouth falls open in wonder. A circular hole in the ceiling is open, meaning I can see the clouds in the sky.

"Is that open?" I ask.

"Yes."

"Does the rain get in here?"

"Yes, the floor is sloped and has drainage."

"It's incredible," I whisper.

He looks at his watch. "Come, it's almost time." He takes my hands and he leads me to the center of the room to stand on a marked spot.

"At 11:11 on the 21st of April every year, the moon shines through the Oculus and creates a beam of light. It is said that, in that light, you speak with the gods."

I look up at the ceiling and then back at him. "Wait, that's today."

"We get to speak to the gods, Olivia."

"What?" I whisper.

"When the moonlight shines on us, you need to say your truth."

I stare at him. "What do you mean?"

"I go first and speak my truth to the gods. After that, you tell them yours."

"Are you serious?"

He holds my hands in his and we stare up at the opening in the ceiling above, waiting for the moonlight.

This is the most incredible thing I've ever done… ever seen.

We wait and wait and wait, and then suddenly, the moonlight dances off the mirrors around the room, shining directly down on us like a magical beam.

We stare at each other.

"What's your truth, Enrico?" I whisper.

He clenches his jaw and frowns, as if troubled by what he's about to say. "I don't think our story ends here."

Tears threaten to form as I stare at him, because this is magical and perfect and how the hell is this real? *Does he feel it, too?*

"Now your truth, Olivia," he whispers.

I pause. What the hell do I say?

"Hurry, bella," he urges.

I stare at him. "I think our story is just beginning."

In a perfect moment of clarity, hope fills me. Enrico takes me into his arms and kisses me in the light… and just as quickly as it came, it disappears as the moon moves on.

The light may have gone but the magic hasn't left the room.

Suddenly, I need him.

I need all of him.

"Take me home," I beg him.

He kisses me with a desperation, and I smile against his lips.

The Pantheon wins the best tourist award of all time.

Holy shit.

4

Enrico

It's dawn, and I'm sitting on the side of the bed watching Olivia sleep.

Her naked breast rises and falls with her every breath, and her long, thick, blonde hair is splayed across my pillow.

Breathtaking.

This woman is utterly breathtaking.

Arousal isn't the only thing I'm feeling. It's a closeness... a strange attachment.

I walk to the window, pull the drapes back, and stare out at the street below as I imagine what would happen if I brought Olivia to meet my family.

An Australian.

It would be frowned upon. Blasphemy!

The Ferrara's eldest son not taking an Italian as a partner? I imagine my grandparents and their reaction.

The gossip that would follow.

It would kill them.

My stomach twists at the thought of letting them down.

For years, I've been set up with every well-bred Italian woman known to my family. Every time, they hope and pray that she will be the one I fall for. They've lined them up—ticked them off their list. The women have come from far and wide as my family try and coax me into who I should be dating.

Someone who is good for me.

Someone who will be the next Ferrara.

So far, nobody has interested me in the slightest.

I exhale heavily. Why the fuck does a woman from the other side of the world who is completely wrong for me finally make me feel something?

Typical.

She inhales sharply as she rolls over and puts her arm out for me. "Rici?" she murmurs in her sleep as she feels around the bed.

I go to her and sit down, brushing the hair back from her forehead. "I'm here, bella."

She smiles with her eyes still closed, and she takes my hand to kiss the back of it. "Come back to bed, baby," she whispers, her voice husky from sleep.

"You have to get up. It's time to go, angel." I smile softly as I watch her.

She scrunches her face up, her eyes closed as she groans.

I stare at her as I fight to hold my tongue. I want her to stay. I don't want to let her get on that plane. I want her to stay here with me... in the moment.

But I won't.

She needs to go, and she needs to go soon.

We drive to the airport in silence. Olivia's hand is in mine on my lap, while I am deep in thought.

"Where are you going again?" I ask.

"Down to The Amalfi Coast with my friend Natalie."

"Who is Natalie?"

"She's my best friend. We met when we were sixteen and have been inseparable since. She's been living in London. She's meeting me there. She's the funniest person I know. I call her Nat the rat."

My eyes drift over to her. "Why is that?"

Olivia grins, her affection for her friend obvious. "She's always getting into some kind of trouble."

So, she fucks around.

I try to hold my tongue. "Meaning what?" I snap, failing miserably.

"Nothing, she's just funny. It's my nickname for her." She leans over and kisses my cheek as I drive.

"What are you going to do down there?" I ask.

"Sightsee. Look around."

"Is she single?"

"Yes."

"Will you be going out at night?"

"Obviously."

I see red and clench my jaw.

Don't say it. Don't say it. Don't fucking say it.

"So, you'll be looking for number four down there?" I snap.

Olivia looks out of the window without a care in the world. "I don't think so."

I turn to her, horrified nearly running us off the road.

"You don't fucking *think* so?" I growl. "What is this? An Italian fuck fest?"

She laughs out loud. "I'm teasing you, Rici." She leans over and kisses my face, while I continue to see red. "Although, I do have to say, I'm loving this jealousy thing."

I hold the steering wheel with a white-knuckle grip...that makes one of us.

"Can I see you when you come back to Rome?" I ask.

"I'll think about it," she says casually.

I glare at her, infuriated beyond belief. No woman has ever played with me before.

She bursts out laughing. "Rici, you are so easy to rile up. I'll be counting the days until I see you again." She picks up my hand and kisses my fingertips. "You're my sun, remember?

"I don't like you traveling alone."

"I'm not alone, I'm with Natalie."

"And what about when Natalie picks up a man? What then?"

"Then I will do what I've been doing since we were sixteen. I'll go home alone. We have our own rooms for this reason."

I watch the road, angered by my sudden outburst of jealousy. What the fuck is this?

"I'm staying at the same hotel when I come back in two weeks," she says.

"You'll be staying with me." Jesus fucking Christ, I can't even act cool for a moment.

"Okay. Will you pick me up from the airport?"

"If I can get off work." I think for a moment, and then hand her my phone. "Can you put my number into your phone, please?" She types it in. "Now put me in yours." She dials her number from my phone, and it registers the call.

"Call me as soon as you get there tonight so I know you're safe."

"Okay."

"And trust nobody down there," I add.

She rolls her eyes. "Rici."

"Don't Rici me. I know how fucking seedy men think."

"Did you just admit that you're a seedy man?" She smirks.

"Olivia," I warn. "I mean it. Don't go anywhere alone. I don't want you in danger."

"I'll be fine." She rolls her eyes dramatically.

We pull into the airport parking lot, and my stomach sinks.

I don't want her to go.

We stand in the boarding lounge, holding hands, looking at each other.

"Last call!" the attendant announces.

"You have to go," I say. Her eyes search mine. "Have a safe flight," I whisper as I pull her into an embrace.

"See you in two weeks."

"Yes."

She smiles sadly. "Will you call me?"

I stare at her as I begin to feel myself lose the battle of remaining silent. "Every day." She wraps her arms around me, and our lips touch. "We had a crazy weekend, yes?"

"Crazy good. Call me tonight?" she asks in a whisper.

I suddenly become aware of the people around us staring at our long-winded goodbye. Self-conscious, I step back from her, our hands still linked. "Safe travels, bella."

She smiles softly and hunches her shoulders together. "See you soon."

I tuck my hands into my pockets. “Not soon enough.”

She gives me a fingertip wave and blows me a kiss. I watch her disappear into the departure gate, an overwhelming sense of dread filling me.

Because she’s gone.

Because I won’t see her for fourteen days.

Fuck.

I turn and leave the airport. I’m crossing the parking lot when my phone rings.

I smile broadly when I see it’s my mother calling.

“Ciao, Mamma.”

“Enrico, devi andare all’ospedale,” my mother’s panicked voice says.

“What?’

“Get to the hospital immediately. There’s been a car accident.”

My face falls. “Who?”

“Your father and your grandfather. They were driving to Roma this morning when it happened.”

“What?” Panic sets in. “Are they all right?”

“Just get to the Gernelli University Hospital, Enrico. The rest of the family are hours away. We are on our way now. Andrea is in Paris for work, and Mattia is still in France.”

My thoughts go to my sister. “Where is Francesca?”

“She’s coming with us. Get there, Enrico—hurry.” She begins to sob, and I know that this is serious.

“Okay, Mamma, I’m on my way. Don’t worry, it will be okay.”

Twenty minutes later, I am running up the corridor toward the intensive care unit of the hospital.

"Hello," I pant to the girl on reception. "Giuliano Ferrara was brought in here, alongside my grandfather Stefano."

Her face falls. "What is your name, sir?"

"Enrico Ferrara. Can I see them?"

"Just a moment. " She picks up the phone and calls someone. "We have Enrico Ferrara here." She listens for a moment. "Yes, he is Giuliano's son."

I look between her and the other nurses as they make eye contact. "What's wrong?" I snap as unease fills me.

"Take a seat," she says kindly. "The doctor is on his way."

I begin to pace as I drag my hand down my face. "I don't want to see the doctor. I want to see them. Now." I'm getting agitated. As a cop, I've been on the opposite end of this conversation way too many times.

Two doctors come into view, and the look on their faces... I've seen it before.

"Mr. Ferrara, can you come into the office with us, please?"

The room starts to spin. "No." I flare my nostrils to try get a hold of my emotions. "You tell me here."

"Please, sir." The female doctor grabs my elbow to lead me into the office, and she closes the door behind us.

I clench my hands at my sides as I brace myself.

"I'm sorry, sir, but your father didn't make it."

I stare at her.

"The impact of the car accident caused massive head injuries. He died in the ambulance on the way to the hospital. They did everything they could to try and save him but in the end, it wasn't enough. Please have comfort in knowing he wasn't in any pain."

My brows rise by themselves as I grab the wall to support myself.

"Your grandfather is in critical condition in the intensive care unit."

I stare at the floor through my tears as my throat begins to close up.

He didn't make it.

No.

Papa.

"Would you like us to contact the rest of your family for you?"

"No." I close my eyes as I try to regain some strength. "I'll tell them. They're on their way." I put my head into my hands.

Papa.

"Would you like to see your grandfather?"

I pinch the bridge of my nose. "Give me a moment, please?" I whisper as tears well in my eyes.

"If there's anything we can do."

"Leave me alone!" I snap angrily.

The door quietly clicks closed, and I screw my face up to fight the tears. I tip my head back to the ceiling. "No, Papa... no."

Then, I lose all control.

My beloved father... gone.

No.

I slide down the wall and sit on the floor in a crumpled heap as my new, dark reality begins to sink in.

My *Papa.*

I stare at the wall through tears...this can't be happening.

Three hours later, the sound of the heart monitor feels somewhat comforting.

Beep…

Beep…

Beep…

I stare at my grandfather Stefano's black and blue face. He is unrecognizable.

The doctors are coming and going. They don't think he's going to make it.

I can tell by the language they're using. It's already past tense.

My mother, grandmother, and Francesca will be here in two or three hours.

How do I tell them?

How in the hell do you tell someone that their husband of forty years has died?

They loved each other… *so much.*

And my beautiful baby sister—the apple of her father's eye.

The tears well again as I imagine her heart when I tell her he's gone.

"Mr. Ferrara," the nurse says softly.

I turn to her, dazed.

"Your grandfather has a visitor. He said he needs to see him as a matter of life and death."

I frown. "Who is it?"

"He said he is your father's best friend. His name is Marcello. He happens to be in Rome by chance."

I stand. "Yes, of course. Let him in."

She goes outside and returns with the man following her, and my face falls.

"Hello, Enrico."

I frown.

He bends, kisses my grandfather on each cheek, and he begins to cry.

"Stefano. Stefano, no, no. You fight, do you hear me? You fight. We need you," he whispers. He drops to his knees and begins to pray.

I watch him as the tectonic plates in my entire existence begin to shift.

I know who he is.

Every policeman in Italy knows who he is.

What the fuck is he doing here?

Marcello Baroni is a hitman—the darkest of dark criminals.

"How do you know my grandfather?" I ask.

His eyes rise to meet mine. "He's my boss, Enrico." Our eyes are locked. "He's *the* boss."

"Liar," I whisper. "Get out. Get out." I walk to the door and open it in a rush to see the ICU waiting room full of men in suits. My eyes roam to them, every one a familiar face.

Criminals.

The worst kind.

The ones you read about in history books.

Some are on their knees praying, while some are gripping rosary beads… but they're all crying.

"What the fuck is going on here?" I murmur.

Beeeeep.

I turn in a rush to see the heart rate monitor alarm going off. Nurses rush in from every direction.

I press my hands to my head as I begin to panic. Loud sobs come from behind me, some of the men openly crying now.

What the fuck is going on here?

The doctors and nurses work on my grandfather.

People are running around and calling out different instructions.

Clear...

Clear...

Clear...

The room is a clusterfuck of panic.

They pump his chest to try and restart his heart.

I feel a strange detachment, as if I'm watching this from way up above.

No, this day cannot be happening. All of this... it can't be happening.

The line on the monitor goes flat, and I hold my breath.

"No, no, no," I begin to chant. "Don't go, don't go."

The doctors and nurses work on him and work on him, until finally, they stop.

The commotion dies down and the room falls still. An eerie silence fills the space.

It's as if I can feel his energy leaving the room.

He's gone.

After a moment, the nurse closes his eyes with her hand, and the doctor turns to me. "I'm so sorry, sir. We did everything we could. His injuries were too severe."

I stare at her, numb.

"We will leave you alone to say your goodbyes."

The medical team turn and leave, and I'm left with a waiting room full of strangers.

I kiss my grandfather on both cheeks through my tears.

"Look after one another," I whisper.

I brush his hair back from his forehead as I stare at his beaten face. My tortured eyes rise to meet Lorenzo's who is now on his knees crying, and I nod.

Granting him silent access to say his goodbyes.

I stand at the back of the room and watch on as one by one the men come and kiss my grandfather goodbye. Each one whispers words of love and respect to him as they openly weep. My mind goes to my grandfather—the loyal, wonderful man I know...

Knew.

Who *was* Stefano Ferrara?

Where the hell does my family's money come from? If it's old money, how far back does it go?

My stomach rolls at the thought. This is a mistake. A terrible mistake.

The walls start to close in. This is too much. I have to get out of here.

I have to get the fuck out of here. I turn to leave, and Lorenzo drops to his knees at my feet. He picks up my hand and kisses the back of it.

I frown as I stare down at him, and then I look up at the men as they all collectively drop to one knee and bow their heads.

"Il capo," Lorenzo says.

"Don," the men all repeat.

Horror dawns.

Don means leader.

I'm the oldest son. With my father gone, I'm next in line.

But next in line to what?

5

Enrico

I SIT in the foyer of the hospital and stare at a spot on the carpet. The carpet is new—recently laid. Why has it been replaced? Did someone tear it up in a grief-fueled rage?

I wouldn't blame them if they did.

I'm waiting for my family—my mother, grandmother and Francesca—to arrive.

It should be any moment now. It' a six-hour car trip. If I'd have known how this was going to turn out I would have suggested they fly.

In hindsight, it's for the best. I wouldn't have wanted them to see what I have today.

Even as a policeman, where death is all around, nothing could have prepared me for this. Nobody should have to see their loved ones on their deathbeds. It's a cruel reality that's better off left alone.

I glance at my watch for the tenth time this hour. I didn't

want to tell them over the phone that our whole world just came crashing down.

How could I?

So, I'll wait here, to tell them in person.

I look around the lounge area, to the few men who have stayed behind to wait for my mother, and I wonder what their role is.

Did mother know?

Did she know what her husband and father-in-law were capable of?

My stomach twists. What *were* they capable of?

It doesn't make sense, any of this. Criminal families bring their children up in the midst of it. They teach their children the ropes—prepare them for the life they will lead.

I didn't know.

I think back to when my father pushed me into the police force. His words come back to me.

You need this life experience, Enrico, trust me. One day, you will need it.

Did he know? Of course, he knew.

I think of the money, the real estate, the lifestyle, and the special treatment everywhere my family go, and I clench my jaw. How the fuck did I not see this? Why didn't it ever occur to me that this was my family's history?

A few times through my life I'd heard rumblings. I once asked my father if the stories were true, too. He told me that most people are jealous of success, and that of course it would be rumored that they were criminals.

Jealousy was the root of all evil, he told me, and I believed him.

Maybe it's not true. Maybe this *is* all a big mistake.

I glance at my watch again. Where are they?

The door opens with a flurry of activity, and I stand and watch as they run in.

"Rico!" my mother cries. "Are they all right?"

I make eye contact with Roberto, my mother's driver, and he drops his head.

He already knows. He isn't a driver at all. He's a bodyguard.

The three of them look up at me, their faces filled with hope, and my eyes fill with tears. "I'm sorry."

"What?" Mother's face falls.

"They didn't make it, Mamma."

"No. Stefano?" my grandmother cries.

I shake my head as my face twists in pain.

"*Nooooo!*" my grandmother cries out. Her step falters, and she stumbles in shock.

Francesca grabs the wall for support as men come in from around me to hold up the girls as they each fall apart.

This is why the men stayed. They knew I couldn't do this alone.

"No, Enrico, no," Mother wails as I hold her in my arms. Her shoulders shake, and I can hardly hold her up. "Tell me it's not true. It's not true! It can't be true."

To the sounds of sobbing, my gaze falls to the carpet once more, and I wish I was anywhere but here. My beautiful family has fallen apart.

It's a dark day.

The darkest.

I stare into space as I sip my amaretto. It's dark outside, and my apartment is quiet.

This afternoon, we went to the morgue to give a formal identification. After that, the doctor had to sedate my grandmother and mother. They completely lost it.

Francesca is lying down, and my brothers are on their way. I'm sitting here with no idea what to do. Lorenzo, my father's best friend, is in the apartment, quietly trying to help. How can he? This is irreparable.

Men are out on the street, subtly surrounding the apartment, and I know we are now under guard. From what, I don't know.

The door buzzes. I go to the intercom and see a familiar face. It's Mario, the family solicitor. We know him well. He attends all our family events. He's been around for years and years. I open the door and wait until he comes into view.

"Rico," he whispers sadly. We hug and cling to each other for an extended time. His presence is only adding to our reality.

"Please come in." I step back, and he walks past me into the apartment before turning to me.

"I need to talk to you."

"Yes."

"Upstairs."

I frown. "I can't leave the girls."

"They're safe. The place is surrounded."

I stare at him, my mind a clusterfuck of confusion. Safe from what?

"There are papers in the offices upstairs that I need to show you. Where is Lorenzo?"

"He's here."

"You will need him."

Our eyes are locked. Why will I need him?

Lorenzo comes into view. He's openly weeping with tears are running down his face. He grabs Mario in an embrace.

"We need to talk to Enrico," Mario whispers as he holds his friend.

Lorenzo's eyes find mine. "Yes, yes, I know."

I follow them upstairs to the top floor to my grandfather's apartment. I don't know what's going on here, but everyone else seems to. I can't focus, I can't feel... I'm numb.

I'm too confused to articulate a single thought.

Blinding anger is all that I can see.

Lorenzo opens the door with his own key and we follow him in. My heart constricts as I look around. This place is so Stefano. He loved it here.

With my chest in my throat, I follow Mario to the office at the end of the hall.

"Please, take a seat," he says.

I sit down at the large mahogany desk. Lorenzo sits beside me, dabbing his eyes with a handkerchief. His tears won't stop.

Mario begins opening locked filing cabinets with his keys, taking out large folders and putting them onto the desk in front of me. I watch him for ten minutes. He eventually sits down opposite me.

He falls silent as he stares at me, and after a while he sighs. "My deepest condolences, Rico. My heart is breaking today."

I exhale heavily as emotion threatens to take over.

"It is with deepest regret that I'm here, but I have strict instructions in the event of this happening. You have been kept out of the family business on purpose."

I glance over to Lorenzo. "Why?" I ask.

"Your father wanted you to have a carefree childhood."

He pauses. "He knew that, in the event of their deaths, you would find out everything you needed to. He had faith that you would have the knowledge you needed and would know what to do. Although it doesn't seem like it, he has prepared you over the years. He thought ahead."

I frown in confusion.

Mario opens a large leather box that has a folder inside. "As the oldest Ferrara son, I must advise you that, as of this moment, all the family business now lies in your hands. You are the sole owner of Ferrara enterprises." He begins to read. "Ferrara Sports Cars, valued at nine billion euro The Flamingo Bell Football League side, and the four football stadiums. Seventy million euro worth of real estate." He slides his finger over the list of assets as he reads them out. "Five hundred and twenty-two high class brothels. Seventy-two VIP strip clubs."

What the fuck?

My phone beeps, and I turn it over thinking it may be my mother. A picture of a clifftop view over the ocean comes to life on the screen, alongside a text.

Arrived safely.
Wish you were here.
Olivia.

I pinch the bridge of my nose, feeling like I'm about to explode. "Carry on."

"Nine casinos worldwide, valued at an estimated fourteen billion euro."

I stare at him as he reads through the list. The room begins to spin.

"Four thousand staff and another eleven hundred personal staff."

"Personal staff?"

Mario looks up over his glasses and closes the book. He clasps his hands in front of him. "You're not a stupid man, Enrico."

I clench my jaw.

"Not all of the Ferrara businesses are reputable." He pauses. "But it has been vital to keep these parts of the business going in order to support the legitimate businesses. Your grandfather was a shrewd businessman. The generations before him, however, were not. It was those businesses, though, that gave Stefano the funds needed to build an empire."

"Drugs?"

His eyes hold mine. "Among other things. You will be briefed on that side of the business."

I drop my head in shame, and Lorenzo puts his hand on my shoulder. "It's all right, son," he whispers.

"You will need to resign from the police force immediately to begin your training," Mario says.

"Fuck you. I'll do nothing of the sort." I make to stand, and Lorenzo pushes me back down into my seat.

A trace of a smile crosses Mario's face. "Your father always said that you will be the best leader the family has ever had. He pushed you to be a policeman to learn how the other side of the law works."

I stare at him, completely lost. "Why?"

"So that you would have an edge over everyone else."

"I want nothing to do with this."

He smiles sadly. "I'm afraid you don't have a choice, son.

There are a lot of people who want to take your throne. We have had word that your father's bodyguards are missing."

I sit up. "You mean?'

"Our men don't go missing unless they're dead. This wasn't an accident, Rico."

Anger begins to surge through my blood.

"We think we know," Lorenzo says, "and we're waiting for confirmation."

My eyes flick between the two of them. "Who did this?" I demand.

"Rico," Mario says as he holds my gaze. "At this point, you have two options. You take the reins, or you prepare to die. Your skin is the next one they will want as a trophy."

I stare at him.

"Take over the empire… or you and your family—your mother, grandmother, and sister—will no doubt be murdered in cold blood. It's only a matter of time."

"Fuck you. I will do nothing of the sort," I hiss angrily.

He narrows his eyes. "So, you'll leave it to Andrea then. Or perhaps Matteo?"

I stare at him as my mind goes to my two gentle brothers.

"Your family assets need to be protected, Enrico. Andrea can't do this job. He isn't strong enough. We both know that, and Matteo is too young."

"Does she know?"

"Your mother?" Lorenzo asks. I nod. "No, and she never will. Unless you don't do the right thing and she wakes up one day with a bag over her head or in the trunk of a car. Or perhaps she'll be mourning the death of Francesca, instead," he says sadly.

My stomach twists.

"How will it feel to have that on your conscience, Enrico?"

Mario says. "The family needs your strength now. Our men need your strength," Lorenzo pleads.

"Shut up," I whisper. "Shut the fuck up."

"You will not be alone. We have men to train you. Your staff are loyal. They loved your father. We will look after you. We are your family. Your grief is our grief," Mario says.

"We?"

"I am a part of the business, Enrico. It's not all bad, and you will be surprised who Stefano has on his payroll."

"Get out," I sneer.

He stands and puts his hand on my shoulder. "In time, you will come to appreciate the choices your family before you have made. You are very fortunate to be a Ferrara."

I stare straight ahead, unable to make eye contact with him.

"Suck it up. You have funerals to arrange. Do your fathers proud." Mario stands, leaves, and the door closes quietly behind him.

My breath quivers on the inhale as I try to control my breathing.

Lorenzo pulls me into an embrace and holds me while tears of rage run down my cheeks.

My entire life has been a lie.

6

Olivia

SORRENTO. What a magical place.

I smile as the sea breeze whips my hair, and I gaze over at the breathtaking view.

The cliff face is covered with beautifully colored old buildings, and at the bottom, a deep shade of turquoise blue, is the Tyrrhenian Sea.

Perched high up above, I'm standing on the balcony of my room at the iconic Grand Hotel Capodimonte.

The room has a timeless feel, like something you would see in an old Hollywood movie. There's Terrazzo tiled floors, luxurious bedding and furniture, and big white windows that swing open so that you can gaze over at the priceless view.

Wow, Natalie really got this booking right. This is a lot better than the hotels I've been staying at. I should have got her to organize my entire trip. She got this for a steal too.

Natalie and I grew up in Sydney together. She lives in

London now. I miss her desperately, even though we speak nearly every day on Facebook. Her flight arrives here in Sorrento this afternoon. This is our much-anticipated two-week holiday together. She couldn't come for the entire time, but we swung it so she could meet me here for the remaining leg of my trip.

I take a seat on the balcony and smile to myself.

I can't believe the weekend I just had.

I pick up my phone and scroll through the photos of Rico and I together when we were sightseeing in Rome.

I look so happy. My hair is tussled, I have no makeup on, and I look flushed. Enrico is laughing in every image. I run my finger over his face. What a beautiful specimen he is. It's been a long time since I've been happy... really happy.

I'm twenty-seven, and I guess I'd kind of given up on men. Lately, I get more enjoyment out of a tub of chocolate ice cream. I was preparing myself to buy an apartment on my own—getting a cat and some potted plants. Work and the gym would probably be my only social life. I was easing myself into the next phase of my life, alone.

I wasn't unhappy. I was just... existing.

As if sensing my despair, Natalie talked me into taking this trip and meeting her here.

I'm so glad I did.

Now, my hunger for adventure has been reignited. I want to travel and go to exotic places. I want to get that dream job I had given up on, and damn it, I want my very own dream man.

I'm a good girl. I deserve a good man.

What if he's in Italy?

That's drastic, even for a good man. Even for the best man.

Could I really give up my Australian home to live here?

I have my job that I love, and I don't want to give that up. I worked too damn hard to get it. But then, I did always want to work with a fashion designer in some shape or form.

Apart from my job, I don't really have anything holding me there. My social life is non-existent, my best friend lives on the other side of the world, and my parents are both dating imbeciles.

Ferrara's marry for life.

Enrico's words come back to me along with my goofy smile. Why do I smile like this every time I think of him?

I'm not going to get excited about it. We only spent three days together... but what an amazing three days they were.

In actual fact, these two weeks away from him is the worst possible timing ever. If only I could have spent the time with him instead.

Stop it, don't get ahead of yourself. It was just one weekend.

I stand and take some photos of the beautiful view, and I send one to Enrico with the text:

Arrived safely.
Wish you were here.
Olivia.

I smile as I imagine him reading it. He's probably at work now and won't get it till later. I'm going to go for a swim in that beautiful pool down there.

I change into my bathers and grab my sunhat. I leave my room, looking for adventure.

Life is good. Really good.

"To us." Natalie clicks her glass with mine as she beams happiness across the table.

"To us." I giggle. "Can you believe we're here?"

"No." She grabs my hand. "It's so good to see you, Liv. I miss you."

"I know. Me, too."

We're on the large balcony of our hotel having dinner. After Nat's flight, we thought we would take it easy tonight. The tables are lit with candles, and the cliff is alive with twinkling lights from the buildings. The sound of the ocean is loud as it crashes against the cliff face.

"So?" I cut into my chicken. "Tell me everything. How's London?"

"Yeah, it's good." She chews her food. "The weather is atrocious, though."

I've never been to London. "It's just raining all the time? Every Aussie goes on about how bad the weather is over there."

"It's overcast every day. The sun is hardly ever out. It gets depressing after a while. I'm so used to eight hours of sunshine every day, all year long."

"Well, it could be worse. Cold is better than hot as Hell, right?"

She laughs. "I guess." She takes a sip of her wine. "Tell me about your trip."

I smile proudly. "I met someone."

"What?"

"In Rome."

"And?"

"And we had the best sex of my life all weekend long."

She puts her hands over her mouth. "You? Had sex with a stranger?"

I laugh at her shock. "Not just any stranger. God's gift to women."

"Fuck off."

I laugh. "Yes." I get out my phone, go to the photos, and pass it over to her. "His name is Enrico Ferrara."

"Sounds so exotic." Her eyes bulge as she sees the photos of him. "What the fuck?"

"Gorgeous, right?"

"Jesus." She scrolls through the images. "Gorgeous doesn't cut it."

"He's a policeman."

She puts her hand on her heart. "Oh, please, it gets better."

"And he took me to The Pantheon and told me he thinks our story isn't over."

She frowns as she listens.

"You know I have nothing holding me in Australia now."

She holds up her hand. "Woah... slow down girl."

"I know it sounds crazy—"

"Because it is. You don't even know this guy." She hands my phone back in disgust.

"Don't wreck this for me by being all sensible."

"Oh God, Liv." She sighs. "Someone has to think clearly around here. It doesn't sound like you are." We eat in silence for a moment. "Sorry. I'm being a bitch. Tell me about your weekend with him."

I smile sadly, hating that she's not as excited as I am. "It was just really great, you know? We connected, and it wasn't just because of the awesome sex."

"The sex was awesome?"

I put my hands on my forehead and then fake an explosion in the air with my fingers. "Mind blowing."

She smiles.

"And I'm not moving here, I'm..." I shrug and my voice trails off.

She watches me intently. "What?"

"My life is shit back home. I'm boring and comfortable and I've always done the safe things in life. Where has it got me until now?"

"This is true." She sips her wine.

"Maybe this trip is to teach me about myself."

She rolls her eyes. "You're not getting all, *Love, Eat, pray* on me, are you?"

I giggle. "Maybe."

"Maybe you should go to Bali, take up yoga and fuck the gorgeous guy in that movie like Julia did."

I laugh. "My guy is better."

Her eyes hold mine. "I'm just saying... be careful, that's all." She grabs my hand over the table. "I don't want you to get all attached to and then hurt by a guy on the other side of the world who you think you know. Not all men are like your ex-boyfriends, Liv. This Enrico could be a huge player. Probably is if he looks like that."

"I know." I sigh, saddened by her reality check.

"Look." She shrugs with a smile. "Actions speak louder than words and I could be completely wrong. Maybe he's great and this could work out."

"I'm not getting excited. I know what you're saying is right. I'm going back to Rome to spend the weekend with him before I fly home, so I'll see what happens then."

She smiles broadly. "Good, take it slow. There's no rush."

"I am."

"Has he called you today?"

"He's working." I rearrange my napkin on my lap. "I'll speak to him tomorrow."

I sip my wine as I try to act casual. *Why hasn't he called me back?* An annoying little alarm bell goes off in the back of my brain. I was sure he would have called me back by now.

"So, what are we going to do tomorrow?" she asks.

I smile up at her. "Everything."

Enrico

The red embers glow in the dark and a sporadic crack signifies the wood's demise. I stare at the flames of the fire with my two brothers beside me.

Shocked, that's what we are.

We're heartbroken that our father and grandfather have left us. We're horrified at what we've found out about our family history. We don't even know who we are anymore.

"Everything is a lie." Matteo sighs sadly as he tips his head back and drains his beer.

"You must have known." Andrea frowns as his eyes come to me accusingly. "How could you have not known? You're a fucking cop, for Christ's sake."

"I heard whispers, but when I asked, I was told it was from jealousy—that people always think the worst of successful people. That all money must be bad, and the businesses were... ***are*** **now all legitimate, except for a few gambling houses."**

We fall silent again, lost in our own thoughts.

I drag my hand down my face. I'm exhausted—too tired to think, and too tired to focus on anything other than how fucked up this all is.

Francesca, our sister, walks in and sit beside me. She's beautiful, with long dark hair and porcelain skin. She's much fairer than her brothers but with the same brown eyes.

I put my arm around her and pull her close. "You okay, baby?"

"Not really." Her tear-filled gaze falls to the fire.

I hold her close. "Where's Mamma?"

"Inside." Her eyes find mine. "Are we going to be all right, Rico... without Dad?"

My heart sinks and I hold her closer. "Of course, angel. I'll make sure of it. You're safe, I'll look after us now. I'm here. Lean on me."

She holds me as she cries, and I close my eyes to my own pain.

The four of us, the Ferrara children, sit around the fire, and we weep.

I sit at the table wearing my black suit. I'm waiting for my mother to get ready for her husband's funeral.

The house is deadly silent.

When my father passed, he left a hole.

His jovial laughter is missing—his wise face, too. His deep voice and the way that he made everyone around him feel loved have gone.

His strength.

He's deeply missed, and I am empty.

I have nothing left to offer. Grief is all I can see.

Lorenzo has stepped up and taken over for us. He's caring for our family, easing our pain as much as he can.

My mother is quiet, pensive, and barely holding it together. The pain on her face is unbearable.

Francesca is heartbroken and won't speak at all. When she does, it's through her tears. She's only fifteen years old—

way too young to be left without a father. I die a little inside every time I look at her.

"Your mother is nearly ready," Lorenzo says behind me.

I nod, the lump in my throat hurting. "How do we do this?"

Lorenzo falls into the chair beside me and closes his eyes. He, too, is in pain.

"How do we say goodbye?" I whisper.

"We put one foot in front of the other and do what we need to do."

"Then what?"

His eyes rise. "We avenge their deaths, Enrico," he whispers. "We have the names. We know who is responsible. Let us take them out."

His profile is blurred as I stare at him through tears.

"We can't go forward without your lead, son."

I drop my head, defeated. "I can't take over. I don't know what I'm doing."

"Yes, you can... and in time, you will. Give us the go-ahead to take care of this, Enrico, I'm begging you."

We've had this conversation every day now. He won't give up. Hunger for revenge is his only goal. I drag my hands through my hair in despair. My father's men want to start a war. They want my approval to kill the men responsible for their deaths.

I'm the only one who can give it, but I know that once I consent, I'm agreeing to taking over. To this lifestyle. To turning into something I despise.

The Don, leader of darkness.

My phone vibrates in my pocket and I glance down. The name Olivia lights up the screen and my heart constricts. My beautiful angel. The only person I do want to see is the one that I can't. I put my phone back into my pocket. I can't speak to her right now. Not until I'm stronger. If I do, I'll cry like a baby.

I don't want her to feel my pain through the phone, because she would. She's so in tune with me that I couldn't hide my heart from her. I'm not whole anymore.

When my father died, he took a piece of me with him.

The best part.

He took my belief that I was good.

I stand and stare at the coffin as it sits in the ground. Dark rosewood against dirt.

My father is inside.

Cold and lifeless.

My mother's soft sobs can be heard beside me. My brothers huddle together in their united grief.

Francesca's hand is in mine. She won't let me go.

We've already buried my grandfather, now it's Dad's turn.

In a daze, I look around and see the thousands of men surrounding us, crying.

They're mourning their leaders. They're pledging their allegiance to us, the Ferrara's.

These men have been loyal to the death.

The priest passes us all a red rose, and I watch on as my mother, with tears streaming down her face, kisses the rose and bends to place it on my father's coffin.

Adrenaline begins to surge through me.

Why?

I hold Francesca's hand as she sobs out loud. My heart breaks watching her. She kisses the rose and bends to copy my mother. She puts her head down, leans onto the coffin, and she begins to sob. I bend and pick her up to hold her tight.

A strange detachment falls over me as we go through the processes one by one.

It's like I'm not even here anymore—as if I'm watching from up above.

Twenty minutes later, with the funeral over and a swell of well-wisher's kissing my family, I look over to Andrea and Matteo, and I nod.

It's time.

They frown in question.

"I need to do this."

They nod, realizing exactly what it means.

I walk over to Lorenzo. "Can I have a moment?"

"Yes, son."

My eyes hold his. "I want it to be painful," I whisper. "I want them to suffer."

He smiles darkly. "You have my word."

"Bring their hearts to me in a box."

He clenches his jaw and nods. "Yes, sir."

"Start the fucking war."

7

Olivia

SIX DAYS later

I pace back and forth on my balcony, listening to the phone ring.

"Pick up, pick up," I whisper.

The call is cut off and my heart drops. Rico rejected it. He usually just doesn't answer but today he actually rejected it—me.

My Italian Stallion *is* an asshole. He's the kind that is too gutless to let me down like an adult. Instead, he's going to pretend nothing happened between us, which makes him the worst kind of fucking asshole.

Weak.

I throw my phone onto the couch and drop down onto the bed.

How could I have been so gullible? There I was, opening my heart and telling him he's my sun, falling to my knees and sucking his dick as a goodbye present, and he doesn't even want to talk to me now.

I fell for his act hook, line, and sinker. I really thought we had something.

I feel stupid that my feelings are hurt, and if this is what the world of casual sex is like, count me out. I want nothing to fucking do with it.

I'm not heartbroken because I really didn't know him, and it was very early days.

But disappointed? Yes. Hell, yes.

My ego has taken a massive hit. I mean, if Rico didn't call me after the chemistry we shared, what chance do I ever have of hearing from someone who I share mediocre chemistry with?

I gave him my best and did all that I could. I was totally myself and still, it wasn't enough. Maybe there really is something wrong with me.

I get a vision of Rico and I laughing and riding around on the bike. I see us making love—fucking like rabbits. It felt so real and raw at the time.

I'm getting angry now.

Screw you, Italian Stallion. I'm too good for you, anyway.

I would rather be single than made to feel like a worthless piece of meat.

You know what? I'm just going to see it for what it was: a great weekend.

It didn't work out. So what?

Maybe something has happened to him...

God, Olivia, can you hear yourself right now? Stop being pathetic.

He hasn't called.

He doesn't care. Onward and upward.

Enrico Ferrara who?

I stand at the luggage carousal in Rome and wait for my suitcase. I watch as, one by one, the travelers collect their belongings and make their way out of the airport.

Why is mine taking so long?

Damn it, I knew I should have changed my flight and flew home from Sorrento. It was going to cost me an extra thousand dollars. I need to get on top of my finances, and putting a thousand dollars onto my credit card just because I didn't want to accidently run into a man seemed so stupid at the time.

Now, not so much.

I find myself keep looking around, scared that I'm going to see him.

I'm embarrassed that I kept calling him. I was sure something must have been wrong for him not to call me. It didn't occur to me that he just didn't want to speak to me until I had already called him six times. Then it was too late to take them back.

What a loser I am.

I stare at the rotating carousal. For fuck's sake, where is my bag? I'm not in the mood for this shit. It's going around empty now. Have they lost it?

It's probably on its way to Antarctica or some shit.

Ugg, this is typical.

Another round of bags roll out, and I finally see mine. Oh, thank God. False alarm. I drag it off the carousel, pop the handle up, and make my way outside to the cab rank.

"Excuse me, signore," a voice says.

I turn toward him. "Yes?"

"Is this your suitcase?" He gestures to my luggage. He has a very strong accent—so strong that I can hardly understand him.

I frown as I look down at it. Don't tell me I picked up the wrong bag. I quickly check the luggage tag.

Olivia Reynolds

"Yes, this is my bag," I say.

He exchanges looks with a man. "Come with me, please."

"What?" I glance up to see that I am surrounded by airport security. There are five of them in total. "Why?"

"Come into the office." He picks my bag up and begins to wheel it back into the airport. "Hey, what are you doing?" I ask. "I don't have time. I have to go."

"You're not going anywhere," he tells me.

"What? Why not?"

A strong hand grabs my elbow. "Into the security office... now."

"W-what's going on?" I stammer as I look between them. They all remain silent as the man on either side of me pulls me along. "I don't understand. Do you speak English?" I ask, desperate for answers. We walk past a woman on the help desk. "Excuse me!" I call to her. "Do you speak English? What's going on here?"

Her sympathy-filled eyes hold mine, and in that moment, I know something's wrong.

"What's going on?" I demand as they lead me into the office. One of the men puts his hand on my shoulder and pushes me down into a seat.

He takes my passport, and then sits down opposite me. "Are you aware it is a federal offence to transport drugs?"

I frown. What the fuck is he talking about? "Yes."

"And are you aware that the imprisonment for such an offence carries a minimum of twenty years imprisonment."

"Why are you telling me this?"

He lifts the cover of a trolley that I didn't see in the corner to expose five big bags of white powder. "Explain to me why this was in your bag? Twenty-five kilograms of cocaine, with a street value of approximately nine million euro." He picks up the bags and counts them one by one.

My face falls. *This can't be happening...*

Oh, my fucking God.

"What?" I gasp. "That was not in my bag."

"It was, and we have footage of the moment it was discovered."

My heart begins to race, and I look between them all in a panic. Why didn't I put the locks on my bag?

"This is a mistake, I don't." I begin to shake my head. "That's not mine. I swear to you, that's not mine."

"Do you have any more drugs on your body?"

"What?" I shriek. "No." I try to stand and am pushed back into the chair. "Those drugs are not mine. You have the wrong person." My heart is beating so hard that it feels like I'm about to go into cardiac arrest.

Suddenly, there's a knock on the door.

"Come in," the security officer calls out.

Three policemen walk into the room.

"Oh, thank God. Officer! There has been a terrible mistake. They think I'm a drug trafficker. You need to help me."

They begin to talk to the airport staff in Italian, and I look between them hopefully. What are they saying? They will know this is a mistake, surely, they will.

"We'll take it from here," the policeman says.

"She hasn't had a cavity search yet," the security guard says.

"What?" I shriek. "I haven't done anything wrong. You have to believe me. I'm not a drug trafficker. I swear to you," I cry in an outrage. I try to stand again and am pushed back into my chair with force.

Fuck.

"We'll take it from here," the policeman says to the airport staff before he turns to me. "Olivia Reynolds, you are under arrest for the possession and trafficking of cocaine."

"I didn't do this. I swear to you. Please, you have to believe me," I beg as tears well in my eyes. This can't be happening. You hear about this stuff in the media all the time, but never in a million years did I think it would happen to me.

"We will search her down at the station."

The police officer drags me to my feet, and I dig my heels into the carpet.

"I did not do this!" I cry. "I want an attorney." Yes, yes. I need an attorney. They will make them see sense. "I have a right to call an attorney."

The policeman grabs my hands and puts me into handcuffs. They snap shut hard—too tight around my wrist. The bite of the metal hurts and I wince. I'm lifted from my chair and yanked out the door with an officer on each arm, I'm led out of the office and through the airport. People stop and stare as we walk past, and my eyes fill with even more tears.

Oh God. Things can't get any worse.

Twenty years imprisonment. This can't be happening.

We walk out of the airport and across to where the police car is parked. I begin to really panic.

They're not going to put me in jail, are they?

They can't.

I can't be locked in.

My chest begins to tighten. "I didn't do this," I whisper as my vision blurs. "I swear to you, it wasn't mine. I've never seen those drugs before in my life, you have to believe me. Somebody has put it in there. Check the security tapes. I promise you. It was not there when I got to the airport." I dig my heels into the concrete. "I didn't do this!" I cry out loud as people around us begin to stop and stare.

I feel a hand go to the top of my head, and I'm pushed into the backseat of the police car. One of the officers climbs in beside me.

The car pulls out, and I stare out the window with tears streaming down my face, but I can't wipe them away because my hands are cuffed. I feel like I'm about to throw up.

What do I do? What do I do? What the fuck do I do?

They speak Italian amongst themselves and I have no idea what they're saying.

Fuck, why didn't I learn this language?

After what feels hours later, although I know it's only a few minutes, we pull into a police station.

I'm lifted from the car and dragged through the front doors.

I go into panic mode and begin to sob uncontrollably.

"I want a solicitor!" I cry as I am bustled through reception. "I need a translator." I glance up and see Enrico at the other side of the desk. He's writing something. He looks up and his face falls when he sees me. His eyes dart to his coworker.

"Cosa è successo?" *Translation: what's happened?*

"Stava trafficando droga." *Translation: She was trafficking drugs.*

"Cosa? Come lo sai?" Rico snaps. *Translation: What? How do you know?*

"Rico!" I cry. "Help me. Tell them I didn't do this."

"La sua borsa era piena, ovviamente colpevole," the policeman tells him. *Translation: Her bag was full, guilty as.*

I'm bustled away quickly.

"Rico!" I cry as I try to crane my neck to see him. "Please, help me."

I am pushed into an office and the door is slammed shut behind us.

Six hours is an eternity when you're locked in a room.

Eeriness is lurking in the air. I stare at the wall through my tears, battling the silence, trying to quieten the sheer terror of what I'm facing.

Drug trafficking in another country.

I've been strip searched, interrogated, humiliated, and then... deserted.

Enrico left.

Well, I'm assuming he left.

He hasn't come to see me. There's been no mention of him or the fact that we know each other from the policemen I've been dealing with. Did he even tell them that he knew me? I stupidly thought he cared. If not enough to carry on our relationship or whatever it was, at least enough to help me as a friend when I'm in need... and I'm in dire fucking straits here.

They allowed me to make one call and I chose to call the Australian Embassy.

They will know what to do; they have to. I'm assuming by now they would have called my parents back home, and I feel sick knowing what they must be going through. This is every parent's worst nightmare. Natalie is in the air, on her way home to London, and she won't have any idea of what has happened yet.

Maybe I'm going to wake up any moment and find that this is all a bad nightmare. Please, please, please let me wake up soon.

The door opens and clicks quietly closed. I close my eyes in dread. Here we go again.

"Olivia."

I turn suddenly to see Enrico standing over me, and my emotions bubble over at seeing a familiar face and my eyes instantly fill with tears. "Rico."

"What's happened?" he whispers.

"I don't know." I shrug sadly. My hope of this being a big mistake is dissipating by the second. "I've no idea. I got on the plane as normal, and then when I arrived, they said I had drugs in my bag."

His cold eyes hold mine. "How did they get there?"

"I don't know." I throw my hands up in the air. "I have no fucking idea who put them there but it wasn't me."

He rolls his eyes and drops into the chair opposite me. His body language tells me he knows it's as bad as I think it is.

"What do I do?" I whisper.

"Just sit tight," he says with a clench of his jaw. He seems angry.

"For how long?"

"Until I get you a lawyer," he snaps.

"This isn't my fault."

"What is the one fucking rule of travel, Olivia?" He holds his finger up to accentuate his point. "One rule."

"Lock your bags." I sigh sadly.

"Exactly. Are you so fucking lazy that you couldn't lock your god damn bag?"

My emotions bubble over. “If you came in here to upset me then don’t bother. I’m upset with myself enough about this.”

He pinches the bridge of his nose and exhales heavily. “I don’t need this shit. This is the last thing I need to deal with. I have enough on my plate without having to worry about you.”

What?

“Are you fucking kidding me?” I whisper angrily. “You don’t need this shit. You think I do?” I slump back into my seat. “Just go.”

“I’ve called a lawyer. He’s on his way.”

I wonder if I ever knew anything about him at all. “Thanks,” I eventually reply. We sit and stare at each other for a moment. He looks terrible with dark circles under his eyes and a pale complexion. “Are you all right?” I ask.

His eyes drop to the floor, and I see the muscles flex in his jaw. “Why wouldn’t I be?”

“Because you look like shit,” I fire back. This hard to get act is wearing thin. “And why didn’t you return my calls?”

“Because....” He stands, suddenly angered. “You’re more trouble than you’re worth.”

What?

My face falls and my eyes fill with tears, I blink to try and hide them. That was the last thing I expected to come out of his mouth.

Without another word, he rushes from the room, and the door slams hard shut behind him. I hear the lock click as he locks me in.

What the hell was that?

I can’t hold it anymore. I can’t act brave for one minute longer. I screw up my face and cry.

Seven hours later

I lie on the cold, hard bed of the jail cell.

It's dark and eerie in here, and I'm scared.

I keep thinking back to all the international drug trafficking cases over the years and how I haven't really paid much attention to them or followed up on what the outcome has been. Drug traffickers in other countries get forgotten. Nobody even questions if they are guilty. It's just assumed that they are.

It's ironic really. I'm one of the people who forgot them. Will they forget me?

The door opens and the light flicks on. A policeman escorts a man in a suit into the room.

"Hello." He smiles. He's older, handsome, and from the look of his suit, loaded.

I scramble to my feet and pull my shirt down. I feel so exposed and vulnerable in here.

"My name is Mario Botecci. I am a solicitor, and I represent Ferrara Industries."

He shakes my hand.

"Hi." I force a smile as I try not to get my hopes up.

"I have secured your release."

My eyes flick between him and the officer. "Really?"

"Yes, but there are conditions. I will be escorting you to the airport, and you will leave Italy immediately."

"Oh." I frown. "I-I missed my flight," I stammer.

"You'll be flying on the Ferrara jet. I will be accompanying you back to Australia."

"That's not necessary." I don't want to go on Enrico's father's fucking plane. That's the last place I want to be. "I'll book a commercial flight. I don't want to put anyone out."

Mario's eyes hold mine. "That is the condition of your release. It's unnegotiable."

I stare at him as the lump in my throat begins to close over. Enrico would know this, and he has chosen to not be the one who accompanies me home.

I nod, unable to push any coherent words past my lips.

The policeman gestures toward the door. "This way. We have some paperwork for you to sign, and then you can go."

Relief begins to flood through me, and I force a smile despite my tears. "Thank you. Thank you so much."

8

Enrico

December, 18 Months Later.

She arches her back, her body straddled over mine as she rides my cock. My hands hold her hips, guiding her to where I want her.

In, out, deep... so deep.

My legs are spread, and our bodies are covered in perspiration as we writhe together. Her long, dark hair falls down her back as she watches me with her big brown eyes in the diluted light.

Sex.

My necessary evil.

At least three times a week I have it. Sometimes with one girl, or two from one of my brothels. Other times, I go traditional and meet a woman. Tonight, it's with one of my general managers, Sophia. She's beautiful—everything a man could need. We fuck often but she leaves me still hungry and unsatisfied.

They all do.

We've been at it for an hour and I'm nowhere near close to coming.

I hate this. I hate that I have this need to fuck, yet can't come when it's happening. It's the worst kind of torture.

Sophia moans, half in pain, I know I have to let her go. I'll have to finish myself off.

Fuck this.

I close my eyes and go to my kink—the only thing that can get the job done.

Olivia.

I imagine it's her on top, riding me. I envision her blonde hair and those big blue eyes. I feel myself relax as I imagine her looking down at me.

Soft and lush.

"Clench," I command.

She tightens and I smile. There she is. My tight girl *Olivia.*

I lose control, and in one motion, I flip her onto her back and lift her legs over my shoulders. I let her have it.

Deep, hard pumps.

I give it both barrels. The bed is smashing against the wall as I take what I need from her body—what I've been trying to achieve for an hour.

I hiss as I tip my head back and come in a rush. My cock jerks so hard that it's almost painful.

I open my eyes and look straight down into brown ones. My heart drops.

It isn't her.

I pull out and fall onto my back beside Sophia, gasping for breath.

She rolls herself so she's half on my body, and she kisses me. I scrunch my face up and pull my lips away. I don't want to kiss.

"Wow." She smiles as she struggles for air. "You're incredible."

I close my eyes, my heart still racing. Disappointment floods me about the only way I can get over the line.... every single time.

This fascination with Olivia needs to fucking stop.

February, 2 months later.

I watch as a boat slowly pulls into port and the passengers get off. The sea breeze whips through my hair.

We are sitting in a bar having a late and lazy lunch in Venice. Our guards are strategically out of sight, up against the walls. Andrea laughs at something on his phone before he shows me a meme as he scrolls through Instagram. I smile.

We've been here for a week. Drea had a break from work and wanted a short getaway. We've laid in the sun, eaten, drank, and laid low. While he's so relaxed that he's nearly asleep... I'm not. I'm not sure I even know how to relax anymore.

It's been such a long time.

"Can I get you anything?" the waitress asks as she smiles down at Andrea.

I smirk as I watch her. She's been circling him for hours, and knowing him like I do, she will be beneath him in his bed tonight.

"Yes," he replies. "Two more Aperol Spritz, please." He gives her a cheeky wink.

"Yes, sir." She smiles.

I look through the crowd and see a woman in a red dress with blonde hair. I sit up suddenly.

Is that her?

"What?" Drea asks as his eyes follow my line of sight. "What are you looking at?"

"That woman in the red dress over there."

We both watch, and then she turns. I exhale heavily and slump back into my chair.

It's not her.

Andrea looks over at me and frowns. "Are you *still* thinking about her?"

I pick up my drink and sip it. I crunch on a piece of ice as my eyes go to him.

"How long has it been?" He frowns.

"Since what?"

"Since you've seen her."

I shrug. "A long time."

"You still picturing her to come?"

I drain my glass, unwilling to answer his question. I don't know why I told him that. Momentary drunken insanity.

"What are you doing?" he asks.

I shrug. Fuck knows. Least of all me.

"You can have any woman in the world you want. Every beautiful Italian woman on the planet is madly in love with you, yet you choose to pine over an Australian who lives on the other side of the world." I exhale heavily. "She's probably happily married to someone else by now, Rico."

"She's not."

His eyes widen. "You've been watching her?"

I pick up my second drink and sip it as I stare out over the sea. "Maybe."

"And?"

I crunch on my ice. "She's still single."

"So, bring her here."

"And offer her what, Drea?" I sit back in my chair, dejected. "We both know..." I pause as I try to articulate my thoughts. "I can't. It's not like she lives here. If I bring her here, I have to have an offer." I sigh sadly. "No woman in their right mind is moving to the other side of the world for a mob boss. Not a woman like her, anyway."

He watches me for a moment. "What if she was working here and you accidently ran into her?"

"But she's not."

He smirks. "You're Enrico Ferrara, aren't you?"

My eyes hold his.

"I'm pretty sure you have most of Italy on your payroll, brother."

I stare at him.

He raises an eyebrow. "Something to think about, right?"

"Hmm." I smirk as his plan begins to play out in my head. I sit back and sip my drink. My mind begins to run at a million miles per minute.

What if I brought her here and 'accidentally' ran into her?

For half an hour, I go through the possibilities in my mind.

"I'm going to the bathroom," Drea says.

"Yeah, sure," I reply, distracted as I begin to scroll through the names in my phone. I get to the one I'm looking for: Giorgio work. I dial the number.

"Hello, House of Valentino," he answers.

"Giorgio," I say. "It's Enrico Ferrara."

"Ah, Rico. Long time no speak, my friend. How can I help you?"

I smile. "I… need a favor."

9

Olivia

April, two months later

I CLOSE my eyes as I stare at the email in my inbox. *"Please let this happen."*

This is it; the moment I've been waiting for. Three months, seven interviews, an hour-long conference call last week, and it all comes down to this.

One email. I either got the job or I didn't.

All my hopes and dreams rest on this.

I'm either moving to New York to take up a position in the designing team for Valentino. Or I'm not.

And damn it, I really, really want to.

It seemed crazy when I applied for the position on the other side of the world, but now I've gotten used to the idea of moving, I'm excited about it. More excited than I've been about anything for a long time. I've been looking at rental apartments over there, and I have worked out the area I want to live in.

Now, it just has to happen.

I'm still designing pyjamas. It's still a great job with a great company, but my life in Sydney is still batshit boring. I've bought an apartment and pottered along for a while, even been on a few dates, but I'm itching. I don't know how I find out what makes me happy but I do know that designing pyjamas and living alone isn't it.

My finger hovers over the email. Okay, just do this. I inhale deeply and hit open.

My eyes skim the letter until I get to the line I'm dreading.

Unfortunately, you have been unsuccessful in your application.

I slump back into my chair.

What?

For fuck's sake. I drag my hands down my face and go back to read it from the beginning.

Dear Olivia

Thank you for your recent application with Valentino.

Your experience and creativity are very impressive, and you were shortlisted for the position of junior designer in the New York division. However, the applicant you were up against had extensive experience and came from a similar established role. It is because of this that we feel that he is better suited to this particular position. We regret to inform you that you have been unsuccessful in your application.

I sit back, dejected and, quite frankly, pissed off.

Great. I read on.

However, we have found something else that we feel you would be perfect for.

The position is to be a fabric consultant to the designers, and it is based in Milan.

Your key role will be to source and negotiate the production of the desired fabrics for our upcoming ranges. You will be required to relocate to Milan in Italy, and extensive travel will be required to fulfill your role.

My eyes bulge. What the hell?

If this sounds like something you would be interested in, please contact me and we can discuss the specifics further. The position is available from the 28th May. Valentino will cover moving costs, and your first six weeks of accommodation will be supplied until you get settled in Italy.

I look forward to speaking with you with regards to this role, and I hope that we can welcome you into the Valentino family.

Have a nice day.

Giorgio Bianci

Valentino, Milan.

"Oh my God." I bite my bottom lip as a goofy smile crosses my face. Picking the fabrics for upcoming ranges? It's a dream come true.

Holy shit.

I get a vision of myself being all professional and traveling the world looking for fabric. It could be the opportunity of a lifetime. My mind goes to the last time I was in Italy, and that stupid bastard the Italian Stallion, Rici Ferrara. It's been a while since I thought about him and his fuckable package.

Asshole.

I can't think of him without getting angry.

Rome is six hours away from where I'm going. If I don't go to Rome, I can't see him. Problem solved.

Excitement begins to sink into my bones.

Italy.

Not quite New York. It's the other end of the spectrum, sure, but it is away from here. It's exotic and new, and not to mention the position is amazing. It's a no-brainer really. I'm stupid if I don't do this. I roll my fingers on my desk as I go over my options.

Fuck it. I'm going.

May, one month later.

"Ciao." I smile at the concierge over the counter.

I'm in the hotel where I'm staying for the next couple of weeks in Milan—The Chateau Monfort. I'm trying desperately to contain my over-the-top excitement. This place is already fabulous; I can just tell. The foyer has huge limestone arches and a marble concierge desk. The floor is an exotic tile. Don't even start me on the artwork in here. Let's just say, I can tell that I'm in Milan.

Over the last month I've been listening to my Italian tapes like a woman possessed. I really want to learn the language while I'm here and I am going to try to converse as much as I can in Italian.

"Vorrei fare il check-in, per favore. Mi chiamo Olivia Reynolds." I smile proudly. Yes, that's right. I speak Italian because I live in Milan and shit. I bite the side of my cheek to stop myself gushing about how cool I have suddenly become.

The man on the counter speaks. "Certo, signora! Ha prenotato online?"

Oh. Jeez, he said that fast. "Ah, può ripetere per favore?"

"Abbiamo aggiornato la sua prenotazione e abbiamo incluso un pachetto colazione," he says way too fast.

My coolness was premature. "Do you speak English?" I ask.

"Yes, Madame." He smiles, knowing full well he just knocked me down from my pedestal. "We have you booked in for a period of six weeks."

"Yes."

He types something, and then reads the notes. "Oh, you are here for Valentino?"

"Yes."

He continues to type. "What do you do for them?"

"I'm a textiles consultant." I beam. That sounds so cool.

"Impressive. You are in room two-three-two on level two." He slides my key over the counter. "We have upgraded you to also have a breakfast package. It's served daily in the restaurant on level two from 6:00 a.m. You have full access to the swimming pool on level three with a gymnasium and a day spa.

Concierge is twenty-four hours, and we will arrange all of your transfers for you if you call ahead. There is around-the-clock room service available with an extensive menu."

I grin brightly. "That all sounds great. Can I please have a kettle, coffee, and tea supplies brought to my room?"

"Of course, I'll order that now." He types something into his computer. "Your luggage will be up shortly, and if there is anything you need, please dial nine."

"Okay."

"Enjoy your stay in Milan, Miss Reynolds."

I bounce my shoulders. "Thanks." I make my way up to level two and down the wide corridor until I get to my room. I walk in and my breath catches.

The room is huge, full of antique furnishings, chandeliers, and gorgeous artwork. Sheer white drapes cover the windows, and the view over the city is spectacular. There's a circular table made from dark wood, and matching chairs with upholstered cream velvet cushions. There's also a large couch in the same velvet, and the carpet is thick and lush. Holy shit, the bed. It's round, king size, and has a white netting canopy over it.

What the heck? A king size round bed? Now I've officially seen it all. I look around in awe. This place is fucking amazing. It's like a fairy tale.

There's a knock on the door and I rush to open it. "Your kettle, coffee, and tea supplies." The porter smiles.

"Yes, please, come in." I open the door and watch on as he sets them up in the little kitchen area. "Will that be all?"

There's another knock on the door.

"Yes, thank you," I say as I open the door. Another porter has arrived with my luggage.

"Your luggage."

"Yes, just put it here."

He wheels my suitcase in, and I tip them both. "Thank you." They leave me alone.

I look around my room with a broad smile on my face. I quickly text my mum.

Arrived safely.
Call you tomorrow.
Love you
xoxo

I'm going to make a cup of tea, put away my clothes, and then go to sleep.

I start work at Valentino in two days.

Holy shit, is this real?

I walk up the street until I get to the big old stone building. The iconic V sits above the door, and I feel my stomach flutter with nerves.

My first day of work.

This is it.

I'm wearing my sensible yet stylish clothes, black business pants, a camel turtleneck with black pumps… all Valentino of course. My blonde hair is in a low ponytail and my makeup is natural. I don't know if I've ever been so nervous. *What if I can't do this?*

You can. Shut up.

I drop my shoulders, stand up straight, and power walk inside.

"Hello, my name is Olivia Reynolds. I'm starting today," I say to the kind-looking woman on reception.

"Of course, hello. Please come through." She stands and shakes my hand with a warm smile. "My name is Maria."

"Hello." Oh, she seems nice.

"Welcome aboard. You are going to love it here. Just go up to level three and ask for Fernando."

"Okay, thank you."

I get into the elevator and smile, Fernando sounds so... *Italian.*

I swear to God, this entire thing is like a dream. The Abba lyrics run through my mind.

There was something in the air that night, the stars were bright... Fernando.

The elevator doors open, and I power walk out into another lobby. It's quiet and a young man is walking through. "Can I help you?"

I clutch my bag tight. "My name is Olivia Reynolds. I'm starting today."

"Oh, you'll need to see Fernando." He looks around. "I'll go find him." He smiles and shakes my hand. "I'm Jason. I'm on internship here in marketing."

"Nice to meet you." I smile. Jason is a lot younger than me, and he's American, although he could be Canadian. I'm not quite sure of the accent. He's cute, and he has light brown curly hair with big brown eyes. He looks like a kid straight out of High School Musical.

I watch him disappear down the corridor.

My nerves bubble in my stomach.

"Olivia," I hear someone call.

I turn and see a man rushing toward me. "Nice to meet you. I'm Fernando, I'm the Human Resources manager." He shakes my hand. "We're so happy that you're here. I hope your hotel is okay."

His English is good. I can easily understand what he's saying. I smile in relief. Phew, that could have been tricky.

Fernando's short, a little overweight, bald, and about fifty years old, but he seems nice and welcoming.

"Yes, I'm excited to be starting." I smile nervously.

"Come through, follow me, and I'll show you around. You're in design."

I follow him as he takes me down the long corridor and opens a double door that reveals a large warehouse style room. Huge tables stand in the middle, and a few people are scattered around at desks and computers.

"Everyone, this is Olivia Reynolds," he calls. "She's from Australia and is taking over from Seraphina. Make it your mission to come and introduce yourself to her today."

"Hello!" they all call as they look me up and down.

I clutch my bag as I feel their eyes on me. Jeez.

He takes me down a flight of stairs. "Design and materials are on the level down but it's easier to take the stairs between these two floors."

"Ah, okay." We get to the bottom and my eyes widen. Holy shit, this is every design graduate's dream. The same big tables that are upstairs are in the middle, but there is also huge timber shelving with rolls and rolls of fabric. Mannequins are everywhere with dresses and samples pinned onto them. Feathers and sequins and buttons and... .my eyes can't take it all in as I look over the magic of this room.

Leather—rolls and rolls of leather in every color of the rainbow. Holy shit!

"Seraphina." He looks around. "Where is she?"

She comes into view, and her face lights up. "Hello, Olivia," she says in a heavy accent as she shakes my hand. I feel myself wither under her gaze. Seraphina is gorgeous, with long dark hair that's styled to perfection. She has a beautiful, curvy figure, and perfect bone structure. She's the epitome of Italian beauty. She's wearing a tight leather skirt that hangs just below the knee and a silk deep red blouse with sky high stilettos. She looks like she's going to a wedding or something, all stylish and glamorous.

Ugh, why did I wear this? I feel the blood drain from my face. I look like her daggy mother.

"Seraphina is transferring to our Rome offices so that she can be with her fiancé," Fernando says as he picks up her hand and shows me her huge rock.

She fakes embarrassment. "Oh, Fernando. Behave." She laughs. "You're such a showoff."

"Ah." I smile awkwardly. "Nice."

Her fiancé lives in Rome?

No, don't be stupid. Why does everything about Rome have to be about him?

He's not the only man in Rome, you know, Olivia, you fucking idiot.

"Great," I push out. "Exciting."

"You will work with Seraphina for the week. She will show you around and give you a feel for the position, and then next week you will begin training with one of our trainers for a week. In two weeks, you will take over the role," Fernando explains.

"Okay."

"Come this way." Seraphina smiles. "I'll show you your new office."

"Great." I smile as I follow her, but I don't feel great. I feel majorly unaccomplished. She's gorgeous, stylish, and she's moving to start a life with her fiancé, while I can't even get the courage to put myself on a dating app.

I really need to pull myself out of this dating funk. It's getting ridiculous.

She opens the door of the office and my eyes widen.

The room has huge burgundy velvet couches in it, a black desk, and a black, leather office chair. There are huge, framed images of models on the runway in exotic clothing on the walls.

"Bella, huh?" She smiles, sensing my admiration.

"Yes, beautiful." My eyes scan the room.

There's a brief knock on the door before a man pops his head around it. "Hello. You must be Olivia?" he says.

"Yes." I smile awkwardly because he is the most gorgeous man I've seen in a *very* long time. He's beautiful actually. There's a golden hue to his thick hair, and he has big brown eyes. He's well-built and a little older. I would say completely and utterly gay, too, damn it. Why do gay men get the cream of the crop?

He walks into the office and shakes my hand. "I wanted to introduce myself to you. My name is Giorgio."

"Hello." I shake his hand. He's wearing a navy-blue suit and a pink shirt. The top two buttons of his shirt are undone, and I can see a scattering of his dark chest hair. Well, that's a little bit sexy for the office. *Very Valentino,* I remind myself.

Seraphina's face falls in surprise. "Giorgio," she says. "Nice to see you."

"All ready for the move?" he asks her.

"Yes, very much looking forward to it."

Giorgio's eyes come to me. "So, you're Olivia Reynolds?"

"Yes."

"Hmm." He smiles as he looks me up and down as if doing an internal assessment., and I feel myself blush under his gaze.

"We must have coffee next week, Olivia. I would love to get to know you."

"Sure." I smile. "That would be great."

A frown crosses Seraphina's face as she looks between us.

"Okay, got to run." He smiles. "Happy settling in, Olivia. Good luck with the move, Seraphina." He disappears out of the door.

Seraphina watches him, and then turns her attention back to me. "Have you ever met him before?" she asks.

"No."

"Huh." She shakes her head and drops into her chair at her desk.

"What?" I ask.

"Do you know who he is?"

"Who, Giorgio?" I frown. "No idea."

"He's the CEO. He's never been in my office before in his life. I'm surprised he even knew my name."

"Really? That's weird?"

"Very." Seraphina shrugs. "Oh, well, great for you, I guess. Where were we?" she asks.

I shrug. "Me feeling completely overwhelmed?"

Why in the hell would the CEO of Valentino want to have coffee with me? I feel my nerves flutter just at the prospect. What would we talk about?

She laughs. "You'll be fine and will hold a very important role in the company. Don't be nervous, get excited. This is the opportunity of a lifetime."

I inhale deeply as the challenge begins to light my fire.

"The Valentino designers are a nightmare to work with," she says. My face falls. "But I'll be working with you from Rome, so we'll help each other deal with them."

I smile, grateful for her honestly. "That sounds great."

She pulls up a chair. "Now, let's get to work." She thinks for a moment. "There's so much to learn, I don't even know where to start."

"The beginning?"

"Yes." She smiles. "Let's start there."

I watch the steam float up to the ceiling in puffs. It's hot, cloudy, and I'm wet with perspiration. I'm in my hotel sauna, wrapped in a white towel and lying flat on my back, staring at the ceiling as I assess my life.

I moved to Italy to change myself.

But did I really think a new job and a new country would change my old habits? Because it hasn't so far.

I've been in Milan for nearly a week. I've been working hard and am looking so forward to the career challenge, but I haven't gone out at night once. Not that I've been asked, I guess. That old saying comes back to me.

If you always do what you've always done, you will always be where you always were. Something needs to change in my life. I need to change. I'm on the other side of the world and living the same way I was at home… alone.

Deep down, I know what the answer is, but it all seems so desperate.

Who am I kidding? I am desperate.

I'm twenty-fucking-nine and I haven't had sex since that asshole in Rome. He turned me off men for life. Either that or his dick was so good that it satisfied me until now. It was definitely a dicking that I need to forget. I exhale heavily, annoyed with myself for being like this.

Fuck it.

I sit up in a rush and leave the sauna.

I'm going to do it. I'm going to do what everyone else does to meet people in this day and age.

I'm going to join Tinder.

If nothing else comes from it but great sex, that's a whole lot of sex more than I'm getting now. Even average sex is better than no sex.

Screw these damn high ideals I have. Where have they got me so far?

Lonely and miserable.

I search through my bag, find my phone, and before I have time to think about it,

I download the app. I watch the dial click around as it downloads. Operation *Meet People* is underway.

Holy shit, here we go.

I sip my coffee and smile at my phone. I have to admit that this Tinder app is kind of fun and great for the ego. I'm getting lots of swipes, although that could totally be because men swipe anything with a pulse. I have a picture of myself from behind, and I put my name as Olly Reynard. That way, I'm not too out there. I've been speaking to this guy for a week. His photo is kind of hot, and he seems nice, albeit a bit pushy. He wants to meet on Saturday night in a bar, but it just seems so weird.

Could I really make myself turn up to a restaurant to meet a stranger? What the heck do you talk about? Talking to someone in texts is so different to sitting and having dinner with them. His message comes through. This is the tenth time he has asked.

So, are we meeting this weekend?

I close my eyes.

If you always do what you've always done, you will always be where you always were.

This is it. Either step up and be brave or get off this fucking app. I can't talk to someone and never have the courage to meet them. Maybe if we meet at a restaurant and take it slow...

I open my eyes and I text back.

Yes, okay. Can we meet at a restaurant?

I hit send. A reply bounces back.

I'll organize the restaurant and get back to you.

My stomach flips. I already regret this. Shit, shit, shit, shit. I text back.

Okay.

xo

"Hi, there." I smirk.

"Oh my God, what are you wearing on your date?" Natalie asks down the phone.

I close my eyes. "Oh, please don't talk about it." I sigh. "I'm five minutes from calling the whole thing off."

"You'll be fine. I go on a Tinder date every week," she scoffs. "Why are you being a baby?"

"Men on Tinder only want sex," I whisper.

"And your point is?"

"I don't want *just* sex."

"Oh, fuck off, you need to get laid... stat. Your vagina is closing up by the hour."

I giggle. "This is true."

"You don't have to sleep with him, just meet him. Talk and see if you feel any chemistry. If not, text me, and I'll call you with an emergency exit plan."

"Yes." My eyes widen. "That's a great idea. Emergency exit plan." I frown as I go over the concept in my head. "Wait, do you have an emergency exit plan?"

"No, I just tell them I'm not feeling it and I go home. I don't give a fuck. I don't owe them anything."

Nat is the most honest person I know. "God, I would hate to date you."

"Me, too. Now, wear something sexy and have a few glasses of wine before you go to loosen yourself up."

"What if I get too drunk and wake up in his bed with him and his flat mate?"

"Then I'm coming over to high five you. About fucking time you let it all hang out."

I burst out laughing. "Will you be serious?"

"I am."

I begin to pace back and forth. My nerves are dancing just thinking about going on this date. "Okay, have your phone on you for my emergency exit plan."

"Yes."

"And if I don't like him, I'm just texting you."

"Yes."

"What else do I need to do?"

"Have you got condoms?"

I frown. "No. Should I?"

"Yes, you can't trust men's condoms. What if they've put a hole in it?"

"Why would they do that?" I ask, horrified.

"I don't know. In case he's purposely trying to spread his sexually transmitted diseases or some shit."

"People do that?" I shriek.

"I'm not finding out. Get your own condoms to be safe."

I put my hand over my eyes. "Honestly, Nat, I can't do this."

"Just shut up and stop acting all innocent. You've done it before."

Him.

I feel anger bubble at the mere mention of Rico's existence, and I roll my eyes. "He was different."

"He was a complete asshole, that's what he was. What are you going to do? Sit over there in Italy and twiddle your thumbs?"

I get a vision of myself still doing the same pathetic things when I'm seventy. "Yes, you're right." I inhale deeply as I try to pump myself up. "Okay, I'm doing this."

"Good, get to the pharmacy."

The good thing about being brave is... nothing. It completely sucks.

I want to run hard and fast across the water and go back to Australia to escape this Tinder date from Hell.

It's Saturday night and I'm in the restaurant, but when my date wasn't here when I arrived, I came into the ladies' bathroom to hide. I can't sit at the table and wait like some desperado. I stare at my reflection in the mirror. My hair is set in big curls. I'm wearing a black fitted dress with a low back and spaghetti straps. I have my smoky makeup on with my red lipstick. I look good. I know I look good.

Tinder fuck-on-first-date kind of good.

I peer around the door and I see him sitting down at our table. He has dark hair, and he seems okay. He actually looks like his profile picture. He isn't hideous, at least. That's something, I suppose.

I exhale heavily and take one last look in the mirror to give myself a pep talk.

"Right, go out there and pretend that you like him. You never know, maybe you will?"

Oh God, this is a disaster already.

I walk out and weave through the tables. He smiles and waves as he sees me. He seems impressed when he stands. "Olly."

"Hi," I push out. "You must be Franco?"

"Lovely to meet you." He kisses my cheek, and I fall nervously into my seat. The waiter arrives. "Can I get you anything to drink?"

"Please." Jeez, I need fucking tequila to get me through this. I pick up the drinks menu and glance up, and then I stop dead still. I feel the blood drain from my face.

What. The. Actual. Fuck?

Chiseled jaw, dark eyes, and curly hair? I would know that face anywhere.

Enrico Ferrara is sitting at a table in the back.

10

Olivia

I QUICKLY PUT the menu up in front of my face so I can hide behind it.

Shit, are you kidding me?

"How are you?" Franco smiles.

I glance back over to see Enrico deep in conversation with a group of men. He laughs out loud and I pinch the bridge of my nose.

"Great," I lie. This is the worst day of my entire freaking life. What the freaking hell is Rico doing in Milan? I frown and pretend to read the menu in great detail, trying to buy some time. "Wow, you have such a great selection of drinks," I mutter to the waiter as I break into a cold sweat.

Franco and the waiter wait for my order. Oh man, I can't hold the menu up any longer. This is getting awkward. "I'll have a shaken margarita, please." I hand the menu over. I should have been polite and shared a bottle of wine with my date, but too bad. The ante just got upped.

It's every man for himself now.

The waiter leaves us alone, and Franco looks over at me. "It's so good to finally see your face, Olly."

I fake a smile. "Yours, too." I look over his shoulder to the level above. Enrico is sitting in the corner with a group of men. He says something, and they all burst out laughing. *What was so funny?* His hair is a little longer than when I was with him. His face is still...

"How are you liking Italy?" Franco breaks me from my thoughts.

I drag my eyes back to my date. "Great, thanks."

I don't want Enrico to see me. What am I supposed to do? Should I leave? What would I say?

"I've been looking forward to our date all week." Franco smiles.

The waiter arrives with our drinks. "Here you go."

I pick the glass up and immediately take a big gulp. "Can you bring me another, please?" I ask. Franco and the waiter exchange puzzled looks.

"So thirsty," I mutter into my glass. "Parched, actually."

"Tell me all about yourself," Franco asks sexily. His eyes focus in on me as he waits for me to speak.

I stare at him. "You want to know about me?" What do I say? I don't fuck on first dates because the one time I did, the guy was a bastard and, *oh, guess what*? He's right over there, leaving me to look for the closest escape route?

"Well..." Enrico laughs out loud. I stop still. He has the most incredible laugh.

I snap my eyes back to Franco, shit what was I saying? I pause as I try to get my bearings. Damn, Enrico has me completely frazzled. “Well, as you know, I’m Australian and I’ve recently moved to Milan for a job.” I sip my drink. I don’t want to tell him too much in case he’s a serial killer or something. “I’m having a great time. Why don’t you tell me about you instead?”

“Okay, I’m in banking...” He begins to talk but I completely zone out as my eyes roam up to the man at the table above us.

Enrico Ferrara.

He’s wearing a dark suit, and he looks different. More... *cultured* or something. Older.

But what the hell is he doing in Milan?

I frown as a distressing thought springs to mind. Oh no. Seraphina!

He is Seraphina’s fiancé. Of course, he is. She’s frigging beautiful.

Oh God, this is my worst nightmare.

I pick up my glass and drain it. I glance up to see Franco frown as if he is waiting for me to say something. Wait, did he ask me a question? My eyes widen. “I beg your pardon?”

“I really like you,” he whispers.

What? I’ve said three words. How can you really like me? I fake a smile. “Great.”

Her grabs my hand across the table. “Let’s cut to the chase.”

I stare at him. Okay.”

“I like you, you like me...”

I take another big gulp of my drink. I wasn’t joking before; I really am parched. It’s bordering on deep dehydration now.

“Let’s have dinner and go home. I know the perfect way to get to know each other.”

I choke on my drink. “What?” I splutter, coughing.

“I mean, we can just fool around if you like.”

“Fool around?” I frown as I glance back up to Enrico. Oh

man, this night is going down in the history books as the worst date ever. I open the menu and gaze at the selections. "Let's just eat, Franco. I'm not that type of girl. I'm offended that you think I am."

"Oh." His face falls. "I didn't mean to offend."

"Well, you did. I'm not going home with you, so get it out of your head right now."

I try to control my racing heart, and I can feel perspiration heat my underarms.

Just act calm, for fuck's sake. You can get the hell out of here as soon as you eat.

"Hmm, what looks good?" I hope I get food poisoning and get taken away in an ambulance. Anything is better than this.

My eyes float back up to Rico. His legs are wide, his back is straight, and everything about him screams dominant male. He's deep in conversation, smoking a cigar as he drinks out of a small crystal tumbler. I've never seen anyone smoke sexily before… but of course, he is. The way his lips wrap around the cigar, his cheeks hollow as he sucks. His eyes are dark, and fuck me, he's so hot.

I imagine him leaning back against the headboard naked after having sex, smoking a cigar. His cock still hard and throbbing… weeping. He could make anything look sexy.

My blood begins to boil as I remember the last words he spoke to me.

You're more trouble than you're worth.

An attractive waitress says something in his ear as she leans over him. He gives her a sexy smile and winks.

Huh, what did she just say? Did she ask for his number or something?

She walks off and he says something to the men. They all laugh again.

"I just really like you," Franco says. "Don't be angry with me."

I stare at Franco, deadpan. I have zero attraction to this man. I'm going to have to text Natalie for an escape plan because this is intolerable.

I glance back up to the table at Enrico. I can hardly drag my eyes away from him.

He's looking around and the restaurant slowly, and suddenly his eyes meet mine across the room.

Fuck.

A frown cross Enrico's face as he stares at me.

I snap my eyes away. "Franco," I whisper. "This isn't probably..."

Enrico stands and begins to stride over to our table.

Franco grips my hands in his tightly. Holy mother of fuck, help me.

"You want me, I want you," Franco continues.

Shut up. Shut up now, you horny freak.

"Olivia," Enrico barks, standing over us.

I look up at him, and the blood drains from my face. He's wearing a perfectly tailored navy suit. His dark hair is in curls, and his big lips are a wonderful shade of fuck me. The bastard has become even better looking than before. How is this fucking possible?

He looks down at Franco and our joined hands. "Who are you?" he barks at him.

"I'm her boyfriend," Franco replies, winking at Enrico.

My eyes widen.

Enrico glares at him, and his jawline moves as he clenches his teeth. "Get away from her now," he growls.

Oh, this night is getting worse. "He's not going away, you go away," I fire back.

Enrico drops his hands to the table and leans down toward me. "Don't push me, Olivia," he hisses.

Who does this fucker think he is? My anger boils. "I'll push you over in a minute. I said... go... away." I roll my eyes and pick up my drink to add to the theatrics.

"I need to talk to you outside... now."

"No. Leave me alone, I don't want to see you. You're annoying me."

But we all know that's not true. I want to jump into his bastard arms and kiss his bastard lips, and then punch him in the bastard face. *Bastard of all bastards.*

His brows shoot up in surprise.

Franco chooses now to speak. "You heard her. Fuck off."

Enrico stands up, his back straightens, and he glares at Franco. He doesn't move, he doesn't say anything, he just glares at him. If death had a stare... this is it.

My heart is beating so hard, and this is beyond uncomfortable.

"I said, fuck off," Franco repeats.

"Stop it," I whisper in a panic. Jeez, does this guy have a death wish? He's going way too far with the aggression. This is my battle. Only I'm allowed to tell Enrico to go away.

Enrico stares down at Franco as he tucks his hands into his suit trouser pockets. "You should be very careful with who you tell to fuck off," he warns calmly.

I swallow the lump in my throat as I look between them.

I need to diffuse this situation. "Enrico, go back to your table. We'll talk after I have my dinner." He narrows his eyes at Franco. "Please, Rico," I whisper.

His eyes find mine. "Outside. Now."

"What?"

He takes my hand and pulls me from my chair without

saying another word. Before I know it, I'm being marched toward the door.

"What are you *doing*?" I whisper angrily.

"What the fuck are you doing? Lui chi è?" *Translation: who is he?*

"Speak English!" I snap as we burst out through the doors and into the restaurant foyer.

"Who is that?" he growls.

Words escape me. What the hell do I say?

"Chi diavolo è lui, Olivia? *Translation: who in the fucking hell is he, Olivia?*

"You're trying my patience. Answer my question. Who is that man?" he barks.

"He's my date."

"*What?*" I flinch. "Vi ammazzo entrambi con le mie fottute mani." *Translation: I'll kill you both with my bare fucking hands.*

The door of the restaurant bursts open, and Franco appears.

I turn toward him in a rush. I know I need to get rid of him. "I need to talk to you. Inside... now."

"I thought I told you to fuck off!" Franco yells at Rico.

Jeez, what is this power tripper on? "Franco, stop, please."

Enrico steps closer to Franco. "Be very careful."

"You be careful," Franco replies.

"Franco, stop it." Ugh, all men are idiots.

"Get away from her," Franco says as he pushes Enrico hard in the chest.

Enrico smiles at Franco, and he has this creepy calmness about him. "Push me again," he dares him.

My eyes widen. "Stop it!"

"Go on," Enrico whispers.

What the actual hell is going on here? "Stop it, you idiots."

"Get on Tinder and find your own date!" Franco yells.

Enrico's horrified eyes come to me. "You met him on Tinder?"

My heart sinks.

Enrico loses control and turns to Franco. He punches him hard in the face, and Franco floats to the ground like a feather.

"Oh my God!" I bend to help Franco. "What the hell are you doing?"

Enrico's nostrils flare as he glares at me. I don't think I've ever seen anyone look so angry. "Ti porto fino a qui e ti trovo con qualcun altro? Che diavolo sta succedendo?" *Translation: I bring you all the way here and find you with someone else? What in the fucking hell is going on?*

"What are you saying?" I cry. "I don't understand you."

"All this time," he whispers, almost to himself. He shakes his head in disgust as his furious eyes hold mine. "And now I find out you're just another Tinder whore."

My face falls.

He turns and pushes out of the foyer and through the front doors, storming outside.

The door bangs as it closes. I watch him leave, in shock. What the hell just happened?

The restaurant door opens in a rush and Franco's cousin comes into view. "What the fuck are you doing?" he whispers angrily as he peers out the glass doors to see if Enrico gone. "Are you trying to get yourself killed?"

"He was being a jerk," Franco huffs.

"Do you know who that is?"

"Who?"

"That's Enrico Ferrara."

"Who's that?"

"The biggest crime boss in all of Italy."

Franco's face falls. "*That* was him?"

"What?" I scoff. "That's ridiculous. Enrico is a policeman."

Vinnie pulls Franco's jacket closed and fixes him up. "I don't know what he told you, lady, but my sister's old boyfriend used to be a driver for them."

"What? That's not true, it's insane." I push out of the front door and I look up and down the darkened street. It's silent, and there is no sight of Enrico.

"I'm going," I tell them before I hold up my hand and a cab pulls over.

"I'll call you," Franco calls out.

"Please don't." I slam the door shut. "I'd rather be single."

My heart is hammering in my chest as the taxi begins to pull away. Shame and adrenaline are pumping through my body.

Who the fuck does Enrico Ferrara think he is?

It's funny that the more you tell yourself not to think about something, the more your mind fixates on it.

I've been going over and over the things Enrico said on Saturday night.

You're just another Tinder whore.

Five words have cut me to the bone.

The worst part is, it's true.

I was never cut out for dating a stranger. How could I possibly think I was?

I keep seeing the sheer disgust on his face. The way he stormed out and left his friends without going back. I didn't sleep all night for thinking about that look on his face. It will haunt me forever.

I'm so flat today, and I know it's stupid. Why on earth

would I let an asshole upset me so much? I don't know him and he doesn't know me. What does his opinion matter, anyway?

I hate that it does.

"So, we're nearly done," Seraphina says, interrupting my thoughts as she looks around her office. She's wearing a fitted woolen plum dress and knee-high black boots. She's channeling Sophia Loren today. "What else do you want to know? Have I forgotten to tell you anything?"

I exhale. "Seraphina, can I even do this job?" I whisper. "I'm so nervous about it. What if I mess this up?"

She smiles at me and takes my hands in hers. "Listen to me, Olivia. You are going to be wonderful at this. You know what you're doing, I've been watching you."

Seraphina has been a big surprise. She's smart, kind, and supportive—not at all like the sex kitten I had her pegged as.

"I wish you weren't leaving." I sigh. "You're the only person I like around here."

She giggles as she begins to pack up her desk. "I know but love calls. When in Rome and all that."

I watch her for a moment, wondering if it's him. Is her fiancé Enrico? I bet it is. I bet it's a strange coincidence that has been sent to test my sanity. Why wouldn't he fall madly in love with her? She's all kinds of wonderful.

Just ask her. "What's your fiancé's name?"

"You'll meet him in a minute. He's collecting me from downstairs."

I stare at her. "He's coming... here?"

"Yes, so grab that box and carry it down for me."

I feel faint. "Really?"

"Yes, really. Everyone else has already gone. Let's go." She smiles as she takes one last look around.

I pick up one of her boxes with my heart hammering in my chest. I don't want to see him. I don't want to see him with her.

We get into the elevator, and she smiles and talks, while I stare at her, crippled by fear.

Please don't be him, please don't be him, I begin to chant in my head.

The doors open, and we walk out into the foyer. My heart drops. Two men are standing with their backs to us.

I follow Seraphina over to them, and then she turns to me. "Olivia, this is Johnathan my fiancé, and his brother Marcus."

I look up at Marcus and he smiles and shakes my hand. "Hello, Olivia."

"Hi." I smile, grateful as he takes the box from me.

It's not him.

Seraphina kisses my cheek. "Good luck, I'll call you Monday morning."

"Okay."

"Goodbye!" they call as Seraphina, her fiancé, and his brother disappear out of the front doors.

I slump against the wall. Thank God.

"Olivia!" I turn to see Giorgio, my boss. He's wearing black business pants and a cream shirt with the top few buttons undone at the top. His honey hair is perfectly styled. He really is lovely.

"Oh, hello." I smile.

He has his briefcase with him. "How about we grab that glass of wine?"

"What… now?" I frown.

"Why not? Do you have other plans?"

"No." I stare at him for a moment. Why is he being so

friendly? Seraphina said this is very uncharacteristic for him. "Yes, okay, sure." I shrug. "Why not?"

He holds his arm out and I stare at it for a moment. Is he asking me out on a date?

"Oh, darling." he scoffs, as if reading my mind. He grabs my hand and puts it around his arm. "You are the wrong sex for me. This is completely platonic."

I smile, embarrassed that he just saw the fear on my face. "Thank goodness for that. I've had more than enough bad dates for one week."

He laughs, and we walk out into the street with my hand linked around his arm. "So, tell me… how are you settling in?"

"Good. It will take a little time to get used to everything."

He gestures to a bar and we walk in. "Is everyone being good to you at work?"

"Uh-huh." I smile, even though that bitch Rosalie on reception is a rude pig.

"Shall we just sit at the bar?"

"Okay." I smile as we go to take our seats there.

"What would you like to drink?"

"Maybe some Prosecco?"

"Great choice. Can we have two glasses of Prosecco, please? Vorremmo anche degli antipasti, per favore," he tells the bartender. *Translation: We will have some starters too, please.*

"How is your hotel?" Giorgio turns back to me.

"Great." I look around the beautiful bar. It's dark and moody, and I'll have to remember to come back to this place. "I'm going to start looking for an apartment this weekend."

He rests his chin on his hand and smiles over at me.

"What?" I smirk.

"You've been to Italy before?"

"Yes, Rome and The Amalfi Coast."

"When was that?"

"Two years ago."

Our glasses of Prosecco are put down in front of us. Giorgio picks his up. "Two years. That's a long time."

I get the feeling he's asking me these questions for a reason. "Why are you asking?"

He sips his wine. "No reason. Just curious."

"Do you live around here?"

"In Milan. I'm originally from Sicily but have been here for ten years."

"Oh." I sip my wine and smile. "Hmm, this is nice."

"It is," he mutters, distracted. "Do you have a boyfriend?"

"No."

"Do you like Italian men?"

I wince against my glass. "Maybe."

"Did you meet someone last time you were in Italy?"

I giggle at his eagerness for information. "I did, actually."

He leans forward. "And?"

"It was just a weekend thing."

"Did you hear from him again?"

"No and I don't want to. He's a total douche."

"Really?" His eyes dance with delight. "Why is that?"

I shake my head. I'm not telling him that story. "He's just a possessive asshole."

He smiles against his glass, clearly delighted. "How wonderful. Don't you just love it when they're all possessive?"

I giggle. "Not really."

"Do you think you'll ever see him again?"

I raise my brows. "Funny you should say that. I ran into him last night."

His eyes widen. "Here. In Milan?"

"Yes."

"What happened? Tell me everything."

"You seem very interested in my love life. Let's talk about yours."

"Mine's boring." He huffs. "I've been with the same man for ten years. I much prefer to live vicariously through my friends."

I giggle. "Well, I was on a date with someone else, and he saw me. He marched over and caused a scene."

He sits back and laughs out loud. "You were on a date with someone else? Oh, this is priceless."

"Anyway, that's all. There's nothing else to tell."

"Well, who knows when you'll see him again?" He gives me a cheeky wink.

"Never, I hope." Just the thought of that bastard makes my blood boil.

He raises his glass in the air. "Oh, I like you, Olivia. We need a toast."

"What are we toasting?" I raise my glass, and smile.

"To making men jealous."

I laugh out loud. Actually, that's a pretty good toast. "To making men jealous."

11

Olivia

I SMILE as I write the text and hit send.

I'm reporting you to Human Resources for being a bad influence.

I am wrecked.

Whose brilliant idea was it to drink four bottles of Prosecco on a Monday night?

I don't know what the hell happened last night, but I left work thinking I was going straight home, and then somehow arrived home six hours later, drunk and disorderly. Giorgio is hilarious, and his boyfriend Angelo ended up coming and meeting us for dinner. He's lovely, too.

I had fun last night—the most fun I've had since I've been here—but there is one small problem.

For the life of me, I can't stop thinking about Rici Ferrara.

It's eating at me. The whole damn thing is eating at me. He is the world's biggest asshole.

After the way he treated me in the police station, he has the nerve to judge *me* for going on a Tinder date. I mean, who the actual fuck does this guy think he is? Who died and made him God? The more I think about it, the angrier I get. At first, I was in shock, but now I just can't believe it.

He marches over to my table, drags me outside, and then calls me a whore.

What the actual fuck was I thinking by standing there and taking it? Why didn't I punch him in the face or something much more satisfying?

I keep hearing my pathetic little whiny voice. *Go away,* I said.

Damn it, I should have marched over and kicked him as hard as I could in his bastard shin. Nobody is that good looking that they can get away with treating people the way he has treated me.

Nobody.

My phone beeps with a text.

Please do notify HR.
Hopefully they will put me out of my misery.
Sick. As. Hell.
G

I giggle. Good. I'm glad he's sick, too.

I sip my tea as I type two words into Google.

Enrico Ferrara

That guy said he was a crime boss.

I was so rattled the other night that I left that major detail out of my thought process. What did Franco's cousin mean by that exactly? Could it be true, could Enrico really be a crime boss? The whole notion seems ridiculous. He's a policeman, and I know he really is because I saw him at the station myself.

But then I think back to how wealthy his family are.

The search results pop up and I read on.

Enrico Giuliano Ferrara

CEO FERRARA HOLDINGS.

Enrico Ferrara is an Italian businessman, aged thirty-four. He took over as the CEO of Ferrara Holdings upon the death of this father Giuliano and grandfather Stefano Ferrara who died in a tragic motor vehicle accident in Rome.

Known for his handsome good looks, sharp intellect, and Playboy lifestyle, he has become one of the most powerful men in Europe, with company assets currently valued at seventeen billion euro.

What the fuck?

His father died in a car accident? When?

I skim the information, until I get to a line that stands out.

For generations, the Ferrara family has been known to have deep roots within the Mafiosi, though no criminal charges have ever been laid and no witnesses have ever come

forward. The Ferrara family is somewhat an enigma and has been a constant source of innuendo and gossip for centuries. Nothing, however, has ever been proven. They are perhaps just shrewd businessmen, and along with their success have come false accusations.

I slump back into my chair. What?

I Google again.

What is Mafiosi?
Noun, Plural noun. Mafiosi
A member of the Mafia or similar organized crime organization.

My eyes widen. The Mafia! He's in the fucking Mafia?

I slam my computer shut. That's ridiculous.

This isn't a crime novel, Olivia, you idiot.

I drum my fingers on the table for a moment. I pick up my tea and take a sip with a shaky hand. I get a vision of Rico holding a gun up while someone kneels and begs for his mercy. I see horses' heads in beds, murders, drugs, killing, death and...

I just can't imagine the Rici Ferrara I know being involved in any of this.

But I really don't know him at all. I never did. He already proved that to me.

Oh shit, I really need to know more. I open my computer again and type in:

What is the Italian Mafia in the twentieth century?

I lean forward as I read on.

The Mafia is a group of men with an allegiance to one family. In Italy, there were four Mafiosi families dating back hundreds of years, although all territory has now been claimed by the Ferrara Family. They have tentacles into labor unions, and many legitimate businesses, including construction, sports car manufacturing, football stadiums, restaurants, nightclubs and strong ties in the Milan garment industry. They have raked in enormous profits through kickbacks and protection shakedowns.

I sit and stare at my computer screen, too shocked to react. I read that line again.

Although all territory has now been claimed by the Ferrara family.

Holy shit, maybe it really is true?

I slam my computer shut in disgust.

Rici Ferrara isn't just an asshole now. He's a bad asshole—one with criminals who pledge allegiance to him.

That's it, I'm forgetting I ever met him. Unlike the five hundred times I've tried to forget him before, this time I really am.

I get up and begin to look for my gym clothes. I just wish I had the chance to tell him what I think of him.

Two hours later, I walk toward the gym with a sense of dread hanging over me. I don't know why, but every time I walk into a new gym it's like the first time I've ever been in one.

This one took a little while to find. It's not the cheapest membership or anything but it's over some shops near my work. I thought this would be good because when I move into my apartment, I'll always be in this area each day because of my job.

I walk through the red door on the ground floor and I take the stairs. I get to the top and walk in through the big glass double doors, and I look around. Wow, I'm pleasantly surprised. It's airy and bright with big glass windows down one side. It has six rows of cardio machines and a large boxing ring. To the left are all the weight machines. Huge plasma screens hang everywhere with music videos playing.

I smile. This place is pretty cool, actually. I walk to the reception where a girl is tidying up some things on the floor on her knees.

"Hello."

She looks up, surprised to see me. "Hi. Sorry, I didn't see you." She's English and has a wonderful Geordie accent. She has dark hair and olive skin. I assumed she was Italian.

"That's okay." I smile. "I imagine not many people come to the gym at 2:00 p.m. on a Sunday."

"Right." She laughs as she climbs to her feet. "I'm Anna." She holds her hand out to shake mine.

"I'm Olivia. Nice to meet you."

"You want to look around?" She gestures over to the cardio machines.

"Yes, please. I've just moved here."

"You're a kiwi?"

"No, Australian."

"Ahh, how are you finding it?" She smiles. "Milan, I mean."

"Good." I shrug. "I find the language barrier a little harder than I thought it would."

"Yeah, I found it really hard to settle in at first. Took me a good six months to feel at home. I moved here three years ago. My fiancé is Italian. We met on a Contiki tour in Germany."

"Oh." I smile. "That's lovely."

"Not really. He's an ass." She rolls her eyes. "I'm off him today. He crawled in at four this morning. He's lucky he didn't wake up with a plastic bag over his head. Stupid twat."

I giggle. I like this girl.

"You'll like this gym, it's very multicultural. It's owned by an English couple. It seems to have a lot of foreign members as well as Italian. It's not intentional, I think it's just the central location."

"Sounds great."

"The first session is a free trial. Do you want to work out today, and then I can show you the rates and memberships at the end?"

"Yes, please."

She gestures to the treadmill, and I hop on. She hits the buttons and it starts up.

"Not too fast," I warn her. "I'm likely to die of a heart attack, I'm so unfit."

"At least you don't work here." She huffs. "I have no bloody excuse."

A head pops around my office door. "Olivia, would you have time to go and pick something up for me?" Tara from the design team asks. "You can take my company car. It's just on the other side of town. I'm just really swamped, and we need this sample for a meeting at four."

"Yeah, sure." I spin in my chair toward her. "What do you need?"

"There's a commercial dry cleaner who is trialing a dry clean on a new fabric we are thinking of using next season."

"Okay. So, it's just a piece of fabric that I'm picking up?"

"No, we've made a very basic dress. We just want to see how it washes and wears. I'll text you the address."

"Great."

She passes me her car keys. "You have a license here, right?"

I take them from her. "I have an international license. How I will drive with it is another story."

She laughs. "Just don't crash, and no rush. As long as I have it by four."

"I'm going on lunch soon, anyway, so I'll get it while I'm out."

My phone beeps with the address. "Addio."

"Addio." I open the text and read the address. Hmm, it seems familiar. I stare at the address in front of me. Where have I seen that before?

Tower 1, 365 Amaro Ave: Level Four
Centro Direzionale di Milano

I shrug. Who knows? I grab my bag and walk out through reception. I'll have lunch on that side of town—something different. My phone rings and the name Natalie lights up my screen.

"Hello." I smile as I take the lift down to the underground parking lot.

"Oh my God. Tell me you love me."

"I love you."

"Ah!" she squeals. "I did it."

"You did what?" I walk through the elevator doors and look around. It's creepy down here. Dark. I look for the designated parking lot and finally locate it on the other side. Of course, it is.

"I'm coming to Milan."

I freeze on the spot. "What?"

"I resigned from my job. I got a six-month working visa."

My eyes widen. "Are you serious?" We have talked about her coming for months but she couldn't get her act together.

"Yes! But don't worry, I'll get my own apartment."

I close my eyes and laugh out loud. Nat and I tried to live together once before, and it didn't go well. I couldn't stand her one-night stands and not knowing who was coming to breakfast, and she couldn't stand my complaining about it. "Thank God. When do you get here?"

"I haven't booked a flight yet. My visa application only just came through an hour ago."

"And you resigned already?" I gasp.

"Fuck, yeah. I'm getting the hell out of here."

I laugh again. "I'm so excited."

"Me, too!" she screeches. "Okay, I gotta go. I have a million things to organize. I'll call you later."

"Bye."

The phone cuts off, and I grin as I arrive at the car. The lights flash twice when I unlock it.

This is awesome. We're going to have so much fun.

An hour later I park the car, turn the air conditioning up high, and I lean my head down on the steering wheel. Holy shit. How didn't I just die?

Thank God I'm here.

Lost, confused, and driving on the wrong side of the road do not make for easy driving. I'm hot and flustered. Hell, I need a stiff drink. I sit for a moment and try to calm myself down. Damn that Italian Stallion for giving me such a short wick this week. I feel like every little thing pushes me close to the edge of losing my cool when it's him I'm really mad at. If only I could tell him so. I'm sure I would feel so much better.

I push the exact building address into Google maps on my phone. I'm parked a few blocks away. I think the dry cleaners must be in a mall or something because this is as close as the maps app would let me get. I make my way down the street and find that I'm in the central business district. It's not trendy and hip like where my workplace is. Skyscrapers are dotted everywhere, and the streets are bustling with people in suits and business attire. It's very city chic without the glamour of my office's neighborhood.

I stare at the address on my phone. It should be just down here. I peer down at a huge quadrangle paved area and see a black glass building. Its super modern, and I glance up, and then I stop dead in my tracks at the huge gold letters above the door.

FERRARA

A man bumps into me from behind and mumbles something in Italian.

"Sorry," I call. I quickly take out my phone and Google again.

What is the Ferrara building?

I feel sick as I wait for the information.

The Ferrara Building is located in Milan
and is the head office for Ferrara Industries.
Address: 330 Amaro Ave
Centro Direzionale di Milano

My eyes widen as I peer up at the glass tower. Holy fucking shit.

That's his work building....... are you freaking kidding me? I stare at the skyscraper, all trendy and perfect, cold and hard.

Suddenly, I'm furious. Furious that he's such an asshole. The fact that he's rolling rich is even more infuriating. Entitled bastard.

You're just another Tinder whore.

How dare he?

I square my shoulders and pull down my shirt. Not today, motherfucker.

Before I can stop myself, I march into the Ferrara building like a madwoman.

My step falters as I walk through a metal detector and past three armed guards.

Jeez, okay. I regain my bravery and walk up to the reception.

The secretary smiles. "Ciao."

"Ciao." I frown. "Do you speak English?"

"I do."

I steel myself. "I would like to see Enrico Ferrara, please."

"Do you have an appointment?"

"No, but I need to see him."

"I'm sorry, Mr. Ferrara only sees pre-booked appointments."

"But is he in his office today?"

"I believe so. You will need to call ahead for a future appointment."

"Call him," I snap rudely. She stares at me. "You call him and tell him that Olivia Reynolds is here to see him."

She frowns and exchanges a glance with the other secretary. Then she glances over my shoulder at the security guard who is suddenly behind me, eavesdropping.

"I'm sorry—" the secretary begins.

"I'm not leaving until you call him."

She raises her brows and then picks up her phone. She waits as it rings.

"Ciao, c'è una donna qui che vuole essere presentata al Sig. Ferrara, dice che lo conosce, Olivia Reynolds." *Translation: Hello, we have a woman down here who wants to be announced to Mr. Ferrara, she says she knows him. Olivia Reynolds.*

I twist my fingers nervously in front of me. My heart is racing, slamming so hard into my chest that I'm nearly breathless.

"Si, va bene." *Translation: Yes, okay.*

"Miss Reynolds, can you turn and face the security camera, please?" She gestures to a camera at the side of us, mounted on the wall.

"Are you serious?" I frown.

"Very."

I exhale and turn toward the camera, giving it my best *fuck you* look. Don't mess with me, asshole. I'll smash your fucking camera over your head in a minute. If he doesn't let me in, I'm going postal and wrecking something.

"Yes, sir." She hangs up and comes back to me, unimpressed. "Junco will escort you up to Mr. Ferrara's office now."

"I can go by myself."

"Nobody enters the building unescorted." She glares at me. "You have an eight-minute appointment."

I glare right back. "I'll only need two."

The security guard approaches us. "This way." He leads me over to the elevator, and I get in behind him. He stays solemn and stares straight ahead. With every floor we go up, I feel a little crazier.

He leaves me in a prison.

He calls me a Tinder whore.

He didn't want me.

Well, fuck him.

The elevator doors open, and I step out like I'm the Devil himself.

Mr. Ferrara messed with the wrong girl.

We arrive into a reception area, and it's not at all what I expected. It's made from black marble, modern, and very futuristic with dark timber finishes. The ceiling has a huge crystal chandelier hanging from the roof. There's another guard on the floor, as well as two receptionists sitting at a long, black desk.

Why does he have so much security?

Mafiosi

Fuck.

"Just take a seat. Mr. Ferrara will be out shortly." A receptionist gestures to a large, leather sofa.

"Is that his office?" I ask, pointing to the oversized, double timber doors.

"Yes. He won't be a moment."

Without another thought, I turn and storm through the doors, forcing them open.

The bang echoes through the space, and I hear the receptionists gasp from behind me.

Oh jeez, so dramatic. I should be on *The Bold and the Beautiful* or something.

"No, no, no." Junco runs in behind me.

Rico looks up at me in surprise from behind a huge black desk. A sexy smirk crosses his lips as he sits back in his leather chair, holding a pen in his hand. "Miss Reynolds."

Another man is sitting at his desk, and he watches me with beady eyes, his interest piqued.

My sanity snaps. "Don't you Miss Reynolds me," I growl.

Junco grabs my arm. "Fuori adesso." *Translation: outside now.* "So sorry, Mr. Ferrara."

Enrico's smirk breaks into a grin, and he holds his hand up. "Esci." *Translation: get out.* "Leave us."

Junco looks between us.

"Now," Rico commands.

Junco bows his head and leaves the room,

"Anche tu." *Translation: you too.*

The other man stands and nods before he exits the office. The doors shut quietly behind him.

I stare at the smug as fuck bastard behind his big desk. He's equally as sexy but I'm choosing to ignore that.

I hate him.

He sits back in his chair as his eyes hold mine.

Electricity crackles through the air between us.

My poor heart may not survive today's activities.

"Olivia."

I grit my teeth, I hate the way he says my name. Husky and deep. *Ol – liv-i-ah.*

It's almost melodic.

Most definitely sexual.

The sound of his voice scatters my senses, and I stare at him as I search for an intelligent response.

He gestures to the chair in front of me. "Please, take a seat."

"Go to Hell." My hands clench into fists as they hang by my thighs. I can't remember ever being this angry at someone.

His tongue slowly darts out and sweeps over his bottom lip. He raises a brow. "Don't you dare come into *my* office and give me that tone."

"I'll do whatever I fucking like."

He stands and walks around the desk toward me. Our eyes are locked, and I swallow the lump in my throat.

His power surrounds me. I feel myself brace as I wait for his angry onslaught.

He leans his behind onto his desk and crosses his ankles in front of him. He's wearing a navy suit and a crisp white shirt. His shoes are the black leather pointy kind, and his chunky, obviously expensive watch sits heavily on his wrist.

He grips the desk beneath him. "Let me guess. You were in the area and thought you'd drop in?"

Damn him and his dark hair, chiseled jaw, and his big red lips. I begin to feel my pulse quicken. This is not in the plan, Olivia.

"Cut the shit, asshole," I fire back, furious that my traitorous body has the audacity to still find him attractive.

Amusement crosses his face, and he breaks out into a low chuckle.

"This isn't funny."

"I would apologize, but I disagree."

I narrow my eyes, contempt dripping from my every pore. "What are you apologizing for?"

"Laughing. What else?" He raises his brow.

I can't believe this. He's fucking infuriating. "How about you start with the caveman act during my date on Saturday night. I would like an apology for that."

He clenches his jaw and stands, angered. "He wasn't your date."

"Yes. He was."

"You met him on Tinder. Don't insult my intelligence, Olivia. Tinder isn't dating."

"What do you care who I date?"

"I don't," he fires back. "Get out. You're not the woman I thought you were, anyway."

"Ha!" I cry. "That's the pot calling the kettle black."

"The what?"

"You're not even a man. Your good looks and money can't hide what a fucking asshole you really are."

He lifts his chin in defiance. "Since when do you curse so much?"

"Since now."

"Go back to Tinder, Olivia." He rolls his eyes. "I am not interested in your dramatics."

I lose control. "How dare you," I sneer. "What man leaves a woman in a prison to rot?"

"I organized for the best lawyer in Italy to bail you out."

"But where were *you*?" I cry as my eyes fill with tears. I swipe them away, annoyed with myself for baring a weakness. "You left me when I needed you the most. I needed a friend." My voice cracks betraying my bravery act.

"I had a lot on my plate. It was a very bad time for me."

"Yes, I know. You and your thousands of lovers. You make me sick."

"You fuck strangers on Tinder," he growls. "I should have left you in that cell to rot."

I lose it, step forward, and I slap him hard across his face. The crack echoes through the room. We stare at each other, hate running between us, and I'm not entirely sure that he isn't going to slap me back. The look on his face is murderous. "You were the last man I slept with, asshole, not that that's any of your business," I sneer. "Yes, I know that's pathetic, and damn it, I'll be rectifying the situation immediately. You left a bitter taste in my mouth, and up until now, I couldn't stomach the thought of being with another. But thank you *very* much for reminding me of what you really are. I am well and truly ready to meet a real man."

His eyes hold mine. His chest rises and falls, as if he's grappling for control.

"Don't come near me ever again," I whisper. "I hate you. I wish we'd never met." I turn and storm toward the door. I open it in a rush to find four security guards waiting. "Move!" I yell, and they quickly jump out of my way.

"Olivia!" Enrico calls from behind me. "Get back here."

I run to the elevator. The doors are still open, and I slam the button to close them.

The numbers start to go down, and I run my hands through my hair as I try to control my erratic heart. Oh my God, that is the exact opposite of what I wanted to say.

Why did I come here?

The elevator doors open, and I run out of the building. I duck around the corner and lean up against the wall, closing my eyes.

What a disaster.

I climb the never-ending stairs, and I drink out of my water bottle. I'm wet with perspiration but nowhere near the end of my workout. I can't stop; I'm too wound up. I didn't expect for Enrico to rattle me the way that he did.

I cringe every time I think of myself tearing up in that asshole's office this morning.

Stupid fool. What on earth was I thinking?

The gym seems like a great place to try and punish myself. I wipe my perspiration with my towel and I keep on climbing. Perhaps this is the secret to working out hard—anger. Maybe all the people who smash it at the gym are really just pissed off individuals who have no other outlet. Makes perfect sense. Right now, I feel like I could take on Rocky Balboa and kick his ass.

My phone rings. It's Giorgio.

"Hello," I pant.

"Where are you?"

"The gym."

"Can you do me a favor?"

"I guess. Although you should be doing me a favor after the hangover you gave me."

He laughs, and I find myself smiling. I have no idea why Giorgio and I have clicked, but he's fun and we seem to have strung up an unlikely friendship.

"I completely forgot that I have a black-tie charity event tomorrow night. Angelo is away and can't make it. Will you be my date?"

"Seriously?" I continue to climb. "I can't, I have nothing to wear."

"You can wear a dress from work. It is a work dinner. You would be on the clock, technically."

I roll my eyes.

"Please. I just have to show my face. We can have dinner, a few cocktails, and be home before ten."

"Giorgio," I sigh. "Really?"

"Great, I'll pick you up at seven tomorrow night."

I stay silent.

"Please?" he whines.

"Fine."

"What's wrong with you? You don't sound your usual happy self."

"I'm at the gym killing myself."

"I should be doing the same. Thank you. See you then." He hangs up before I can change my mind.

Jeez, this is the day that keeps on giving.

I smile to myself as I unzip the first suit bag. My breath catches as my eyes roam over the gorgeous red evening dress. It's fitted with spaghetti straps and it is backless. I've never seen anything so beautiful, let alone imagined I would have the chance to wear it. I unzip the second bag to see gold and sequins. The third bag holds black lace. It goes on and on.

Wowsers.

I have a dress you can wear, Giorgio said. That was the understatement of the year. Being friends with the boss of Valentino seems to have its perks. Perks that come in the form of gorgeous evening wear being delivered to your hotel room in your exact size.

My blonde hair has been styled in big, loose curls, and pinned back on one side. My makeup is smoky, and I even pulled out my sexy underwear for the occasion.

I look through the six dresses that have been sent over but my eyes keep going back to the red one. The fabric is embossed, the detail on the stitching, the way it falls at the back, the shade of red—it's all so incredible. I hold it up in front of my body and stare at my reflection in the mirror. A big smile crosses my face.

Maybe this week isn't a complete disaster after all. I'm going out in Valentino.

Who have I become?

I look around the big ballroom in wonder as Giorgio leads me by my arm. We weave through the beautiful people and make our way over to the seating arrangement chart. He studies it in great detail.

"Wow." This place is ridiculous with over the top chandeliers hanging low and huge candelabras lining the walls.

"These things are always over the top," Giorgio says as he looks around, distracted. "This is our table here."

We make our way over and he pulls out my chair. We take a seat at the large, round table, set with ten places. It's covered with white table linen and set with fancy silverware. There are dozens of fresh flowers, all in different shades of cream.

A waiter arrives. "Can I get you a drink, sir?"

Giorgio's eyes flick to me. "Champagne to start?"

"Sounds great." I smile.

"Two champagnes, please."

I smile as I look around. I recognize some people from my design studies. Never in a million years did I think I would ever be the in the same room with them.

"I feel like a celebrity or some shit with all these famous people here," I lean in and whisper.

He chuckles, clearly amused. "Well, those famous people were all staring at my gorgeous date. You're the most breathtaking woman in the room."

"Why *am* I your date? I'm sure you have a million girlfriends you could have asked."

"This is true," he says as our drinks arrive. "Although, unlike them, I have an invested interest in you."

"Why?"

"Let's just say that I find you fascinating, Olivia Reynolds."

"Me," I scoff. "Fascinating?"

He glances down at his watch. "All will be revealed shortly."

"Giorgio!" someone calls from afar. A man standing with a group of people waves him over.

"Marcel." He laughs. "I'll be back in a moment, darling. Are you all right here for a moment?"

"I'm fine. Go do your thing."

He stands and goes to the other side of the ballroom. I watch on as he kisses everyone on both cheeks.

"Buongiorno," a voice says.

I turn to see a man in a black dinner suit standing behind my chair. He's dashingly handsome with a honey-colored hair and big brown eyes.

"I don't speak Italian, I'm sorry. Do you speak English?"

He sits down in the seat beside me and holds out his hand to mine. "Hello, my name is Sergio."

I shake his hand. "I'm Olivia."

"Are you new to Milan, Olivia? I haven't seen you around before."

"Yes." I smile. "Although, I'm sure you don't see everyone in Milan."

"When a woman is as beautiful as you, I would have remembered her." His eyes hold mine. "And I would have most definitely approached her to introduce myself."

I open my mouth to speak but no words come out. I feel my face flush. "Are you here alone?" he asks.

"I'm here with a friend." I gesture to Giorgio who is now watching the two of us.

"Ah." He smiles. "I have competition." I tuck my hair behind my ear. "If only I wasn't working tonight."

"You're working here tonight?" I ask.

"Yes, my boss is on his way."

"You work in fashion?"

He grins, amused. "A little."

"Do you work for a design house?"

"I'm in..." He pauses, as if searching for the right word. "Security."

"Oh. You're someone here's security?"

"Yes." He smiles, reaches over and picks up my hand, lifting it to his lips. "Can I have your number? I would like to call you tomorrow."

I frown as I watch his mouth dust my skin. "I... oh, I..."

He pushes something in his ear, and it is then that I notice he's wearing an earpiece.

"Me ne vado subito." *Translation: I'll be right out.* His eyes flick to me. "I have to go. My boss is here. I shall be back later." He kisses my hand again as he stands. "Don't have fun without me, Olivia."

He rushes off, and I smile as I watch him disappear out of the room.

He was... interesting.

Giorgio falls back into the seat beside me. "What did he want?" he whispers.

I smile against my champagne glass. "My number, apparently."

He rolls his eyes and picks up his drink, unimpressed. "I'm sure his boss would be thrilled about that."

I glance over at him and frown. "Why, who's his boss?"

Giorgio lifts his chin to the door, and I see Sergio walk into the room with a group of men. Someone is trailing behind them while speaking to another man, and I crane my neck to see who it is. He slowly comes into view.

Black dinner suit.

Square jaw.

Power that emanates throughout the room like a shockwave.

Fuck.

Enrico Ferrara just arrived.

12

Olivia

MY STOMACH FLUTTERS and I snap my eyes away, angry that his presence still affects me.

"So, that's his boss, hey?" I mutter.

"Yep." Giorgio's eyes dance with delight. "Enrico Ferrara, the king of Italy. Do you know him?"

"Why would I?"

He smiles and picks up my hands. "I thought we were friends."

"We are."

"Then why are you lying to me?"

I stare at him. "Why would you think I know him?"

He shrugs. "Just a hunch."

"Mr. Ferrara doesn't interest me." I don't want to have this conversation.

"That's his mother on the other side of the table and his two brothers and his younger sister," Giorgio continues.

My eyes float over to his table, his mother is talking and smiling with a man, she's very attractive with a gorgeous figure, I noticed her before I even knew who she was. She has perfectly styled shoulder length dark hair and is wearing a black Gucci dress, the epitome of style. My eyes then go to the young girl, his sister. She's talking to one of his brothers, the one that I met in Rome, what was his name? The doctor, Andrea, that's it. She tips her head back and laughs out loud, she's absolutely stunning and is wearing a modest ice pink dress with long sleeves.

"Fascinating...aren't they?" Giorgio smiles as he sips his wine.

I push my chair out. "I'm going to the bathroom. Where are they?"

"Over to the back wall and down the corridor." He points in the direction.

"Thanks." I grab my clutch and make my way out of the ballroom. I walk down the corridor and sigh in relief when I get into the privacy of the cubicle.

Damn him.

What's he doing here?

Is this how it's going to be in Milan? Every time I walk out of the door I run into his building, his workers, or worse... him.

Just the sight of him infuriates me.

I finish up in the bathroom, wash my hands, and I reapply my red lipstick. I tuck my boobs back into my dress and turn to look at my behind in the mirror. Suddenly, it's become super important that I look amazing.

I'll show the bastard what he missed out on.

Go out there, have a fun night and don't even look his way, don't give him the satisfaction of even glancing toward him, I tell myself as I smooth my dress down.

I stare at the blonde in the mirror.

To the outside world, she looks so put together. What a joke that is. Little do they know I'm still thinking about a man who treated me abysmally two years ago. I can't get him out of my head no matter how hard I try. Seeing him yesterday or should I say fighting with him yesterday seems to have opened up old wounds. I feel raw and open, it's as if he has just left me in the police station.

What's wrong with me?

I just need to snap out of it, as soon as Natalie gets here it will be much easier. I'll have a friend and a social life. To hell with Enrico Ferrara.

With a deep exhale, I drop my shoulders and leave the bathroom. I take a wrong turn and arrive at a doorway on the other side of the ballroom.

Near his table.

I stop and watch him for a moment. He's smiling and talking to the people he's sitting with. I watch him pick up his scotch and take a sip, and my stomach clenches.

Why does he have to be so gorgeous?

The beautiful woman next to him says something. He listens to her and then laughs out loud.

Is she his date?

She has long dark hair and is exotically beautiful. But he didn't arrive with her.

He came alone.

Stop it. Who the hell cares if she's his date?

I know I should stop watching him like a stalker from the corridor, but I can't make myself. My feet won't move.

A man walks up behind him, puts his hand on his shoulders, and says something. Rico smiles broadly before he stands and the two of them shake hands.

He's so much taller than everyone around him, and muscular, but it's the unbridled power that comes from within him that draws me in.

Is the weirdest thing.

It's like he has this magnet inside of his body and I have the other magnet inside of mine.

Every instinct inside of me wants to walk over to him and take him in my arms.

But then I remember that he's an asshole and I can't.

I drop my gaze to the floor.

Go back to your table, Olivia, you're pathetic.

His loud laugh surrounds me. I glance back up to see him greeting a woman. He leans in and kisses her on the cheek. *Who's she?*

With a disgusted shake of my head, I go back out into the corridor and make my way around to the other side of the ballroom. I eventually take a seat.

Giorgio smiles over at me. "You all right, darling?"

"I'm fine."

He passes me my glass of champagne. "I propose a toast."

"What to this time?"

His eyes dance with delight. "Same as last time."

"To making men jealous?"

He winks. "Would be such a shame to be in that dress and not make a man jealous, don't you think?"

I smirk. "What exactly are you talking about, Giorgio?"

He leans in and kisses my cheek. "I know that you have men circling this table watching you. Use it to your advantage."

I don't know what he's up to, but I like his thinking. "Perhaps you're right. Why don't you introduce me to some of your friends?"

He pushes his chair back with a big smile and holds his hand out to mine.

"This way, darling." Giorgio leads me through the crowded ballroom and over to the bar where a group of five men stand. "Gentlemen, may I introduce Olivia Reynolds. I adore her. She recently started with Valentino and is new to Milan."

"Hello." They all smile, and one by one they introduce themselves and kiss me on the cheek. They're all breaking their neck as they try to talk to me, and we fall into a conversation about my work and where I'm from. They're all similar ages to me, and quite good looking, too. Perhaps it's the black dinner suits talking.

Can any man be ugly in a dinner suit? I don't think so.

Giorgio gives me a not so subtle wink before he discretely moves to the bar.

Snake. I'll kill him later.

For ten minutes, I stand and talk politely. One man in particular named Pedro has taken a liking to me.

The group falls silent, and I glance up from Pedro to see Enrico has approached the group. "Enrico, my friend," one of the men greets him nervously.

They all shake his hand, while I sip my champagne. His eyes eventually find mine. "Hello, Olivia."

"Hello."

The men's eyes all widen as they look between us, realizing we know each other.

I try to talk to Pedro again but Enrico holds his gaze across the circle, and Pedro becomes flustered. "I'm going to the bar," he announces suddenly.

"Yes, I'll come," offers another man.

"Yes, I need to get back to my table," someone else mutters.

"I'm going to the bathroom," another says.

Suddenly, I'm left alone with Rico. *Wimps.*

Enrico steps toward me. "Hello." His voice is velvety and deep.

I squeeze my champagne glass so tight that it may smash in my hand.

His eyes drop down my body, and then back up to my face. "You look breathtaking."

My stomach clenches. "Thanks."

"I wanted to talk to you."

"About what?"

"Many things."

That damn electricity crackles in the air between us again.

"You asked me yesterday why I left you in the police station two years ago," he says quietly.

My heart stops. "Yes."

He opens his mouth to speak.

"Here you are." Giorgio smiles. "Rico, darling, it's been too long, my friend. Where have you been hiding?" He grabs Rico's hand and kisses him on both cheeks. They hug.

"You're interrupting us," Enrico tells Giorgio as his eyes come back to mine.

"What's new? I'm always interrupting you." Giorgio laughs, and I can tell he and Enrico are friends. He isn't scared of him like the other men are. "Olivia, our entrees are at our table, sweetheart." He pulls me by the hand. "Goodbye, Rico, we shall talk later, darling."

Giorgio pulls me back to our table, and I glance back to see Enrico glaring after us, unimpressed that I've left our conversation unfinished. Damn it, I wanted to know what he was going to say. Not that it would make any difference, but still.

We take a seat, and Giorgio smiles over at me like the cat that got the cream.

"Our entrees aren't at the table." I smirk. I'm not discussing Enrico Ferrara with him, but I have sneaking suspicion that he already knows.

Giorgio's eyes hold mine. "How many times do we need to toast before I teach you the lesson, Olivia?"

"Am I a bad student?" I smile and raise my glass to his.

"The worst."

Three hours later, I spin around on the dancefloor with Giorgio.

"Thank you for bringing me tonight, I've had fun." I'm not lying, either. We've laughed and talked. I've met a lot of new people, and it has honestly been fun.

"The formalities are over now. Shall we go soon?" he asks.

"Yes, it *is* a school night."

He smiles down at me. "Did I tell you how gorgeous you look in that dress yet?"

"A few times." I giggle.

"You wear it better than our models. Maybe you could be the next Valentino girl."

"Ha." I laugh out loud. "I will need to lose twenty pounds before I would even fit into the sample."

"Can I cut in?" a deep voice asks. We turn to see Enrico standing beside us.

"Why, of course you can." Giorgio smiles and steps aside.

Enrico takes me in his arms. He pulls me close, and my body awakens from her dormant sleep.

Shit...

We sway to the music for a moment as I hold my breath. If I inhale, I'm sure to smell his pheromones—the ones that make me weak at the knees. He towers above me, one hand on my lower back holding me close to his body. The other is holding my hand.

"I had forgotten how good you feel in my arms." He smiles down at me as everyone around us disappears.

That look… I had forgotten it.

I gently ease my body back from his but he pulls me close again.

"Don't pull away from me."

"Don't tell me what to do."

He leans closer, his lips resting on my temple, and I begin to feel a warmth seep into my bones.

He feels so good.

"What were you going to say before?" I ask. "When we were at the bar, you started saying something."

"Does it really matter now?"

"It does to me. I…" I stop myself from speaking.

"Can I see you tomorrow night?"

I stop dancing.

He moves my body with his hands, and I begin to dance again.

"No."

"Why not?"

I shake my head. "Why would I want to see you after last time?"

"It was out of my control before."

I roll my eyes.

"I never left you in a prison to rot."

"That's exactly what you did."

"I ensured you had the best legal team available. It was all that I could do at the time."

I stop, angered at his piss poor excuse. "That's not good enough. Whatever. This is pointless." I pull out of his arms. "Rico, I told you to stay away from me."

He pulls me close again. "Don't go," he whispers. His lips drop to my temple, and I close my eyes at the feel of him there.

"It was a very bad time for me, Olivia. I wasn't thinking clearly."

"Why?" I breathe.

"The day I put you onto the plane to Sorrento, my father and grandfather were killed in a car accident."

I stop dancing and stare up at him. "On that very day?"

He clenches his jaw. "I got the call as I was leaving the airport."

"Why didn't you tell me?"

"I didn't want to burden your trip. I was someone you had just met."

I watch him struggle with this conversation. This subject is obviously hard.

"Every time you called me that week, I was with a lawyer or my grieving mother. The timing was all wrong, and then everything got too hard."

My heart hurts. "I could have helped you," I whisper up at him.

He pulls me close, and we dance for a moment. Regret swirls between us.

"I saw you with that man and I..." His voice trails off.

"I'm not on Tinder. That was my first date, Rico. You know me. I'm not like that."

He pulls me closer. We don't speak, we just sway to the

music. After just one excuse and five minutes of dancing, I feel myself melting against his body.

Mafiosi.

He isn't good for me.

Nothing about Enrico Ferrara is good for me.

His questionable lifestyle, his money....and the hold he has over my wimpy heart is one big recipe for disaster.

"Can we go for a drink after this? I would like to talk to you," he says quietly.

I stare up at his handsome face. "No, Rici," I whisper sadly. I wish things were different. "It's too late."

He stops dancing. "You said that our story was just beginning." His eyes search mine.

"That was before you burned the book."

Our eyes are locked, the music finishes, and everyone claps while I step back from him.

"Olivia."

"Goodbye," I whisper.

His gaze drops to the floor, and before I cave, I turn and quickly walk back to my table.

Giorgio smiles as I arrive, and we both turn to see Enrico leave the ballroom in a rush.

My stomach drops.

Giorgio watches him leave and then turns to me. "Why do you think you're in Italy, Olivia?"

I turn to him, confused. "What do you mean?"

"Your application was successful in New York."

I frown. "What?"

"You got the job in New York—the first one you applied for."

"Then why did I end up in Milan?"

"Mr. Ferrara sent for you." I stare at him, lost for words. "I brought you here at his request."

"What?" I splutter. Horror dawns. "So, my whole job is a sham?"

"No." He puts his arm around me. "Darling, you got that position fair and square, and I got them to hold the position in New York for three months in case things don't work out here."

I stare at him. "Why would you do that?"

"For Rico."

"He asked you to send for me?"

"Yes."

The room spins. "But why?"

He chuckles as he picks up my purse and hands it to me. He links my hand around his arm and leads me toward the door. "Connect the dots, sweetheart. It seems Enrico Ferrara has a tendre for you."

We walk out of the front door and straight into the back of a waiting cab. I stare out of the window as the taxi pulls out into the street.

"I haven't seen him for two years, Giorgio."

"And yet, he hasn't forgotten you."

I stare at Giorgio, my mind a clusterfuck of confusion. "He's an asshole."

He smiles and puts his arm around me. "They all are, darling."

"I can't believe you're here already." I smile across the table at Natalie.

"My boss decided he didn't want me to work my notice, and then the airline had a half price special for this week only. I had nothing holding me back. May as well get here so I can start looking for work."

"I'm so excited you're here."

"Me, too."

It's Saturday night, and in an unexpected turn of events, Natalie has arrived in Milan earlier than we expected. We're in a cocktail bar and we have just had dinner. We're going clubbing tonight after this to celebrate.

Natalie frowns. "So, tell me this story again. I'm confused."

"Well, that makes two of us." I sip my margarita. "Apparently, Enrico asked for my job to be in Milan instead of New York."

"How does he have that pull?"

"I don't know, he's friends with Giorgio and, well... there are stories about him being the head of the Mafiosi," I whisper.

"The mafia?" she gasps out loud.

"Shh." I look at the people around us, hoping nobody heard. "Keep your voice down."

"What do the stories say?"

I wave my drink in the air as I try to articulate myself. "That the Ferrara family has been linked to Mafiosi, but nothing has ever been proven or any charges laid." I shrug. "I don't know. It's some fucked up shit that I can't make head nor tails of."

"Oh, that's crap," she huffs. "As if you would listen to the internet. Anyone can load something onto Wikipedia, Olivia."

"But he is really, really rich, Nat. Like horse's head rich."

"Because all rich Italians must be criminals, right?" She rolls her eyes. "This isn't the 1940s, Liv. He probably just comes from a really smart family."

"You think?'

"It's a lot more plausible than the frigging mafia rumors.

Didn't you say his brother was a doctor and that he was a policeman?"

"Yeah." I sip my drink, fascinated with her theory.

"Since when have you ever seen a policeman and a doctor in the fucking mafia?"

"True."

"Oh, hang on." She holds up her hand. "I can't kill criminals today, I'm in heart surgery."

We giggle. "It does sound ridiculous when you say it like that."

"But then he sent for you."

I smile softly. I hate to admit it, but I love that he sent for me.

"He must have been thinking about you all this time."

"I don't know. He asked to see me the other night and when I said no, he left in a huff."

"You haven't heard from him since?"

"Nope."

"Hmm." She purses her lips. "What about how his father died on the day you left?"

"I know."

"This is like a movie or something. El Caspase Blanco."

"Is that a movie?" I frown.

"Yeah, maybe, I don't know. Something like that." She sips her drink. "I mean, you thought he hated you. He was broken. Huge misunderstanding. He sends for you two years later." She puts her hands over her heart and bats her eyelashes. "My faith in romance has been restored."

I stare at her, deadpan. "He's still an asshole."

"Totally, but at least now you can fuck him without regret."

I grab her hand over the table. "Nat, thank you for coming to stay to Milan for me. It means the world."

"Baby, I'm not here for you. I'm totally here for the men."

Two hours later,

The club is pumping. The dance music is as loud as can be, and we are outside on the terrace. Inside there's a large dance area, three or four bars, and a second lounge area. Outside here is a marquee, a big pool and bar area, and it's not as crowded as inside.

"God, will you look at this place?" Nat whispers.

"It's something else."

There's beautiful people everywhere, and fairly lights light up the sky. "This will be where all the cool people hang," Nat says.

"Yeah, I guess." I smile as I glance up at the door in time to see Enrico walk through to the outside bar, with two men ahead of him.

"Shit," I whisper.

Natalie looks over in the direction of where I'm looking. "What?"

"That's him."

"Who?"

"Enrico."

"What? Which one."

"The tall one at the back."

Her eyes widen as she eyes the perfect specimen. "That's... him?"

He towers over everyone. He's wearing black jeans that fit in all the right places, and a slim cut black T-shirt. His shoulders are broad, his jaw is... *fuck.*

Nat stares at him, wide-eyed. "That's him? That god there is the guy who you met in Rome?"

I nod.

Her mouth falls open. "The rich one?'

"Yes."

"Holy fuck, no wonder you were heartbroken. I'm a bit in love with him myself. He's gorgeous, Liv."

I can't take my eyes off of him, and unexpected excitement rushes through me.

He's here.

"Talk about a trifecta," Natalie whispers. His two friends are gorgeous too. "Now that is one Italian sandwich. Who's he with?" she whispers.

"I don't know. Neither are his brothers. I met one in Rome."

"You met his brother?" She frowns.

"Briefly. He was out with his brother on the night that we met." One of the men has honey-colored hair and is wearing a white collared shirt with blue jeans. The other is dark like Enrico, wearing a sports coat over jeans. All three of them are super handsome. Every woman around them does a double take.

But it's Enrico that I can't take my eyes off. My stomach rolls with nerves as I look down at myself. I'm wearing a tight black strapless dress and sky-high stilettos. Do I look okay?

"Go over there. Go over there right now," Natalie whispers.

"He's an asshole, remember."

"Who cares when he looks like that?" I laugh. "Tell me he fucks as good as he looks," she whispers with her eyes glued to him.

"You have no idea," I reply as we continue to watch from our spying spot across the pool.

"Right, here's the plan," she says. "Walk past him, let him know you're here."

"You think?" I frown.

"Yes. Definitely." She shoves me in his direction, and I start to walk around the pool to the bathrooms. A gorgeous redhead stops to talk to him. She says something and he laughs out loud, as if he knows her. They begin to talk. I immediately turn back to Nat.

"He can walk past me. I'm not chasing him. Maybe we should go to another club?" I turn my back to him.

Natalie narrows her eyes as she watches them over my shoulder.

"Is he still talking to her?" I ask as I sip my drink.

"Yes." She rolls her eyes. "She's getting all touchy and putting her hand on his chest."

"Stupid bitch," I whisper.

"Yes, hands off, mole." She frowns.

"What's happening?"

"She grabbed his hand."

My eyes widen. "What?"

"Oh no."

"What's happening?"

Natalie puts her hand on her chest and sighs in relief.

"What?"

"I thought they were going to kiss."

"Are you kidding me?" I snap as I spin toward them. The redhead is wearing a white dress that's super low cut. She has the best body I think I've ever seen—huge boobs and a tiny waist. She looks like a sex kitten on crack. "Fuck this," I whisper. "I'm not standing here and watching him with her. I'm going inside to the bar. Do you want another drink?"

"Yes, please." Her eyes are glued on them. "I'll stay here and keep watch."

"You do that. Push her in the pool if you need to."

"Copy that."

I drain my glass, put it on a table, and walk inside. I want to waste some time. I go to the bathroom and walk around the club looking at all the bars and lounge areas. This place really is amazing.

Don't let him get to you, I remind myself. I eventually head to the bar and stand in line, which is huge. I'm going to be here for a while. I text Nat,

Line is huge

A text bounces back.

Oh my God.
He knows you're here.
He watched you walk inside.

My mouth falls open.

What?: Are you sure?

A message comes in.

Positive.

Excitement runs through me. Oh, this is ridiculous.

MAYDAY.
Ahh, he's coming inside.
Look Fucking Sexy!

I'm in such a fluster that I go to shove my phone in my bag

and completely miss it. The phone falls on the floor in the darkness.

I bend down and feel around looking for it. Oh hell, where is it? A man steps on my hand.

"Ah!" I cry out. I find the phone, stand, and come face to face with Enrico Ferrara.

He smirks right at me. "Hello, Olivia. We meet again."

13

Olivia

"What are you doing here?" I blurt out.

"Looking for you."

I frown. That's not the answer I was expecting. "You're looking for me?"

"Yes, and here you are."

Thump, thump, thump goes my heart.

"You look beautiful." He takes my hand and holds it out as his eyes roam up and down my body. "Very nice," he purrs.

"Thanks." Nerves steal my breath as I stare at him.

"Next!" the bartender calls. I turn and step forward, and Enrico comes up snug behind me.

"I'll have two margaritas, please," I tell the bartender, totally distracted by the man behind me. Enrico's hand goes to my waist and electricity shoots through me. "Do... do you want a drink?" I ask him over my shoulder.

"I'll have an Amaro, please." He digs out his wallet and hands his card to the waiter.

"That's not necessary. I'll get it," I say.

His hands fall to my hips, instantly silencing me. He bends and puts his lips to my ear. "You will get it." Goosebumps scatter over my skin at the feeling of his breath on my neck. "But I'll get this one."

Oh jeez...

I stand and watch the bartender make the drinks as Enrico's hands stay fixed on my waist. The heat from his touch feels like it's starting a slow burning fire.

Shit, shit, shit, *shit*.

The waiter puts the drinks on the counter.

"I'll help you carry them," Enrico says. He picks up two and I pick up one. He follows me outside.

Natalie glances up as I approach. Her eyes widen when she sees him behind me.

"Here you are." I smile awkwardly and hand over her drink.

"Thanks." She smiles.

I turn to Enrico. "Natalie, this is Enrico, a friend I met in Rome."

Enrico's eyes hold mine for an extended beat and he raises a brow. Finally, his manners surface, and he smiles. "Nice to meet you, Natalie." He shakes her hand and then passes me my drink.

Natalie goes back to the man she was talking to, and Enrico bends to whisper in my ear. "So, I'm your friend?"

"What would you prefer I introduce you as?"

He sips his drink with a straight face. "Not that." Unable to help it, I smile over at him and he smiles back. "How has your week been, Olivia?"

"Good. Yours?"

He shrugs. "Okay."

"Just okay?"

"Just okay."

We fall silent, and I don't know what to say. He makes me so nervous.

"Let's go and sit down." He gestures to a bench seat beneath a canopy.

My eyes flicker to it. "Okay."

I follow him over to the corner of the courtyard. It's darker here, but the space is lit with fairy lights. We find our spot and sit beside each other.

"Closer, bella." He grabs my hips and drags me to him. The dominance of the act starts a series of memories to flood my mind. The way he moved me while we made love. He just flipped me around like a feather. My body was at his disposal.

"Tell me why your week was just okay," I say.

He smiles as he looks out over the other clubbers. "Let's just say that having you in town is very... distracting. I've been unable to focus on anything knowing you were so close."

Hope blooms in my chest. I don't know what I'm hoping for, but it's most definitely there.

I look out over the club, searching for something intelligent to say. "I'm sorry about your father," I whisper. "I was so shocked when you told me, I didn't offer my condolences."

A soft smile dusts his face.

"I wish you'd told me back then," I say softly.

He clenches his jaw and stays silent.

I twist my fingers in front of me. "Do you come here often?"

We turn back to each other, and his dark eyes hold mine. "No."

"Oh."

An awkward silence falls over us. I have to concentrate to

remember to breathe. He's not chatty like he was before. He seems more intense, or am I imagining it?

"You're different," I whisper.

"How so?"

"You're quiet now."

He smiles sadly. "I just…." He stops himself from saying more.

"You just…?"

He shrugs. "Words escape me sometimes."

I smile as I catch the first glimpse of the man I met. "Did you organize for me to come to Milan?"

"Yes," he confirms without hesitation. "And you weren't ever supposed to find that out. Damn Giorgio and his big mouth."

I smile. "Why did you want me here?"

"I needed to see you." His eyes hold mine.

"Why didn't you just call me?"

A frown crosses his brow. "Because I knew you wouldn't come for me alone."

Does he even know me at all?

We stare at each other and I feel this connection that just shouldn't be there. Not after this long—not after the way he treated me.

"What are you thinking?" he whispers.

"I don't know." Thump, thump, thump goes my heart. "What are you thinking?"

He leans toward me. "I'm thinking that you're the most beautiful fucking woman I have ever seen, and I……" His voice trails off.

"And you *what*?"

"I need to kiss you."

I stare at him as the air swirls between us. "So, do it."

He frowns and his eyes lift to the people around us. "I can't. I can't kiss you here."

"Why not?"

He gives a subtle shake of his head and clenches his jaw. "I don't get to choose what I do in public anymore."

Fuck, *he doesn't want me.*

I fake a smile and stand. "That's okay, I get it."

He frowns and stands abruptly. "You get what?"

"I'm not playing this game, Rico. You don't have to say pretty things. You don't have to kiss me. I'm not going to beg. How pathetic do you think I am?"

"You think I don't want you?"

I roll my eyes. "Just leave it."

He grabs my hand and pulls me through the club quickly. "What are you doing?" I cry out. We cross the dance floor, walk through the hall, and we enter another room. I glance around to see we're in an office of some kind.

Enrico slams me up against the back of the door. "I said I can't kiss you. Not that I didn't want to."

His lips take mine aggressively. His tongue slides through my open lips, and I melt against him. He pushes his hard body up against mine as he moans into my mouth. We lose control. My hands are in his hair when he slams me harder against the wall. I feel his hard length up against my stomach. He bends and runs his hand up my thigh, under my dress. His tongue seductively dances with mine as he pushes my panties to the side.

We fall silent as his fingers slowly circle through my dripping wet flesh.

"Solleva la gamba, lasciami entrare." *Translation: lift your leg, let me in.*

"What?" I pant.

"Wrap your leg around me."

I slowly lift my leg, and he pushes two thick fingers inside me. My head falls back. *Oh, fuck.*

"Cazzo, sei un fuoco" *Translation: fucking hell, you're on fire.*

His grip on my hair is painful. His tongue in my mouth mirrors his thick fingers, pumping to a slow, erotic dance. The sound of my wet arousal hangs in the air.

His teeth slide down my neck with a sharp hiss.

"So... wet... fucking tight," he whispers, accentuating the Ts. "I've missed you and this beautiful cunt."

Oh God.

He really begins to work me, and I hold onto his forearm as my mouth hangs open. Our eyes are locked, and I can feel the muscles in his forearm contract. Oh yes, it's been too long.

I shudder, and he immediately pulls out.

"Don't stop," I plead.

"You won't come here." He kisses me again, but this time it's slow and deliberate. Then, as if the last five minutes didn't happen, he regains composure. He straightens my dress, pulls it down, and drops it back into position. He runs his fingers through his hair, and before I can protest, he's pulling me out of the room. He drags me back through the club, and my mind is a blur. How is he even functioning right now?

I'm so close to coming that the smoke machine might set me off. My body is contracting as she searches for those fingers. I grit my teeth as I try to focus on where he's taking me.

"Olivia, please meet my friends." He presents me with a cool, calm, and collected smile. "This is Matteo, my brother, and Fabien, my best friend."

I smile as I look between them. I'm flushed and messed up. Can they tell that their friend has just finger fucked me in an office?

"Hi," I offer.

"Hello." Matteo smiles as he kisses my cheek.

"Lovely to meet you." Fabien smiles, too. "Do you live in Milan?"

"Yes, I'm new here." I glance over to Enrico. With his dark eyes locked on mine, he brings his fingers up to his nose and inhales.

The air leaves my lunges in a rush. *What the fuck*?

I watch on as he slowly puts his two middle fingers deep into his mouth and sucks them clean. His eyes flicker with arousal at my taste, and he licks his lips as if savoring every last drop.

My stomach flutters. Good God.

I lose the ability to speak. All coherent thought leaves my mind, and my sex begins to throb. Hell, I need him. I need all of him. I don't give a damn about Mafiosi or tomorrow or anything to do with reality.

I need Rico tonight.

"Do you live here?" I ask Fabien, distracted. I get a vision of Rico naked… in my bed.

Fuck, yes.

His friend keeps talking but I can hardly hear them over the heat of his stare on me. I can't speak, I can't do anything. My body is in complete meltdown.

It's on a mission to fuck.

I glance over to see that the man Natalie was talking to now has his hand on her hip. She's looks settled for the night. I can't stand here like this for one moment longer.

It's now or never.

I crook my finger, and Rico leans in. "Let's go," I whisper.

A dark smirk crosses his face. "We're leaving," he announces immediately. "See you tomorrow."

Before I can hardly say goodbye to them, he's pulling me by the hand over to Natalie.

"Hi." I smile as I get to her.

"I'm going to get something to eat with Rico," I lie.

Nat smiles mischievously. "Sure." She looks over to Rico. "Take care of her."

Rico eyes hold mine. "I intend to."

We walk through the crowd and my body starts to hum. I know what's coming, and goddamn it, I can't wait. We arrive at the front doors of the club and he drops my hand.

"My car is this way."

I follow him down the steps, and I go to grab his hand again.

"Don't," he whispers, discretely pulling his hand away.

I frown. "Why not?"

He looks across the road to a parked car with men sitting inside it. "My security guys are here. I don't feel comfortable being affectionate in front of them." He begins to walk faster.

"Oh." I nearly have to run to keep up as my eyes dart around. "Is that why you wouldn't kiss me inside?"

He nods once, and we arrive at a black sporty-looking car. He opens the door for me, and I get in. I look around at the black leather interior. It has that new car scent with all the bells and whistles inside. Wow, this thing is swanky.

He gets in, and without a word, he starts the car and pulls out into the traffic. Once alone, he grabs my hand and lifts it to his lips. He kisses me tenderly as his eyes come to me.

"That's better."

"Where are we going?" I ask.

His eyes go back to the road. "My place."

"What's wrong with my hotel?"

"Nothing," he replies casually as he turns the corner. "It's just safer at my house."

I frown, safe from what? "Why do you have security now?"

"It's a necessary evil." His hand slides up my thigh and he inhales sharply. "Let's talk about how fucking edible you look in that dress tonight."

I smile and glance behind us to see the two cars trailing behind us. We drive on in silence. He seems lost in thought, and my mind is on the security cars behind us. Why are they here? Is he in danger of some kind? I turn again and look out the back window to make sure I'm not imagining it.

Two cars both filled with men trail at a safe distance behind. "Where do you live?" I ask

"In the Magenta District. It's not far."

The farther we drive away from the club, the more a little of my sanity returns.

Shit, what am I doing?

I told myself to stay away from him, yet here I am on my way to his house. I get a vision of us in that office and how incredibly hot he felt. How dominant he is... hard. *Damn my body and her carnal needs.*

Horny bitch.

He pulls into an underground parking lot and the cars pull in behind us. I feel like I'm in a James Bond movie or something. He parks the car, and then comes around to open my door.

The men get out of their cars and pretend not to look at me, although I can feel their assessing eyes.

"This way," Rico says, void of emotion. I follow him into the elevator and the door shuts behind us. He instantly grabs my hand and smiles softly.

There he is...

"I don't like you not touching me in public."

"I don't like not touching you."

He leans in takes my face in both hands, and he kisses me. It's soft, with just the right amount of suction. My feet nearly lift off the floor. He kisses me again as he begins to walk me backwards, and then the ping notifies us of our arrival.

The doors open up and Rico pulls me out. I look around in wonder. The elevator doors opened up directly into his apartment.

It's huge with a mezzanine level upstairs. City lights twinkle through the expansive glass wall, and there's a pool outside on the private terrace.

"This is your house?" I whisper, wide-eyed.

"Yes." He puts his hands into his pockets, giving me time to look around and get my bearings. "Do you want the tour?"

I nod, suddenly too nervous to speak.

He pulls me through the foyer and down a few dark timber stairs.

"Living area," he says. I look around in wonder. There are navy and chocolate slouchy leather couches, a huge bluestone fireplace, and beautiful colored artwork. We walk through double timber doors.

"Dining area." A beautiful pale wood dining table that seats twelve sits in the middle of the room. "Kitchen." The kitchen doesn't even look like a kitchen. It looks like an exotic restaurant that you would see in a travel brochure. Chunky metal light fittings hang from the ceiling, and large benches take up the floor space.

"Did you pick all the furnishings?" I ask him.

He smiles softly as if imagining what I must see through my eyes. "Yes."

What are you doing here, Olivia? This is out of your league.

His eyes come to mine. "Do you want to see my bedroom?"

Butterflies flutter deep in my stomach. “I don’t know, do I?”

He steps forward and takes my face in his hands. “Your body told me earlier that you do.”

“You shouldn’t listen to her. She’s…” I stop talking, distracted by his big lips that are suddenly on mine.

“She’s… what?” he breathes.

“She’s good to go and trying to get me into trouble.”

He chuckles, and it’s deep and raspy. “I like that about her.

“She doesn’t know what’s good for her.”

His eyes dance with mischief. “I have no doubt about that.” He kisses me again. “Although, I’m sure she knows what does feel good.” He gently bites my bottom lip and stretches it out. My sex contracts at the feel of his teeth on my skin.

He pulls back and looks at me. His eyes are dark, and he licks his lips in anticipation. “My bedroom is this way, Olivia.”

He takes my hand and leads me up an expansive hall. I’m sure I’m supposed to be taking in my surroundings right now, but I can’t concentrate on anything other than the beautiful man holding my hand.

The Devil himself, leading me to his den.

My heart is beating so fast that I have to concentrate on my breathing. I don’t want it to sound like I’m running a marathon, although it totally feels like I am.

His bedroom is big, modern, and minimalistic. The walls are a dark gray, almost navy blue. The linen on the huge bed is white, and white chunky sofas surround another bluestone fireplace. The artwork on the walls is all monochrome photography. It really is something else.

“Wow. You have impeccable taste.”

He steps forward, bringing us closer. “I do.” He kisses me with such passion that I can’t keep my eyes open.

Damn this man and his magic tongue.

Our kiss turns frantic, and my hands go to his hair, while his hands go to my behind. Suddenly, he lets me have it both barrels. We slam up against the wall as we lose control. He turns me away from him and unzips my dress. It falls to the floor and I stand before him in a black strapless bra and lace panties.

His eyes drop as he drinks me in. When they rise to meet mine again, they're blazing with fire.

He wants me. Every inch of him wants me.

I can feel it.

He undoes my bra and tosses it to the side. My large breasts fall free. He slides my panties down my legs. His chin rises, and he hisses in appreciation. His dark eyes burn holes in my skin.

"Hmm, there she is." His voice is deep and guttural—a hushed whisper.

My sex begins to throb. "Take it off."

He holds his hands out. "If you want me, you come and get it."

Suddenly I'm frantic. I tear his T-shirt off over his head and I throw it. I'm met with the sight of his broad chest, scattered with dark hair, and his muscular shoulders, too. His skin is a beautiful honey shade of tan.

Oh, God, yes. Spurred on by the sight of him, I unfasten the zipper on his jeans and push then down—his boxers, too.

His stomach is washboard hard, his legs muscular and strong, and his black pubic hair is short and well-kept. His large cock hangs heavily between his legs.

Thick veins run down the engorged length of it. Rico is rock hard and ready to go. I've never seen anything more beautiful.

Good grief, this man is one hell of a specimen.

He stands still, his hands by his side as my eyes roam over his skin.

My chest rises and falls as I struggle for air. I place my hand on his chest, and then retract it quickly and close my fist as if he burned me.

Maybe he did.

This man is white hot. The kind you read about in romance books… the kind that breaks your heart.

"Rici." My eyes drop lower. "You've become even more beautiful," I whisper to myself. "How is this even possible?"

His eyes hold mine and if I'm not mistaken, he seems nervous. Is he waiting for my approval?

"Baby," I whisper as I step forward. I rise up on my toes and softly kiss him. His hand curls around my waist. "Show me," I breathe against his lips. "Show me what I've been missing."

His eyes close and he moans against my lips as our kiss reaches a new level.

As if that's the green light he's been waiting for, his hands grab my behind with force, and he grinds his cock against my pubic bone and walks me back to the bed. His dark eyes hold mine as he lies me down and arranges me exactly how he wants me.

On my back with my legs wide open.

His hand moves to his cock, and he strokes it slowly as he looks down at me.

Pre-ejaculate drips from the end of his cock, and my back arches as I begin to lose control.

This is ridiculous. He's hardly touched me, and I swear, I could orgasm at any moment by just watching him pull himself. His grip on his cock tightens, and he gives himself three hard jerks, and then drops his head and kisses my inner thigh with an open mouth. I buckle beneath him.

The sensation is too much.

He holds my legs open and kisses his way up to my sex.

I stare at the ceiling as I gasp for breath, my rib cage rising as my lungs search for air. Oh God.

He spreads me apart with his fingers and hisses in approval. Then his thick tongue swipes through my flesh with force.

Holy fucking fuck…

He begins to suck, his eyes closed, and I begin to shudder. Oh no.

Not this again.

He reaches up and kneads my breast. "Watch," he commands.

I lean up onto my elbows and watch him suck and lick on my most private parts.

His eyes are dark, his tongue a perfect pink, and I watch the muscles in his jaw contract as he eats me.

I've died and gone to Italian Heaven.

I know now why the men I've been with over the last two years couldn't get over the line with me. They were all shit—very poor substitutes for the real thing.

Nobody came close to giving me the high of Rici Ferrara. He's a designer drug all of his own.

The best kind of high.

He bites my clitoris, and I buck off the bed as a freight train of an orgasm tears through me. I cry out in ecstasy and grab the back of his head.

Both his hands are splayed on my stomach as he holds me down, but his tongue doesn't stop. He hasn't finished. He wants to suck every last drop of the orgasm from my body.

My legs are quivering, and I try to close them. I'm too sensitive. "Rici," I breathe. "Now. Give it to me… please."

He stands, takes a condom from the drawer, and I watch as he rolls it on.

Thump, thump, thump, goes my heart as he climbs over me.

"Olivia. My beautiful Olivia." His lips take mine and his tongue moves in a slow, erotic dance. I can taste my own arousal in his mouth.

My heart freefalls from my chest.

No. No. No.

This is wrong. This isn't supposed to feel special. This is supposed to be brutal fucking. A getting him out of my system kind of fuck.

With his lips pressed tenderly against mine, he lifts my left leg and puts it around his waist.

"Open for me, baby."

I do as I'm told, and in one strong movement, he pushes forward and slides in deep. My mouth falls open as his possession takes over. I exhale slowly.

"You all right?" his deep, hushed voice whispers.

"Yeah." I close my eyes to try and deal with him—to block him out—because, hell, this man doesn't just make love. He fucks my soul.

He pulls out slowly and then pushes back in. I wince at the size of him. What the hell kind of man is he?

He clenches his jaw. Dark eyes hold mine, and I know he's clinging onto his control.

His breath is quivering and his tongue is sliding between my lips, begging for me to let him in fully.

What a beautiful, virile beast he is.

Sexual perfection has a name, and it's Enrico Ferrara. The king of fucking.

With his knees wide on the bed, he pulls out again. This time with purpose, he slams back in, and I cry out.

"Ahh!"

I cling to his broad shoulders and feel the muscles contract beneath my hands.

"Shh," he whispers, realizing he has to slow it down or he'll hurt me. "Okay, okay. Shh," he breathes. He gently begins to ride me, knowing that we have to work up to what he wants.

And like the perfect student, my body loosens with every pump as he holds himself up on his elbows.

"Olivia," he whispers darkly as he watches my lips. "Fuck me, Olivia. Let me in."

My eyes roll back in my head as I lift my legs up on either side of his body.

God, yes.

Fuck me, all right.

We keep going, gradually getting harder, and the bed begins to rock. My hands relax enough to roam over his back and up to the back of his head.

His beautiful face stares down at me, and I know that this is it. This is what sex is supposed to be like. I'm positive that when it was invented by whoever it was back then at the dawn of time, it was with this man in mind.

He lifts my leg a little higher to his shoulders and his eyes flash black. He's on the edge of sanity.

"Go," I pant. "Give it to me." I put my hands onto his behind and pull him in deeper.

He lets out a guttural moan, straightens his arms, and then slams me hard. My entire body jerks up the bed, and I can feel every vein on his thick cock.

Oh shit...

The sound of our damp skin slapping together bounces off the walls, and the heat from his thrusts burns me from the inside out. I begin to thrash beneath him. I can't hold it as I cry out. My orgasm tips him over the edge, and he holds himself deep. I feel the telling jerk of his cock deep inside my body.

He slams into me three more times—each time deeper than the last as he tries to empty himself completely.

And then he kisses me with such tenderness, and it's so foreign to the way he just was with me.

Enrico Ferrara fucks with his body but he kisses with his whole heart.

I can feel it. Every cell in my body tells me that he is as into this as I am.

That this is something more than it's supposed to be.

"Sei davvero fottutamente perfetta," he whispers. *Translation: you are so fucking perfect.*

I don't know what he said but it was in reverence—words of worship.

I smile up at him as he pulls out and lies over me. He carefully drops his lips to my clavicle and trails kisses up my collarbone.

"Olivia," he murmurs against my skin.

I feel his dick reharden against my thigh, and I smile up at the ceiling as I bring my arm around his broad shoulders.

I get the feeling that the night is just beginning, and that he is nowhere near done with me.

We kiss again, and I am done.

Perfection.

14

Olivia

I WAKE to lips brushing my shoulder blade. It's dark, but my bladder is telling me it's morning. I roll over to find Rico leaning up on his elbow.

"Good morning, bella." He smiles sexily.

Oh God. *Shit.*

"Hi."

What the hell happened last night? One minute I vowed to hate Enrico Ferrara for all of eternity. Not seven minutes later I'm getting finger fucked in an office.

I think we said all of twenty words together before we were at it like rabbits. Horror dawns. For fuck's sake.

"I have to go to the bathroom," I whisper as I climb out of bed and go into the en-suite bathroom. I lock the door, sit down and put my head in my hands. I didn't even make him work for it. I'm weak, a pushover.

What am I doing here?

My heart is beating fast and I'm filled with regret. I need to get out of here, pronto.

I wash my hands and stare at my messed-up reflection. My blonde hair is wild, my makeup is smudged all over my face and don't even talk to me about how much I smell like sex.

Like him.

How did this happen? I mean, I was fine... and then he sucked his fingers and the sky turned red until I couldn't see anymore. No horny woman should ever have to watch that while he's giving her his best *come fuck me* look. It's unnatural. It's like a go button or something. It should come with a warning. Do not go beyond this point...sure as hell fucking follows.

I wash my face and run my hands through my hair. I look around and borrow his toothpaste to brush my teeth.

I really need a shower, but damn, I just want to get out of here. I don't want to walk back in there naked. I grab his robe from a hook on the back of the door and I throw it on.

Here goes. I've always heard about this, although it's much worse in reality.

The walk of shame.

I open the door in a rush and find Rico leaning up on his elbow. His dark, tanned skin is on display, and his top leg is bent at the knee, displaying the most beautiful thick thigh muscle I've ever seen. The white sheets are pooled around his groin, although the tip of his cock is peeking out up against his stomach.

Hard again.

Fuck.

His eyes hold mine as I nervously sit down on the side of the bed.

"Come here, bella." He taps the space beside him.

"Um." I feel the blood drain from my face. I pause as I try to think of a lie. "I have to go. I might grab a cab."

"What?" He frowns.

I shrug. "I'm really busy today."

His chin rises. "You're really busy today?"

"Uh-huh."

His eyes hold mine. "Doing what?"

"Stuff." Stop talking. Stop talking now.

"What's your problem?" He sits up slowly.

"Nothing, I just have to go." I scoop my dress and underwear up from the floor and go back into the bathroom. I'm not fighting with him here in his house. He'll just somehow talk me onto my back again. It's obvious I have zero willpower where he's concerned. He has leg opening superpowers.

I quickly get dressed back into my whore bag dress. This thing is going in the bin. How do people do this on the regular? It's appalling.

I walk back out into the bedroom to find him zipping up his jeans. "I'll drive you."

"No, it's fine." I slip on my black high heels.

He glares at me. "Don't piss me off, Olivia."

What?

My hackles rise. "Fine. Drive me home, you control freak."

With another dirty look, he throws on a T-shirt. I follow him out of the bedroom and into the apartment. All the windows are open, and I quickly glance around the beautiful pool and its surroundings. Well, it was nice almost swimming in you.

We get into the lift. He bangs the button hard and stares straight ahead.

Animosity is oozing out of his every pore. God, this is awkward.

I twist my fingers in front of me as I watch the dial. The

doors open into the underground parking lot, and he storms out. I follow him over to a black sports car. I see the Ferrari symbol and I inwardly cringe. He drives a Ferrari. Of course, he does. I couldn't make this shit up if I tried.

He opens the door abruptly for me despite his anger. I climb in and he slams the door hard before he walks around and gets in to start the car with a large rev of the engine.

I glance over at him. Maybe this isn't such a good idea.

He tears out of the parking lot at full speed and I hang on for dear life. Oh hell, get off the road, we're all going to die.

"Slow down!" I cry.

He pushes in the code of the security gates, and the door slowly rises up.

He stares straight ahead. I can see his jaw ticking as he clenches his teeth together.

Oh fuck.

The gates rise, and he screeches out onto the road at full speed.

"What is your fucking problem?" he snaps as his furious eyes flick to me.

"Watch the road!" I screech. He changes gears fast, overtaking two cars. I cling onto the dashboard for dear life. "You're the problem," I cry as I watch the oncoming traffic zoom by. "You treat me like crap, don't call me for two whole years, and then turn up in a nightclub. I go home with you like you're a fucking rock star. I'm disgusted with myself."

"I told you why I treated you the way I did." He changes the gears again and I grip my seatbelt.

"Will you slow down?"

He stares at the road.

"Why didn't you call me all this time? If you wanted to see me, why didn't you just call me?"

"Because you wouldn't have come! I told you that. Listen to me when I speak, woman."

I throw my hands up in the air. This is pointless. He's an arrogant bastard.

"Well, I'm not staying. I'm taking the job in New York. How dare you think you can just wave your magic dick around and I'll be putty in your hands?"

His glances at me. "I didn't see you too angry last night when you were riding my magic dick," he sneers. "In fact, you moaned on it all fucking night."

"See?" I shake my head around in disgust. "It's this arrogant fucking asshole attitude that turns me off you."

He punches the steering wheel hard, and I jump. "You haven't seen a fucking asshole yet, Olivia." The veins are prominent in his neck. "Don't fucking push me!" he growls.

"Stop it!" I scream. "You're being crazy."

"You make me fucking crazy," he yells.

"Let me out of the car. This was a big mistake. I wish I never laid eyes on you."

He glares over at me. "Yeah, well, that makes two of us."

He pulls into a parking space at my hotel. I get out and slam the door hard. He tears off into the distance. I watch the car disappear to the sound of his tires screeching, and then I look up to see everyone has stopped and is staring after him.

Hmm, that went well.

I drop my head and continue my walk of shame.

Great.

The thing about bastards is that they get under your skin. They're like a poisonous rash.

Insidious, festering, and begging for attention.

I don't feel like I have that *I won the fight* feeling.

It's Monday afternoon, and I haven't heard from him.

I mean, I don't want to. It's not like I'm checking my phone every ten minutes or anything. I pick my phone up and check it again.

No missed calls. I exhale heavily.

Asshole.

I spent yesterday afternoon with Natalie analyzing this situation over copious amounts of alcohol and tapas in a bar.

She thinks I'm being a drama queen—that his father had died, and he wasn't thinking straight back then. She thinks him bringing me here is romantic.

She thinks this is a second chance love story waiting to happen.

I think he's a control freak.

Part of me wishes I handled yesterday differently—that I just sat and talked to him.

Why was I so angry? I acted like a crazy person.

And why was he so fucking angry? He acted like no woman had ever asked to leave before.

Probably haven't.

I glance at the clock and see it's 5:00 p.m. I've achieved nothing today. Giorgio isn't even here because he's in New York working for the week. I can't wait to tell him about my weekend from Hell.

This is one fucked-up situation.

I close down my computer, pack up my desk, and make my way downstairs.

I'm supposed to be going to the gym but a bar of chocolate seems much more enticing.

I walk out of the building and glance up to see a black Ferrari parked across the street. Rico is standing beside it, his behind resting on the door. His eyes are locked on me.

My heart skips a beat at the sight of him. Just go and speak to him. Be an adult.

I cross the road and approach the car. "Hi."

"Hello."

The wind blows my hair around, and I tuck it behind my ears. "What are you doing here?"

"Waiting for you."

We stare at each other. "Why?"

"I want to talk to you."

"No, you don't, Rici, you want to scream at me."

"You can't blame me for being angry. After the night we spent together, I wake up to that."

I cross my arms in front of me. "I'm know, I'm sorry." I sigh, disappointed in myself. "I don't know what came over me."

His eyes hold mine. "Can we get a drink?"

"I guess." I gesture up the street, and he falls inline beside me. The two of us walk in silence until we get to a bar and restaurant.

We take a seat and the waiter comes over. "What would you like to drink?'

Rico gestures for me to order first.

"I'll just have a mineral water, please?"

He frowns subtly. "I'll have a blue label scotch, please."

"Sure." The waiter leaves us alone.

Rico's eyes hold mine as he waits for me to speak… so I don't.

"Well." He opens his hands to me. "Start talking."

I shrug.

"You obviously have things to say. Say them."

This is it; the moment I know I have to be completely honest or I have to cut my losses and walk away. I can't keep harboring this resentment toward him.

"You really hurt me when you left me in jail. It's not something I can forget so easily. And it wasn't in a lover kind of hurt, it was a humanity hurt kind."

He drops his head, taking a moment to himself.

"I thought we were friends," I whisper.

"Bella, I couldn't deal with you and the drug thing back then. My whole world had collapsed. I was battling many demons—too many to name."

Empathy wins and I put my hand on top of his on the table. "Why didn't you just talk to me?"

"I couldn't."

"Why didn't you call me when you had calmed down?"

"I was ashamed of the way I treated you." He looks back up, and his eyes search mine. "For that, I'm truly sorry. I can't turn back time. If I could, I would."

"But you didn't even call me when I got here. It doesn't make any sense."

"I was letting you settle in for a week, and then I was going to accidently bump into you." I frown. "But then I saw you on that date and I went..." His voice trails off. "Things haven't gone to plan."

We sit in silence for a moment, staring at each other. "You know you're a really bad driver when you're angry," I tell him.

He smiles and turns his hand over to take mine. "Then stop making me angry."

I smirk, and that buzz between us is there again.

"How does this go, Enrico? What is this between us?"

"Rici. You call me Rici."

I look down as I try to articulate what I want to say. So clear in my head, so clunky in real life.

"You said we had more story between us," he says.

"I did."

"Can you honestly say that you feel like you turned the last page? Because I can't."

"No," I say. I watch as the twinkle returns to his eyes, and I exhale heavily. "I'll make a deal with you. You pick me up and take me on a date tomorrow night, and I'll wipe the slate clean."

"How about we just talk about it tonight?"

"And stop doing that."

"Doing what?"

"Hypnotizing me with your sexiness."

He smiles brightly at me. "No promises."

I stand. "I'll see you tomorrow?"

His face falls. "You're leaving already? Your drink hasn't even arrived."

"Yes. I'm leaving."

He opens his mouth to object, and then shuts it, silencing himself. "See you tomorrow night."

I kiss him on the cheek. "Tomorrow."

Enrico

I would have preferred to stay in with her tonight but I need to make an effort, so here I am. I knock on the door and Olivia opens it in a rush.

My breath catches at the sight of her. She's wearing a red strapless dress. Her long blonde hair is up, and I've never seen anyone more beautiful.

"Bella," I whisper as I look her up and down. "So beautiful."

She performs a twirl for me. "You like?"

I take her in my arms as my cock hardens. "I love."

I can't stop myself; I lean in and kiss her softly. Not kissing her feels unnatural. It's the weirdest thing. I want to talk her out of going out, but I won't because I know she wants this. "Let's go."

She grabs her purse and shawl, and I take her hand and lead her downstairs. My car is waiting in the parking lot, and I glance over to see the four cars parked with my bodyguards inside them.

My every instinct is to drop her hand, but I know I'm already skating on thin ice. I grit my teeth and let her hold my hand. Just this once.

"What's this car?" she asks as she takes in the black Audi.

"This is my sensible car." I wink as I open the door for her.

"Are you going to be sensible tonight, Mr. Ferrara?" she teases.

"Yes." I smirk as I slam the door shut. I go around and get into the driver's seat. "I'm only going to make love to you once in the missionary position instead of fucking you six times on your knees."

"That's presumptuous." She smirks as we pull out into the traffic.

I take her hand and put it on my thigh. I want her hands on me when she sits next to me... wherever she is. I have to be touching her. It's an urge I cannot control.

"Where are we going?" she asks.

"To my favorite restaurant."

"Tell me they have pasta."

I pick up her hand and kiss her fingertips. Her joy is contagious. "They have the best pasta in all of Italy."

"It's a wonder we got in on a Friday night then."

I smile. She's oblivious to the pull that I have. "Yes, very lucky," I reply as I keep my eyes on the road. I glance in the rearview mirror at the security cars trailing us. There's trouble brewing at work with threats coming in left right and center now. Security around me has never been so high. It's not exactly the right time to start a torrid affair of the heart.

I pull into the parking lot, open her door, and we walk into the restaurant.

"Mr. Ferrara." Mario smiles. "Come in, come in, sir."

We weave through the tables until we get to my favorite spot. He pulls out Olivia's chair and she takes a seat. He hands us our menus.

"We will have a Margarita and a Amaro please," I ask.

"Of course, sir. I'll leave you alone and come and take your food order soon."

Olivia smiles as she looks around at the glamorous space. "Well, this is special."

"Like you." I kiss her hand. "What are you eating, my love?"

Her eyes linger on my face.

"What?" I ask.

"I like it when you call me your love."

You are.

Stop it.

I open the menu to distract her. "The linguini is spectacular."

"Hmm, all my cardio training is going down the drain tonight. Carbohydrate coma, here I come."

"Your drinks." Mario puts our drinks on the table. "I will give you some more time."

Olivia holds up her margarita glass, and I clink it with mine. I smile and go back to reading the menu.

"I've had a good day, you know?" Olivia says.

"Why is that?"

"I went to the gym and found an apartment."

I look up. "You found an apartment?"

"Yes, it's lovely, and not far from my work and my gym."

I keep reading my menu and exhale as I try to keep my cool. "I don't know where I want you to live yet."

She looks up, surprised by my statement. "What is that supposed to mean?"

"It means I don't know where I want you to live yet. I want tight security around you. I will organize something for you. I'll look into what properties of mine are vacant first thing in the morning."

"This is our first date, what are you talking about?" She rearranges her napkin on her lap. "I don't want to live in one of your apartments, I'm not."

I glare at her across the table. "Why are you so difficult?"

"Why are you so domineering?"

"It's a safety issue, Olivia."

She rolls her eyes. "You are overdramatic, Mr. Ferrara."

I sip my drink as I try to reign in my temper.

She shakes her head as if shaking off her annoyance. "Anyway," she continues. "Let's talk about you, for once. We always talk about me. You know everything about me, and I know nothing about you."

I feel my chest tighten and I sip my drink. "I think I'm having the linguini," I say to change the subject. "What are you having?"

"Tell me about your work," she asks.

"What do you want to know?"

She frowns as she thinks for a moment. "After the accident, you took over the family businesses, yes?"

"Yes."

"All of them?"

"I became the CEO of the company, so yes. But there are many staff under me that had worked alongside my father and grandfather, and they continue to do what they did before."

"It's a lot of responsibility."

"It is."

She puts her hand under her chin and studies me. "It must be terrifying. The thought that you could fuck everything up."

I stare at her for a moment. "You're the first person who has ever said that to me."

"Well, is it?"

"More than you know."

Her eyes hold mine, and she waits for me to go on.

"The pressure of expectation is suffocating. Some days are better than others. It is what it is."

"We could always run away," she offers with a goofy smile.

I laugh out loud. "Don't tempt me. The prospect of running away with you and being normal would be a dream come true."

Her face falls. "Do you feel trapped in your life?"

"Yes," I answer without hesitation.

"Oh." She thinks about it for a moment. "You don't have to do this you know?"

"Yes. I do. My life is already mapped out for me."

She looks around the restaurant and frowns. "I thought you said this was the best restaurant in Milan."

"It is."

"Why are we the only ones here?"

I smile as I rest my face in my hand. I booked the whole restaurant so I could have her to myself. "Just lucky, I guess."

I stand in the corridor as I fumble with the key to Olivia's room. It's late now, and we've had too many drinks. I had to leave my car at the restaurant. We caught a cab home. She's standing behind me running her hands up and down my body. She's hot for it. *She's always hot for it.*

She unzips my pants from behind, and I bump her with my ass.

"Let me open the door, woman."

She laughs and begins to pull my pants down.

"Stop it," I whisper as I struggle with the lock.

She slides her hand down my briefs and grabs my hard cock. I struggle with the key some more. "Open, fucker." I give it a swift kick.

She laughs and strokes me hard, and the door clicks open. I stumble in and before I can even close the door behind us, she's on her knees in front of me.

"Time for dessert," she whispers darkly as she licks her lips.

She takes my cock into her mouth and my breath catches at the sight of her.

She slides my pants and briefs right down, and I kick them to the side along with my shoes. I take my shirt off over my head while she takes me deep down her throat.

My legs nearly give way beneath me. I gently sweep the blonde hair back from her forehead. Her eyes are closed, and she hums at the taste of me.

Fuck, she's hot.

Some women give head to please men. Olivia gives head to please herself. She loves it.

I love it more.

I can honestly say that watching her suck my cock is the sexiest thing I've ever seen. She opens her throat and really takes me deep as she cups my balls in her hand. Her other hand roams up and down my thigh.

My stomach tightens, and a gush of pre-ejaculate makes her eyes close.

Fuck, fuck, fuck.

She begins to fist me hard, and I grab her head in my hands as my primal instincts take over and I begin to ride her mouth—desperate for the release that only she can give me.

I need her. Fuck, I need her. I need to be so deep inside of her that she can't breathe.

I drag her to her feet and take her dress and underwear off. I sit back on the bed.

"Condom," she pants.

"Are you on the pill?"

She frowns. "Yes, but..."

"I've never had sex without a condom on before. You're safe."

She pushes me on the chest, losing the last of her control. I hold the base of my cock up and slide it through her swollen, wet flesh. She gently rocks back and forth.

"Fuck me," I whisper up at her.

She slides down onto my cock, and her mouth falls into the perfect O shape.

Oh God, she *is* perfect.

The feeling of her, flesh-to-flesh, without anything between us, is too much.

I need more. I need to fill her everywhere. I reach around and push my finger into her back entrance, and she quivers. Our eyes lock.

My smile darkens. "You like that, my beautiful girl?"

"Hmm," she moans with her eyes closed. "Fuck, yes."

I grab her hip bone and slam her down hard, knocking the air from her lungs. She clings to me.

"Knees up," I order.

She does as she is told, and I feel her beautiful cunt contract so hard around my cock that waves of pleasure run though both of us.

"I'm going to fuck you all night, baby," I promise her.

"God, yes!" she screams. "Do it. Give it to me harder."

I wake to the feeling of the bed dipping beside me. I snap my eyes open and reach out.

"Just going to the bathroom, baby," she whispers.

I close my eyes again. Within moments, she slides back into bed and lies half over me. I smile as I kiss her forehead.

"What a night," she whispers.

I smile with my eyes closed. What a night is right.

Incredible doesn't even come close to describing it.

"What's on for you this week?" I ask as I mindlessly run my fingers through her hair.

"Just work."

"I have to go away today." I open my eyes.

"What?" She looks up at me. "For how long?"

"Until Friday."

"Oh." She lies back down. "Okay."

I roll her onto her back and drop my lips to her neck. “Let’s go away next weekend when I get back.”

“I am away.”

“I’m not. I need a break. I can be back early Friday, and we can leave as soon as you finish work.”

“Really?” she asks.

“Yes, really.”

She smiles, and I drop my lips to her nipple to give it a hard suck. “I’ll look forward to it.”

15

Olivia

"So?" Giorgio sits back on the chair in my office. His mischievous eyes hold mine and I have a sneaking suspicion that he already knows. "What have I missed?"

"Nothing much." I roll my lips to hide my smile.

"I've missed nothing?"

I pretend to type.

He lets out an exaggerated sigh. "Why must you torture me, my darling?"

"Torture?" I smile as I type. "How so?"

"Have you seen Mr. Ferrara?"

I turn my attention to him for the first time since he's been in my office. "What do you know about Mr. Ferrara? How do you know him?"

"Rico and I have been friends for years. I knew his father."

"And how exactly did it come about me coming to Milan?"

"Rico called me."

"And said what?"

"He asked me if you had applied for a job there two years earlier. I said I would check it out. I found when I searched your name that you actually had a current job application in place. I called him back, and he asked me if I could arrange for you to be in Milan."

"But why wouldn't he call me himself? Why would he need the excuse of Valentino?"

He cringes. "I know, I thought that, too. How exactly did you two meet?"

"Our eyes met across a crowded room. He came over and translated the menu for me, and then he joined me for dinner."

Giorgio smiles as he listens.

"We ended up spending the weekend together before I left for Sorrento. I'd arranged to meet my girlfriend Natalie there. Enrico and I agreed to meet up again two weeks later."

"Natalie is your friend who is moving here?"

"She's here already. She arrived on Friday."

"Wow." He swings on his chair, clearly happy for me.

"But get this; the day I left for Sorrento happened to be the same day his father and grandfather were killed."

His face falls.

"I didn't hear from him for the entire time I was away, and then when I got back to Rome, someone had planted drugs in my bags."

Giorgio's mouth falls open. "Was it him?

"I hope not," I scoff. "But I didn't know any of this when I was arrested at the airport."

Giorgio's eyes widen. "You were arrested?"

"Yes, and I saw Rico at the police station, but he left me."

"What do you mean… he left you?"

"He organized for a lawyer to get me off the charges, and he called the embassy, but he never came back and saw me again. I was put on a plane home by his lawyer, not him."

He presses his fingers against his lips. "Extraordinary."

I shrug. "I mean, even if we were nothing to each other but friends, you wouldn't just leave someone that you spent the entire weekend with in prison, would you?"

"I wouldn't have thought so, and especially not him. His loyalty is his strongest trait." He thinks for a moment. "So, you hadn't spoken to him since?"

"Not until I ran into him when I was on my Tinder date and he went feral crazy."

Giorgio's fascinated eyes hold mine. "What did he say about all of this? How did he explain this?"

I shrug. "He said that he was dealing with the deaths and he just couldn't handle me and drugs. He said he was in the grieving crisis."

He frowns. "In all fairness, he was."

"Did you see him back then?'

He nods. "He was very angry for a long time. He disappeared from the social scene altogether. His brothers both moved back home to help him."

"Help him with what?"

"As the oldest child, he had to take over the family business. This would have been traumatizing for him."

I frown. "What do you mean?"

He sits up and straightens in his chair. "Nothing really, just a lot to get his head around, I imagine."

"I guess. Anyway, we had a big fight, and then he came to work and waited outside. I don't know. We're seeing how things go."

"Oh, I love this story." He claps his hands together. "It's like Cinderella going to the ball."

I roll my eyes.

"So, what now?"

"He's away for work for the week. He wants to go away for the weekend."

"Oh." He stands. "I'm fitting you out with a new wardrobe. You must look incredible for Mr. Ferrara. You are now officially my hobby."

I smirk and turn back to my computer. "Actually, his favorite outfit for me is my birthday suit. He prefers me naked."

Giorgio presses the back of his hand to his forehead and pretends to faint. "Dear God, darling I can't even imagine what he would be like in bed. His intensity is on another level. You can feel it from across a room."

I giggle. "Giorgio, you have no idea."

It's late on Thursday night. I scroll through my phone, flicking from Facebook to Instagram and back again. Earlier tonight, I went to the gym with Natalie and noticed two men in a car across the road.

I think that maybe they were his men.

Rico hasn't called me, and to be honest, I thought he would. I mean, if he cares enough to have me watched over like I think he did, I would have at least thought he would check in once in a while.

Stop it. Stop being so needy.

I hate that he brings out this side of my personality. For two years, I've blissfully hated him from afar. Now, after one weekend with him, I'm whisked back to the beginning, waiting for him to call.

I scroll through the numbers on my phone and smile when I come to his name.

ENRICO FERRARA

I go back to Instagram, and I see the green light come up. What? Oh shit, I'm calling him. I quickly cancel the call. My phone immediately begins to ring, and his name lights up the screen.

I cringe with regret. "Hello," I say.

"What's wrong?"

"Nothing. Sorry I didn't mean to call you."

"You're all right?"

"Yes." I frown. "Why wouldn't I be?"

"Ah." I hear his voice relax. "I thought something was wrong."

Something is wrong. You're not here. "No." He hangs on the line, silent. "Are *you* all right?" I ask.

"Yes," he sighs. "I would prefer to be there with you, but it is what it is."

"You can come home if you want?"

He chuckles. "I'll be there tomorrow, my love."

My love.

"Yes," I breathe.

"And I'll whisk you away."

I smile. "I can't wait."

"Me, too."

The line falls silent again, and I wonder if he's smiling goofily down the line like I am.

"You looked lovely in that photo you posted this morning. I've stared at it all day."

I bite my bottom lip. I posted a picture of me at my work

desk this morning. Giorgio snapped it when I wasn't looking. But, wait, what?

"How did you see it on my Facebook account? It's private," I ask.

"Do you know Beverly Whalen, Olivia?"

"She's my mom's friend." I frown. "Isn't she?"

"Maybe." I can tell from the sound of his voice that he's smiling.

I suddenly want to get off the phone to see who in the heck Beverly Whalen really is.

We fall silent again.

"I'll see you tomorrow then?" he says.

"I've been banking my hours this week so I can leave at three."

"Good girl. I'll pick you up at three."

"Okay." I smile as butterflies dance in my stomach. I get to see him tomorrow.

"Goodbye."

"Bye." I hang on the line. After a few moments, he hangs up.

I instantly open Facebook and look up Beverly Whalen on my friend list. The profile pic is a woman. She is one of my mums' work friends, I'm sure of it. Huh?

I click on her profile. No friends, no address, no details. This *is* weird. I look up the date we became friends.

I got a friend request from her four weeks after I returned to Australia from Italy. I didn't even look into her profile because I knew the face on the photo. Holy shit.

Beverly Whalen is Rici Ferrara.

With a stupid, huge smile on my face, I go through all my images over the last two years. He's liked every single one.

He's been watching me from afar. I should be appalled, disgusted... outraged.

Instead, I'm utterly thrilled.

He cared. Even though he may be wrapped in a bastard suit, I know he isn't a bastard. I think that, deep down, I've always known that, and maybe that's why it was so hard to move on from him. I don't know what happened back then with us, or why he handled things the way that he did, but I don't think I care anymore. I'm going to try my hardest to take him at face value moving forward.

I stand with a renewed excitement.

I need to pack. I've got a dirty weekend with a sex god on the horizon.

I can hardly wait.

The clock strikes three and I have to stop myself from running from my office.

He's here, just outside. After waiting all week to see him, it's finally time.

I play it cool and take my time to pack up my desk up. Giorgio swings his head around the door. "Have a wonderful weekend, darling."

"Thanks."

For once, everything is going to plan, and not just for me. Natalie seems to have hit it off with her guy, too. She's going on a date with him tonight that will hopefully last the entire weekend. I'm so relieved. I don't know if I would have been comfortable going away if I knew she was sitting back here alone.

Giorgio saunters into my office and sits on my desk. "Have you got everything?"

"I'm all packed." I swing my handbag over my shoulder and kiss his cheek. "Wish me luck."

He assesses me. "No luck needed." He stands and straightens my scarf. "Knock him dead."

My heart begins to race as I make my way downstairs. Finding out that Rico has been stalking me on Facebook for the last two years has made this seem real, and all that more important to get right. I walk out of my building, and I look around.

Where is he? I don't see him. Panic begins to set in.

Then, a black Ferrari comes around the corner. It drives past me and pulls into the loading bay.

He's here.

My stomach dances in excitement and I have to stop myself from running to him. I casually walk up to the car as if gorgeous rich men pick me up in black Ferraris every single day.

Calm, calm, keeping fucking calm.

I open the passenger door and lean in. "Hi."

He smirks. "Hi."

"Going my way?"

"If I wasn't already," his tongues sweeps over his bottom lip, "I am now." He has a certain twinkle in his eye and seems excited, too.

I bounce into the car, and he grabs my hand. I lean over to kiss him and his eyes flick to the rearview mirror. I sit back in my seat, instantly reminded that we're not alone.

He pulls back out into the traffic, and then picks up my hand to kiss my fingertips. "It's good to see you."

"You, too." I smile.

I see another two cars pull out behind us, but I push it to the back of my mind as I pretend not to notice. My stomach is dancing, alive with nerves. For the first time since we've been together, I actually have hope. Maybe this can be something more?

I didn't imagine it when we were in Rome. He did feel it too, and I don't feel near so foolish now. Maybe I'm being presumptuous. I don't know, but this feels real.

We drive along with my eyes flicking between Rico and the road. He has this smirk on his face, like the guy that got the girl.

"What are you smirking at?"

"Just you."

"Why?" I smile broadly.

"Are you packed?" he asks as he pulls into my hotel and parks the car.

"Yes, where are we going?"

He turns the car off. "Monte Carlo."

My eyes widen. "In Monaco?"

"I have a yacht down there."

"You have a yacht?" I squeak, wide-eyed.

He chuckles, gets out of the car, and comes around to open my door. He takes my hand and helps me from the car. "Yes, I have a yacht."

"Of course, you do." We begin to walk into my building. "You have all the toys."

We get into the lift and he stares straight ahead, while I stare up at him.

Touch me, damn it.

I'm really beginning to hate this no touching in public rule. I want him draped all over me like a scarf. We arrive at my room, and as I unlock the door, his hand takes my hip from behind.

There it is. Touch.

It's not sexual, not sleazy, but somehow it sends tingles all the way down to my toes. Maybe that's because I know it's a prelude of what's to come. The door opens, and his hand comes from behind me. He pushes it open with force, unable to wait a second longer.

Then he's on me. His hands are in my hair and he's kissing me like his life depends on it. I smile against his lips.

"That's more like it," I whisper. "Took your time."

For ten minutes, we kiss, and then he takes me into his big, strong arms and holds me tight. We stand cheek-to-cheek for a long time just enjoying holding each other. *I've missed him.*

His lips take mine, slow and deliberate, and I find myself clinging to him as he leads me into temptation.

"Let's take a shower," I suggest.

"We can't, our plane leaves at five. We have to get to the airport."

"What?" Damn it, I want to have *I missed you* sex.

"We can relax once we get there." He kisses me again. "I promise."

"Fine." I step back from him and begin to gather my things. Did I pack right for Monte Carlo? What even happens in Monte Carlo? I definitely don't have any Princess Grace wear in my suitcase.

"Do you wear that dress to work often?" he asks as his eyes skim my body.

I look down at myself. I'm wearing a tight black, woolen turtleneck dress. It has long sleeves and a lower neckline. "Yeah, why?"

His brows crease. "Please don't."

"Why not?'

"Because it shows your every curve."

"And?"

"And I want to be the only one seeing those." He steps forward and takes me into his arms again. "Your body is for my eyes only."

"Is that so?" I smile up at him.

"That's so."

I love that my body is for his eyes only…this is going very well indeed. "You know, you can't tell me what to do," I tease.

He gives me a slow, sexy smile. "Would you like to place a bet on that?" He pumps me with his hips.

I giggle. "I would, actually. I'm in the betting mood. Isn't that what they do in Monte Carlo?" I bat my lashes.

He chuckles and turns me away from him, and he playfully slaps my behind. "Get your things. We need to go."

"Stop rushing me. I want to stay here and be naked and playful."

"Well, I want to get there so you can be naked and under me."

Our eyes lock, and he gives me the best *come fuck me* look of all time.

"Okay then. That's definitely more of an incentive." I begin to rush to get my things together.

"Like I thought."

I pass him my travel suitcase, and then I grab my makeup purse and tuck it in my handbag. I do a quick last check. "Okay, let's go."

He smiles, then leans in and takes my face into his hands to kiss me slowly. "It's good to see you, Olivia Reynolds," he whispers.

I run my fingers through his dark stubble and stare into his big brown eyes. He's so hard and masculine, yet soft to my touch. Just like his personality. He can act hard with me all he wants, but I know the real him. I want to blurt out that I missed him…. *stop it.*

Don't be a pushover, play it cool I remind myself.

Calm, calm…keep fucking calm, I pull out of his arms. "Let's go, Mr. Ferrara."

We walk down the dock in Monte Carlo, and my heart is in my throat. Gorgeous boats are lined up, one after the other. I don't know much about boats, but I do know this is some serious boat porn.

This afternoon has been quite daunting, I met Rico's four closest staff: Lorenzo, Maso, Marley, and George. They seemed nice, although Lorenzo stands out as my favorite. His smile was warm and welcoming.

We caught our flight here in a private jet. We drank champagne, talked, and I have to admit that I'm having a hard time not openly staring at Enrico Ferrara. He seems to be getting more and more handsome by the hour... or perhaps that's just my lady parts swooning at his masculine ways.

"This way." Enrico leads me down the boardwalk. Unable to help it, I link my arm through his. A smile crosses his face.

We walk up a private jetty. I frown and stop on the spot.

"That's your boat?" I ask him.

"Yes." He continues toward it. "Come, Olivia."

It's huge, white, and I count the floors by the rows of windows. One, two, three, four... five. It's a five-fucking story boat.

Are you serious?

There are five staff waiting at the boarding gate to welcome us aboard, and Rico shakes their hand as he boards.

"Please meet Olivia," he tells them. "Dote on her this weekend."

The captain smiles and nods. "Yes, sir." He turns and shakes my hand. I feel like the queen or something and slipping into the sea with embarrassment. I go along the line and shake everyone's hand as Rico leads me onto the boat... yacht... whatever the hell this thing is.

He turns back to them. "We would like privacy all weekend."

The captain nods. "Yes, sir, of course."

The deck is made of beautiful, light timber, and huge deckchairs face out to the ocean. The entire level is glass, and when we get to the doors, I stop still again.

What the fuck?

There's a grand living area filled with big luxurious couches and a mini grand piano. The carpet is a gorgeous coffee color, and chandeliers hang wherever possible. I look over to the stairs golden balustrade, and I see a glass elevator sitting to the right of it.

An elevator? On a boat?

Are you freaking kidding me?

"Come, Olivia," Rico says casually, holding his hand out for me. "We will put our bags in our room." He begins to walk up the stairs.

"There's a bedroom?" I whisper as I stop on the bottom step.

I look out of the huge glass windows to see the twinkling city lights dancing on the water.

Rico smiles down at me. "There are eight."

"Eight bedrooms?" I squeak. "Are you kidding me?"

He chuckles and comes back down the stairs to grab my hand.

"This way."

He leads me up two sets of stairs before he opens up a huge set of black doors. My mouth falls open. It's the master bedroom suite. There's a huge king bed in the center, and the room is made entirely of glass on all sides with the most breathtaking views over Monte Carlo. I look out onto the deck below to see a full-sized swimming pool there with a bar and lounge chairs....what the actual fuck?

"A pool?" I gasp.

Rico laughs. "A pool."

I walk into the bathroom to find a huge sunken spa bath in the center, the walls and floors are all white marble.

"Holy shit. This is unbelievable. Who knew that boats looked like this?" My eyes find his.

He walks over, closes the bedroom door, and then flicks the lock. "Alone at last." Like a predator, he steps toward me, and my stomach dances with nerves.

"I like your boat," I breathe.

"I like you." He bends to lick the length of my neck, and he bites my ear. Goosebumps scatter up my arms. "Now you can have a shower." He takes off his suit jacket and throws it onto the chair.

I close my eyes. The heat from his tongue steals my ability to think. He leads me into the bathroom and turns the shower on. Steam begins to fill the room, and in one swift movement, he lifts my dress over my head.

I stand before him in white lace underwear. His hungry eyes drop down my body. "I've waited all week to have you." He unclips my bra and slides my panties down my legs.

I stand before him, naked and vulnerable. "Now that you have me, what are you going to do with me?"

He smiles darkly and unbuttons his shirt. My chest constricts when I see his broad chest and dark hair. He kicks his shoes off before he unfastens his trousers and slides them down. I'm blessed with the sight of his cock hanging hard between his legs. A smile crosses my face, and I bite my bottom lip to stop myself from blurting out words of praise. I need to try and remain cool here. I can't be his fan girl, but it's pretty damn hard to stop myself when he's so fucking gorgeous.

Our lips connect, and he walks me into the shower. The hot water tingles my skin. He pins me to the wall, lifts me, and then in one sharp movement he impales me deep. His cock jerks, and we stare at each other in awe.

"I like your shower," I whisper.

He smiles darkly. "I'm about to get you dirty in it."

Hours later

The room is warm and the steam rises in puffs. It's late, long after a respectable bedtime but we can't seem to go to sleep.

I smile at the man sitting opposite me in the bath. His hair is wet, hanging sexily over his forehead. His legs are spread, and my feet are resting on his chest. We've been in here for an hour. We keep letting the water out as it goes cold and topping it back up.

"We need a bigger bath," he sighs.

"I think it's the largest you can get." I smile dreamily.

It's perfect. I'm in a steamy hot bath with a sex god. I mean, what else is there in life?

"Tell me about your family?" he says to me.

"What do you want to know?"

"You said your parents got divorced when you were young."

"Yes." I pick up a sponge and squeeze the water out of it. "They did."

"Why?"

"My father had an affair. He..." I pause. It's been a long time since I've thought about this. "He was in love with someone else and... he left us."

Enrico picks up my foot and kisses it, not saying anything in response.

"It changed me. I've never been the same since."

"Why not?"

"A piece of my love for my father died with his admission." I splash the water up over my breasts as I think back to my painful childhood. "I felt like my whole life was a lie. If he didn't love my mum, how could he possibly love me?"

Enrico watches me intently.

"I remember crying myself to sleep, wishing I'd been better behaved because then he wouldn't have left us."

He picks my foot up and kisses it again.

"I'll never understand how a person could be married to someone and have feelings for someone else," I sigh. "I mean, how can that happen?" I sigh.

We stay silent for a while.

"He's definitely not you," I add.

"Meaning what?"

"Ferrara's marry for life." I smile softly. "Remember when you told me that?"

He clenches his jaw.

"It was one of the most honorable things any man has ever said to me." I smile.

His eyes hold mine as his face falls.

"Dad went on to marry some other woman. He didn't even marry the woman he left us for."

"He didn't leave you," he says.

"He did. He left us because my mother was never the same, either. She went a little crazy herself, dating every man that looked her way."

He runs his hands up my legs as he listens.

"As soon as they brought other people into their lives, it felt like my brother and I didn't matter to them anymore. I know we did, deep down, but they had a separate life to us then—one we weren't included in. A secret society for lovers. Children weren't invited. I knew they both looked forward to their weekends without us so that they could do what they wanted with their new flings. I always felt in the way, and so did my brother."

Enrico exhales heavily.

"I'm not going to be like them," I whisper. "Over my dead body will I ever be like them."

"Is that why you don't sleep around?"

I think on that for a moment. "I don't know. I don't think so. I'm just not wired like that. I have to really feel something to want to have sex with someone."

"You sleep with me."

"It's the weirdest thing. I feel like I know you," I whisper.

Our eyes lock.

"Have you ever had that feeling that you already know someone, but you don't?" I ask.

"Yes." He smiles softly. "I have it with you. I had it from the moment we met."

I sit up in a rush, and water sloshes everywhere. I lie over his broad body, and his hands come to my behind. "Maybe we were lovers in ancient Roman times."

He grabs my face and smiles against my lips. "I know we were."

I smile up at my partner as he twirls me around the dance floor.

The room is lit by candlelight, and there are beautiful people everywhere.

The mood is sultry and romantic, like my outfit. I'm wearing a smoky gray backless dress with spaghetti straps that falls to the floor. It's Valentino, of course. Giorgio really has injected some serious sexiness into my wardrobe. Not that I'm complaining.

Rico is wearing a black dinner suit. We are in the swankiest restaurant club I've ever seen. We've had the most amazing day. We woke up late and had a lazy breakfast. After that, Rico took me sightseeing, we've laughed and talked and my poor heart may never recover. Having his undivided attention has been perfect in every way. He's different here—more relaxed. Only a few men are trailing behind us. I didn't realize how different it is for Enrico in Italy. He has a reputation to uphold there. Everyone double takes when they see him, he is so well known. Here, he can go relatively unnoticed.

This afternoon we went back to the yacht. We made love and drank cocktails on the deck as the sun set over the water.

This is living.

Monte Carlo is beyond incredible. I now know why it's known as the playground for the rich and wealthy.

It's the weirdest thing, when I'm with Enrico, I don't feel out of place. Wherever he belongs, I do, too.

I smile up at him as he moves us to the music.

Wearing his black dinner suit, Enrico's back is rigid, and his hand is at a respectable height on my waist. Always the perfect gentleman in public—polite and respectful— but he's always the Devil in private.

He's two versions of the same song. The good and the bad. I like the good in him, but it's the bad that I love. He brings out the bad in me, and I happen to love this new version of myself. I'm keeping her.

A song comes on, and I smile as soon as I hear it. "I love this song," I say. "It's called 'Someone You Loved.'"

He frowns as he listens. "Hmm. Not my taste."

"Why not?" I laugh. "It's a beautiful song."

He spins me to the music. "It's about a man having his heart broken. It's a sad song."

"And?"

"I don't want to dance with you to a sad song. I don't feel in the least bit sad. Quite the opposite, actually."

I smile up at my man, his big brown eyes look down at me. Everyone else in the room disappears. "Tell me something about you," I whisper.

"Like what?"

"Tell me something I don't know yet."

He thinks for a moment as we sway to the music. "I hated being away from you this week," he murmurs softly.

"You did?"

"I had to force myself every day not to come home to you." I put my head onto his chest and smile against him. He pulls me closer and kisses my temple. "Are you ready to go home, my love?"

My love.

"I am so ready."

The plane comes to a slow stop on the tarmac at Milan airport, and Rico inhales deeply, as if steeling himself for what's to come.

Once given the go ahead by the captain, he stands, and I

watch him walk around the cabin, talking to Lorenzo, who happens to be multitasking on the phone. Lorenzo seems to be his right-hand man, and most of the details are managed by him. He's a good-looking man in his mid-fifties, at a guess. He's handsome and obviously proud. He and the other men speak only Italian to Rico and each other. I'm unsure if they can even understand me. If they can't, they've given me no indication other than a polite nod when I look their way.

I sit and stare out of the window. It's 11:00 p.m. on Sunday night.

What an amazing weekend.

Work tomorrow, though. Ugh. I could live on that yacht for all of eternity and never miss a thing.

Rico comes back to me. "Are you ready, Olivia?"

My heart drops. I'm Olivia again now. He's back to being guarded. I much prefer my private man to the one he shows the world.

He takes my hand and helps me out of my seat. I see a black SUV drive onto the tarmac.

Lorenzo bends to look out of the window.

"L'auto è qui." *Translation: the car is here.*

"Ok. Andiamo." *Translation: okay let's go.*

Rico presses his hand on the small of my back and leads me from the plane. We are ushered into the back of the car.

"Il mio appartamento." *Translation: my apartment.*

"Where are we going?" I whisper.

Rico takes my hand and squeezes it on his lap. "My place."

"Where is this place?" I mutter as I walk down the street with my heavy garment bag.

Damn this, I now know why nobody else jumped at the opportunity.

It's Monday, and today, at work, some dresses needed to be put in at the dry cleaners on the other side of town. I offered to do it, thinking it would get me out of the office for a while. I got dropped off by the cab three blocks too early, and now I have to walk a mile.

The sequins on these stupid dresses weigh a ton, and my arm is killing me. I sling it over my shoulder and continue to look at the map on my phone. It says it's five hundred meters away now.

"For fuck's sake." I look back up at the road in front of me and stop still.

Enrico just walked out of a restaurant with a woman. He's wearing a dark navy suit, and he looks every bit the Playboy millionaire.

The woman is beautiful with long, thick dark hair. She's wearing a fitted grey dress with a plunging neckline and high heels. She has big maroon lips, and her makeup looks perfect. Her Prada bag is tucked securely over her arm.

He has his hand at the small of her back and he is talking to her as he leads her out to a car. He says something. She laughs and kisses his cheek before he opens the door of the black Mercedes and she gets in.

He walks around to the driver's side and gets in. They pull out and drive away, still deep in conversation.

I watch the car as it disappears down the street.

Who the fuck was that?

16

Olivia

I STAND on the spot for a moment as I watch the car disappear with my man and a beautiful woman inside. I'm not sure if I'm in shock or disbelief. Probably both.

Don't be stupid. It's his sister or something. It has to be. Enrico's not a sleazebag. I know he isn't.

I struggle down the street with the heavy garment bag, my mind running wild. Maybe I should just call him and put my mind to rest. Yes, I'll do that.

I take out my phone and have another thought. He doesn't touch me in public.

Is there a reason?

A sick, suspicious feeling washes over me, and my heart begins to race.

Is he married? Of course, he isn't married.

Fuck.

"Don't be dramatic," I whisper, spotting the dry cleaners up ahead. I drop the bag off and return to work by taxi, with every conspiracy theory running through my mind.

He took me away this weekend. I thought it was to be romantic. What if he was hiding me?

I've been so hypnotized by his company that I haven't asked any questions.

Is he with somebody else? Is that why he didn't call me in Australia and ask me to come here for him?

No. He's not.

Ferraras marry for life.

I go over our weekend together. The laughing, the making love, and the closeness we shared.

Just get back to work and stop thinking the worst. There is a completely logical explanation.

We'll see what happens tonight when I ask him.

It's 8:00 p.m., and I'm waiting for Enrico to knock on my door.

He called me earlier and said he was working late.

Was he?

I played dumb. I want to see his face when I bring it up. I'm still convinced that this is all in my head, but my gut feeling is setting off alarm bells.

Something is going on. There are just too many holes in our time away from each other and what he's told me about himself. I have questions that have had me pacing back and forth in my room for the last two hours.

Knock, knock.

This is it. I open the door in a rush.

Enrico's sexy eyes hold mine. "Hello, bella."

My heart skips a beat at the sight of him. "Hi."

He leans in and kisses me before he takes me into his arms. "I missed you today."

I pull out of his arms and he walks past me into my room. "What did you do today?" I ask.

"Worked," he says as he takes off his jacket and throws it on the bed. "How was your day?"

"Good," I say as I watch him. "Where did you have lunch?"

His eyes come to me and in that moment, I know the woman he was with wasn't his sister.

"Downtown," he replies calmly and sits on the bed. He taps his lap for me to go him. "Why do you ask?"

I remain standing. "I saw you." Our eyes are locked, and he remains silent.

"Who is she?"

After a beat, he replies, "Her name is Sophia." I stare at him as I wait for him to elaborate. "She works for me."

Relief begins to flood through me. I knew there was a logical reason.

"She's the General Manager of..." He pauses.

"Of what?"

"Our high-end brothels."

"She's a Madam?" I whisper. "You're spending time with a whore?"

He clenches his jaw, angered by my outburst.

"Why didn't you tell me about this?" I snap. "Why did I have to see you in the street with another woman?"

He stands and goes to the window to stare down at the street below. He puts his hands in his suit pockets. "We needed to talk about this, anyway," he says calmly. "I have been waiting for the right moment to bring it up and this is as good a time as any. I want to get you your own apartment. Pick somewhere, anywhere, and I will buy it for you."

I stare at him. He's different, detached and calculating. Or maybe that's just because my rose-tinted glasses have been smashed to smithereens and I'm seeing the real him for the first time.

He owns brothels.

"You don't need to work for Valentino. You can have your own fashion label. I'll back you financially. Anything you want is yours. No budget. You can have everything."

"Where will you live?" I ask.

He stares at me, but stays silent.

"Will you live with me?"

"No."

"Why not?"

He inhales sharply. "We cannot be in a relationship in a traditional sense, Olivia."

My brows rise.

"I have..." He pauses, searching for the right words. "More than ever, I need to hold onto my Italian heritage."

My skin begins to crawl.

"I am not just a man who lives in Italy, Olivia. I am an Italian man in all senses. I need to carry on my traditional bloodline. It is very, very important to me—non-negotiable."

What?

We stare at each other. "This is why you didn't come for me in Australia?"

He clenches his jaw. "Yes."

I can literally hear my heart as it breaks.

"What you're saying is that you can fuck an Australian... but you can't marry one?" I whisper as tears form.

His cold eyes hold mine. "I'm sorry."

"So, you'll have your Italian wife and keep your bloodline with her, and I will be your girlfriend on the side?"

He drops his head, ashamed of what he has asked of me.

My throat hurts as I try to hold it together. If he hit me with an axe it would be less painful. I grab the table to steady myself.

"Olivia," he whispers. "Think about it. You will have me in every sense other than marriage. I will be yours." He cups my face in his hand. "I don't want to lose you." His eyes are crazy, panicked. "I can't lose you."

"You just did." I push out through gritted teeth.

"No, bella." He grabs for me, and he holds me tight in his arms as I struggle to break free.

"Get out."

He holds me. "No, no, no. Per favore, no. Non posso perderti," he whispers as he clings to me, desperate to hold me in place so that he can talk me into this. "Non posso vivere senza di te."

I know he's losing control because he's talking Italian. He only does that when he can't think.

I break free from his grip and push him hard on the chest. He stumbles back.

"Get out," I sneer.

"I'm not leaving you. I can't. Don't ask that of me."

I pick up a glass from the table and hurl it at him. "Get the fuck out!" I scream.

His eyes hold mine for an extended moment, and then, as if conceding defeat, he drops his head.

I turn my back on him as my tears begin to pour free.

I've never felt so fucking cheap in all of my life. Here I was thinking we were falling in love, and he was just lining me up to fuck me behind his future wife's back.

The only sound is my heartbeat as adrenaline courses through my veins, trying desperately to calm me down.

Thump, thump, thump.

Eventually, I hear the door click closed as he leaves.

I turn and see a white business card on the table.

Enrico Ferrara
02- 99889002

His number… in case I change my mind.

I already have your number, asshole.

I slide down the wall and sit hunched up on the floor as I cry out loud.

What the fuck just happened?

Enrico

I lean my forehead against Olivia's door, the palms of my hands flat against it.

I can hear her crying. I just shattered any dreams she had of a future with me. Any dream that I ever had, too.

Everything she thought I was no longer exists. I knew she wouldn't go for the arrangement, but I had to at least try.

If only things were different.

Her sobs are loud, and my chest constricts at the sound. I hate that I disappointed her.

"Bella," I whisper as her cries escalate.

I can't stand it. I can't stand listening to her being hurt and alone. I grab the door handle to go back inside her room. I can't leave her like this.

And offer her what, Enrico? A sleazy arrangement where you pretend to love your wife and secretly spend time with Olivia? One where you have children with someone else and always wish they were Olivia's?

I don't want that life for her, but I was too selfish not to

offer it. I knew the consequences if I did. I will be forever tainted in her eyes.

I deserve to be.

I listen to her cry for half an hour with regret swirling deep in my stomach. I hear something bang, and I listen, knowing she's thrown something at the wall.

She's angry.

Good.

Angry is better than heartbroken.

I hear something else bang, and I close my eyes in relief. She's okay. Anger, I can deal with. Heartbreak, I cannot.

I drag myself away from her door and make my way downstairs to head over to the car. Maso and Marley are inside. I trust these two with my life. They wind down the window as they see me approaching.

"Hey, boss."

"Hi." I force a smile. "I'm heading home, but I want you to stay and watch over Olivia."

"Sure thing." Marley looks across the road at her building. "How long for?"

"Just stay with her until further notice. I want her guarded around the clock. Arrange for a team to look over her."

"Okay."

"I want to know where she is at all times," I add.

"Yeah, okay."

"Ciao." I make my way over to my car in the parking lot and I pull out into the traffic. Another car with my two guards inside follows me.

Never alone.

With every block farther away from Olivia, I feel a little more darkness creep in.

It's 1:00 a.m. and I'm sitting on my bed, resting against the headboard. With a shaky hand, I pour myself another scotch. I've drank most of the bottle trying to take the edge off of my sadness.

I feel more alone than ever.

My mind is a swimming pool of memories… every one of her.

I get a vision of her talking and flicking her long, golden hair over her shoulder. Her big blue eyes. The way she looked up at me when we made love. The way she laughs. The way she feels. Her voice. Her smile.

She's gone.

You did the right thing.

But did I? Because it sure doesn't feel like it. Being in her arms over the last weekend has only shown me how empty my life really is.

Ferrara.

My name, my entitlement… my prison.

I feel soft skin against my back, and a gentle dusting of lips on my shoulder.

I smile in my sleep. *Olivia.*

Her hand reaches around and takes my cock. She gives it a long, slow stroke. My eyes flicker. "Hmm."

She kisses my shoulder again and rolls me onto my back. I'm having trouble waking.

The scotch.

"Hmm," I moan again as my legs open to allow her access.

She strokes me, harder this time, and my balls contract. My back arches off the bed. Mmm, this feels good.

She softly kisses my shoulder as she works me, and my eyes flutter. *Olivia.*

My body begins to quiver with need, and I spread my legs to touch the mattress as I feel the blood rush to my cock.

Yes… yes.

The bed begins to rock from her hard strokes.

God, yes.

I need to fuck.

"Ti piace il mio uomo?" she whispers.

Italian.

My eyes snap open at the sound of her voice.

"Sophia?" Fuck! I forgot she has a key. I push her off me in disgust.

"Cosa c'è di sbagliato, Enrico?" *Translation: what is wrong Enrico?*

"What the fuck are you doing in my bed?" I growl as I jump up, furious. "Do not touch me. Do you hear me?"

"Che problema c'è?" *Translation: what is the matter?*

"Everything. Get the fuck out of my bedroom!" I push her out of the door. "Get out!" I scream.

"I don't understand!" she cries in an outrage. "You want me, I know you do. You always want me."

"What I want is for you to get out of my house. Get out!"

Her face falls. I push her out into the hall, slam the door shut, and flick the lock.

My breath is labored. I'm physically rattled.

I get into the shower and under the steaming hot water. I'm shaken that I nearly just accidently fucked Sophia. How do you nearly accidently fuck someone?

I nearly cheated on my darling Olivia.

I close my eyes, and I can hear my Olivia crying from last night through the door. I can hear the hurt in her voice.

She's not your Olivia.

What the fuck is happening to me?

Olivia

I stare out of the window of the café in a daze. My coffee and breakfast are getting cold on the table, but I can't bring myself to start them.

I've cried all night, and my eyes were too swollen to go to work today.

This isn't the first time I've been hurt but it's definitely the deepest.

I know there's no way around this.

I'm not Italian. I will never be Italian, and he will never make a future with a woman who isn't.

My heart wants me to call him so that he can come over and make us better—so he can hold me and tell me that he's never leaving. I want to be warm and safe in his arms.

My brain wants to bomb his office for daring to think that I would be his mistress.

He drew a line in the sand last night, and now I know what kind of man I'm in love with. A womanizing pimp who sleeps with his whores. One who has zero respect for me.

I want to pack up and go home to Australia, but I know I can't. I won't let a man ruin everything in my life. Nobody has that power. This is the opportunity of a lifetime, but honestly, who cares about the job if it costs me my sanity to stay here? Is the job even really fucking mine? I got it at his request.

I can't be here in Milan with him and his Italian wife. I'll choke on my own fucking vomit.

"Is everything all right?" the waiter asks as he looks down at my untouched coffee and breakfast."

"Yes, thank you." I pick up my knife and fork. "I'm eating now."

He smiles, pretending not to notice my swollen eyes, and he puts his hand on top of mine as it sits on the table, knowing I need comfort. Unexpectedly, my eyes fill with tears at his kindness. "Are you all right?" he asks softly.

"Yes." I nod as I fumble around in my bag for a tissue. "I will be." I dab my eyes and drop my head in shame. He leaves me alone and I go back to staring into space.

I've hit rock bottom.

I'm on the other side of the world from home, alone, and heartbroken.

I get a vision of Enrico and the week we have spent together, laughing and making love, and it only makes it worse.

I can't even hate him.

"Fucking hell," Natalie whispers as she rests her cheek on her fist. Her eyes are glued to mine, and she softly shake of her head. "I can't believe this."

I've just dropped the bombshell. It's Tuesday night, and I am relaying the Ferrara fuckface chronicles to Nat as we eat at our favorite restaurant.

"I can," I sigh sadly. "Think about it, Nat. It never really did add up. Something was always amiss. If he wanted me in the true sense, he would have come for me in Australia. It's not like money was ever an object."

Her shoulders slump. "I'm sorry, baby. I know you really liked him."

My eyes fill with tears, and I swipe them away angrily.

"I just feel like a fool, Nat." I stare out over the people in the restaurant. "What's that old saying? Fool me once, shame on you. Fool me twice, shame on me. I'm so embarrassed about the whole thing that I can't even tell Giorgio. I feel like an idiot. I'll just tell him in a few weeks when I'm stronger and not at risk of crying like a baby." I shake my head. "I should have known better than to trust my stupid heart."

Nat rolls her eyes. "Yeah, that bitch sure is tapped."

I smile sadly. "Enough depressing talk about rich pricks. Tell me all about your man."

Nat twists her lips. "Meh, I'm kind of off him, to be honest."

"What? Already? I thought you liked him."

"He got all needy and stuff." She fakes a shiver.

I giggle and put my head into my hands. "What the hell is wrong with us, Nat? Every guy you date is too nice. Every guy I date is a fucktard."

She laughs and shakes her head. "He's got one more weekend to toughen up. If he's still being pathetic, he's gone." She dusts her hands together.

I smile. "Poor bastard."

We fall serious, and her eyes hold mine. "So, what are you going to do now?"

I exhale heavily. "Forget I ever met him… again."

My phone rings and I pick up with a sad smile. "Hi Mum." I always hate talking to my mum when I'm feeling blue. It's like she has a sixth sense and can tell what's going on with me from wherever she is in the world.

"How are you?" I ask, faking happiness.

"I'm good darling, missing you. How is everything going?"

"Great," I lie, my heart drops, it's actually the polar opposite.

My life is a total mess, I've cried myself to sleep the entire week.

"And how's the romance going?"

My stomach drops.... romance? Ha, what a joke? He wanted me to be his mistress and fuck me behind his wife's back. I close my eyes, the reality of telling my mother that yet another relationship has failed is just too hard at the moment, I'll tell her when I'm stronger. "It's going good. Ticking along."

"Oh, exciting, this could be the one, love."

My eyes fill with tears, I thought so too. "I doubt it, mum," I sigh. "It's just a holiday thing, don't get excited."

"How's Natalie settling in?"

"She's looking for work, going well." I smile broadly. "Met a guy already."

Mum laughs. "That's not like our Nat now, is it?"

"I know right, she's like a man magnet."

"What's he like?"

I screw up my face. "Not my type."

"What's this guy your seeing like?"

I roll my eyes, this again. "He's nice." I really don't want to get into this today, I need to get off the phone. "I have to run mum, I'm going to be late for my gym class."

"Okay dear. Love you. Call me later."

"Love you too, bye."

"Would the Sedan be suitable?" the girl on the car hire desk asks.

"That will be great, thank you."

It's Friday afternoon, and I'm hiring a car to get out of Milan for the weekend. With Nat busy and my life in a fucking shamble, I need to get the hell away. I've decided to drive up to Heidelberg in Germany. It's about a five-hour drive from here, so not too far for a weekend. I always wanted to go there, and I'm not lying around in my hotel room in Milan being depressed all weekend. I've booked a hotel and will drive there tonight with the intention of coming back Sunday night.

It's not like I have anything on other than feeling sorry for myself, and I'm sick of doing that.

I'm better than this. *I'm better than him.*

I deserve a man who loves me and, damn it, I won't take anything less.

Fuck Enrico Ferrara. He can go to hell on a broomstick for all I care.

I sign for the car and the woman shows me all of the settings and how to work the navigation system. I throw my bags into the back and get in. I drive around the corner before I program in where I'm going.

Heidelberg, here I come.

It's just on 10pm when I drive into the hotel in Heidelberg. I've had a good trip; the traffic was good and I'm excited to be here.

I've always had a fascination with Heidelberg since the tenth grade when I did an assignment on Heidelberg Castle. I vowed to myself then that I would one day see it in the flesh with my own eyes, and here I am.

I'm going to spend the day there tomorrow and I have to admit I'm feeling very proud of myself for ticking something off my bucket list.

Even when things are shitty, I'm still okay. I'll make it through this rough patch, I always do.

I walk through Heidelberg castle in awe. It's so much better than I could have ever imagined. I'm fully aware that I only know this place because of my stupid assignment when I was a girl, but I feel an affinity to it, as if I were meant to come here one day.

I spent the morning looking around by myself, and then this afternoon I signed up for a guided tour. I'm fascinated by its history. The building is red brick and sits on the side of the hill overlooking the gorgeous town below. It was built in the early 1600s and has been destroyed by lightning, fire, and war, yet it still sits proudly on the mountain, as if guarding the town below.

The ten members of the tour group are wearing earpieces while our tour guide is pointing out the facts about the castle. We get to the main quadrangle.

"And this here..." The tour guide points out a deep footprint in the stone below a window that is two-stories high. "This footprint is a bit of a legend." He smiles. "Apparently, the queen was tired of the king always being away, waging wars and what not. So, she took a lover—a knight—and they began a torrid affair which led to them falling madly in love. Their affair went on for years until, one night, the king came home early to find the knight in bed with his wife. The knight had no choice but to jump from the window or the king would have had him killed instantly. When the knight jumped out of the window in his armor, he made this footprint in the stone. Now, for the really fun part. It's said that any man whose foot fits in this hole is a fantastic lover."

The group laughs and we move onto the next point of interest. I stand and stare at the footprint in the stone, and my mind begins to drift back in time.

What would it be like to have been that queen? To be married to one man and yet be in love with another? Her husband's knight. One of her protectors. I look up at the window above and imagine the nights that they spent together in her quarters.

The love that they shared would have been sacred and special. They literally risked their lives to have it.

In all the places I have been, with the all of the history I have learnt, it's the stories of love that truly fascinate me. Did the king kill her knight? Or was she beheaded for having a lover?

What happened to them?

Did they die in each other's arms?

I walk over to the balcony and look out over the town. The breeze whips through my hair, and my mind goes to Rico. So much was left unsaid between us.

I didn't ask enough questions. When we spoke in my hotel room and he told me his wishes, I was so shocked that I didn't ask why. Why does he feel the way he does?

Why does he feel that he has to marry an Italian?

What's hurting the most is that I know he wants me— I felt it in every touch.

It's eating at me, the not knowing why. I understand his wishes, and I know it won't change the outcome for us, but for him... it's sad. This is *his* life. In the twentieth century, why does he still feel so obliged to follow ancient tradition?

Why should his life be a sacrifice to his ancestors?

I can't call him and ask, but if I had my time again and he came to me with that proposition, I would have asked more questions to try and get an insight into his inner thoughts so that I could understand them and move on.

I stare out over the town and wrap my cardigan around me. I guess it doesn't matter anymore, anyway.

I need to stop thinking about him.... our time together is over.

17

Enrico

"She's at a castle in Germany," Marley says.

I frown. "What's she doing there?"

"Sightseeing, by the looks of it. I've emailed you some pictures just now."

I click open the email as I sit at my desk, and a barrage of images come up of Olivia Reynolds.

"Is she alone?" I ask, transfixed by her beauty.

"Yes, she arrived late last night. She got room service and has been pottering around town all day."

I stare at the image of her looking over the balcony of what looks like a castle. She's so deep in thought. Her blonde hair is up in a high ponytail, and she's wearing a cream sweater and blue jeans.

She's so beautiful.

I click to the next page of images. There's one of her

drinking coffee in a café, another of her eating an ice cream, followed by one of her driving a car, and then arriving at the hotel.

A scribe of her actions, all laid out for me to look at. I run my fingers over my lips as I stare at her images.

"Will that be all, boss?" Marley asks, snapping me out of my daydream.

"Yes, sorry. Stay with her. Let me know of any changes."

"Okay."

He hangs up, and I sit back in my chair, staring at the woman who's become somewhat of an obsession to me.

The one I can't have.

Knock, knock.

I minimize my computer screen. "Come in."

"Hey," Sergio says. "You got a minute?"

"Yeah, take a seat."

Lorenzo and Sergio take a seat at my desk—my two right hand men. Lorenzo's family has worked for my family for years, meaning he is my family now, too. Sergio had just started moving up the ranks before my father died. He's been out on the field for ten years with them. He knows what he's doing.

"What is it?" I sigh, not in the mood for working at all.

"We've got problems in Sicily," Sergio informs me.

"Why?"

"When you gave up our cocaine ring down there—"

I cut him off. "No drugs. I fucking told you I won't sell drugs."

Sergio's eyes hold mine. We have fought over this many times. "Let me finish."

Lorenzo and I roll our eyes.

"By giving up our reign of that side of the business in Sicily, it went to someone else. His name is Luciano Lombardi, and he's been making quite the name for himself."

"How so?"

"They call him Lucky Lombardi. He's into stand over tactics: torture, rape. There isn't anything he won't do to be the top dog."

"He isn't our concern." I turn my computer on.

"He has his sights set on our brothels."

I frown and turn my attention back to him.

"We have twenty-seven down there, as well as five strip clubs. Him and his growing band of men have started frequenting them as clients."

I stand and pour myself a glass of scotch, my interest piqued. "And?"

"Last night he went into one and demanded the girls come and work for him. When they refused, he roughed a few of them up."

My back stiffens. "He hit them?"

"Bashed the living fuck out of a couple of them. Three ended up in hospital."

I inhale sharply. "Nobody hits a Ferrara girl and gets away with it."

"What do you want us to do?" Sergio asks.

"Beef up security, send more men down there."

"We need to take back the cocaine," Lorenzo says.

"No!" I snap. "We're not drug dealers anymore. We are better than that. That time is over." We keep having this same argument. "How many fucking times do I have to tell you? No. More. Drugs."

"If we let him take that, he will take the rest." Sergio shakes his head. "The more blow he sells, the more power he gets. How long will it be before he infiltrates our other areas?" Lorenzo snaps. "This isn't about the drugs, Enrico, it's about the power that it gives whoever has it."

"We have reputable businesses now. We do not need that side of the business. Stop thinking with fear. I will not be a lowlife drug dealer. That time is over for Ferrara. We are smarter now."

"What about the girls? They're in Sicily with a fucking madman who's trying to take over our turf. Are you just going to let him?"

I stand and walk over to the window, and I look out at the city below. "Beef up security. Every girl is to be protected and I want to know everything there is to know about this Lucky Lombardi."

"Yes, sir." They both stand and leave the room. I sip my scotch as anger begins to seep into my bloodstream.

Nobody hits a Ferrara woman and gets away with it.

Nobody.

I sit in my car and stare across the street as she walks down the pavement.

I have a new pastime.

Stalking Olivia Reynolds.

Like a drug that I can't have, I find myself thinking about her night and day.

Day and night.

I'm furious with Sophia, as if this is all somehow her fault. I can't even talk to her at the moment. She doesn't have what I need.

My drug has blonde hair, blue eyes, and the morals of a saint.

My drug made me feel worthy of her affection.

My drug is gone.

I watch on as she sits down onto a park bench and takes out her phone to scroll through it. She does this sometimes, as if not wanting to go back to her hotel.

My phone vibrates on the seat beside me, and I look over at the screen and frown.

Olivia Reynolds

It's her, I scramble to answer it. "Hello, Olivia."

"Hi," she says softly. I smile as I watch her across the road. "Are you okay?"

"Yeah. Are you?"

"It's so good to hear your voice," I whisper before I turn my mouth to brain filter on. I scrunch my eyes shut… *stop it.*

She pauses for a moment. "Can we meet up for a coffee sometime?

My heart flips. "Of course." I smile, she wants to see me. "When. Now?" I offer.

"No, I'm at work now," she lies.

"I see." I run my finger along the side of the steering wheel as I watch her. "Tonight?" I ask.

"No. In the daytime is better."

I clench my jaw, knowing that means it's platonic. She feels safer in the day. "Okay, tomorrow?"

"Yes. Two o'clock?"

"The café near your hotel?"

"Yes. See you then." She hangs up, and I watch her stare at

her phone for a moment before she stuffs it in her bag and begins to walk away.

"I'll see you tomorrow, bella. I'll see you tomorrow," I whisper with a smile.

She wants to see me. There's hope.

I sit in the café and glance at my watch. It's 2:10 p.m.

Where is she?

I've been antsy all day. What if she doesn't come?

I sip my coffee, while her coffee sits on the table opposite me, going cold. I got here early. I couldn't wait any longer.

She breezes in and gives me a little wave as she approaches the table. I smile like a puppy as I scramble to my feet.

"Hello."

"Hi," she replies as I kiss her cheek.

She's wearing a white linen shirt and navy capri pants. Her blonde hair is in a low ponytail, and she is wearing minimal makeup.

Natural perfection.

She sits down opposite me.

"I ordered you a coffee but it's probably cold. I'll order you another."

"It's fine."

I stare at her, lost for words. What do you say to someone you've been following around all week? "How are you?" I ask.

"Good." She smiles. "Getting there. How are you?"

My face falls. I hate that she's fine. Am I alone in this? "I'm okay." I fake a smile. "You wanted to see me?" I ask.

"Yes, I did." She pauses and sips her coffee. "I have a few questions that I need answered."

"Okay." She wants to keep seeing me. She's going to agree to it. "Anything, ask me anything."

Her eyes hold mine, as if she's steeling herself to speak. "Why do you think that your heritage depends on who you marry?"

I frown. "What do you mean?"

"Well, you... you said that..." She stops herself. "I know these seem like stupid questions to you, but I didn't ask you them the other day and they are eating away at me."

"I'm the head of my family now, and with that comes responsibilities. It's in my hands to ensure that my family continues on as it has for centuries."

"And you were taught this as you grew up?"

"Yes. When I have my own children, it is very important for them to know my language and their culture, and what it means to be Italian."

"I see." She smiles sadly.

We sit in silence for a moment.

"So, that's your magnet?" she asks.

I frown, not understanding. "What do you mean?"

"When you meet someone, they have a magnet that attracts you to them. Everyone has a magnet. Some are stronger than others."

I stare at her, fascinated by her theory. "What's your magnet to me? What attracted you to me?" I ask.

She chuckles. "Funnily enough, my magnet to you is the exact reason that we can't be together."

"Such as."

"I loved how you are so proud of being Italian."

My heart drops.

"And how you care for your family and love your parents. How I felt so safe in your arms."

I frown and take her hands over the table as emotion overwhelms me.

Baby.

"But it was your stance on marriage that caught me off guard. You told me that when you marry, it's going to be for life."

I clench my jaw. She's here to say goodbye.

No. please no.

"But then you ruined it in spectacular fashion by telling me that you own brothels, and then wanting me to be your mistress." She shrugs. "I'm wiping that from my memory bank permanently, by the way. I've never been so insulted in my entire life."

"I didn't buy the brothels. I took them over from the family. Don't judge me on that. And..." I pause. "I just didn't know how to walk away from you. I was trying to find an answer to this mess—one where we can stay together."

"I know." She smiles sadly. "And if my self respect was for sale, I would sell it to stay in your arms."

We stare at each other, sadness and regret hanging in the air between us.

I wasn't joking. I really don't know how to walk away from her.

She pulls her hands out of mine with renewed determination. "What was your magnet to me?" she asks. "Just for interest's sake."

Sadness begins to roll in like a thick fog.

I raise my brows as I think. "When I'm with you, I forget

who I am. You remind me of who I was before," I whisper. "When I could be who I wanted to be." Her eyes search mine. "You are the only honest thing left in my life, and I'm scared that if I lose you, I will lose myself." I frown. Where the hell did that come from?

I drop my head, rattled by my own admission.

"Baby," she whispers. "You are a good man. You don't need me or anyone to prove that to you. And when you meet her and fall in love, you will know that too."

"I don't want to fall in love with anyone else," I whisper as fear grips me. "What if I'm already in love with you?"

"You're not." She smiles sadly with a shake of her head. She cups my hand to her cheek.

"How do you know?"

"Because when you love someone, they instantly become your family. It isn't a choice. Your family presents itself."

My face falls. "I'm so sorry," I whisper. "I never meant for this all to happen but I couldn't stay away."

"I'm sorry, too." She smiles as she takes her hand from my face, coldness fills the void.

"So, this is it?"

"Yes, this is it. I just wanted to say goodbye and tell you that I understand."

I get a lump in my throat. "You do?"

"Of course, I do." She gives me her first genuine smile of the day. "I wish you the best. She will come."

I stare at her, unable to push a word pass my lips. *She's already here.*

"And if I find out you have a mistress behind her back, I'm coming back here to kick your ass."

My face falls. "You're leaving?"

"I'll stay for the three months for the experience, but them I'm going to New York."

My gaze drops to the table, unable to look her in the eye, and reining in my every instinct to drop to my knees and beg. "If it's any consolation, I knew you would never become my other woman." I pause for a moment. "But I had to try. I can't change my heritage and what's expected of me." My eyes search hers. "If I could, I would."

She gives my hand a reassuring squeeze. "I understand. It doesn't make it any easier, but I understand. Thank you for explaining everything."

I smile, relieved that she doesn't hate me. I hate me enough for the both of us.

She stands.

"You're leaving already?" I murmur as I stand with her. "Can we just be friends? Stay and drink your coffee."

"We both know where that will lead." She smiles sadly.

I take her in my arms, and we stand cheek-to-cheek for a long time.

I close my eyes in regret.

Don't go.

"Goodbye, Rici." She tries to walk away and I cling onto her hand.

"What if I won't let you go?"

"But you will."

The truth hurts.

She turns, walks out of the restaurant, and out of my life.

I slump back into my chair and drag my hand down my face.

I inhale with a shaky breath. It will be fine.

I'll be fine.

It needed to come to an end.

I'll be fine.

I sit at the table and stare at the bride.

Traditional white dress, madly in love with her groom.

Italian to the bone.

It never bothered me before, and I've been to a lot of weddings. This wedding is different. I can't take my eyes off the newly married couple. I keep envisaging myself kicking the ten-tier wedding cake down. Smashing it to smithereens.

Screaming to the whole world that it's a façade.

The groom leans over and kisses his bride, and my stomach twists with jealousy.

Italian blood.

The lifeline of my heritage.

Fernando, my cousin, can marry her because of the blood that runs in her veins.

I tip my head back and drain the scotch from my glass.

Stop fucking thinking about it.

I feel two warm hands on my shoulders. "Enrico."

I glance up and smile as I see my mother. She's dressed in her mourning black and as beautiful as ever.

"What is it, son?" she asks softly as she takes a seat beside me. "What's wrong with you?"

"Nothing, Mamma." I fake a smile. "Busy."

"That's not true. I've seen you every day this week. Something is wrong, I can feel it. A mother knows these things."

I clench my jaw and look out over the party. "Leave it, Mamma."

"Andrea told me."

I run my tongue over my teeth as my attention drifts back to her. "Told you what?"

"You've met someone."

"I said leave it."

"What's the matter, Enrico? Talk to me."

I shake my head. "Nothing, I'm fine."

"She doesn't love you?"

I roll my eyes.

"She loves another?"

"No!" I snap, angered by the mere prospect. "She does not." I drag my hands through my hair.

"Why can't you have her?"

"Because I am Italian. Because I choose to honor my ancestors."

Her face falls. "Oh, Rico," she sighs. "My darling boy." She watches me for a moment. "You are your father's son. Honorable and brave."

I stare into her big, brown eyes, and I see sympathy.

"Your father would want you to choose love, Rico. What good is tradition if your love is untrue?"

I stare at her, confusion setting in.

"When you find your love, you must fight to keep her." She leans over and kisses me on the cheek. Without another word, she stands and walks away.

My eyes go back to the married couple. I don't even know what true is anymore.

Olivia

Two weeks later

I look at the three swatches of fabric as I try to work out what I'm putting on this vision board for an upcoming dress I am delivering next week. One is browner than I thought, and damn it, I thought it was going to be perfect. I hold the sequin swatch over the fabric. They do still look good together though.

"Delivery for Olivia Reynolds," someone says.

I glance up to see a delivery man with a big bunch of red roses. "What in the world?"

"Are you Olivia?"

"Yes."

"Sign here, please." I sign the card, and he hands over the heavy crystal vase filled with beautiful roses.

"Thanks." I smile in surprise and open the card attached. It reads:

I need to see you tonight.
Luciano's Italian at
7:00 p.m.
Rici
xo

What the fuck?

I walk into the restaurant just after seven. I've been a bundle of nerves all day.

What does he want?

It's been two weeks since I said goodbye to Rici. I would love to say that I haven't thought of him once, but I would be lying.

He's the first thing I think of in the morning and the last thing I think of at night.

His love has lingered on my soul.

The restaurant is dark and moody. Candles sit on top of every table.

I catch sight of him sitting at the back, and I smile as I make my way up to the table.

He stands and smiles. "Bella."

Unable to help it, I smile at the mere sight of him. He takes me into his arms. "Hello." We are genuinely excited to see each other and we hug and take a seat.

He has this twinkle to his eyes, and he pours me a glass of champagne.

"What's this about?" I ask. "You wanted to see me."

"I did." He takes a sip and seems in a rush. "I'm just going to get straight to it. I have a proposition for you."

"Do tell."

"Although there are some conditions that you will need to adhere to."

"Conditions?" I frown. What the hell is he on about?

"You will become a practicing Catholic."

Huh?

"You will learn Italian and speak it as your first language."

I frown and sit back.

"You will be under guard twenty-four hours a day, and will not go anywhere unaccompanied."

"I'm sorry… what?" What the heck is he talking about?

"You will move to Lake Como with me, into my main residence."

I raise my brows… speechless.

"You will become an Italian citizen."

"Enrico, what are you talking about?" I whisper.

"I can't live without you, Olivia."

"What?"

"I have been fucking miserable since you left, and I am not giving you up. Not for my country, not for anyone."

Has he lost his mind?

"I want you, in every sense of the word."

"You want me to become… Italian?" I frown.

"Yes."

"Why would I do that?"

"So that I can love you."

18

Olivia

I STARE AT HIM, lost for words, while his face is filled with hope.

"This is why you wanted to see me?" I ask.

"Yes." He reaches over and takes my hands in his and lifts one and softly kisses my fingertips.

My stomach clenches. "What makes you think we will work now, when two weeks ago, you were so sure that we had no chance?"

"You could at least act a little excited," he whispers half annoyed.

"Talk to me, please." I sit back in my chair and pull my hands from his. "Last week, it was a completely different story. Help me understand this. I don't understand your thinking."

He rearranges the napkin on his lap. "I was thinking about what you said about our magnets and why we like each other. Our conversation last week had a deep impact on me. Our wants are what makes us special."

"Enrico, me reminding you of your old life is not enough to build a future on," I huff.

"Don't call me Enrico, and it's more than that. I can't leave you alone. I think about you all the time. I can't drop this, Olivia, I tried. God knows how hard I tried." He pauses. "I'm not leaving someone I want for something I should. What good is all the money in the world if I can't have who I truly care for? What we have is sacred…and you know it is."

I stare at his hopeful face. Unable to help it, I smile softly. "Olivia, I know I'm asking a lot but we can make it work; I know we can."

"I'm not Italian, Rici."

"You are if you're with me." He smiles. "Don't you see?"

"It will take me time to learn your language."

"That's fine."

"And besides, I don't know if I want to even live with you." I frown.

"That's non-negotiable. I need you with me." He squeezes my hand in his.

I like that he needs me with him. My mind begins to race. There's so much to consider.

"So, we'd never live In Australia?" I ask.

He purses his lips. "No."

My face falls.

"But we can have a house there and holiday whenever you want. Your family are always welcome here, too. Olivia, I am under no illusion that this is going to be easy for you. I will be patient and try my best to help you, you have my word on that. I've thought long and hard about this and I know it's what I need to do. There is no other way around it."

"Rici…" I sit back to distance myself from him. "You're asking a lot of me."

"I know, bella."

I sip my wine. I really want to pick up the whole bottle and start pouring it down my throat.

"What I'm asking is if you care enough to build a future with me."

I stare at him, and emotion begins to pump through my system.

"Do you?" he asks.

"What about your family?"

"I'll deal with them."

"What if I make a bad Italian?"

He grins then breaks a deep belly laugh, and I smile as I watch him.

"I'm serious, Rici. This is petrifying. What if I do all this for you and you leave me anyway?"

He falls serious. "I won't be leaving you. Nobody will be leaving anyone. We have to make it work, and we both know we have a very strong base to work from. Yes, it will be tough sometimes, but I adore you and you adore me. What we have is precious. You never forgot me. I know you didn't. I never forgot you."

I smile over at the beautiful man opposite me. He has so much hope in his eyes and pride and love and, oh God, I can feel myself caving in.

"Do you want a life with me or not, Olivia? It's a yes or no answer."

I stare at him, the word yes on the tip of my tongue.

"I can teach you my world, Olivia. I will show you Italy through my eyes. All you have to do is love me."

My eyes fill with tears, because I do. I love this man, and the fact that he is so determined to talk me into this only adds another layer to that love.

I can feel myself falling off the cliff and into the Italian abyss. "Okay," I whisper.

His eyes widen as if surprised by my agreement. "Okay?"

I nod with a smile, and he taps his lap for me to go around and sit on him. I look around us at the people in the restaurant.

"Get over here, woman," he whispers darkly.

I giggle as excitement runs through me. He doesn't even care who can see. I climb onto his lap, and he wraps his arms around me tightly. He kisses me, his tongue sweeping through my open lips.

"I've missed you, Rici Ferrara," I whisper down at him as I brush the hair back from his forehead.

He smiles against my lips. "I've missed you more, my love. Don't leave me again."

He gifts me with the perfect kiss, full of emotion and promise. I giggle. "Everyone is looking at us."

"Fuck them." He smirks. "Fuck them all."

It's after 9:00 p.m. when we leave the restaurant. We've been acting like lovesick teenagers all night. I can't wait to get him alone. All this pent-up heartbreak and back and forth love means I'm about to lose my damn mind.

Enrico looks over to a car parked, and I see a man give him a thumbs up.

"Who's that?" I ask.

"Marley. He's my bodyguard who, unbeknown to you, has been guarding you since we broke up."

"What?" I look over to the car and the two men inside it who are staring at us.

Rico opens my door, and I get into the car while still looking at the two men. I've never seen them before in my life. He closes the door and gets into the driver's seat. "I've been guarded?" I frown over at him.

"Yes." He starts the car and pulls out onto the road. I turn in my seat and see the car pull out behind us. "I needed you safe."

"Why wouldn't I be safe?"

He puts his hand on my thigh. "I'm a very wealthy man, Olivia. With that comes security issues. If somebody wanted to hurt me, they would hurt you. You will have a bodyguard twenty-four-seven now. Marley will be with you. I trust him with my life."

No words are in my head—only shock. "They've been following me?"

"Guarding you, not following you. How was Germany, by the way?"

"Rici." My mouth falls open to say something nasty about my lack of privacy, but I decide to stay silent instead.

"We'll go back to your hotel now and pack up your things. You will move to Lake Como tonight."

"What? That's crazy. Why tonight? What's the rush? I want some time to sit with this."

"I want you to move there tonight."

"Why can't we just go tomorrow?" I ask. Damn it, I want a whole heap of bone-shattering make-up sex first. Not to be moving frigging house.

"Olivia, I want to start our new life together in Como... tonight. Our first night together will be in our bed, not your cheap hotel room, and not in my apartment, but in our new home."

I smile over at him.

"What?" He smirks.

"I was just horny, that's all."

He throws his head back and laughs out loud as if shocked by my statement. "Don't worry, you will be well and truly fucked tonight... but in my bed, and on my terms."

I smile as I look through the windscreen in front of us.

"What are you thinking?" he asks.

"I'm thinking that you're very bossy, Rici Ferrara."

"I just know what I want."

I look over at him. "And what is it that you want?"

"You, bella." He puts one of my fingers into his mouth and sucks it slowly as his dark eyes hold mine. My sex clenches. "Only you."

The cavalcade of cars pulls into a driveway. Huge wrought iron gates greet us, and Enrico stops at the little security house. They open the gates and wave him through. We are at his house in Lake Como—the one he was desperate to get me to right away. At his insistence, we packed up my hotel room life into my suitcase and made our way here.

It's late—just past 11:00 p.m.

We drive through the gates, up the long driveway, and I peer out the window like a scared child.

"This is your house?" I ask as I feel the confidence drain from me and run down into the car seats. The property is incredible, with manicured gardens and spotlights lighting up the beautiful trees.

"Yes, this is where we will live."

"Why don't we just live in Milan?" I frown. It took us an hour to get here.

He smiles over at me. "You'll see."

We turn the corner, and I see a stone pillar covered in vines with a large copper sign hanging from it.

Villa Oliviana

I turn to him. "Your house is called Oliviana?"

His eyes dance with delight. "*Our* house, and yes. This house was the first thing I bought when I took over the family business."

"After we met?"

His smirk is slow to rise. "The name of the property was why I bought it. It reminded me of a beautiful woman I once met."

I smile dreamily. Oh, man, could this guy get any swoonier if he tried? "Only a bit fancier than me," I add. From the back of my mind a little voice whispers

Slow down.

He smiles to himself as we continue up the driveway. At the top of the hill is a gigantic cream-colored house. It's classically Italian. Out the front is a large, circular driveway with an undercover awning. It's so grand, it looks like a hotel.

He parks the car undercover, and two men come out. Rico gets out of the car.

"Ciao, per favore, porta i bagagli di Olivia al piano di sopra."

"Si, signore."

Rico opens my door and grabs my hand to help me out. I smile nervously at the men.

"Ciao, Miss Olivia." They nod in greeting.

"Hi."

I look around at the opulent luxury. It's like a movie. Sandstone pillars and marble floors and gorgeous hanging lanterns line the space. Large, impressive potted plants are positioned all around. I don't know where to look first.

This place is out of this world. Next level, fucking insane.

"Come, my love." Rici leads me up the stairs, where two lion statues sit proudly, guarding either side of the house. Gosh, this place is like ancient Rome. We go up onto the sandstone terrace, and in through the large double doors. I look up in awe as we pass through them. They would have to stand thirty-feet tall, and they're black with a big gold knocker on each one.

Enrico watches me, and I tighten my cardigan around my shoulders.

"You're very quiet," he says. He smiles softly. "Thoughts?"

I have no words in my head—none that will make sense, anyway.

This doesn't look like a house. It looks like a national museum.

"It's... big."

He smiles and continues to lead me through the foyer. It has a gorgeous fawn-colored marble floor, and a huge staircase that splits in two on the first floor, dividing into two wings of the house.

"Say something."

"This is... I... you... I mean..." I sigh.

A door opens to the left and, a man and woman come out in a rush. They're in their early fifties, at a guess.

"Rico." The man smiles happily.

Enrico's face lights up. He grabs the man in an embrace. It's obvious he is close to him.

"Ciao, Manuel." He presents me to the two of them. "Olivia, please meet Manuel and his lovely wife Antonia. They look after this house while I'm not here. They have a home on the property."

"Hi." I smile nervously.

"Questa è olivia, viene a vivere qui, d'ora in poi riferirai a lei" Rico says as he gestures to me.

Their faces fall.

"Please meet my Olivia," Rico translates for me.

The woman claps her hands together before she takes me into her arms. "Hello, hello," she cries.

The man kisses both of my cheeks. "Hello, bella Olivia."

"Hello." I smile. My eyes dart to Rico nervously. I don't know what he just said to them, but they seem awfully happy about it. Manuel holds me at arm's length as he looks me up and down. "You look like a beautiful…" He hesitates as he searches for the right word. "Asshole."

"Angel," Rico corrects him.

I laugh and put my hands over my mouth.

Rico laughs out loud, as if that's the funniest thing he has ever heard. Well, it kind of is. I can be a real asshole.

"Hai appena detto che era uno stronzo," Rico says to them.

Their faces fall as they realize what Manual has just said to me.

"Oh, no, no, no. Sorry, so sorry." Manuel slaps himself across the face, and his wife and I laugh.

"Andremo subito a letto. Ci vediamo domani," Rico says.

"Si, si, buonanotte, piacere di conoscerti, Miss Olivia." Antonia smiles before they disappear.

"They said good night," Rico tells me.

"Buonanotte," I say, feeling proud of the two words I *do* know.

Rico's eyes glow with affection, and he leans in to kiss me softly.

"Are you hungry, my love? Do you want a drink or anything?"

"No." I look at our opulent surroundings. I feel everything but hungry.

Out of place? Hell yeah. I feel that and then some. But hungry? No.

"I'm fine, thanks."

"Let's go upstairs."

He takes my suitcase and I follow him up the grand staircase, where we veer off to the right. The balustrade is a chunky dark timber, and the carpet is a deep crimson tapestry; the kind you see in exotic movies. We walk down a long, wide corridor, and then through a double set of timber doors.

Holy shit.

It's a huge bedroom, with an already lit fireplace in it. It has two big armchairs and a couch in front of it. At the back is a large four-poster, king size bed.

"This is your wardrobe in here," Rico says as he pulls my suitcase in through the door. I follow him, and it leads to another room. The walls are all mirrored with black floor-to-ceiling wardrobes. There is also a pink, velvet ottoman couch. A beautiful chandelier hangs low in the middle over a large mirrored chest of drawers.

My mouth does drop open this time.

"This is my *wardrobe*?"

"Yes." He puts the suitcase down.

"I only have one suitcase, Rico."

"That will be changing." He kisses me and pulls me out of the wardrobe and into the bedroom. "I haven't spent much time at this house yet. Decorate it as you wish. Get an interior decorator or whatever you want, bella."

I stare at him. I have no words. None.

Slow down.

He leads me through another set of doors just off the

bedroom—a mirrored version of my wardrobe—only this one is already filled with his things.

"Your things are already here?" I ask him.

"I come here on weekends."

"You don't live here full-time?"

"I haven't yet." He puts his hands into the pockets of his expensive suit pants. "I didn't want to move in permanently until I started a family."

I stare at him. Okay, how many times can a man steal my words in one night?

"You want a family?" I gasp.

"No, just you." He kisses me softly as he squeezes my behind. "For now."

He pulls me out of his wardrobe and into the bathroom. The floors and walls are white marble. There is a huge round stone bath sitting in the middle of the room, and behind it is a large walk-in triple shower with a bench seat. The taps and fixtures are gold, and the entire back wall is mirrored.

"Holy fuck." I put my hands over my mouth.

"I like this bathroom. This bathroom can stay," he says casually.

I look over to him. "Can you hear yourself, right now?"

"What?" He takes me into his arms and bends to kiss me.

"You sound like a rich snob," I mumble against his lips.

He chuckles. "Maybe I am." He pulls me again back into the room. "I hope you'll be happy here."

My eyes fall to him. "You are the only thing I care about in here, Rici. The rest is just..." I stop myself from saying something derogatory. "If you lived in a shack, I would love it just as much."

He stands tall, his hands in the pockets of his expensive

navy suit, he seems so in control and powerful. An enigma, all of his own.

I can't believe this night, I can't believe he wants me.

Is this real?

As if he's been waiting all night to get me alone, he steps forward and kisses me, his tongue sweeping through my open lips, and he grabs the back of my head to guide me where he wants me.

I know this kiss.

I crave this kiss.

He closes the door, flicks the lock, and then turns toward me.

"Voglio la mia donna, nel mio letto intorno al mio cazzo," he purrs.

Hearing his whispered Italian voice does things to my insides. "Translate for me?" I whisper.

"I want my woman in my bed... around my cock." He kisses me hard. "Right fucking now." Our teeth clash as he pulls me toward him with urgency. "Get it off. Get your fucking clothes off." In one swift movement, he lifts my dress over my head.

I stand before him in a black, lacy G-string and matching bra. His eyes darken as they drop down my body. He puts his hands on my shoulders and pushes me down to my knees in front of him. Desperate to please him, I wait for his instruction as I try to control my erratic heartbeat.

There are two men in my life. One is carefree and gentle. Rici, the man who makes beautiful love to me. The other one is the man who fucks me like he hates me. My body is his. He takes what he wants, how he wants, and it's so fucking hot, I can't stand it.

Enrico Ferrara is here in all his glory tonight, and anticipation is thumping hard through my body.

He takes his suit jacket off and throws it to the side. He loosens his tie with a sharp snap, and he tears it off. With his eyes locked on mine, he unzips his suit pants and takes his cock out. He gives it a slow stroke, and my insides clench hard.

"Apri la bocca," he says.

My legs open wider, knees scratching on the carpet.

"Sto per scoparti la bocca."

He kicks off his shoes and drops his pants. I'm blessed with this sight of his huge cock at eye level. Thick veins course down its engorged length as it hangs heavily between his legs. Pre-ejaculate drips from its end as it searches for swollen wet flesh.

My eyes close, and I hold my breath. He walks around me, sizing me up. Working out how he wants to fuck me.

"Succhia il mio cazzo."

"Translate," I whisper. "I don't understand you."

He grabs a handful of my hair and tugs my head back sharply so our eyes meet. "Then learn, because I only fuck in Italian."

"Yes," I pant up at him as the grip on my hair becomes painful.

His dark eyes hold mine, and he aggressively jerks my head again. "I said... suck my fucking cock."

My insides melt and my body screams to be dominated.

God, I love him like this.

I lean forward and take him deep down my throat. He hisses in approval and tenderly pushes the hair back from my forehead as he watches me. I gag, struggling to take him.

"All of it," he commands. "Take me whole."

He pushes himself deeper, and I instantly gag again. He smiles darkly. The bastard is loving watching me struggle with his size.

I close my eyes to calm myself, and we get into a rhythm. He grabs my hair in his hands and begins to ride my mouth, and I watch him begin to come undone. With every pump, there's something a little more animal in his eyes.

He's turning me inside out.

"Up," he commands as he pulls me from the floor. "In ginocchio."

I stare at him, desperately wishing I knew what he wanted.

"On your hands and knees on the bed."

I motion to undo my bra, and he holds his hand up for me to stop. "Leave them on."

I hesitate for a beat, and then get onto the bed on my knees.

"Drop to your elbows."

I drop to my elbows.

"Legs wider apart."

I shuffle my legs wider apart, and I drop my head to try and regulate my breathing.

He circles me on the bed, stopping directly behind me. He rubs his hand over my bare ass and down my thigh, and then over to the other side. I hold my breath. Goosebumps scatter over my skin, and then he gives me a sharp slap.

"Ahh!" I cry. I'm pushed forward into the mattress. He rubs the sting affectionately, and then slaps me hard again. He inhales sharply, and I know he's nearing the edge of his sanity. What the hell is going on here? His dominance over me has risen another notch. I've not seen him like this before.

My body begins to throb, and I can hear my heartbeat in my ears. My knees part farther apart. I just need to be fucked.

Hard.

He pulls me back to the edge of the bed and pushes his cock between my cheeks. He leans forward and takes off my bra. He cups my breasts as his teeth nip at my shoulder. He lifts my hair to one side and latches onto my neck. He sucks as he squeezes one of my nipples hard, and I nearly come.

Holy fucking shit. What kind of sex is this?

I'm panting and dripping wet as he takes full control of my body.

He continues to suck the back of my neck as his hands roam up and over my breasts, his large cock writhing between the cheeks of my behind as the weight of his body forces me farther into the mattress.

I quiver. I'm going to come. I can't hold it.

He bends and pulls my G-string to the side. I smile into the mattress, and I feel his breath on my cheeks. He blesses me with a tender kiss.

His tongue reaches out and brushes over my back entrance.

I flinch.

What the fuck?

I try to move but he holds me in place and licks me again.

My eyes close, and I moan against the mattress. Oh, my fucking God.

"Rici," I whisper.

"Shh." He breathes into me as his large hand holds me in place. "I want all of you."

I can see his cock between my legs. It's dripping and rock hard. He licks me again, and I can feel his whiskers on my behind. He begins to really eat me, and all I can do is screw up the blankets beneath me.

Holy fucking god......what the hell is going on here?

He slowly slides my panties down my legs and takes them off. My heart is racing so fast. What the hell is he going to do to me?

He spreads my legs wider, his tongue really tempting me,

and then he slides his thumb deep into my ass at the same time he puts his thick cock into my sex.

My eyes roll back in my head, and I cry out...

In pleasure.

In pain.

In total fucking ecstasy.

My knees buckle, and he slaps me hard with his free hand.

"Stay up," he barks.

His cock slowly slides out, and my mouth falls open. He slides it back in time with his thumb. He gets harder and faster with both cock and thumb. Then he takes his thumb out and slowly eases himself into its place.

Deep, where no man has gone before.

A claiming. . .my eyes roll back in my head to the sound of his hiss.

I can't talk.

I can't hear.

I can only feel him.

Enrico Ferrara, the god.

My god.

"Oh, mia bella ragazza, mi sei mancata."

With the sound of his whispered words and the feeling of his cock, I begin to moan as his pumps get deeper and deeper and it feels so fucking good that I can't stand it.

It sends me over the edge. I cry out as an earth-shattering orgasm rips through my body.

"Ah!" he cries as he loses control, he grabs my hipbones with force.

He begins to fuck me hard. The sounds of our skin slapping together echoes around the room.

"Fuck. Fuck, ohh," he hisses as he holds himself deep.

I feel the jerk of his cock deep inside of me as he fills me with his thick semen.

He continues to slowly pump me as he completely empties himself deep inside of me, and then he leans over me and turns my face to his.

I have nothing left. I am completely spent—wet with perspiration, my morals smashed to pieces.

"I'm going to make you happy." His lips take mine, and we kiss. I feel the last of my sanity fall away.

"Rici," I whimper into his mouth.

"I've waited all my life for you, Olivia," he whispers.

My eyes fill with tears. "Thank God you found me."

He pulls out of my body as his lips hold mine. I wince at the loss of his body. It hurt coming out as much as it did going in.

He leads me into the shower and holds me tightly in his arms as he turns it on. I'm speechless.

I can only cling to him, my emotions raw.

I never expected that, I never expected to want it.

Everything about today is new.

We get in under the water, and he soaps up his hands and takes his time. He washes me as we kiss. It's not sexual; it's loving, caring, and everything I thought we would never be.

We don't speak. Words are irrelevant right now.

He missed me. With all of his heart he missed me. I can feel it with every touch.

For a long time, we stand under the hot water in each other's arms, and I feel so warm and safe that I'm falling asleep against him. It's like the torture of the last few weeks without him have come to an exhausted head and I can hardly keep my eyes open.

"Come, my bella. Bedtime, baby." He helps me out of the

shower and dries me carefully with a towel before I get into bed.

He turns off the lights and climbs in behind me. Then he lovingly pulls the blankets up over me. “Sleep, my love.”

I close my eyes, completely exhausted.

“Non ti lascerò mai andare via,” he whispers into my ear. “I’m never going to let you go.” He puts his arms around me from behind and kisses my shoulder.

I smile into my pillow.

I’ve died and gone to Ferrara Heaven.

19

Olivia

THE NEED TO go to the bathroom wakes me from my deep sleep, and I roll over in the darkness.

What time is it? It's pitch-black. I sit up and rise out of bed, feeling my way around the room. I fumble until I find my handbag and take my phone out. It's nearly 9:00 a.m. Why is it so fucking dark in here?

I put the torch on my phone and go to the bathroom and return to bed as my eyes finally acclimatize.

Rici is lying flat on his back, fast asleep, one hand behind his head and the other safely holding his dick. His black hair is messy against his pillow. His dark eyelashes flutter, and his big red lips part as he inhales. I smile as I watch him.

So peaceful and perfect.

I lie onto my side to face him. My mind goes to last night and the love that we made.

I feel myself blush.

He's so dirty, and it's so damn hot.

I've never been with anyone even remotely like him.

Never in a million years did I think I would like the things that he does to me. When we have sex, I completely forget who I am.

Because I am his. His to do what he wants with.

My eyes roam down his broad chest and dark hair. Over his rippled abs, too, and then lower to his perfectly kept pubic hair and dick. Even when fast asleep and flaccid, he's one hell of a man.

He begins to stir, and I have to stop myself from cuddling up to him and waking him up.

Maybe I should go and make breakfast for us?

Yes. I'll do that. I get up and look for something to put on. Rici's pale blue shirt from last night is still on the floor. I throw it on, grab my phone, and make my way out into the hallway.

The entire house is pitch black. What the hell? Why is it so dark? I don't get it. There must be some kickass drapes on the windows. I put my cell's torch back on and tiptoe toward the stairs. Finally, the sensory lights come on and light my way down the grand staircase.

Once at the bottom, I flick the light on, and I look around in wonder. I've never been anywhere like this.

Money is no object.

Everything is over the top luxury. Everything is perfect.

Like him.

Enrico Ferrara, you are one major mindfuck.

Yesterday, I was heartbroken over you. Today, I've moved in.

What the hell?

Natalie is going to lose her shit at me.

I make my way into the kitchen, turn the light on, and stand for a moment as I take it all in. It's an all-white state of the art kitchen with beautiful coffee-colored marble floors. The best appliances money can buy sit on every surface, and there's a huge copper range hood that hangs over the triple oven and hotplates.

Wow, what the hell could you cook in this kitchen? *Hopefully good food.*

I smirk at the thought of serving up something crappy. I wonder where I could buy packet pasta.

I peer into the fridge, only to be pleasantly surprised to find that it's fully stocked. There's lots of fresh fruit, vegetables, and meat. I open the pantry and find a selection of breads and oils. Antonia must have bought all this stuff for us coming here. Or maybe it's just constantly stocked, and the food goes to waste half the time. I search through the cupboards to find the pots and pans, and then I get to work.

Rici likes fruit for breakfast, but when he's with me he's been having eggs and bacon. All those ingredients are here. I'll make him a smorgasbord—try and impress him with my culinary skills.

Half an hour later, I have a plate of freshly cut up fruit, poached eggs on sourdough with a side of bacon and avocado. There's also a cup of the strongest coffee known to man. I don't know how to work that fucking coffee machine. This is the fourth cup I've made, and they all taste like shit, but it's the thought that counts right?

I load it all onto a tray and make my way upstairs.

I carefully place it down on the table in his room and, feeling proud of myself, I lay myself down beside him.

He inhales sharply as he wakes. "Hmm, bella," he sighs sleepily.

I swear, Rici Ferrara's bedroom voice should be used for all voiceovers. That deep, raspy tone sends shivers down my spine.

He kisses my forehead and holds me close as he begins to doze back off.

"I made you breakfast." I smile against his chest.

"Hmm." He frowns. "What?" He peels his eyes open.

"I made you breakfast." I stand and go to get the tray. I put it down on his bedside table.

He leans up on his elbows and smiles sleepily. "You spoil me."

"Baby, you have no idea how spoilt you are going to be." I lean in to kiss him softly and he wraps his arms around me and pulls me down on top of him. In one quick movement, he flips me over so I am beneath him.

"I wanted to have you for breakfast."

I giggle up at him. "You have me all day."

He gives me a sharp pump with his hips. "And I will."

He rolls off me, sits up, and then hits a button on his bedside. I hear a motorized sound. I look around to see the shutters over the windows rising. Natural light begins to flood through the room.

"What the heck is that?" I frown.

"Security shutters."

"On every window?"

He sips his coffee. "Yes, bella."

"What on earth for?"

"So that people can't shoot through the glass."

My mouth falls open. "Are you serious?"

He smiles, amused by my horror. "Yes, security shutters are for security." He raises his brows as he sips his coffee. "Shocking, isn't it?"

"Smartass." I point to his plate. "Eat your breakfast."

He smiles and starts to eat. I walk over and pull the drapes back to look outside. My breath catches.

"Oh my God," I whisper. He chuckles and I turn to him. "That view?"

"Beautiful, huh?" He chews his food casually.

I look back out of the window to the huge bed of water in front of us. "That's a lake?" I ask, unsure if it's the ocean or something.

"Well, we are at Lake Como." He smirks against his coffee cup.

I turn. "You're being very cheeky this morning, Mr. Ferrara. You want to be careful I don't smack your behind."

He chuckles and continues eating. I look back out the window. There's a huge manicured garden and a little boat house that sits on the edge of the water, and a wharf. "You have your own wharf?"

"Yes." He keeps chewing, totally uninterested in all the wonderful things I can see through the window. I look directly down and see a deep blue pool. "You have a pool?" I shriek.

He smiles as he finishes his breakfast. "Yes, bella."

I press my hands on the glass as I peer down into the yard. "Oh, Rici, this place is divine," I sigh dreamily.

He smiles and taps his lap. I go to him. "I hope you will be happy here."

I kiss him. "As long as I'm with you, I will be." He inhales deeply into my hair. "Is this where *you* want to live, though?" I ask.

"Yes."

"Why? I mean, I can see that it's beautiful, but don't you need to be closer to work? We can come here on weekends."

"We will have an apartment in Milan, too, but I feel closer to my father here. It's why I love it. This place is good for my soul."

I smile softly. That's so sweet.

"This was my father's favorite place on Earth. He brought my brothers and I here all of our lives. It feels like home. Both of my brothers have holiday houses here, too."

"Your mother lives here?"

"No, she lives on a large property just out of Milan—the house we grew up in. She doesn't come here often. She's more of a city person and prefers Roma. She lives near my grandmother."

"Oh." I think for a moment. "When will I get to meet your mother and grandmother?"

He smiles as he lies me down on the bed and moves over me. "When you're totally in love with me and it's too late to run."

I laugh. He bites my neck hard, and I wriggle to break free from his grip. "Do you think your mother is going to like me?"

He nips down my neck before he bites hard. I try to buck him off me, and notice that he doesn't answer my question.

"Rici," I prompt him. "What does that mean?"

"It means I like you enough for the two of us. Let me worry about my mother." He growls against my neck, and I squeal in delight. He pins me to the mattress, his eyes darken. "Open for me, bella."

I smile up at him, lift my legs and wrap them around his waist. He begins to slide his cock through my open lips as his mouth drops to my neck—softly this time. "What do you have planned for me today, Mr. Ferrara?"

"I'm going to show you around your new home, and then we'll go sightseeing." He kisses me again and slides his dick deep inside my body. My head falls back onto the pillow. "And there'll be a whole lot more of my cock." He slides out and pushes back in with a hard pump. "How does that sound?"

His possession creates a hot feeling through me, and I put my hands on his behind and push him back in. "Heavenly."

I sit at the table and smile over at my handsome date.

It's Saturday night, and I think I have had the best day in history. Rico showed me around the gigantic house. We went for a walk around the expansive gardens of his property, and then this afternoon we came into town and ambled through the shops. We're now sitting in a seafood restaurant after eating a beautiful dinner. Dessert, and drinking Limoncello cocktails.

"This place is dreamy." I smile.

"Like you." Rico's face is resting on his hand on the table, he gives me the best come fuck me look I've ever seen.

"What are the chances of me having sex tonight, Mr. Ferrara?" I lean toward him. I pick up his hand and put his index finger in my mouth to give it a slow, sensual suck.

"I'd say one hundred percent." I suck his finger again, and his nostrils flare. "Finish your drink."

I smirk.

"Before I finish you on the table."

"Maybe I want to be finished on the table."

His dark eyes hold mine. "You're a sex manic, Olivia."

"Takes one to know one."

The afternoon sun flickers through the branches of the tree overhead. It's Sunday afternoon, and I'm lying on the daybed next to the pool. I'm wearing a white bikini, and my man is half asleep next to me in board shorts, his beautiful olive skin on display. He's calm; more relaxed than I've ever seen him. We haven't left the house today. I made us breakfast and then he worked out in the gym on the grounds while I explored the garden some more. I did some washing and we ate lunch. I get why he loves it here. It has a real holiday feel to it, and it's so far removed from the hustle and bustle of Milan due to the sounds of the water lapping and the birds flying overhead. The wind in the trees and the distant sound of a boat engine on the lake help, too. It's a sensory cleanse. If peace had a sound, this would be it.

Seeing my man so happy and relaxed makes me appreciate his affinity with this place. The hour to travel to and from work each day is a small price to pay.

I sit up to lean on my elbows as I look out over the lake and catch sight of someone in the boathouse.

Security.

I know they're always around, but somehow Rico seems to make it all seem normal. Like he said, they keep their distance, so I need to forget that they're here.

It will take me a while to get used to, I'm not going to lie.

I think back to the security shutters.

What in the hell is all that about? Who the fuck would shoot through the windows, anyway? Why would anyone need that in their home? It just doesn't make sense.

A little voice from deep within me whispers, *Mafiosi.*

Rici reaches over and rests his hand on my thigh. I roll onto my side to face him. I push his hair back from his face. The shadows are flickering over him as the sun moves through the trees.

"You're sleepy today, baby," I whisper.

"Hmm." He smiles with his eyes closed.

"Do you want a drink or anything?"

He pulls me closer and snuggles into my neck. "No, I want you to sleep here with me."

"That, I can do."

My lips dust his temple, and I listen as his breathing slowly returns to a regulated pattern. He's drifted back off.

I stare back out over the water and come to the conclusion that it doesn't get much better than this.

I've found him.

It's not Lake Como that brings me peace. It's Rici Ferrara.

Enrico stands in the bathroom mirror and ties his tie. Gone is my relaxed Rici from yesterday. The businessman is back. Enrico. He's wearing a navy blue, perfectly fitted suit, with a crisp white shirt, and a stupidly expensive Rolex watch. It's 5:30 a.m. and he's getting ready for work while organizing me left right and center.

"Lorenzo is going to collect you in two hours to drive you to work," he says as he stares into the mirror.

"Okay."

"I'm flying to Sicily today. I have an issue down there I have to take care of. I'm flying out of the airport from here, so Lorenzo will collect you after work, too. I'll meet you at home."

"Oh." I pause. "I wanted to go the gym after work in Milan."

"You have your own gym here now. You don't need to go to a public gym."

"I know, but I want to. I'm going to go with Natalie. She's just moved here for me, and I can't abandon her. I want to include her in my life. She's my best friend."

I sit on the basin in front of him and take over tying his tie. He stares at me. I can almost see his brain ticking.

"What?" I ask.

"Can you just not go to the gym today, please?"

"Why?"

"Because I don't want you out and about in Milan when I'm not there. I'm hours away."

"Why don't you want me out and about?"

"Olivia," he sighs, in frustration.

"Okay, fine," I concede. "I'll use the gym here tonight, but I do want to keep my membership there. I want to make some friends."

"Strangers?" he scoffs. "You will not be friends with strangers."

"Why not?"

"You have no idea who they are. You can't trust just anyone. This isn't Australia."

I roll my eyes. "You're so dramatic."

"Cautious," he corrects me with a kiss.

"What are you doing in Sicily?"

"We're putting in new security into our clubs down there. I need to meet with the security company and go through our requirements."

"Oh, okay."

"So, Lorenzo will be with you today," he reminds me. "Pick up is 7:30 a.m."

"I know." I roll my eyes. "You told me already."

"If anything is wrong, call him immediately. He'll be outside your office all day."

"That's not necessary. Besides, I thought Lorenzo works with you. Why aren't you taking him to Sicily?"

"Maso runs this side of things. He's coming with me. I wanted Lorenzo to stay with you today."

I stare at him for a moment. "Why do you think I need a guard now?"

"Because if someone wanted to hurt me, they would hurt you."

"Why would someone want to hurt you?"

He shrugs and turns away from me. "Just in case." He walks out of the bathroom and into his wardrobe to collect his briefcase.

I go to hit the shutter button.

"No," he says. "Leave them down until daylight. Never put the shutters up in darkness if I'm not here."

I stare at him as a small thread of fear runs through me. "What's this about, Rico?" I ask. "You're beginning to frighten me."

"Precaution, that's all. I have to go, bella." He kisses me quickly. "See you tonight."

I sigh. "Have fun… flying around, I guess."

He walks out and I follow him. I drop to sit on the top step of the grand staircase, and I watch him walk downstairs. He sets the alarm and closes the door behind him. I hear the lock click as he locks the deadlock with his key.

I can't even look out of the window to watch him leave.

This feels so weird.

"Hi, mum," I answer the phone.

"Hello love, how's my favorite daughter today?"

I giggle. "I'm your only daughter."

"Oh, that's right," she says and I can tell she's smiling. "I'm good, battling a dreaded cold."

"Oh, are you alright?"

"Yes, I'm fine. What's new?"

"Well." I walk out of the bedroom and down the big grand staircase. "Things are going well with Enrico."

"Really? That's great."

"I've been staying with him at his house in Lake Como."

"Oh, isn't that where the rich and famous live?"

I shrug, embarrassed and completely unsure how to warn her about him. "Yeah." I try to sound casual. "His parents come from money. Lots of family businesses and things. He does alright too for himself." I wince, does alright for himself is the understatement of the year.

"Is he being nice?"

"Yes, mum." I roll my eyes.

"I've heard these Italian men can be very possessive when they want to be."

I smirk, she hit the nail on the head. "He's lovely, mum. I really like him." I smile broadly. "In fact, I think I might be in love with him."

"Oh Olivia, let's just see how it goes," she sighs as she senses heartbreak. "Don't go giving your heart to anyone just yet. It's only early days."

"I know." I scrunch my eyes shut, it's too late. He has my entire heart in his suit pocket at his disposal.

"How's work going?" I ask. Last time I spoke to her she was hating on her boss. "Is Gerrard still being a micro manager?"

"Oh god yes, he's going around the twist."

Mum has worked for the same man for thirty years as his personal assistant, he's in his eighties now and becoming senile. "Maybe he'll retire soon?" I smile.

"I wish, I've been hanging on for five years in hope."

"You can just find another job you know!" I remind her.

"Oh, I couldn't leave him, he needs me."

I smile, that's mum, loyal to a tee. It makes me sad that she let my father's shortcomings taint her view on men. She never has really trusted anyone since him.

No one has ever come close to measuring up except for short dating bouts, she has been mostly alone over the years.

It's a shame because she of all people deserves to be adored.

"Do you need to go to the doctor about your cold?" I ask.

"No, I'm on the mend, I'm fine."

"Okay, I'll call you later."

"Good bye, love. I'm glad you sound so happy."

I smile broadly. "Me too."

Enrico

I walk through the club with the three security team staff with Maso directing them.

"We need a camera system that instantly links back to base at our security office upstairs. See this, here? This isn't good enough coverage," Maso continues as he shows them around.

We've gone over the strategies, and they are now working through the placement of the cameras.

Sophia and I trail behind.

"Do you want to grab some lunch while they work this out?" Sophia asks. "I'm famished."

I glance at my watch and see it's 2:00 p.m.

I'm hungry, too.

"Yeah, sure. Maso?" I interrupt. "We'll be back in an hour or so."

"Okay." He keeps walking and talking with the men.

Sophia and I leave the club and make our way across the road into a restaurant.

It's awkward between us. We've hardly spoken since I kicked her out of my bed in the middle of the night.

We take a seat by the window and I order a scotch. She orders a glass of wine. We sit in silence for a while, and I lean back in my seat... waiting for it.

"You met someone?"

Here we go. "I told you I had."

"Who is she?"

"You don't know her."

Her eyes hold mine. She stays silent, and it makes me feel like a prick.

"We used to date a few years back. She has recently come back to me."

"And you care for her?"

"Yes. I really don't want to sit here and explain myself to you, Sophia."

"I want to know why."

"I met someone and want to be with her. End of story."

She runs her fingers through her hair. I watch her. She's a beautiful woman—Italian to the bone with long, dark hair and a gorgeous, curvy figure. With her long, red nails, and her stilettos, she's always perfectly made up.

"We were never like that, Soph, and you know that," I remind her softly.

"What will she be to you?"

"I am only taking her."

She frowns, confused. I have never been loyal to only one woman before.

"She will—"

"Yes," I cut her off. "I am only having her. I don't want anybody else."

"Where is she from? Milan?"

I roll my eyes, wishing I was anywhere but here. I have to get through this conversation. Sophia is good at her job and I need her. We need to be amicable. "She's from Australia."

Her face falls. "Australia. She's Australian?"

"Yes."

"Dear God, Enrico," she whispers, full of horror. "A man with your bloodline cannot date a common criminal from Australia."

I sip my scotch as my anger begins to grow deep in my stomach.

"You know that, don't you?" she continues. "Australia's colony started from the English sending their convicts there."

"Criminals for stealing food for their children," I sneer. "Not quite the crime we Italians are accustomed to, now, is it?" I raise my glass to her sarcastically.

"And you think you want this woman?"

"I know I do."

She sits back in disgust. "You can't marry her."

"I'll do whatever I fucking like."

"A Ferrara cannot marry a foreigner." She pinches the bridge of her nose. "You will have to take her as your comare."

A comare means a mistress in Italian. "No, when I marry, I'm only having my wife, just like my father did."

She throws her head back in disgust. "Oh, please, your father had a goomah for thirty years. Don't pretend you don't know her," she scoffs.

"He did not."

"He did, Enrico. I know her very well."

"You lie. My father adored my mother."

"And he loved his comare. I went to the funeral she held for him. It was beautiful."

"What?"

Her face falls. "Don't tell me you didn't know?"

I stare at her as I begin to hear my heartbeat pounding in my ears.

"I'm sorry," she whispers. "I thought you knew—everyone knew. Even your mother."

I sip my scotch with a shaky hand.

"She lives in Lake Como with their son."

What?

"They had a son?" I whisper.

"Yes, they had a boy. He was only seventeen when your father passed."

I stare at her as I begin to feel my pulse raging throughout my body.

"He was with her long before he met your mother, but he wasn't allowed to marry her. She was the love of his life. He was loyal to her to the very end."

I clench my jaw... in distain. My mother was the love of his life.

"Liar," I sneer.

"Why do you think your father had a house in Lake Como that he took you and your brothers to every weekend, Rico?"

I stare at her as a missing piece of the puzzle falls into place.

"Why do you think your mother hated the place? Why does your mother prefer to be in Rome?"

"My mother married my father for love."

"Your mother married your father because of his name. She knew he loved another. She always came second to

Angelina. She was happy with the arrangement and his money."

I drain my scotch and slam my glass down onto the table. I stand in a rush, and without another word, I storm out of the restaurant and around the corner into an alleyway. I'm hot, clammy, and disorientated. I push my hands onto my knees. With the realization that my whole life is a lie, I throw up.

Olivia

I stand at the 3D printer and fold my arms in a huff.

It's Monday afternoon. I hate this machine. Why does it print so slow? Where is the normal photocopier? Why is it all so technical?

"How was your weekend?" Martin from accounts asks me.

"Great. How was yours?" I smile.

Great doesn't come close to describing my weekend. I had the most fabulous weekend in history, and I am on a Ferrara high. I'm so high, I can't even see the ground.

Rico and I turned the corner in a big way and I just can't wait to see him tonight. He won't be back until late, but that's okay. This will be my new normal.

My design finally prints, and I make my way back to my seat. My phone on my desk rings.

"Olivia, this is Torino from reception downstairs."

"Hi." I smile. "How can I help you?"

"You have someone to see you down here."

"Who is it?"

"Um." She pauses. "Yes, just go into the conference room on level two—take the elevator," she says to whoever is waiting. "Olivia will meet you up there."

I frown as I wait on.

"It's the police," she whispers.

"What? And they're here to see me?"

"Yes, two of them. They're detectives. They're in the conference room waiting for you now."

"Shit, okay. Thanks."

I make my way to the conference room, and I open the door. Two men are sitting at the table, and they stand as I walk in.

"Hello, Olivia. We're Pedro and Michael. We're detectives, and we'd like to ask you a few questions, please."

They're older and classically cop-like. One is short and bald, while the other looks like a stripper who hired a suit.

"Okay." I smile as I shake their hands. I gesture to the table and chairs. "Please, take a seat."

We all sit down.

I cross my legs in front of me as I wait for them to tell my why they're here. "I'm sorry, you have me at a loss. How can I help you?"

"We are investigating a missing person."

"Okay..."

"Franco Macheski."

"Am I supposed to know who that is?" I ask, confused.

"You probably should," Pedro says sarcastically. "You went on a date with him three weeks ago."

Oh shit. Mr. Tinder. "Sorry. Mental block there for a moment." I feel like a total whorebag.

"He hasn't been seen since," he tells me.

I stare at them. "What?"

"You were the last person to see Franco alive. Tell us what happened on the night you went out together. We want to know everything."

20

Olivia

I SCREW UP MY FACE. "What do you mean he hasn't been seen since? I don't understand."

Pedro replies, "You went on a date with him, and then he vanished into thin air."

"Oh. I thought it was weird that he never contacted me again." I shrug with a subtle shake of my head. "I just assumed he didn't like me."

The men glance at each other. "Tell us what happened that night."

"Well..." I pause as I try to remember. "We'd been talking on Tinder for a few weeks and he wanted to meet. We had dinner, and then..."

Shit... then he had a fight with Rico. Do they know that? My eyes rise to meet theirs as horror dawns. Did Enrico have something to do with this?

Holy fuck.

"Go on," Pedro urges as he takes notes on a small pad of paper.

Goosebumps scatter up my arms.

"Umm." I stare at them as my brain begins to misfire. I can't lie for shit. I scratch my head. "He wanted me to go back to his house, and I wasn't really into him, you know?" I look between them guiltily. "We ended up having a fight about it, and he left in a rush."

"Did he say where he was going?"

"No."

"What restaurant did you have dinner at?"

"Ah." I snap my fingers as I try and remember the name. I'm beginning to perspire from the pressure. "It's the one down on the main street, next to the theatre."

"Apocalypse?" Michael asks.

"Yes, that's it." I smile awkwardly. "Maybe check the cameras of the parking lot?" I offer.

"We did. The entire night of security footage has been wiped."

"Oh." My face falls as my heart begins to thump hard. "That's... weird."

"Very," Pedro replies calmly. "Where are you staying at the moment?" he asks.

"I'm at a hotel a few blocks down. I just moved here from Australia."

They both stare at me, as if they're waiting for me to slip up. "Where were you all weekend?"

I swallow the lump in my throat. "Lake Como."

"Who with?"

I have a momentary brain slip. "Alone."

What the fuck did I say that for?

They exchange looks. "You were alone all weekend?"

I look them straight in the eyes. "Yes, I was."

Oh, fuck.

I don't know what the hell is going on here, but I need to get away from them. "I have no idea where Franco is. Have you searched his Tinder profile? He's probably shacked up with someone."

"Do you have any friends in Italy, Olivia?"

"Just one, a friend from Australia just moved here."

"Are you dating anyone?"

Our eyes are locked. "No."

Fuck, fuck, fuck.

"I really have to get back to work." I stand. "I'm sorry I couldn't be more useful. Please let me know when you find him." I shake their hands.

Pedro hands me a business card. "If you think of anything, please call us."

"I will." I turn to walk off.

"Oh, and Olivia."

I turn back to face him.

"Obstructing justice and lying to the police is a criminal offence in Italy, just so you know."

I fake a smile. "As it should be. Goodbye, gentlemen."

With my heart in my throat, I turn and walk out of the room. Oh, my fucking God, what the hell is going on?

Three hours later and I'm sitting at my desk with my mind in overdrive.

Where the fuck is Franco?

Why would they be asking me, and why did I immediately think that they were suspicious? I know Rici had nothing to do with this, so why did I feel compelled to lie on his behalf?

With shaky hands, I Google

Who Is Enrico Ferrara

Enrico Ferrara is a thirty-four-year-old billionaire. Well known for being hard and driven, this Italian thoroughbred is head of the infamous Ferrara dynasty.

The CEO of Ferrara Enterprises, Enrico became the sole heir to the company on the death of his father Giuliano, and his grandfather Stefano Ferrara, who were both killed in a tragic car accident near Roma two years ago.

Known for his striking good looks and womanizing ways, Enrico is fast becoming a global force to be reckoned with, having a sharp intellect and impeccable work ethic. He continues to work unbelievably hard. In the midst of accusation and scandal, he has been forced to find new strength in order to face the accusation of bribery, corruption, and hacking by subsidiary firms.

The Ferrara family have been linked to, but not accused of, having deep ties within organized crime throughout Europe.

I knew all this from when I researched him before.

Womanizing ways.... hmm, I hate that description. That's kind of disturbing.

He's not a criminal. Just because his family own brothels, it doesn't mean he's a criminal. He wouldn't know where that stupid fucking Franco is. Franco is probably balls-deep in his next Tinder date somewhere.

I read over the text again.

Enrico is fast becoming a global force to be reckoned with, having a sharp intellect and impeccable work ethic.

I smile proudly. That's my man. Go, baby.

My phone rings at 5:30 p.m., and the name Lorenzo lights up the screen.

"Hello," I answer as I pack up the last of my things and close my computer down.

"Olivia, is everything all right?"

"Yes, sorry, I'm coming now."

"See you soon."

I grab a bunch of swatches for my fabrics appointments tomorrow, and I head toward the elevator. Moments later, I exit my building to see Lorenzo standing next to the black Mercedes. It feels weird being picked up by a stranger.

"Hey." I smile as I walk across the road.

"Ciao, Olivia." He opens the car door for me. "How was your day?"

I climb into the backseat. "Fine, thanks, how was yours?"

"No complaints." He closes the door, and moments later, we pull out onto the busy road.

I sit in the backseat and twist my hands in front of me on my lap. I feel like I should be making conversation or something, I didn't even know he spoke English until this morning when he drove me to work. It feels rude just sitting here and being chauffeured around. I don't want to get into the habit of having to jabber on the entire trip every day, though. I take out my phone and flick through it. There are no missed calls. Rico hasn't called me at all today. He must be busy down in Sicily.

"What time is Enrico due home?" I ask Lorenzo.

"I'm picking them up from the airport at 8:10 tonight."

Them? Who did he go with?

"Who went with him today?" I ask.

"Maso and Sophia. They met others down there. I believe they had meetings all day."

Sophia.

What the hell? Enrico spent the day with fucking Sophia?

I clench my jaw and glare out of the window. Lorenzo's eyes flicker to me in the rearview mirror, as if he's suddenly realizing that he maybe shouldn't have told me that. "Sophia is the general manager of that division in Sicily," he adds.

"I'm well aware of that," I reply, annoyed by my petty jealousy. And even more annoyed that Lorenzo can see it upset me.

For God's sake, Olivia, can't you at least act cool?

I scroll aimlessly through my phone, and my mind goes back to the police who visited me today looking for Franco. Where is Franco?

I download the Tinder app again and try to find his profile. I search his name and find him, although he's changed his profile pic since I last looked.

Hmm, okay.

I scroll through the info, but I can't see where it shows when he was last active.

Can I even see that info in here? I click on every damn button I can find with no clue as to when he was on last. Stupid, useless app. I click out of it in disgust and go back to staring out of the window.

My mind goes to that night and how aggressive Franco was to Enrico—how he kept telling him to fuck off, and then how Enrico punched him.

Oh, jeez, this is all one big mess.

But I do know for certain that Rico has no idea where Franco is, either. He has a lot bigger things on his plate than that fool.

He's with Sophia... right now.

Stop it, they work together.

The annoying little voice from my subconscious whispers... *yeah, and they fuck.*

Gah!

I'm so insecure about her, I can't stand it.

She's a prostitute. She'll be well experienced in pleasing men.

If he wanted her, he would be with her, I remind myself.

I pull my cardigan around myself, lean back, and close my eyes. I'm having a really shitty day today. I'm going to sleep to try and forget that my boyfriend may or may not be in the Italian mafia, and that he may or may not have done something to a weirdo date of mine... and he may or may not be fucking his private whorebag general manager on a desk in Sicily right now.

Who, I might add, is fucking Italian—something I will never be, no matter how hard I try.

Why can't he just be a normal policeman in Roma? An

average broke man with a motorbike and no ex-girlfriends? I would love him just the same... maybe even more.

But he has an entourage, houses, staff, questionable businesses, and beautiful whores who work for him.

It's damn annoying.

"How long till we get there, Lorenzo" I ask.

"Forty-five minutes, Olivia, go to sleep. I'll wake you once we arrive."

It's 9:30 p.m. now, and I'm sitting on the window seat in the spare bedroom, staring out at the dark driveway below. I have this uneasy feeling in my stomach that won't go away. Where is he?

Lorenzo said his plane landed at eight. How far is the airport from here?

I try to call Rico's phone and it goes straight to voicemail... again.

Maybe I should call Lorenzo.

No, I don't want to be the crazy girlfriend, even though I know I am one.

My mind is going crazy with thoughts of Enrico and Sophia. I'm sick with jealousy.

Did they have lunch together today? Did he kiss her hello? Did she look as gorgeous as I know she is? Do they talk? Laugh?

I feel like an insecure fool, and this is not who I am.

We've been back together for one day, and already I feel like I'm going crazy.

I am the one he has asked to move in. I am the one who is waiting at his home for him. He'll be here soon...

Please be here soon.

I head to the bathroom and run myself a steamy hot bath.

Stop thinking crazy thoughts, Olivia.

He'll be home soon.

It's 12:30 a.m. and I'm pacing in the kitchen.

What the hell is going on?

I'm sick with worry. What if his plane crashed? This isn't like him. He's never not called me before.

I hear car doors slam, and then a commotion outside. I run to the front window.

There are three cars, all in a line, and three men are dragging Enrico out of the back car by his arms. He climbs out, staggers, and falls to the side. They all rush to catch him.

He's blind drunk.

What the hell?

I open the door in a rush to hear his deep, slurred voice as he tears his arms from their grip. "Get away from me."

The men are fussing around him. "Rico, Rico."

"Take me home," he growls.

"You are home," Lorenzo tells him. "Calm down."

He takes a swing at one of the men, and they all struggle as they try to contain him. "Olivia!" Enrico bellows as he looks up at the house. "*Olivia!*"

I wrap my dressing gown around me. Oh, jeez, I'm not really dressed for this.

"I'm here!" I call from my place at the front door.

The men each turn toward me, and Lorenzo's face falls. "Go inside, Olivia. We'll take care of him."

"Olivia!" Enrico bellows again, oblivious that I'm standing right here.

"What's happened?" I ask.

"He's had a bad day," Lorenzo sighs. "Too much to drink on an empty stomach."

"Olivia!" Enrico bellows again. His deep voice is angry—almost frightening.

"I'm here." I rush to him, and his face immediately softens. He wraps his arm around me. "Il mio amore." He buries his head in my neck. He holds me tight, and the men all look on as if unsure what to do.

"I love you," he slurs with a drunken smile.

"Shh Rici," I whisper.

Oh, jeez. This isn't quiet the romantic first I love you that I had in mind.

"I love this woman," he tells all the men. "But not you," he cries, as if he's suddenly outraged at something. He breaks free from my grip. "You can all go to Hell. Traitors!" he sneers in disgust. "How many lies have you told me today?" He leans forward and pushes one of the men hard in the chest.

"Jesus Christ," Maso groans as he drags his hand down his face in disgust.

I grab Enrico's hands in mine. "What's happened?" I ask.

"I hate these bastards," he slurs. "Go!" He throws his hand up in disgust. "Fucking liars. Get out of my house!"

"Come inside," I whisper softly, I put his arm around my shoulder and I begin to lead him into the house. The men follow behind us. Enrico staggers and sways as I try to keep him upright. He trips up the step and stumbles. The men all jump in to catch him and help me lead him inside to the couch, where he falls spectacularly onto his back.

He laughs up at me and grabs his dick. "I got something for you, bella."

I try to hold a straight face. He couldn't have sex right now if his life depended on it. The men shake their heads in disgust. I don't think I've ever seen anyone so drunk.

He reaches up, grabs my hand, and pulls me down on top of him.

"Stay here, my love," he slurs.

"I'm here," I say, knowing he's restless and agitated.

The men begin to quietly converse in Italian as they walk into the kitchen so that we can't hear them.

"Shh." I rub Rico's face as I try to calm him. "I'm here, baby," I whisper, watching as his heavy eyes close. I push his hair back from his forehead and see him fall into a deep sleep.

God, he smells like a brewery. It's as if someone has poured straight sambuca all over his clothes. After a while, once I know he's asleep, I get up, take his shoes off, and drape a blanket over him.

Lorenzo and Maso walk back into the room. "What happened?" I ask.

"Nothing," Maso replies coldly. "He's a violent drunk. I'll stay and care for him. You go upstairs to bed. You can't be alone with him right now."

I frown. "He would never hurt me."

Maso rolls his eyes.

"I will care for him," I tell him.

"I said go to bed!" Maso snaps angrily. "I know what I'm talking about. I've been around a lot longer than you."

I put my hands on my hips and glare at him. Who the fuck does this guy think he is?

"And yet, you still don't know him at all. He would never hurt me. I said, I'll take care of him."

"Maso!" Lorenzo snaps.

"Non puo essere solo con lei," Maso growls back.

"Stop speaking Italian around me!" I snap. "I want to know what you're saying."

Maso's eyes come to me, evidently angered that I questioned him. "I said, you are not safe, and I'm not leaving you alone with him."

"He would never hurt me," I repeat. This guy is seriously pissing me off. Actually, they all are. I walk to the front door and open it in a rush. "He's safe, thank you for seeing him home. Now, I must ask you all to leave."

They stare at me, shocked.

"Now!" I snap as I hold my hand up toward the door. "Right now, leave."

The men exchange looks, confused. After a beat, a smile crosses Lorenzo's face, and he turns to the men who have been rendered speechless. He claps his hands. "You heard the lady. Everybody out."

The men begin to talk in Italian again but slowly and surely, one by one, they leave. Lorenzo is the last one out of the door, and he smiles and kisses my cheek.

"Put the shutters down, Olivia," he reminds me softly.

"I know."

"I'm staying in the other house on the property tonight. If you need me, I'm two minutes away."

I squeeze his hand, grateful for his support. "Thank you."

I close the door behind them, flick the lock, and turn toward my drunken man.

He's now snoring and dead asleep, flat on his back.

I stare at him for a moment. What happened to make him so angry? I've never seen him like this, and I know by the way they were all acting that they haven't seen him like this, either. He's going to be cold down here with that thin blanket.

I walk upstairs and grab a quilt from one of the spare beds, and then I make my way back down to cover him up. I gently kiss his forehead as I tuck him in and rearrange the cushion under his head.

"Sleep, baby," I whisper, holding my cheek to his.

Relief fills me that he's home safe. I'll have a cup of tea and go to bed. It's been quite a day.

Ten minutes later, I'm standing at the kitchen sink and I hear a bang behind me. I turn in a rush. Rico is standing at the door watching me, his face murderous. It's obvious he has no control over himself. Uneasiness fills me at once.

"Rico, what's wrong?"

He glares at me but stays silent.

"Are you feeling all right?" I ask as Maso's words float through my mind.

He's a violent drunk.

He steps forward, and I take a step back.

"What's wrong... Olivia?" he sneers. I stare at him as my heart begins to beat faster. "Do I scare you?"

"No."

"I should."

"Why would you scare me?"

He steps forward.

I take a step back.

"Rici," I whisper softly. "It's me, baby. Olivia."

"I know who you are." He takes another slow step toward me. "But, do you know who I am?" he whispers.

Our eyes are locked. "Who are you?" I ask.

He holds his hands out wide. "Let me introduce myself... bella." His voice is a hushed tone, filled with darkness and despair.

I watch him. Fear is coursing through my veins. He doesn't even resemble the man I know.

"My name is Enrico Giuliano Ferrara." He pauses and licks his lips. "The head of the Ferraro underworld." His eyes are dark. "I run all crime in Italy." He holds his finger up. "The Don," he sneers as he staggers to the side. "And the son of a fucking *liar*."

21

Olivia

I STARE AT HIM, lost for words.

He raises his chin in defiance.

What?

I mean, I had my suspicions, but to have him throw it in my face as if he's looking for a fight is not something I ever imagined.

"Now, pack your things and leave," he growls, he turns away from me.

I stare at his back for a while, my mind in freefall. What the hell is going on here? "Why?"

He turns back, curls his lip in disgust, and shakes his head. "I'm no good."

I stay silent, unsure where he's going with this.

"This." He hits his chest with both hands. "This! My story doesn't end well. Leave while you can." He sidesteps as he tries to keep upright. "I don't want this life for you, Olivia."

My heart breaks.

What's happened that has upset him so much?

I step forward and take his drunken face in both hands. "I'm not going anywhere. Not without you."

He blinks slowly, trying to focus on me.

"I love you," I whisper, and I kiss him softly.

"Don't," he sighs. "Don't love me, bella. You can't love me."

"Why not?'

"It's only a matter of time."

"Until what?"

"My days are numbered." His haunted eyes hold mine. "They'll kill me, like they killed my family."

I stare at the beautiful man in front of me, so heartbroken and forlorn. "Then we go down together," I whisper up at him.

I kiss him, and his face screws up in pain as he wraps his arms around me. We stand in each other's arms for a long time. His head is in the crook of my neck, and I hold him tight. He desperately needs comfort. I can feel the pain oozing out of him. I have no idea what transpired today, but I know it's upset him greatly.

After a while, he's heavy in my arms, and I know I have to get him upstairs.

"Let's go to bed." I take his hand to lead him through the house, and slowly up the stairs. He's quiet and placid as he lets me lead him—nothing like the raging bull who was downstairs only half an hour ago, fighting everyone.

I pull the covers back and take his clothes off. "Get into bed."

He stands still, staring at me.

"Get into bed, baby. I'll just have a quick shower and be back," I whisper with another kiss. "I'll be right back, I promise."

He nods, mollified for the moment, and he flops down. I cover him over, and his heavy eyelids close.

I stand at the foot of the bed as I watch him.

Holy hell... what just happened?

Enrico

The banging of my head wakes me with a start. I frown as I try to get my bearings.

Where am I?

I reach out and feel Olivia's bare behind beside me as she sleeps. I immediately relax. *I'm home.*

***Bang, bang, bang* goes my head.**

I slowly sit up and swing my legs over the side of the bed as nausea fills me. I'm hot, clammy, and the taste of cigars and liquor is pungent in my mouth.

Hell, I need a shower.

I get up and stagger. What the...? Am I still drunk?

I make my way to the bathroom and get under the hot water. I lean against the tiles and try to get my bearings.

How did I get home last night?

I can't remember anything.

I concentrate as I go back over yesterday.

There was lunch with Sophia, and then I went back to the club and poured myself a drink... more drinks.

I frown as I get a vision of myself punching someone. Who did I hit?

Fuck.

I put my arm on the tiles and lean my forehead against it as the water runs over me. I still feel as bad as yesterday—perhaps worse—because now I have the hangover of all hangovers.

He had another family and everyone knew. I feel so stupid, so betrayed. *Humiliated.*

I've never been so disappointed in my entire life. I always hero worshiped my father, and to find out he's just another bastard who used my mother is soul destroying.

I didn't know him at all.

The men—*his men.* They knew. They kept his dirty secret for him. For two years, I've worked beside these men, day in, day out, and not a word has ever been mentioned about her...

About his other son.

The one I don't know.

With a heavy heart, I wash my hair, brush my teeth, and desperately wish that yesterday hadn't happened. The memories of my father are forever tainted. Was he watching the clock every time he was with me? Was he counting down the hours until he could leave to go and see them?

I knew my grandfather had multiple mistresses; everyone knew. He was a typical Italian bastard who wouldn't come home for days. I expected nothing more from him. It was just how it was. He and my grandmother were hardly on speaking terms. She lived a life of luxury and was happy enough with that.

But my father... he adored my mother. He doted on her... loved her. To know that he spent thirty years loving another woman on the side *hurts*. I feel betrayed.

So, so betrayed.

Did our family mean nothing to him? It mustn't have. If he loved us, he wouldn't have strayed.

I think back to all our times at Lake Como, where he brought me and my brothers to our house here, while my mother always stayed at home.

He came here to see her.

Did he sneak her in once we were all asleep?

My stomach rolls as I get a visual of him having sex with someone else in his bedroom upstairs, while my mother waited for him at home.

Fury begins to pump through my bloodstream like never before. He never told me because he knew I would hate him for it.

Everyone knew. Even Sophia. She went to the funeral. He had a second funeral. What the fuck?

Everyone knew to keep it from me. I feel so stupid, and I've never been so humiliated.

I turn the shower off in disgust. I dry myself and walk back into the room to see my blonde angel still fast asleep. She's lying on her side, and I crawl in behind her and pull her into my arms. I kiss her temple and she slowly wakes. She turns her head and kisses me.

"Morning," I whisper.

"Mmm," she moans. "You're alive."

I smirk.

"Were you trying to kill yourself yesterday?"

I kiss her neck as I feel my arousal begin to creep in.

"I thought you were going to die of alcohol poisoning," she says.

"Sorry." I hate that she saw me like that. "I don't know what happened."

She rolls toward me and leans up on her elbow. She's all mussed up and looks so beautiful.

"Can we finish our conversation now?" she asks.

I frown. "What conversation?"

"You told me everything, Rico."

I stare at her as panic begins to scream through my system. "About what?"

"I know about the crimes you're involved in. I know about the Ferrara family business."

My face falls. I'm rendered speechless.

I wouldn't have told her. No way I would have told her.

"I know that you think you're going to die soon."

I open my mouth to say something, but there are no words. I roll onto my back as I put my forearm over my face. Fuck. I can't even look her in the eye.

She's leaving.

We lie in silence for a while.

"I'm sorry about my behavior last night. I'm appalled that you saw me like that. I'll have Lorenzo pick your things up and return them to Milan for you," I say as I climb out of bed in a rush.

She sits up. "Can we talk about this?"

"No."

"I want to know what I'm dealing with here."

"It's more than you can handle, Olivia." I pull my boxers up in a rush. "Trust me." I storm from the room and downstairs as my heart goes into panic mode.

She's leaving.

I hit the shutters, and the sound of them rising echoes around me. Light begins to slowly flood the house. I flick on my coffee machine and close my eyes as I mentally prepare myself for her exit. My heart's racing. I'm sucking in deep breathes to try and calm myself down.

Warm arms come around me from behind. "Rici," she whispers, and she kisses my back.

I close my eyes. The thought of her knowing what I am is too much.

Disappointing her is my worst nightmare.

"Just go," I sigh. "It will be less painful if we just get this over and done with."

"Just talk to me."

"And tell you what?" I cry.

"I'm not judging you," she says calmly.

"Aren't you, Olivia?" I spit and turn to her. "'Because it sure fucking feels like it."

"You grew up in this life..." she asks.

"Yes... and no."

Her eyes hold mine. "What does that mean?"

I exhale heavily. "I found out about everything when my father died."

She frowns. "Up until then you thought Ferrara was a reputable family business?"

"It *is* a reputable business," I snap. "There are just some unsavory aspects of it, I'm going to clean it up... but it takes fucking time."

"Like what?"

I shake my head in disgust. "I'm not discussing this, Olivia. Leave it."

"Like what, Enrico. Tell me what unsavory means."

"Brothels, strip clubs, illegal gambling." I shrug. "Shit like that."

"Drugs?"

"No. That was the first thing I stopped."

Our eyes are locked.

"Murder?" she whispers. "Do you kill people?"

I roll my eyes. "This isn't the fucking Godfather, Olivia. In the past, yes, but not anymore. We run reputable businesses in seedy places. That's it."

"I'm just so confused by this all."

I throw my hands up in the air. "That makes two of us."

She steps forward. "Why do you think you're going to die?"

"I don't!" I snap. "I was fucking blind drunk. Why would you listen to anything I said?"

"Because for the first time since we've been together, last night, you were actually making sense." She puts her hand on my chest. "I knew something was off. Too many things don't add up, and I knew with the amount of security you have..." Her voice trails off.

I clench my jaw as I watch her. She deserves the truth, I know she's going to leave me anyway. I may as well tell her.

"For centuries, the Ferrara family have run Italy. They've done some pretty fucking appalling things. I didn't know anything about it. I still know nothing. My father's staff are limping me through it all until I learn enough to completely take over."

She frowns. "Why were you so upset yesterday? What happened to make you like that?"

I stare at the floor for a moment, disgusted by what's come to light. "I found out my father had a comare for thirty years. It turns out everything he told me was a lie and... I didn't know him at all."

"Comare?" She frowns.

"Another woman. Another family. They had a son."

Her face falls.

"Even my mother knew."

She stares at me, horrified.

"My brothers and I were the only ones who didn't. I'm humiliated."

Her face falls as she stares at me. "Oh, baby." She wraps her arms around me, and I close my eyes at the comfort, even if it will be short lived. I need to get on with it. I step back from her.

"I haven't been gifted a normal life, Olivia. I'm sorry I dragged you into this. Your discretion would be greatly appreciated."

"I'm not leaving you, Rico."

I swallow the lump in my throat, unable to speak.

"I love you," she whispers.

"You shouldn't."

"It's too late."

Emotion overwhelms me, and I blink as my vision blurs from the realization of her loyalty. "I don't even know who I am anymore," I whisper.

"You're the man I love." She kisses me softly. "Just be him."

My arms curl around her. "I wanted to tell you I loved you first," I say into her hair.

"You did."

"When?"

"Last night, in front of about twenty people."

I close my eyes in disgust. "Oh."

She smiles softly.

"Was I appalling?"

"Completely. But understandably so." Our lips meet again, but this time I hold her tight, her tongue dancing with mine as an emotional need warms my blood. "I love you," I whisper. Our kiss turns desperate, and I push her back against the kitchen counter. The need in me is escalating by the second. I need to taste her, and my attention drops to her neck as I suck and kiss on her perfect, creamy skin. She smells so good. She always smells so fucking good.

"Bed," she breathes. "Back to bed."

Before I know it, I'm dragging Olivia up the stairs, desperate to be closer to her.

Inside of her.

The need to share myself with this beautiful woman takes over, and I tear her robe off, throw it to the side, and lay her down on her back. I open her legs, and my eyes roam down over her body. Her full lush breasts. Her flat stomach.

I reach down and spread her sex open.

Perfect pink lips glistening with arousal.

I slowly slide two fingers deep into her sex, and she clenches around me. Her big blue eyes are alive with want.

My cock starts to thump, weeping in appreciation.

Olivia Reynold's is every man's wet dream.

Mine.

She knows everything… and she stayed.

I pump her with my fingers, and the bed begins to hit the wall with force.

She loves it when I do this—when I fuck her hard with my hands before I give her my cock.

She's addicted to the pain.

Her back arches, and she begins to shudder. Close.

A deep moan leaves her lips, and my cock is painful with need.

I move to hover over her, and she wraps her legs around my waist. With one hard thrust, I'm deep inside my woman.

"Rici," she moans.

I clench to try and hold it as her body ripples around mine. She's wet and throbbing around me.

Perfect.

My lips take hers. "I'm here, Olivia. I'll always be here."

Our body's writhe together, each of us chasing the ultimate goal.

The rush where we become one.

I lift her leg and pull it up around my chest as I lose control. I begin to hit her hard. The sound of the bed banging on the wall is almost deafening around us. She loves it, sucking me in as she moans beneath me, begging for more.

I hold myself deep, and we both cry out in ecstasy as her body contracts around me.

My breathing is labored. My body covered in perspiration. Her hands in my hair, her soft lips on mine.

But it's my heart that's floating...it feels like it just left my body and nestled itself inside of hers.

She's now a part of me—the calm, sweet, good part.

The best part.

And I am hers.

Two hours later, I stare at my reflection in the mirror. I straighten my tie and dust my hands over my pants.

"We'll talk more tonight, okay?" Olivia says as she kisses me softly. "Try and be calm." She straightens my collar. "Just don't say anything more until you cool down."

"Okay." I kiss her goodbye and walk out of my house on a mission. After two hours with Olivia in bed, I'm centered again. She calmed me enough to at least get through the day.

I head down the front steps to see Lorenzo, Maso, and four men leaning on the cars out the front, waiting for me.

I walk up to them, stoney-faced, and they all stand.

"Rico." Lorenzo smiles hopefully.

"Olivia is going to work. I want you all with her today."

"Okay, I'll send a car with her. I'm staying with you."

I glare at him, imagining myself breaking his neck. I'm so angry with him I can hardly stand it.

"That won't be necessary." I storm to my car as he follows me.

"Rico, you have to understand—"

I turn on him like I'm the Devil himself. "I understand. I understand everything. You have no loyalty to me or my mother, and I cannot stand the fucking sight of you."

I turn to continue to my car, and he steps in front of me. "Rico, listen to me."

"We will have a meeting in the morning to discuss your termination. You are no longer needed," I growl.

"Rico, I have been loyal to your father for thirty years. You cannot fire me over this."

My eyes hold his. "My father is dead. If he wasn't, I would kill him myself today. I'm in charge now."

I get into the car and slam my door. He bangs on the window.

I exhale heavily as I try to control my anger. I roll down the window. "What?" I growl.

"Go see her."

I frown.

"Her address is 347 Lakeview Road. Go there, Rico. Please. Go now."

I clench my jaw and speed off. My anger escalates as I change the gears with a crunch. I fucking hate them all. Tomorrow everyone goes, and I start with new staff.

An hour later, I pull the car up and peer across the road. The impressive house is gated, and I can see a security guard inside. I drove around and around as I tried to resist coming here. In the end, I couldn't.

I needed to see this for myself.

Pain tightens my chest. His other son is guarded. His other life is guarded.

Was it so well known that even our enemies know?

Or are they guarded from me?

As I sit and watch, I see a woman and a boy walk down the street toward the house. They're deep in conversation. She punches in the code to the gate and it opens.

That's them.

She is blonde… *blonde.*

She's wearing tight denim jeans and a navy puffer jacket. She's in runners, and has on a New York Yankees cap, with her long, blonde, thick ponytail hanging down her back. She's laughing. She seems carefree.

She takes the football from the boy and kicks it over the fence to annoy him. He says something, and she laughs out loud.

I stop breathing all together as I watch her. She's the exact opposite of my mother.

My mother is Italian, with long dark hair. She's always in designer clothes and high heels. She's always made up to look exotic—gorgeous. A Ferrara to the bone.

I frown as I watch the enigma across the street. I can't even imagine my father with someone like her.

My eyes roam to the boy. He would be late teens. He has dark hair with a curl to it, and he looks exactly like I did at that age.

He had a football in his hand before she kicked it away. Maybe he just came from training or something.

I watch them walk in and talk to the man on the gate.

I frown as pain sears my chest. I know him. He's one of my father's men.

He works for me.

I drop my head, unable to watch on any longer.

I start the car, and with a million vile visions of my father with her and him, I drive to Milan.

This can't be happening.

There must be something. I've missed something. How didn't I notice this in the will?

When I arrive at my offices, I head straight in.

"Good morning." Rosalie smiles.

"Morning," I say. "No visitors today, please."

"Yes, Mr. Ferrara."

I walk into my office, move the light switch and hit the button. The bookcase slides to the side, and I put the code into the safe. The will. I want to look at the will.

The large metal door clicks open, and I walk inside the room-sized safe. It's filled with transactions, money, and paperwork.

I know where the will is. I saw it in here last week when I was retrieving something else. I look over the shelving until I see a large, dark brown, leather box way up high.

It's in there, I remember it from back when they were going through everything with me. I stand on the stepladder, take it down, and go back to my desk to open it. It's a large leather-bound book. I flick through the handwritten pages, and I frown. Title deeds, ownership papers, the properties I own... businesses...

What the fuck am I looking for here?

At the bottom of the box are loose papers. I take them out, and that's when I see a large yellow envelope.

FOR ENRICO FERRARA TO OPEN
WHEN HE FINDS THIS.

My heart stutters.

I stare at it for a moment.

How haven't I seen this before?

I tear open the large envelope to find three smaller envelopes in side, titled in my father's handwriting. Each one has a name on it.

Enrico
Andrea
Matteo

I put my hand over my mouth, hesitant to open it—Frightened that every memory of my father is about to be crushed.

I open the letter addressed to me.

My darling Enrico,

If you are reading this my son, I have left this world.

I want to start this letter by telling you how proud I am of the man you have become.

Emotion overwhelms me and I blink through my tears.

I miss him.

God, how I miss him.

Hopefully, you will never read this and we will have had this conversation face to face. But, in the tragic event that both my father and I go together, I needed to leave this letter for you.

I'm guessing that you are reading this letter in the days after my death...perhaps weeks.

I didn't want this handed to you until you were searching for answers. I know you would have had enough to deal with at the time of my sudden passing.

I'm so sorry, son. I wish we had more time together.

I can hear his voice.

I have no idea how to write this or what to say, so the beginning seems like a good place to start.

You may ask why I kept the Ferrara business from you, Enrico—why I didn't prepare you better.

It was my greatest dream that, by the time you learned of this, I would have held the helm for a good period of time and the violence would have been a distant memory for our family. I knew that one day you'd find out who your ancestors really were, and I wanted you to be prepared.

Although I didn't train you for our business, I did prepare you in my own way. The day you became a policeman,

Enrico, was the proudest day of my life. You learning that side of the law will help Ferrara greatly in future generations.

I'm guessing that you are searching for this because you have found out about Angelina.

I'm sorry I disappointed you, son. I felt this burden every day of my life.

A tear drops on the letter in front of me, and I stop to try and focus on the familiar handwriting.

Your mother and I were promised to each other on your mother's birth, when I was only three years old. We met a few times over our lives, and we were to marry when I was twenty-two.

When I was seventeen and visiting an aunt, I met an English girl in Lake Como who was an exchange student. Her name was Angelina Linden, and she was the most beautiful woman I had ever seen. We talked, and I convinced her to let me take her on a date. One turned into two, two turned into three.

I fell hopelessly in love with her. We spent two wonderful years together in Lake Como, and when she had to return to England, I ran away to go to her. I couldn't stand the thought of a life without her in it.

My family were appalled. I was promised to another. Many financial deals had been negotiated from this arranged marriage. Stefano came to London and made me return to Italy without my beloved Angelina.

It broke my heart. I never thought I would recover.

Your mother and I began the courting process and I told her I loved another. We spoke often of Angelina. There were no secrets between us. She was a dear friend who helped me through the process. In fear that I would run away again, the marriage was brought forward, and your mother and I exchanged our wedding vows. By this time, we were close friends and I began to have feelings for her. Not the same as my feelings for Angelina, but feelings all the same.

Your mother is the most beautiful, selfless person I have ever met. I adore her with every sense of my being. Over the next four years, we had three beautiful sons together. We traveled along and I was comfortable... but there was a part of me missing.

I close my eyes. I don't think I can read on. After a moment, I force myself to.

I went to France for business. You can imagine my shock to run into my Angelina, who was there for business also.

In the ultimate act of betrayal, I spent a week in Angelina's arms and fell deeply in love with her again.

This time, there was no end in sight. I couldn't live without her.

I returned home and told your mother everything. I asked her for a divorce, to which she declined. She wanted me to be with her for our children's sake. She wanted the security of having me at home. Your mother didn't want me to leave her completely. She put forward the idea of Angelina moving to Lake Como, and that I live between the two houses. At first, I declined. It wasn't fair to either woman. But my heart was with Angelina, and I couldn't leave your mother with three small children alone.

Finally, it was agreed on. I would become your mother's companion. I moved into the spare room of our family home. Your mother and I became just friends, and Angelina became my partner.

For many, many years, the three of us were happy with this arrangement. Your mother had my full support and devotion, and I got to live with my sons as they grew. Angelina had my full heart. But Angelina was missing a part of her life.

At the age of thirty-two and running out of time, she wanted a child.

I begin to hear my heartbeat in my ears as I read on.

I wanted to give Angelina a family of her own. She had given up her whole life and family to be with me.

To have half of me.

Angelina's family disowned her when they found out she had moved to Italy to be a married man's mistress.

When I wasn't with her in Lake Como, she was completely alone.

It was a heavy burden to carry for her, and yet her devotion to me never wavered... not once.

She paid the ultimate price for my love: her dignity.

I loved her desperately, Enrico, please understand that this was not something that was created out of lust. I am a bigger man than that. I couldn't fight my love for her.

I tried. For six years, I tried.

It only got worse with time, not better.

I agreed that she could have a child, and a year later, Angelina became pregnant. For the first time in my marriage, your mother was furious—crazy like I had never seen her before. She wanted to have my only children and she didn't speak to me for three months. We fought. She showed me a side of her I hadn't seen before. Heartbroken, I worked desperately hard to get my best friend back. I missed her. I missed your mother's love, and then the unthinkable happened. For the first time ever, I fell in love with your mother. It was a different love to what I had with Angelina, but love nonetheless.

She deserved better than I gave her.

I don't know how my life turned out the way it did. I was in love with two women.

My beloved wife and my devoted soul mate.

The three of us suffered, but Angelina ultimately sacrificed the most.

How could fate be so cruel?

The day Giuliano was born, my heart sang with happiness.

The joy that he brought to my Angelina was indescribable.

My biggest regret in all of this is that he didn't get to grow up with his brothers. Enrico, when I look at him, I see you.

Brave, strong, and loyal.

I love you, son... more than you could ever know.

I drop my head as the tears roll down my face.

I hate to admit it but I can relate to this story. It was almost my own.

I sit and stare at the bookcase in front of me as I try and prepare myself to read on.

You may ask why I didn't tell you any of this, Enrico.

The answer is simple: it changes you. It changes every part of who you think you are. Knowing that your family's money comes from crime, knowing that your father has committed adultery for all of your life... it's soul destroying.

Trust me, I know first-hand.

I was eleven years old when I found out about the family business. I was eleven years old when I witnessed my first murder. I was eleven years old when Stefano brought his mistresses into my life and paraded them in front of me as if I should be proud. There were multiple women—too many to remember. Sometimes three or four at once. This was his normal. This was how he was brought up. This was how he was going to bring me up.

He had no respect for my mother or me. It changed who I was, and for a long time, I hated him for it.

I vowed that I would never let my sons be tainted and bitter the way I was.

I wanted my sons to be proud of who I was.

I'm not perfect.

I know I loved two women, Enrico. The three of us were victims of circumstance. I know that I am still a Ferrara.

But I hope you remember the good in me, and how much I loved you.

My face creases together as pain tears through me.

Please listen to what I am about to tell you. I know you will be angry, but I have my reasoning.

Giuliano does not know anything about my other life. Like you, I have tried to protect him. He knows me as Papa—his father who worked away for a few days a week. The one who idolized his mother.

Enrico, I need you to be the strong man I raised and step up and look after my beloved Angelina and Giuliano.

They are all alone.

I have taken precautions, and they have been guarded up until you find this letter, but they are now in your care.

I have thought long and hard about this, Enrico, and I have made my decision based on personality alone. I have four sons, but only two are strong enough to be leaders. Giuliano is to be your successor, Enrico.

He will one day follow in your footsteps and lead Ferrara.

"No, Papa," I gasp.

When Giuliano Ferrara Linden is twenty-one, and not a day before, he will receive a letter similar to the one you are reading now, and he will learn of everything. He will be publicly claimed as my son, and his name will be legally changed to Giuliano Ferrara. He will then hate me, I have no doubt.

I need you to take him under your wing and remind him of how much he was wanted and loved.

My love for his mother has not waned in death, he was my gift to her. Love personified.

Care for him, love him, and teach him what I have had the time to teach you.

Look after my beloved Angelina, and your beautiful mother.

I miss them both dearly.

I love you, my son. More than anything, I love you.

Be brave, be strong, and try to understand my life and why I haven't always been honest with you. My only goal was to protect your sense of self.

I pray that I have.

All my love,

Papa.

x

Jessica

I hook the microphone onto my shirt. "Can you hear me?" I ask.

The large screen flickers in front of me, and three men come into view. They're sitting in a boardroom with a screen behind them.

"Ciao, Jessica."

"Hi." I smile.

"My name is Alexander, and this is Smithson and Ray. As you know, we are in the Carabinieri."

"Hello." I smile as nerves bubble in my stomach. The Carabinieri is the Special Forces of Italy. This call up is a big deal.

"We've gone over your resume with the Australian Federal Police with great interest, and we feel that you are perfect for this mission."

"I'm excited about the opportunity. How can I help?"

He brings up an image onto the screen behind him. It's an Italian man. He's very handsome—in his thirties.

"This is Enrico Ferrara."

I stare at the man on the screen as I listen intently.

"He's the head of organized crime in Italy. The Don. His family has been untouchable for centuries, even though they are involved in gambling, prostitution, murder, money laundering, and narcotics."

"Okay," I reply.

"Enrico is different to the past Dons. He's smarter, more

business-minded, and…" He pauses. "He's an ex-policeman. He has inside knowledge that nobody has ever had. If his reign over Italy continues, we are in dire straits of losing all control. He controls most of the police force and judging system as it is now. This mission is top secret."

"Ouch," I wince. "I'm confused, though. How can I help from Australia?"

"Up until now, we've had no way of getting close to him." They bring up an image of a beautiful blonde woman. She's around my age, and she's getting out of a car with what looks like a bodyguard beside her. "Meet Olivia Reynolds. Enrico's new love interest."

I stare at the woman on my screen.

"We interviewed her on Friday, under the guise of a missing person she knew."

"And?"

"She lied for Enrico. She pretended she didn't know him."

"Which means she's on the inside."

"Exactly. We want you to become her new best friend. You will move to Italy. Go to her gym, pretend that you, like her, have moved to Italy to be with your boyfriend. You will mix with her socially."

I smile.

"You're the same age as her, come from the same country, and you will have a lot in common. You need to gain her complete trust."

I smile broadly.

"We need full access to Enrico Ferrara to be able to bring him down. Can you help us, Jessica?"

Excitement rushes through me. "Assignment accepted."

22

Olivia

Three hours earlier.

Rico stares at his reflection in the mirror. He straightens his tie and dust his hands over his pants.

"We'll talk more tonight, okay?" I kiss him softly. I can feel the anger oozing out of him like a volcano that's about to explode. "Try and be calm." I straighten his collar. "Just don't say anything more until you cool down."

He stares at me flatly, and his jaw ticks. "I have to go." He kisses me, and I cling to him, trying my hardest to give him some of my strength.

"I love you." I smile up at him.

He exhales heavily. "That's the only light in my life at the moment." He kisses me again. "Stay with your guards today. I'll be rotating them with new ones to replace Lorenzo and Maso."

"Why?"

"I'm done with their deception. I'm letting them both go."

"Rici," I whisper. "Just wait for a week and see how you feel about it then. Besides, I'm comfortable with Lorenzo. I don't want another man with me."

Rico picks up his briefcase. "You will do as you're told. Goodbye, Olivia."

I smirk at his bossiness. "Bye."

I go to the window and look out through the sheer drapes. I watch him leave the house in a rush. Lorenzo approaches him and they appear to exchange heated words. There are four men standing around, all hanging back, as if too scared to say anything. Enrico goes into the garages, and then drives out in his Ferrari. Lorenzo taps on the car window and says something before Rico speeds off at a million miles an hour.

I exhale heavily.

I continue watching the men down on the front lawn. There's Lorenzo, Maso, and two new ones today. I watch them for a moment when I realize one of them is the guy who asked for my number at the ball.

Imagine if Enrico knew that he asked me out. I wince as I imagine the tantrum he would have. The guard is handsome, with brown hair that has a honey hue to it. What was his name again?

I haven't seen him before—only that night that we met at the ball.

I grab my briefcase and my big bag of sample swatches. I make my way downstairs and out the front door. Lorenzo glances over and sees me struggling with the large bags, and he runs to help.

"Olivia, let me take this for you."

"Thank you, that would be great." He takes my bags and puts them in the trunk.

"Olivia, this is Sergio," Lorenzo introduces us.

Sergio smiles mischievously and steps forward with his hand held out. "Nice to meet you, Olivia."

He's pretending we never met before, which makes sense, I suppose. It's a lot less awkward.

I smile as we shake hands. "Likewise. Nice to meet you, Sergio."

Lorenzo fusses around, putting my things into the car, while the other men get the second car ready. Yet, Sergio's eyes stay glued to mine. He tucks his hands into his suit pockets, and then raises his eyebrow at me. It's playful and a little seductive with a twist of *we both know a secret*. His eyes hold mine for an extended time. In fact, he's giving me the look... *what the hell?*

I snap my eyes away in a fluster. Jesus, he's ballsy.

Enrico would literally kill him if he saw him look at me like that.

I climb into the back of the car, and I watch on as the other men get into the car behind us.

Sergio walks up to the front porch of the house.

Lorenzo gets in and slams the door shut. "Are you ready?" He pulls slowly out of the driveway. My eyes stay glued to the naughty man on the porch. "Is Sergio not coming with us?" I ask.

"No, he will work from here today. Someone has to guard the house at all times. He will work out of the boat house."

"I see."

Sergio waves, and then heads inside the house. *My house.*

Uneasiness fills me.

I'm not sure if I like having strangers in my house all the time. Especially ones that give me the fucking look.

I'm going to have to talk to Rico. I want some privacy. This is ridiculous.

I watch the scenery fly by as I think about the last twenty-four hours. Enrico's words from last night come back to me.

The Don, and the son of a fucking liar.

Fuck, does a sentence get any heavier than that? I don't even know how or where to begin to process it. He said his family have been criminals in the past, and that there are still elements that are seedy. Prostitution, but that's a legal business. Gambling, also legal. He said there are no drugs anymore. He also said that he's trying to clean everything up, but it's going to take time.

I feel like I have the weight of the world on my shoulders. Then there's my poor Rico who really does have the weight of the world on his shoulders. All these staff—staff who lie to him. His father and grandfather left him with this mess, and he feels burdened with such heavy responsibilities.

But I love him, and his burden is my burden.

This isn't ideal, by any means. I would much prefer him to be a broke policeman in Roma...but he isn't, and if I want to spend my life with him, I need to get my head around that. I take out my phone to text Natalie.

Oh my God, can we please meet up today?
I have so much to tell you

My finger hovers over the send button. Who am I kidding? I can't tell Natalie any of this. She can't keep a secret for shit. I erase my message and type it out again.

Hi, Nat,
How are you?

What time is your job interview?

I wait for a few moments and a text bounces back in.

My interview is at two.
I really hope I get it.
I think I found an apartment.

I smile and text back.

Rico asked me to move in with him.

A reply comes in.

What the fuck?
Are you going to?

I smile at the ridiculousness of my life right now. Am I on Netflix?

I already did.
Apparently, I now live in Lake Como.

I smirk as I wait for her reply.

Oh, get fucked, you're like Amal Clooney
or some shit.

I giggle out loud and Lorenzo's eyes flick up to the rearview mirror to see what I'm laughing at. What I really want to write back is: *except for the small fact that she's a human rights lawyer and married to a movie star, while I'm an Australian nobody, dating a Don.*

I won't, though. I'll keep that part of Rici Ferrara to myself. I can't trust anyone with his secrets. It's my man and me against the world now. When I told him I loved him, I meant it, warts and all… and boy, are there some warts.

His words from last night play on my mind.

It's only a matter of time before they get me, too.

What did he mean by that? Who's going to get him? Is that why there's so much security around him? And me? Why am I guarded too now?

Maybe I'm in danger by association. To be honest, it's kind of freaking me out.

I snap myself out of my worried thoughts and text Nat back.

Do you want to catch up for drinks and dinner?
Tomorrow after work?

She replies.

Sounds great, see you then.

I write:

Good luck today, babe.
Knock them dead.

It's 2:00 p.m. when we pull into the driveway of Villa Oliviana in Lake Como. My fabric sample finding mission didn't take all day like I expected. It's amazing how quickly you can get things done when you have four personal assistants driving you everywhere. They all seem lovely, and we even stopped for lunch. The maintenance man is tinkering with the lock on the big iron gates, and they are off their hinges.

Lorenzo pulls the car to a stop in the driveway. He seems unimpressed that the work isn't finished.

"I'll just walk in," I say.

"My apologies. It won't take them long to put the gate back on," he tells me.

"It's a beautiful day. I'll walk. Thanks for taking me today." I smile.

He turns in his seat toward me. "You are most welcome." His kind eyes hold mine, and I can tell he's concerned about Rico and his grudge but doesn't want to speak out of turn.

"I'm going to try and talk to Rico tonight," I say.

He exhales heavily. "I only tried to protect him, Olivia." He shakes his head sadly. "I love him like a son."

"I know." I reach forward and put my hand on his shoulder. "He'll come around. He just needs some time."

He shrugs as if knowing I'm right but he only half believes it.

I get out of the car and walk through the gates. I make my way up to the house. The gardens here truly are spectacular. I walk in through the large front doors. The wind catches them, and they slam harder than I thought.

"Oops."

I walk into the living area and put my handbag onto the side table, and then something catches my eye at the top of the stairs.

Sergio is looking flustered and coming down the stairs.

"Hello, hello." His face is flushed. "I thought you weren't getting back till late?"

I frown. His demeanor is off, or maybe that's just me being suspicious of him.

"What were you doing up there?" I ask.

He glances up the stairs. "I was checking one of the security shutters. It was making a crunching sound. The maintenance man wanted it checked so, if needed, he could fix it before he left."

"Oh." I frown. "I didn't hear any crunching."

"Manuel mentioned it." He smiles. "How was your day?"

"Good." I feel a wave of discomfort sweep through me at being alone with him in the house. Especially after the look he gave me this morning.

Maybe I'm imagining this entire thing. Did he even give me a look?

"I'll just be out the front if you need me," he says before taking off through the front door.

I stare at the closed door he has disappeared through. I'm having a serious discussion with Rico about the amount of people around here. It's like a revolving door with different people coming and going all the time. I hate it.

Manuel and his wife are different. They're the caretakers and live on the property. But the rest of them, quite frankly, give me the creeps.

I walk into the kitchen, put the kettle on, and I slip my shoes off. What will I do with my early mark of an afternoon? I wish I was in Milan. I could have gone to the gym. Actually, I might use the gym here. Yeah why not? Rico isn't going to be home until later. I may as well. I make my cup of tea and head up to get changed into my gym clothes. I smile when I walk into my wardrobe.

It's pitiful. Three measly drawers are filled with my things, because that's all I own. This walk-in is bigger than most people's bathrooms. I open Rico's wardrobe and see all his beautiful suits and designer clothes displayed perfectly. It's like a shop. I look over his expensive watches and his aftershave. I count his shoes. Forty-three pairs!

"What man owns forty-three pairs of shoes?" I scoff. "That's just ridiculous."

I grab my gym clothes and walk into the bathroom, and I freeze. The tube of lubricant is on the sink as if it's just been washed.

Wait...

I thought I put that back in Enrico's side drawer this morning when I got out of bed specifically so that nobody would see it. We use it when we get super naughty, he's too big and likes it too rough.

I open the lid of the clothes hamper and peer inside. There's a lone pair of my panties sitting in the bottom. I reach in and dig them out. I did not put these in here.

I carefully inspect them... they're dirty. These were in my suitcase with my other clothes that needed to be washed.

I look around the bathroom, knowing something is off here.

My eyes widen at once. What the fuck? Was Sergio in here jerking off to the smell of my dirty panties?

Is that what he was doing upstairs?

A cold shiver runs through me. No... surely not.

I drop to a sit on the bed—dirty panties in hand. This is fucking weird.

What guy would go into his boss's bedroom and jerk off to his boss's girlfriend's panties?

My phone rings. It's Natalie.

"Hey, how did you go?"

"Oh my God, I have to get this job. The guy who interviewed me is fucking orgasmic."

I smile as I look down at the panties in my hand. "Really?"

"He looked like Elvis. Love me tender, baby."

I burst out laughing. "You're hilarious. What did he say?"

"He said he's going to call me tonight and let me know if I got it."

"Great. How do you think it went?"

"Good, I guess. When I wasn't imagining myself sucking his dick under the table."

I shake my head as I laugh. "Tell me I'm crazy over here. I need you to talk me off the ledge." I close my bedroom door and go into the bathroom so that nobody can hear us.

She laughs. "No, I can't do that. You are completely mental."

"Listen, do you remember the other night when I told you that a guy asked me for my number, and then he said 'I have to go, my boss is here' and his boss was Enrico?" I whisper.

"Yeah."

"Well, he turned up here today to work, and his name is Sergio."

"At the house in Como?"

"Yes, and he was giving me the look."

"What look?"

"You know. *The* fucking look."

"There are a lot of looks. I need specifics."

"Like the *I think you're hot* kind of look."

"That's a given. All guys give that look. They're horny fucktards."

I nod. This is true. "I got home early today, and the gate was being fixed, so I walked up the driveway by myself. When I came in, Sergio came out from upstairs."

"Who?"

"The fucking guy I just told you about," I whisper.

"He was inside your house?"

"Yes—said he was checking the shutters or some shit."

"Okay, so?"

I look around guiltily. "I just came into the en-suite bathroom and the lubricant is out on the side, and my dirty panties are in the basket. I didn't put them there."

"Get fucked," she whispers. "You think you interrupted him jerking off to your panties?"

"I... I don't know," I stammer. "Maybe?"

She gasps.

"I know," I whisper.

"Oh, I know this is appalling for you, but that's so fucking hot. Send him my way, I do love a kinky man."

"*What*?" I whisper. "That's not fucking hot, Natalie, that's creepy."

"How do you smell?" she asks. "I hope they smell good. Sniff them and see."

I burst out laughing. "Will you be serious for one minute, please?" I look around again. "And, of course I smell good... I hope."

"I'm sure Mr. Ferrara will love the thought of his staff sniffing your vag."

I put my head into my hands and laugh. This really does sound ridiculous.

"Maybe I got it wrong." I frown.

"Enrico could have put them there," she offers as an explanation.

"I guess."

"It is random." she adds.

"It is random, isn't it?"

"Completely."

I drag my hand down my face. My imagination is running wild. "Okay, I'm going to go work out and do something useful."

"Wash your undies."

I laugh. "Yeah, that too. Bye. Call me if you get the job."

"Okay, see you."

It's just after 5:00 p.m. when I walk into the house from the backyard. I've been keeping myself busy and trying not to imagine someone creeping around our bedroom, dick in hand. I've run on the treadmill, done our washing, and now I'm about to cook dinner. Antonia wanted to cook, but I told her I would like to cook.

Fuck this. I want a home not a football stadium. Things are changing around here.

I pour myself a glass of wine and take the chicken out of the fridge. I begin to chop it up. On a serious note, I really need to learn how to cook some good Italian food.

And speak Italian...

And do every fucking thing in Italian.

If I prepare dinner now it will give me a chance to freshen up before my man gets home.

There is so much to do and learn. God, this day is overwhelming.

The doorbell rings throughout the house.

I wash my hands, grab a tea towel, and walk out into the living area. It rings again.

I open the door to see a beautiful woman standing there. She's wearing a tight camel- colored dress, with sky-high stilettos. Her long dark hair is styled and glamorous. Her rich perfume is overwhelming.

It's the woman I saw Enrico with at lunch.

His madam. Sophia.

I'm instantly aware that I look like shit, and the blood drains from my face. I'm still in my gym clothes, with a messy bun on top of my head, wearing no makeup and completely barefoot.

I fake a smile. "Hello."

A frown crosses her face as she looks me up and down. "Hello, my name is Sophia."

I pull my T-shirt down. "I'm Olivia." I look down at my damp hands and the tea towel I'm holding. "Can I help you?"

A trace of a smile tugs at her lips. "I'm here to see Enrico."

Her Italian accent is heavenly.

"Um, he's not home yet."

"Can I wait?"

"I don't know how long he's going to be."

She brushes past me into the house. "That's fine. I don't mind."

I watch her march into the house. Rude. "Or that," I whisper under my breath.

I close the door behind her and glance out to see three men leaning up against the parked cars. They are laughing and talking without a care in the world.

I feel my agitation rise as I walk back into the kitchen. "Would you like a cup of coffee or something?"

Oh shit, why did I offer her coffee? I don't know how to work the stupid coffee machine.

Sophia glances down at my glass of wine. "I'll have a glass of wine."

Will you now? The word is please, bitch.

Yep, it's official, this woman annoys me. I take another glass from the cupboard and pour her some wine.

"Thanks." She fakes a smile as she looks me up and down.

"What are you doing here?"

She frowns. "I'm here to see Enrico, I already told you."

"He was in his office in Milan all day."

"This is of a personal matter." She sips her wine.

"Anything I can help you with?" I smile sweetly.

Her eyes hold mine. "No." She fakes a smile. "I need to speak to him... alone."

Our eyes are locked.

Game on, mole. You may be gorgeous, sexy, a Madame, and Italian...

But he loves me, so put that in your pipe and smoke it.

I pick up the knife and go back to chopping the chicken.

"You cook?" she asks, amused.

"Don't you?"

"No." She lifts the wine glass to her lips. "And I most definitely wouldn't if I had the staff that this house carries."

I smirk.

"What's that look for?" she asks.

"You think you're above cooking?"

She flicks her hair behind her shoulders and gives a conceited shrug.

"That's funny, because in your line of work I would have imagined that you'd be used to getting your hands dirty." I smile sweetly.

Shit, did I say that out loud?

"What do you know about my line of work?" she fires back.

"Only what Enrico has told me. That you're a Madame, and you work for him."

She smiles. "And what else did Rico tell you about me?"

My hackles rise at her use of Rico as his name. "Everything," I lie.

She lifts her chin in defiance. "So, he told you about the two of us?" She sips her wine and smiles sarcastically.

I get a vision of myself diving over the counter and strangling this whorebag.

Our eyes are locked.

"He did, actually," I lie.

I chop the chicken with force, imagining it's her head on the chopping block.

Hurry up and get home, fucker.

I knew he was sleeping with her.

She smirks. "Can I use the bathroom? I would like to freshen up. Where is it?"

I'll freshen you up, bitch. I'll flush your damn head down the toilet. Lucky for me, I'm in my activewear, because this could be an all-out brawl soon.

"Behind you to the left." I point with the knife.

I continue chopping when she disappears. Hmm, she didn't know where the bathroom was, which means she hasn't been here before. Good. This is her first and last visit.

The front door opens, and I keep chopping. This place is like a fucking airport. Great, probably another woman from his whorebag harem.

"Hello, my love." I hear Rico's deep voice from behind me, and I turn. He drops his briefcase and rushes to take me into his arms. He holds me tight, tighter than usual and it's clear that he's upset.

"What's wrong?" I ask quietly.

He holds my face in his hands, and his lips take mine. "It's been a long day," he eventually murmurs against my lips.

"Hello, Enrico," Sophia says from behind us.

Rico jumps back from me in surprise, and his face falls.

"What the hell are you doing here?" he growls.

Oh shit. My eyes widen as I look between them both.

"I… I came to see you," she stammers, shocked by his obvious anger.

He glares at her like a hunter. "Get out," he orders through gritted teeth.

"Rico," I say quietly. God, this is a bit extreme.

"How dare you come here?" he cries.

"I wanted to see if you were all right," she says.

"Liar. You came here to intimidate my fiancée. Tell the fucking truth."

My eyes widen. Holy shit. He's nailed it; that's exactly what she's doing.

"I was at my office all day. If you wanted to see me in regards to work, you come there. Do not ever fucking step foot into one of my homes again." He grabs her by the arm and begins to drag her out.

"Rico!" I cry. Oh shit, what's he going to do? "Calm down, will you?"

He marches her to the front door. "You come near Olivia again and see what happens to you." He pushes her out of the door. "This is your first and last warning."

"Rico," she cries. "You've gone crazy. You're pushing away everyone who cares about you."

"With friends like you, who needs enemies?" he bellows.

He slams the door so hard in her face, it nearly comes off the hinges. He glares at me, and without a word, he marches upstairs and I hear the shower start.

Oh hell, that was unexpected. Although, if I'm honest, I'm kind of glad he did it.

I go back to the kitchen to continue chopping the chicken with my heart racing in my chest. I'll give him a moment to calm down before I go up and see him.

I wait for ten minutes, and then I hear the shower turn off.

The doorbell rings again.

Damn that doorbell! He's going to go postal if she's come back.

I walk out into the living area and see a blonde woman at the door.

He must know her, or the guards wouldn't have let her in.

I open the door. "Hello." I smile, relieved that it isn't that whorebag Sophia.

The woman is in her fifties at a guess. She's naturally pretty. She twists her hands in front of her nervously.

"Hello," she says softly. "My name is Angelina."

Someone with manners, at last. "What a beautiful name." I shake her hand. "Hello, my name is Olivia."

Her eyes dart into the house. "I was wondering if Enrico is home."

"Um." I frown. "Yes. He is."

"Could...?" She pauses before finding her bravery. "Can I see him, please? We need to talk."

"No!" Rico snaps from behind me. "Leave," he barks.

Her face falls.

"E-Enrico," I stammer as I turn toward him, shocked by his rudeness.

"Please, we need to talk, Enrico," she says softly.

He glares at her with such contempt. "I want nothing to do with you. You or your bastard son."

23

Olivia

He steps in front of me and slams the door shut in her face, and then he storms back up the stairs.

Oh my god.

Horrified, I open the door back up in a rush.

"I'm so sorry," I whisper. "I don't know what's come over him today. This is just a really bad time." I glance up the stairs. "Shall I get him to call you or something?" I ask, looking back at her.

Tears well in her eyes, and she nods. "Thank you." She steps back and turns to Lorenzo who's standing at the bottom of the steps. His face is solemn, and he shakes his head, angered by Enrico's rudeness.

"Come, Angelina, I'll take you home," he tells her.

Visibly upset, she walks down the stairs. Lorenzo puts his comforting arm around her, and they walk out to one of the cars before they get in and drive away.

Bastard son…

What did he mean by that?

My eyes widen as I connect the dots. Holy shit, that's her! His dad's lover.

I glare up the stairs to where he's disappeared. I'm suddenly furious. What is his fucking problem today, anyway? How dare he take his anger out on her? This isn't her fault. She never lied to him. That was his prick-faced womanizing father. Angelina's only crime was to love someone too much for her own good.

I take the stairs two at a time, eventually finding him in his wardrobe slamming things around.

I march in. "You know what?" I snap. "You're a judgmental bastard, and a fucking hypocrite." I storm into the bathroom. "Do not be so rude to people in my house!" I yell as I slam the door. I turn the shower on, take my shirt off, and the bathroom door bangs open.

"How the fuck am I a hypocrite?" he growls.

"Are you kidding me?" I throw my hands up in disgust. "Was that her? Your dad's mistress? Was that her?"

He glares at me, and I know for certain it was.

"So, let me get this straight," I sneer. "You hate her for being a mistress, when not three fucking weeks ago you asked the same thing of me?"

"That's different."

"It's *exactly* the same."

"You don't know what you're talking about."

"You think there's one set of rules for you, and one set for everyone else, and quite frankly, this spoilt brat attitude you have going on is fucking pathetic."

"Fucking pathetic?" he gasps.

"You wanted me on the side."

"I did not."

"Yes, you did." I get under the hot water, and then I remember something. "And why didn't you tell me that you were sleeping with Sophia? I felt like a fucking idiot downstairs before."

He trips on the bathmat and kicks it with force across the bathroom. "Fuck off." He snarls to it.

I rub the soap across my shoulders. "How about this? Before you throw a tantrum and start being a rude prick, you stop and think about how you treat people around you, Enrico?"

The veins are popping out of his forehead now. "Do not dare tell me how to treat people in my own fucking house, Olivia."

"This is supposed to be my house, too." I lose the last of my patience. "Angelina deserves your respect. Your father did what he thought he had to do." I wash my arms with vigor. "I don't know why you're taking this so personally."

His eyes bulge. "You don't know why I am taking this so personally?" he yells. "You want to know why I came back to you, Olivia?"

I roll my eyes, unaffected or intimidated by his angry outburst. *So dramatic.*

"Let me tell you right now, it wasn't because I wanted to marry an Australian." His face is furious. "I still don't want to do that."

What the hell?

"Then don't!" I scream. I hurl a bar of soap at him. Good God, he's a bastard. "Just get out."

"I came back to you because, if I were to marry another woman and had children with her…" He pauses, trying to calm himself down enough to say what he wants to say. "I knew that every time I would look at those kids, I would only see the reasons why I can't be with you." His nostrils flare.

"And I would fucking despise my own flesh and blood," he whispers.

Oh...

My eyes fill with tears.

"So, excuse me for being devastated," he blinks away his own tears, "for now knowing that that's how my father saw me." His voice cracks, betraying him. "I was the reason he couldn't have the life he wanted." He hits his chest. "I was the reason he wasn't happy. I am the Italian child he was forced to have."

My heart drops.

Seeing such a powerful man reduced to feeling like an insignificant child.

"Oh, Rici." I step out of the shower and take him into my arms. His breath quivers, and I know he's on the edge, trying to hold it together. "Shh." I hold him tight as I try to calm him down. I'm wet and water is dripping everywhere, but I don't care. I hold him for a long time. We stay silent, and with every breath, his arms tighten around me.

I don't know what to say, because I know that I'll probably say the wrong thing. He's thought much deeper into this than I had realized. He thinks he knows how his father would have felt about a child with a woman he didn't love. Although, I'm sure it's not as black and white as he sees it, I know for certain that he was loved dearly.

"Rici. Let it go. Let all this anger go. Let's concentrate on our life together and how we're going to do things. We have so much to look forward to. Don't let your father's mistakes cloud your judgement or make you unhappy. Make a conscious decision to let it go." His eyes search mine, and I take his face in my hands. "It's time for us to move forward. For you to bring Ferrara into the next phase. For me and you to love each other *our* way."

"I don't know how to be anything other than angry," he whispers.

"You talk to me about it and we figure this out together. That's what partners do. They're a sounding board for each other. Firing everyone and going crazy is not going to bring him back so you can have your final say. Getting new staff is only going to make your life harder, not easier. You haven't made the same mistakes your father did. He would be so proud of you."

He pulls me closer. What I just said meant a lot to him, I can tell.

I search my mind for something I can I say that will make him feel better.

Wait, how do I say it?

"Puoi lavarmi la faccia sotto la doccia?" I ask *Translation: can you wash my face in the shower?*

He pulls back, his eyes search mine, and he smiles softly.

"Laverò non solo il tuo viso, bella ragazza," he whispers back.

I stare at him, confused. I don't understand his reply.

Typical.

He tilts my jaw up so that he has full access to my lips, and he kisses me. His face has softened, and my sweet Rici is back.

"I'll wash more than your face, my beautiful woman."

I frown in question. "My face?"

He breaks into a broad smile and my heart melts. I haven't seen that smile in a long time.

"I wanted you to wash my back." How do you mix up the words face and back?

He takes his shirt off over his head. "I can wash that, too, my love," he says softly.

I smile, hopeful that I've made him feel even the tiniest bit better.

"Ti amo."

"Ti amo di più," he whispers as he kisses me.

I smile against his lips. He said he loves me more. *I understood.*

Suddenly, the anger that's been raging around inside of him all week is gone.

It's just him, me, and what we have between us.

He slides his shorts down his legs and leads me into the shower. The hot water makes my skin tingle. I run my hands up over his broad chest as he stares down at me with tenderness.

We just had a moment—a defining moment in our relationship. I think from the way he is looking at me that I got it right.

His hands go to my behind, and he pulls my hips closer. I can feel him hardening against my stomach, and his kiss holds a hunger that tell me he needs to be fed. His hands go to my breasts and he begins to knead them as his cock begins to slide between the lips of my sex. His kiss becomes desperate —hungry.

God, I love him like this when I can feel the physical need he has for me.

Every inch of his being becomes focused on one thing... the need to fuck.

He grabs a handful of my hair at the nape of my neck, and he drags my head back, granting himself access. His teeth begin to nip and bite my skin as his animal instincts take over. He nudges my opening, and then in one sharp movement, he lifts me and pins me to the wall as he slides in deep.

Our mouths fall open as we stare at each other. No matter how many times we have sex, that first moment of entry is always out of this world.

Perfection.

I grab his face in my hands. "Give it to me," I moan. "Fuck me."

He pulls out and slams back in hard. While his eyes are focused on my lips, I watch as his body takes over. Clicking into another gear, a higher level.

Enrico Ferrara was born to fuck.

The harder the better.

Virile and athletic, his body is a well-oiled machine built for female satisfaction.

I bounce as he holds me up against the tiles, and he hits me hard. The air is knocked from my lungs, and his hips are working at speed. The sound of our skin slapping echoes through the bathroom.

His eyes are focused on where our bodies meet. "Fuck me, Olivia," he growls. "Take it all. My cock is yours. It will only ever be yours."

Hearing his words tips me over the edge, and my body convulses. I clench and shudder as an orgasm rips through me, making me cry out in pleasure.

He grips my shoulders for leverage and really lets me have it, slamming my body down onto his with such force, I don't know how I'm not breaking in two.

His mouth hangs slack as he lets out a deep guttural moan. His head tips back, and he holds himself deep. I feel the heat as he fills me full of semen.

He grabs my hair and drags my face to his to kiss me.

Deep, slow, and tender.

"I love you," he whispers.

My eyes fill with tears, because I really do love him. After the week we have just had, I really needed this connection.

"Ti amo di più," I murmur against his lips.

I put my head down on his shoulder—his body still deep inside mine. His lips are resting against my temple.

And I know that I'm home.

It's 7:30 a.m. when I walk into the gym. I came into to Milan early this morning so that I could come before work. I want to try and make this my new routine. That way, my workout is done and dusted before the day begins. It feels like months since I was last here, and so much has happened since then, but it's good to be back. I know I could use the gym at home, but I really want to keep my independence as much as I can.

"Hello," the girl on reception says as I walk past her.

"Hi." I smile.

I put my things into the locker and make my way over to the treadmill. I start it up and it begins to slowly roll. I walk to warm up, and I glance over as Michael and Rocco arrive and head over to the weight section—close enough to watch me but far enough away that I won't feel crowded. I hate that I have to have them with me, but then I feel safe that they are here, too.

It's a fine line between the two, and I'm not sure which is the lesser evil.

For ten minutes, I walk as I listen to my Italian audio lesson. I'm determined to master this language. I need to know what the hell is going on around me.

"Ciao... hello. Goodbye... addio. Good morning... buongiorno. Good night... buonanotte."

In my peripheral vision, I see a girl get onto the treadmill beside me. I give her a smile and keep walking. She has light brown hair that's up in a high ponytail, and olive skin. She doesn't look Italian. She fluffs around beside me for a while, pushing the wrong buttons.

I take my earplugs out to help her. "You need to push the workout button," I say.

"Oh, thanks." Her treadmill begins to move. I frown at her accent.

"You're Australian?" I ask in surprise. I haven't met any other Australians yet.

"Yes." She smiles. "Just moved here this week. You, too?"

"Yes." I smile with excitement.

"Have you been here long?"

"About six weeks."

"How are you liking it?"

"I mean, what's not to love, right?"

She shrugs. "I'm hoping to get to that stage. I'm so nervous about everything so far. I've moved here to be with my boyfriend—he's Italian. We met when he was travelling in Australia. I don't know anybody else but him."

Sounds familiar. "Really?" I smile. "Mine, too."

"I'm Jennifer," she introduces herself. "Everyone calls me Jen."

I lean over and shake her hand. "Hi, Jen. I'm Olivia."

"Nice to meet you, Olivia."

We walk in comfortable silence for a while.

"Did you get a program made up?" she asks.

"No, I like doing my own thing."

She looks over to the girl on reception. "I think I will. I need a structured workout or else I just schmooze around. Do you know how much it is?"

I giggle. "Yeah, I get the schmooze thing, and I've no idea about the price, sorry."

"Do you come in the mornings every day?" she asks.

"I'm hoping to. I'm trying to get into some kind of routine."

"Me, too." She hits the stop button. "I'm going to go and ask about a program and their pricing structure." She gives me a friendly smile. "Nice to meet you, Olivia. I might see you tomorrow morning."

"For sure," I say.

I watch her walk over to the girl on reception. They talk for a while.

Hmm, she seems nice. I put my earphones back in and continue with my lesson while I walk. "Motorbike... motocicletta."

Enrico

I walk into my office at 9:00 a.m.

"Good morning," I say to my two receptionists.

Greta looks up and smiles. "Good morning, Mr. Ferrara. Mrs. Ferrara is waiting in your office for you."

I exhale heavily. My mother is here. Great. Just what I need. "Thank you." I open the door and find her sitting at my desk.

"Hello, Mamma."

She stands. "Hello, darling." She smiles and kisses both my cheeks.

She's immaculately put together, as always. It's funny, you know; I didn't realize that women weren't always perfect like this. Until I met Olivia, I never knew a woman who was so comfortable in her own skin. So naturally beautiful without all the window dressing.

"And to what do I owe this pleasure?" I ask as I take a seat opposite her at my desk.

Mother's eyes hold mine. She holds her hand out and

looks at her manicured red nails. It's something she always does when she's uncomfortable. "I'm here to talk about the last few days and the things that have come to light."

Her eyes rise to meet mine, and I raise my chin, angered.

She's the last person I want to discuss my father's infidelities with.

I rearrange the papers on my desk to try and distract myself. "Such as?"

"Enrico. Stop it."

"What do you want me to say, Mamma?" I get out of my chair in a rush and walk to the window to stare out over Milan. "That my father was a great man?"

"Your father *was* a great man," she replies calmly.

"Who I now have zero respect for."

"Stop it!" she snaps, and she stands in a rush. "Don't you dare disrespect my husband."

I look her up and down and give a subtle shake of my head.

"What's that look for?"

I put my hands into my suit pockets. "Just looking at you in your widow wear. Two years is a long time to wear black for a man who treated you with nothing but disrespect."

The sharp sting of her hand burns my face, and the slap echoes throughout the room.

"How dare you?" she whispers. "How dare you judge him... or me? You know nothing about our relationship, and you will never understand. You couldn't possibly."

Adrenaline floods my body. That is the first time in my entire life that my mother has raised her hand to me.

"Oh, I understand," I sneer as my anger escalates to a dangerously high level. "I understand that my father has cut both my brothers out of his will completely. That one day, a bastard child of his will lead Ferrara Industries. Tell me mother… when Giuliano is announced as a Ferrara, how are you going to explain this to Francesca?"

Her eyes hold mine.

"How do you explain to a sixteen-year-old girl that her father had two women pregnant within a year of each other?"

"Stop it," she whispers angrily. "Stop being vile."

My eyebrows rise in surprise. "Vile? You think the truth is vile?" I give her a slow smile. "Funny, because that's my point." I walk over with renewed purpose and sit down at my desk. "I'm letting some of the staff go. Ferrara is starting afresh."

"You will do nothing of the sort. Your father worked incredibly hard to recruit the staff that you have. Your gripe with him is not their fault."

I sit back in my chair. "You see, if you were left in charge, that would be your decision to make… but you weren't."

She squares her shoulders. "Lorenzo has been nothing but loyal to our family. He's staying."

"Oh, Lorenzo," I scoff in disgust. "Lorenzo is nothing but a fucking liar."

"Do not curse in front of me. It's disrespectful."

"You think cursing is disrespectful?"

She raises her chin in defiance.

I glare at her. "I'll tell you what's disrespectful, Mamma: leaving two sons out of a family business as if they don't exist. Leaving three sons a letter after your death, but not one for your only daughter." My voice rises along with my anger. "Lying to your children for their whole *fucking* life about who you really are."

"Enrico," she whispers. "He had his reasons."

I slam my hand onto the desk, causing her to jump. "Do not defend him to me!" I yell.

She stares at me through her tears. "You fire anyone you want, get rid of the whole damn company, but if you care for me at all, Lorenzo stays. He's in his sixties now, and after thirty-five years of loyalty to Ferrara, this is how you are going to repay him? He is too old to get another job, Enrico, you know that."

"It's a business decision." My eyes hold hers. "You'll have no say."

"I'll never forgive you if you do this. I would mourn the breakdown of our relationship," she whispers. "Please don't do this."

My eyes hold hers. "Would you wear your widow blacks for me? Or is that a privilege saved for lying bastards?"

"You've gone insane."

"No. I'm defending my brothers' rights. This company is as much theirs as it is mine."

"They don't want it," she whispers through tears. "Have you lost your mind, Enrico? This isn't about your brothers, and you know that. This is about the deception, and I promise you, they only did it to protect you at your father's insistence. I understand why you are angry with him, but for God's sake, don't make your staff pay for his mistakes."

I glare at her, my anger rising dangerously close to the surface. "Giuliano and Stefano Ferrara are dead. I'm in charge now."

We stare at each other in a battle of the wills. For the first time in my life, I've seen a fiery side of my mother I didn't know existed.

"Why?" I ask. "Why did you stay married to him when you knew he loved another?"

She wipes away a tear, and guilt fills me. I hate that I'm upsetting her.

"Because, out of all the men in the world, nobody loved you and your brothers as much as your father did. He would have died in an instant to save your life."

This time, it's my eyes that glaze over.

"And I know that you feel betrayed, Enrico," she whispers, "but one day, when you have a son, you will feel the love that he had for you. You will understand that everything he did was only ever to protect you."

We stare at each other. So much hurt and regret swirls between us.

"It's true, your father and I didn't have the marriage you thought we did. Our love was unconditional. We adored each other until the day he died. He was, and still is, my best friend. He never lied to me, Enrico. Not once. I knew where he was during every minute of every day. He loved another, yes, but that wasn't his fault. You can't choose who you love. But he chose to stand by me—to honor our vows and care for his sons. Our relationship was special because we both knew what he sacrificed to have it."

Her silhouette blurs, and I blink to hide my tears. She stands, and with one last, lingering look, she walks quietly from the room.

I stare at the door to which she has just left through.

My heart hammers hard in my chest, and I pinch the bridge of my nose. Regret hits me hard. I've never been angry with my mother, but how can I not be? She's lied, covered up the truth, and chosen to protect him over us. We shouldn't have learned those things from a letter. She should have told us herself. Once again, she put his needs before anyone else's, including her own.

I stare straight ahead, and contempt runs through my blood like poison. I can feel its tentacles taking a hold of my soul, purging the last of the good memories from the part of my heart where my father lived for so long.

I've never despised him more than I do at this moment.

I hate that he's hurt me so deeply.

I hope he's rotting in Hell.

24

Enrico

I STARE at the computer screen in front of me. I've achieved nothing today.

My mind keeps going over and over my mother's words from earlier.

Don't you dare judge me.

Is that what I've done? Am I angry with her because she didn't stand up for herself like Olivia did with me? Does this have anything to do with my mother... or anyone but him? Is my anger being directed at the wrong people?

I exhale heavily and click into the spreadsheet that I'm supposed to be working on. My head is anywhere but here. Like my heart, it's scrambled.

I'm full of emotion, anger, hate, and sadness. But the biggest, is regret. A man I hero worshipped isn't who I thought he was... and now he's gone. I feel like I need to get to know him all over again but I can't. It's too late.

He's dead.

It's 1:00 p.m. when my intercom sounds. "Miss Reynolds is here to see you, Mr. Ferrara."

My heart somersaults at the sound of her name. This woman brings me so much happiness. "Send her in."

The door opens, and my love comes into view. Her beautiful face and high ponytail bring an instant smile to my face.

I stand. "Hello, bella." I take her into my arms and kiss her lips softly as I study her face. Big blue eyes smile up at me, filled with such love.

"I thought I would come and check on my man during my lunch break."

"Who brought you here?" I ask as I lead her over to my chair. I sit down and pull her onto my lap.

"Maso. Have you eaten?" she asks, concerned.

"I'm not hungry."

She pushes my hair back from my face. "You need to eat."

I bite her nipple through her blouse. "I'll eat you tonight."

She smiles as she wiggles away from me. Her eyes hold mine. "I've been thinking, and I've had an idea."

I chuckle. "Ah, the real reason you're here." I kiss her shoulder. "You didn't come to see if I'd eaten. Do tell."

"You know how we haven't had a very good week?"

"I think *that's* an understatement." Since the day after she moved in, I've been in Hell. My entire life seemed to fall apart with news of Angelina.

"Well, the thing is, I don't really like everyone around us when you're going through stuff. I think we need privacy."

I frown. "What do you mean?"

"There are too many people at Lake Como, and it's all the time. They walk in and out of the house. They gather out the front, they gather out the back, and it feels more like an airport than our home."

"It bothers you?"

She begins to fiddle with my tie. "More so now that you have things you are dealing with. I want us to have some time alone. We're just starting our lives together. I don't want us to have to share ourselves with anyone."

I watch her as I listen.

"Can I get a small apartment in Milan for the week?"

"What?"

"I want to get a place for us. Something... different."

I frown in confusion. "If you want to stay in Milan, we have an apartment here. In fact, we have, like, twenty."

She shakes her head. "No, I want a place without things."

"Huh?"

"I don't want fancy. I want to bring us back to basics, just you, me, and the clothes on our back. I want to simplify our lives completely."

"Olivia." I roll my eyes. "I am not staying in a dump just to prove a point."

"It won't be a dump." She kisses me softly and runs her hands up the back of my neck to try and sweeten the deal. "Please?"

"Olivia," I sigh. "This is unnecessary."

"Baby... please? It's just one week."

"No."

She bounces on my lap. "For me?"

My eyes hold hers. "Why?"

"I want to show you something, but I can't do it in a fancy house."

"It will be unsafe."

"No, I'll get an apartment, and the guards can stay downstairs. Lorenzo will check it over." She smiles, as if suddenly relieved. "Thank you."

"I didn't say yes."

She bounces off my lap. "Yes, you did."

"When did I?"

"Just now." She kisses me quickly. "I could see it in your eyes. I'll organize something and we'll go there tomorrow after work."

"You know, most women would be happy with your house in Lake Como and my property portfolio."

She smiles. "I'm not most women." She kisses me again. "Oh and, Lorenzo is here to see you. I brought him with me. I think you two need to talk."

My eyes hold hers.

"You need to make this right, Enrico."

I swing on my chair, and I exhale. "I don't like it when you call me that."

"Why not?"

"Because you only call me that when you're angry and scolding me."

"I love you, Rici," she whispers as she runs her fingers through my stubble.

I smirk at her. I would literally walk through fire to make her happy.

"That's better."

She kisses me one last time. "I'll send Lorenzo in."

"How are you getting back to the office?"

"Maso is going to take me."

"Have a nice afternoon."

"I'll be counting the hours until I see you." She blows me a kiss.

I smile, her playfulness is contagious. "Get out of here,

troublemaker, before you get yourself into *real* trouble." I tap the desk in front of me with my open palm.

"I wish." She gives me a sexy wink and disappears out of the door.

I turn back to my computer, and there's a knock on the door.

"Come in!" I call.

Lorenzo comes into view, and emotion fills me.

"Hello, Enrico," he says with caution.

I point to the chair at my desk, and he closes the door behind him. He walks in and takes a seat. We stare at each other. His eyes are sad.

Out of everyone I know, Lorenzo is someone I never thought would lie to me.

"Enrico. I know you feel betrayed."

I drop my head and stare at a random mark on my desk.

"Your father wanted you protected. We only followed his wishes."

I stay silent.

"This has all been a shock for you, and I understand that you're angry. I know that you don't like how this has come to light, but believe me, your father grew up with no secrets kept from him. He knew too much from a young age—too young. He battled through his childhood every day, and he despised his father for it. He didn't want that for you."

My eyes rise to meet his. "So, you lied to me?"

"We protected you. There's a big difference." A frown crosses his face. "And I stand by that decision." His jaw ticks. "One day, you will look back and understand that you wouldn't be the honorable man you now are if things had been different. If you knew then what you know now, it would have changed the way you saw the world. Your childhood was happy, and you were well adjusted. That was all your father ever wanted."

My breath quivers on the inhale.

"I will resign, if that's what you want." His eyes search mine. "But there is one thing you will have to do for me first."

"What?"

"You have to come and meet Angelina."

"Forget it."

"Enrico," his voice sharpens. "You are thirty-three years old and look how upset you are over this. Giuliano is going to find this out when he is only twenty-one. He is the child of a mistress. His whole world will crumble. Every single thing the thinks he knows is a lie... even his name. His father isn't the man he knew. He is your baby brother, Enrico. Whether you like it or not, you have to look after him. He is the true victim in this story. Him and his beautiful mother Angelina."

"Did you know her?" I whisper.

"Yes."

I frown.

"She's an incredible person, Enrico, and she deserves our respect. Stop looking at this like you're a hurt child, and begin thinking of it as a man who needs to step up and protect his family."

"She's not my family."

"Whether you like it or not, she is." He shakes his head. "She is a Ferrara. Maybe not by marriage, but most definitely by heart. She bleeds your father's blood, and he bled hers."

I drop my head.

"She gave up her entire life to be with him. She has been nothing but respectful and loving... even to your mother."

I frown as my eyes rise to meet his. "They know each other?"

"Of course, they know each other. They're friends—part of a family. It's not ideal, but they made it work. We all did." He stands and holds his hand out to me. "Come."

"Where to?'

"I'm taking you to Angelina. I don't care if you fire me, but as my promise to your father, you will meet your other family —the ones you didn't know."

The car pulls up to the gates of the house in Lake Como.

"Thank you," Lorenzo says from his place behind the wheel.

The guards look into the car and see me in the passenger seat. Their eyes widen, and they all stand back, granting us access.

"I thought the guards were taken off this house," I say as we drive through the gates.

"Your mother demanded they stay. She wanted them to remain safe. She's concerned for their wellbeing."

I begin to pale as another piece of my reality becomes lost.

The car pulls to a stop, and Lorenzo turns to me. "Do you want me to come in with you?"

I stare straight ahead. "No. I have to do this alone."

I get out of the car and walk up to the front door to ring the bell. I can hear the blood thumping throughout my body as the rest of the world seems to stop.

The door opens and Angelina stands before me. She's blonde and beautiful. "Hello, Enrico." She smiles sadly.

I nod, unable to push a word past my lips.

She steps back and gestures to inside. "Please, come in."

I walk in the door and look up. My step falters as I'm taken aback, and my eyes instantly fill with tears. A huge painting hangs on the wall in the entryway. It's at least six feet tall, and it's a hand-painted picture of my father with her and their son.

He's squatting down in a field of white flowers. The small boy, who looks only around three years old at the time, is sitting on his knee, looking up at him. My father's arm is wrapped lovingly around the woman who is sitting on the grass beside them.

Her.

They look happy. So in love.

I drop my head, unable to move from the spot. Unable to speak through the lump in my throat. This is too much. I need to leave.

I can feel him. His spirit is here... with her.

Angelina gives me a sympathetic smile. "Just this way," she says softly. We walk into the living area, and I frown as I look around. There are photos of my father everywhere. It's like a shrine.

My thoughts go to my mother's house, and how she has not one photo of him anywhere.

So different.

"Please, take a seat." She offers me a chair, and I sit down awkwardly. "Can I get you a coffee, tea?"

Scotch, I think to myself. "No, thank you."

She sits down opposite me, and I inhale as I try to calm myself down. I just want to hurl abuse her way.

"I know this isn't what you wanted," she starts.

I clench my jaw. My eyes roam over her coffee table, and I count the candles to try and distract myself.

"I'm scared for my son," she says quietly.

My eyes rise to meet hers. "You should be."

Her face falls. "I know you hate me."

"Yes… I do."

"Please don't take this out on him." Her eyes fill with tears. "He needs you. He needs your support."

"What makes you think that I would want anything to do with him?"

"He's your brother, and you're a loyal man. I've watched you grow up."

"From my father's bed."

She screws up her face and I close my eyes in regret. "This is pointless." I stand and turn to walk out.

She stands in a rush. "Don't go, please. I don't know how to navigate this with Giuliano. I need your help."

I stop still.

"Hate me all you want, but please don't turn your back on him. You are his only family. He is your brother, Enrico."

I close my eyes, disgusted with the position I find myself in.

"Can I bring him to you? Just meet him. Please. Just once. I won't tell him who you are. He doesn't find out anything for another three years yet, but I do need to prepare him. When the time comes and he finds out the truth, he will turn his back on me. If he doesn't have the love and support of his brothers, he will be all alone in the world." Her voice cracks. "He is just a child."

I stare at the wall in front of me.

"Please, Enrico. If not for us, do it for your father."

I close my eyes, knowing my conscience is getting in the way of my better judgement.

"Bring him to my house on Sunday afternoon," I say flatly with my back to her.

"Thank you."

I stand with my back to her for a few minutes, we don't speak, we don't move…eventually when I can't take the silence anymore, I walk out of the house. That is the first and last time I will ever come here.

Olivia

"So?" Natalie raises her glass my way. "Tell me everything."

I smile at my inquisitive friend. We're in a bar, after work, having a few drinks. Enrico is picking me up in half an hour. "About?" I ask.

She leans in and whispers, "You know…the creepy bodyguard."

"Him." I roll my eyes in disgust. "He's not a bodyguard. He works for Enrico."

"Doing what?"

I frown. "I don't even know to be honest."

"Are you sure he was in your bathroom?"

"No." I shrug and glance around at Maso and Marley who are leaning up against the wall at the front of the bar, watching me from a safe distance. "Maybe I imagined the whole thing. It does seem random, doesn't it?"

"Did he seem creepy the night you met him? When he asked for your number."

"No, but then he gave me the look that day at Enrico's. It seemed so out of order, and it threw me."

"The come fuck me look?"

"Uh-huh." I sip my drink and shrug. "I don't know; I'm probably imagining the entire thing. He could be married with five kids."

"Where's your other friend gone—the gay guy?" She frowns.

"Oh, Giorgio has been in Roma. He comes back this week."

"How long has he been gone for?"

"Two weeks, I think. He works between the two offices. I'm looking forward to him coming back. I've missed him." I smile as I watch my friend, and I tuck a piece of her hair behind her ear. "You look well, Nat. Milan agrees with you."

"Thanks." She smiles. "You, too. How's it going with Mr. Italy?"

"Good. Great, actually." I smile back at her. "He's so fucking beautiful, Nat."

"Liv, just be careful. This guy broke you twice already."

"I know, but it's different now."

Her eyes hold mine. "Have you met his family?"

"No."

She rolls her lips, unimpressed.

"Only because it's been hectic. He's had so much on, and there are people in the fucking house all the time."

"What do you mean?"

"There's security, drivers, cooks, and house maintenance. I'm lucky to get him alone for two minutes. If we do, we go to bed and end up fucking all night and I forget everything I wanted to talk about."

She gives an over exaggerated eye roll. "Oh, poor you, cooks and cleaners and a sex god. Sounds woeful," she mutters dryly. "How do you cope?"

I smirk. "When you put it like that."

She raises her glass and we clink them. "To Italians." She smirks.

"To Italians," I repeat with a giggle. My phone vibrates on

the table, and the name Rici lights up the screen. "Hello," I answer.

"Hello, my bella," his deep voice purrs down the phone.

A goofy grin erupts at the sound of his voice. "Hi," I breathe.

Natalie rolls her eyes at me.

"We are just coming out of the offices now. I'll be there in five minutes," he says.

"Okay, see you soon."

He hangs up.

"Look at you," Natalie sighs. "You're like all starry-eyed when you speak to him."

I smile as I drain my glass. "He's the one, Nat. I'll bet my life on it. I'm marrying him."

"Oh, Jesus. Just calm down for two minutes. It's, like, week six."

"I know, but sometimes you just know these things. I have to go. Are you coming to the gym with me in the morning?"

"What time you going?"

"Seven—seven thirtyish."

"I can't, I'm starting at eight."

"I'm so excited you got the job."

Her eyes widen. "Can you believe it? Me! A personal assistant to a judge."

"So, you're going to wear what we talked about? The black suit."

"Yes." She scrambles around under the table and finds the plastic bag. "Thanks for the shoes. I'll give them back as soon as I have time to buy some new ones."

"It's a pleasure loaning you sensible work heels so you can look hot for your new boss."

She giggles. "Oh my God, you should see this guy."

"I can't wait to." I glance up and see Maso on the phone. His eyes meet mine across the bar, and I know Enrico is here. "Got to go." I give my friend a hug and a kiss, and make my way out of the bar.

Maso and Marley fall in beside me. We walk out and see the black Mercedes wagon parked in the loading bay. Maso opens the back door, and there he sits. My man is wearing a navy suit and a white shirt. With his black, curly hair, and the most perfect chiseled jawline in all of history, it's a sight to behold. His big brown eyes meet mine.

"Hello, my darling," he says softly.

My heart stops...knowing that I am the only person who gets this side of him.

Enrico Ferrara hates most of the world...but he loves me.

With all of his heart, he loves me.

I have to stop myself from diving across the seat to him. "Hi." I get into the car and shimmy across the back seat to kiss him softly. He glances at the rearview mirror, reminding me we are not alone. Annoyed, I go back to my seat and put my seatbelt on. He smiles and his eyes linger on my face. He picks up my hand and kisses the back of it as the car pulls out into the traffic.

"How is your friend?" he asks.

"Good," I breathe. *I've missed him today.* "How was your day?"

"Average." He gives me a slow sexy smile. "Better now."

My eyes search his. I try to send him a telepathic message telling him how much I've missed him. I wish these damn men in the front seat weren't with us all the time.

"Me, too," he whispers.

My heart somersaults. He understood what I wanted to tell him. I put my head back onto the headrest and smile dreamily.

With our entwined hands resting on his thigh, we drive through the night, back to Lake Como.

He falls silent as he stares out the window, deep in thought. I watch him. What was it like to grow up in these conditions? To never have the freedom to say what you want, when you want. My thoughts go to his mother. She would have been guarded around the clock, too. How did she feel when her husband left her to go another woman? I mean, it's bad enough that she knew where he was, but to have all these spectators bear witness to it must have only magnified the horror.

God.... I feel sorry for her. That poor, poor woman.

Everyone says that Enrico is the vision of his father—like him in personality, too. I can't imagine loving him like I do, while he loved another. To have him leave me every week to go to her would remove a piece of my heart every time he left.

It seems like the slowest, cruelest form of torture.

"Aye, aye, what's this?" Maso asks.

Lights flash on the road ahead, and we look up to see a man with an orange roadworks flag pulling cars over. He directs us to pull to the side, and the men in the front all shuffle about in their jackets.

Enrico immediately bends and rustles around under the seat. He takes a gun out and tucks it into his suit jacket.

My eyes widen. *What the fuck?* What's he doing?

Is something happening right now?

I hold my breath as my heart begins to thump hard in my chest.

The man comes up to the window, and Maso smiles casually as he winds it down. "Buonasera, agente." *Translation: good evening, officer.*

The policeman nods and looks into the car with a torch. He shines it in everyone's faces.

"Qual è il problema?" Maso asks. *Translation: what seems to be the problem?*

"Ha un documento d'identità?" *Translation: do you have identification?*

Maso takes his license out and passes it over. The policeman studies it.

"Apra il bagagliaio." *Translation: open the trunk.*

Maso motions to open his door.

"Rimanga dentro la macchina." *Translation: stay inside the car.*

Another policeman comes over, and they look through the trunk together while we all remain silent.

"Dove sta andando?" the officer asks. *Translation: where are you going?*

"Riportando a casa il signor Ferrara. Sono la sua guardia del corpo." *Translation: driving Mr. Ferrara home. I am his security.*

The policeman's face falls and he looks into the backseat with his torch. He immediately bows his head.

"Mi scusi, signor Ferrara. Buonanotte, signore." *Translation: my apologies, Mr Ferrara. Have a nice night, sir.*

"Cosa state cercando?" Enrico asks. *Translation: what are you looking for?*

"Abbiamo un evaso che si ritiene stia fuggendo in questa direzione. Fate attenzione stanotte." *Translation: we have a prison escapee who is believed to be heading this way. Be careful tonight.*

He hands Maso's license back to him and waves his flag. We pull back out into the traffic. Enrico and the men continue on as if nothing has happened.

I stare out the window into the darkness with my heart

hammering in my chest. He has a gun. He has a fucking gun in his car. They all have them.

Who do they think is coming for them?

And why are they all so fucking prepared for it?

For the rest of the trip, I pretend to sleep. My mind, however, is anything but relaxed. I just saw it with my own eyes, as casual as casual can be. The crime. It's still alive and well.

They honestly believe that someone is coming for Enrico.

They thought it was an ambush, and they were armed and ready. They were calm, cool, and collected. Fear is filtering through my bloodstream. Who would want my man harmed, and what the actual fuck is going on around here?

I feel sick.

Enrico reaches forward and tucks his gun back under his seat. He picks up my hand, kisses my fingertips, and rests it down onto his thick thigh.

I watch him in the darkness as he stares straight ahead, unrattled.

Focused.

Who the hell am I in love with?

25

Olivia

HALF AN HOUR LATER, the car pulls into Oliviana.

"We are home," Enrico says with a soft smile.

I wait in my seat as Maso comes around and opens my door. I get out and look around me. Two other cars have pulled up behind ours. They were obviously following us home. Enrico begins to chat with one of the men in the car behind us, and I watch him converse with them. He chuckles at something someone says, and they all break into chatter.

Totally at ease.

This is his normal. This is his safety net. He turns and notices me standing on the spot, and he comes over to take my hand.

"Come, Olivia."

He leads me into the house and shuts the door behind us. He puts his arm around me and pulls me close, kissing my temple carefully before we turn and walk through to the kitchen. Antonia is cooking dinner.

She turns to us with a big smile. "Ciao, signorina Olivia."

"Ciao." I smile. I've been practicing what to say to her. "Grazie per aver cucinato la cena." *Translation: thank you for cooking dinner.*

Enrico's eyes glow with tenderness as he watches us.

"Ha un profumo straodinario," he says. *Translation: it smells amazing.*

Her mouth falls open and she claps her hands together. "Signorina Olivia, così bella in italiano." *Translation: Miss Olivia, so beautiful in Italian.*

I smile bashfully. "Grazie."

Enrico goes to the fridge and takes out a bottle of wine. He collects two crystal glasses, too, and I watch as he pours us both one.

"Let's go sit on the terrace," he says, handing me my glass.

We walk outside and take a seat at the table. He lights the candles in the center.

His eyes watch me as he takes a sip. "You're very quiet."

I'm feeling overly emotional—like I might burst into tears at any moment.

I sip my wine.

His eyes stay glued to me. "What is it?"

I shrug, feeling stupid. I knew all this about him. Nothing new has come to light tonight, but for the first time, I'm unsettled. I'm feeling a new emotion.

I'm frightened.

I stare down at the table. "I wish you were just a delivery man."

His eyes hold mine.

"I wish you and I had a chance to be normal."

A frown crosses his brow. “You wouldn’t love me if I were normal, Olivia.”

“You’re wrong.” I smile as my eyes well with tears. I sip my wine, disgusted with my dramatics. “Ignore me,” I sigh. “I’m hormonal or something.”

“I’ll talk to the staff. They’ll be more discrete.”

I nod.

He leans over and takes my hand across the table. “Tell me about your plan—the one where you show me something.”

I shrug. “Doesn’t matter now.”

“Why not?”

“Because I would be beside myself with worry about you the entire time.”

He exhales and turns his gaze to the lake.

“How did your father and grandfather die, Enrico?” I ask.

“Car accident.”

“What caused their car accident?”

“They were run off the road.”

My heart constricts as I watch him, so detached and cold.

“Is that why you have so much security?” I ask.

“Yes.”

“Are you in danger?”

He clenches his jaw but stays silent. I can see his answer as clear as day in his eyes.

That means yes.

My eyes well with tears again. Damn these hormones. Why am I such a crybaby today?

“What did you want to show me, Olivia?”

“I wanted to take you to a little one-bedroom apartment with no fancy furnishings, no staff, and nobody around. I wanted to show you that our love was enough. That that’s all we need.”

His eyes search mine. "I already know that, my love," he whispers sadly.

"You scare me."

He gives my hand a reassuring squeeze.

"I know how our story ends, Rici," I whisper.

"How?"

"You're either going to be arrested and put in jail... or you will be killed."

Our eyes are locked.

"Either way, we don't get a happy ending... do we?"

He drops his head, saddened by my epiphany. "I'm not going anywhere, Olivia. This is who I am, though, and you need to get your head around that. I've tried to protect you as much as I can from my working life at Ferrara."

"I know," I mutter.

"I just need you to love me—to not ask questions. Let me handle business, and you handle our relationship. Keep me in check when I'm working too much." He smiles softly. "Keep the two things separate. When I come home, I just want to be happy with my family and forget everything else."

"How can I keep it separate when we do nothing else?"

He frowns. "What do you mean?"

"We have no friends outside of Ferrara. Your staff are everywhere I look. I just want a normal Saturday night date with friends and to..." I shrug. God, I don't even know what I want. "I just want you to be a boring old delivery man and for us to live completely alone."

He chuckles. "Okay."

"Okay?" I frown.

"Let's go and stay in Milan at my apartment for a few days. It's a lot more private there. I'll speak to the staff about being more discreet for when we come back home to Lake Como. You have to remember, I have never had a partner. They aren't used to keeping my woman happy."

I smile over at him. "Thank you."

"But I don't want you worrying yourself sick over me."

"I can't help it."

"You need to stop, Olivia. If you begin to think negatively about my line of work, you will drive yourself insane. I am a Ferrara. I can't change it. I wouldn't even if I could. This is your life now, and you need to adjust."

I nod as his words sink in. "I know."

His eyes hold mine and he gives me a slow, sexy smile.

Butterflies dance in my stomach at the intensity of his gaze, it could start a fire. "What?"

"You are completely delusional if you think anything could drag me away from you."

I smile softly.

He shrugs casually. "It's just not happening."

"You know, for a big, tough guy, you say some pretty romantic things, Mr. Ferrara."

He pats his lap, and I go to him. "Do you feel better now?" he asks as he slides his hands around to my behind.

"Yes."

"Do you still wish I was a delivery man?"

I giggle as I get a vision of him driving a delivery truck. "Actually, I do."

My back arches, and I wake to the feeling of my toes tingling.

His strong, thick tongue sweeps through my sex, and my legs open wider instinctively.

Fuck. A Rici Ferrara wake up call.

I put my hand on the top of his head and look down at him. His eyes are closed as he licks me up. He lifts my legs over his shoulders.

"Good morning, Rici," I whisper.

He smiles against me. "Hmm," he hums. "It is a good morning."

He pulls back and, with his eyes locked on mine, his pale pink tongue licks me slow and deep.

My insides clench. He is so fucking hot, I can't deal.

He loves this. He loves my taste. He loves the act. He loves to give me pleasure.

And, dear God, does he ever.

With his eyes locked on mine, he begins to flick his tongue in a way only he knows how, and I lose my mind. His big red lips are glistening with my arousal.

I've never seen a more gorgeous man.

My man.

He begins to really eat me as I writhe beneath him. He goes up onto his knees, puts his hand down to his cock, and he begins to stroke it.

I can see the pre-ejaculate beading. His strokes get harder, as does his tongue, and I can't hold it.

I love this about him, I love that he has to touch himself when he touches me.

It's the ultimate turn on.

"Get up here," I whisper.

He smiles into me, and I grab a handful of his hair to drag him up to me. He brings my legs with him, still over his shoulders.

He slides in deep, and we both moan as we fall still.

Hearts are banging hard in our chests against each other. Our eyes are locked. He's so broad that he stretches me to the max, every damn time.

The burn is so fucking good.

"Oh, bella," he whispers by my ear. "You fuck me so well, baby."

I smile as he slowly slides out.

"I can feel every muscle inside this beautiful cunt." He pushes back in hard, and I convulse with a deep shudder. As soon as he starts talking dirty, it's all over.

His lips take mine aggressively, and I can taste my arousal.

"Fuck me," he growls. "Fuck me hard."

Oh God.

Nobody fucks like Rici Ferrara.

Nobody.

I bounce into the gym just past seven.

"Good morning." I smile at the receptionist as I walk past.

"Hello," she says as she winds the vacuum cord up. "Nice day, isn't it?"

"Gorgeous!" I call as I get onto the treadmill and crank it up.

To be honest, I hadn't even noticed the weather. Every day is a good day to me lately. Mr. Ferrara is an expert at putting a smile on my face. I've never felt so adored in all my life.

I walk briskly as I try to warm up.

"Good morning." I look over to see the girl I met when I was in here last time.

"Oh, hi." I smile.

She frowns at me. "I'm sorry. What was your name again? I'm terrible with names."

I laugh. "I'm crap, too. I'm Olivia. What's yours?"

"Jennifer."

"Hi, Jennifer." I smile. I like this girl. It's nice having an Aussie around.

She climbs onto the walker beside me and starts it up. "Bring on the cardio." She huffs as she turns it up. "I swear, I've put on five kilos since I moved here. I'm eating pasta with every meal, topped off with wine and cocktails. I'm going to be a fat cow."

"Me, too," I chuckle.

She walks briskly, her high ponytail bouncing behind her. "We went to this restaurant last night and it was incredible. Dominion. Have you been there?"

"No." I frown. "Good?"

"They have this soft-shell chili crab. It's to *die for*, and worth every fucking calorie." She puts her hand over her heart and closes her eyes.

I laugh at her dramatics. "I'll have to try it."

"You seriously do."

We walk in silence for a few minutes. "What are you doing today?" I puff.

"Looking for a job," she says. "I had a week off and the plan was to wait until I found something that I really love, but I'm getting homesick." She pants as she walks briskly. "I figure I need to keep busy."

"Yeah, I get that. The time difference does my head in. Every time I want to chat, my parents are in bed."

"Right?" she huffs.

"So, your boyfriend's family are here in Milan?" I ask.

She shakes her head. "No, he's from Naples. He moved here for a new job. Started three days after I arrived so he doesn't know anyone, either. We're like complete losers with no friends."

"We'll have to have to go out for dinner sometime—the four of us. Oh, and my best friend is here from Australia, too. I'll introduce you to her. She's lovely. Mad as all hell, but so much fun. I tried to get her to come this morning but she's starting a new job today."

"Where did she look for her job? Is there a website or something? I have no idea where to even start."

"I'll ask her and text you. Remind me to get your number before I leave." I'm so unfit, I can hardly talk while I walk.

"That would be great. I think when I find a good base of friends, I'll be fine. What's your boyfriend like?"

Oh jeez, what do I say to that. "Quiet and bossy." I smile. "He likes to get his own way."

She laughs. "Don't they all?"

"I guess."

"How did you meet him?"

"We met in Rome two years ago. Things didn't turn out, so I went home to Australia. I moved back here for a job just recently and we ran into each other."

Jennifer smiles as she listens. "Sounds romantic, and it's obviously serious?"

"Yeah, it is. It turned serious really quick, actually. We fell in love last time we met, and then as soon as we reconnected and we got over a few teething problems, it was all systems go."

"It was obviously meant to be."

"I think so." I smile. "I moved in with him nearly immediately." I walk up the incline on the treadmill. I don't know why I put this thing on such a steep setting.

"Yeah, well I'm not sure about this living with him thing yet. Maybe we're about to have teething problems, too. As in, me knocking his out."

We both laugh. She's funny.

"Okay, my warmup is done," she says. "I have to do arms

today. Thanks for that. Just ask your friend if she used a job agency or what way she thinks I should go."

"Okay." I smile. "I'll come get your number before I go so I can text you later."

"That'd be great, thank you so much."

I watch her walk over to the weights area. A guy says something to her, and she laughs out loud. She's so typically Australian—relaxed and carefree.

I like her. I'm going to make an effort to get to know her better. It would be nice to have another friend here. I'll have to remember to call Nat for her later.

I turn up the speed on my treadmill and start to run.

Hot body, here I come.

It's 1:00 p.m. when Giorgio comes swanning into my office with two cups of coffee in hand.

"Hello, my darling. I came for our afternoon tea." He holds up a brown paper bag and gives it a shake.

I look up from my computer and smile. "Is that cake?"

Please let it be cake. I'm tired of eating healthy already. It's been eight whole hours and I'm feeling weak.

He passes my coffee and hands me the bag over. "Almond biscotti."

"Thank you."

He sits on my desk and sips his coffee. "This place is so dull today. I miss the Roma office."

"What's it like? The Roma office. Did you see Seraphina?"

"Yes, Seraphina and I had cocktails last week." He smiles wistfully. "She's divine."

"She really is," I sigh. "I wish she'd stayed in Milan. We really clicked."

I smile, remembering that heart attack she gave me.

"What?"

"You know, when I met her and she told me that she had a fiancé from Roma, I was sure it was Enrico. I was having a heart attack over it."

He chuckles. "What a coincidence that would have been." He watches me for a moment and narrows his eyes. "She is not good enough for Enrico Ferrara."

"She's beautiful. Are you high?" I scoff.

"She's not as beautiful as you." He smiles wistfully. "You have an inner quality. There is something very special about you, Olivia. You were sent from the gods for him. I could feel it from the moment we met."

"Do you mind?" a deep voice says from the doorway.

We turn to see Enrico standing at the door. He raises a brow. "Hands off, Giorgio."

I smile and stand. "This is a pleasant surprise."

Enrico walks in and kisses my cheek. "Hello, bella," he says softly as his hand falls to my waist.

Giorgio leaps up from the desk. "My darling Enrico." He kisses both his cheeks, and Enrico smiles.

"You're visiting me at work?" I ask. "This is lovely."

"Just delivering a package." He places a little black box with a gold ribbon tied around it onto my desk.

I smile as my eyes hold his.

He gives me a sexy wink.

Enrico turns to Giorgio. "Last night, Olivia told me she wishes I was a delivery driver."

Giorgio face falls as he looks at me, and then he claps his hands and bursts out laughing.

"Can you imagine that?" Rico says, clearly amused as his sexy eyes hold mine.

"You? A delivery driver?" Giorgio scoffs. "Now I've heard it all."

"Don't laugh, you two," I huff as I fall back into my office chair. "I actually do wish you were a normal, podgy old guy with a boring job."

Enrico laughs heartily, it's deep and loud and permeates through the room. "What is podgy? It does not sound in the least bit appealing."

I try to think of an apt description. "Sort of fat and pig like."

They laugh again, thinking this is the funniest thing that they have ever heard. It's annoying that the thought of him being fat and pig like is so amusing to these two. I hate that he's so damn gorgeous. I want what's on the inside. I couldn't care less about his fancy packaging, and I'm not even joking. I really do wish he was a podgy delivery driver because then we could have a normal life.

My phone rings.

"Excuse me for a moment," I say to them before answering. "Hello."

Enrico

I watch Olivia answer the phone. She begins to write in her diary, and a smile crosses my face.

"Oh, Rico," Giorgio whispers. "Look at you." He grabs me by the elbows and inspects my face. "Happiness suits you, my friend."

I glance back at Olivia still on the phone. I find it hard to look anywhere else. "What are you doing this afternoon?" I whisper to Giorgio.

Giorgio frowns. “Why?”

“I want to go shopping. Olivia needs a new wardrobe and I could use your help.”

Giorgio clasps his hands together. “She does. I’ll cross myself off for the afternoon.”

“Meet me in the foyer in ten minutes?”

Giorgio winks and blows Olivia a kiss. She gives him a wave, and he disappears out the door.

“Goodbye,” she says, ending her call.

Her eyes find me again. I close her office door and take her in my arms.

“Rico,” she whispers. “I’m at work.”

“I know.” My lips drop to her neck. “But, as the delivery driver, I didn’t get a signature yet.” I take her lips in mine, my tongue slowly sliding through her mouth. I feel my arousal begin to flutter.

She pulls back from my kiss. “Rico, not now.”

I smile and give her behind a hard squeeze. “It has come to my attention that delivery drivers are seriously underpaid and underfucked. Where is my motivation to deliver more packages?”

She giggles. “Well, one would hope that you don’t expect sex for every parcel you deliver. What kind of delivery man are you? Go home, I’ll see you tonight.”

With one last kiss, I turn toward the door.

“Rici.” I turn back and stare into her eyes. “Ti amo.” She smiles.

My heart somersaults, and I move to take her back in my arms. “Let’s go home now,” I breathe.

“No, I’m working.”

“Resign, you don’t have to work here.” I kiss her again.

“You are an awfully distracting delivery driver.”

I stare down at my beautiful girl, she brings me a happiness that I never knew was possible.

I kiss her one more time. "Until tonight, my love."

I walk down the corridor toward the elevators and my phone rings. It's Sergio. He's in Sicily.

"Hey," I answer.

"We've got a problem."

I roll my eyes. I don't need this shit today. "What is it?"

"Lombardi has been going around town stating that he owns Sicily and Roma now—that he has run Ferrara out. He's boasting that we have retracted with our tails between our legs. People are beginning to stop and take notice of him. His cocaine is top quality."

I exhale heavily. "We know that's not true, don't we?"

"My intel tells me that he's coming to Milan."

"Why?"

"He wants our brothels. He's coming to scope them out."

"I won't let that happen."

"We need to take back the blow, Enrico."

"No." I feel my anger rise. We have been arguing about drugs for months.

"We need the cocaine market. We cannot pick and choose what we own. We either own everything, or we have nothing. You know that it's only matter of time before he becomes so powerful that nothing will stand in his way. He has five hundred men on his team now, and that number is growing every day. If he gets even more power, if he takes the reigns, we know what happens next."

I clench my jaw.

"What happened last time when someone became power hungry, Enrico? What happened when they tried to take the crown?"

I close my eyes.

My father was killed in cold blood.

"I'm not a drug dealer, Sergio. I will never be a lowlife fucking drug dealer," I whisper angrily.

"Ferrara has fought for thirty fucking years to hold our territory, and now you are going to just let them waltz in and take it without a fight?" he growls.

"We are smarter than that."

"You are not being smart. You need to fucking level up, Enrico. Our girls are living in fear of him coming into our brothels. We have all but handed him our cocaine racket. What's next? The gambling? Then what? Then what's he going to fucking take?"

I clench my jaw as I stare at the wall. "Barr him."

"What?"

"He and his staff are not to step foot in our brothels or gaming lounges again."

"He'll go crazy. His favorite girl is one of our high-end units. He won't not see her without a fight. You'll start an all-out war."

"Then we go to war."

I sit in the parking bay outside Olivia's office.

It's after 6:00 p.m. now, and she's finished work for the day. I watch for the moment she sees me. Her eyes light up before she makes her way to the car.

"Hi." She beams as she bounces in. "You finished work already?" She leans over and kisses me.

"I took the afternoon off." I pull out into the traffic.

"Oh." A frown mars her face. "What did you do?"

"Picked up a few things, delivered a few parcels."

"Well, I hope I'm the only parcel recipient." She smirks.

I take her hand. "One and only." I kiss her fingertips.

Her eyes hold mine, and she gets this dreamy smile on her face—the one that makes me want to be a better man.

We drive in comfortable silence for a while as I navigate through the traffic. Olivia eventually begins to chatter and talk about her day. She tells me about her new shoes giving her blisters, and a man at work who annoys her. A movie she wants to watch on Netflix tonight, also. Basically, anything that pops into her head. I smile as I listen to her. She's so disarmingly normal.

"Have you been back to the apartment yet today?" she asks.

"Yes." I pull into the underground parking lot. The two security cars pull in behind us. I park the car and take Olivia's hand. We make our way into to the elevator. "Feels like ages since we came here."

"Hmm," I mutter, distracted. "Did you like your present?" I ask, noticing that she hasn't mentioned it.

"Oh, I love it. I just didn't open it yet."

"How do you know that you love it then?"

"Because you gave it to me. Besides, you know material gifts aren't really my thing."

I frown. "What do you mean?"

"Material things aren't the type of present I want from you."

Great. Now this night may not go the way I had planned. "What does that mean?"

"Nothing, sorry. I sound ungrateful. I'll open my gift as soon as we get to the apartment." She leans up onto her toes and kisses me. "Thank you. You're very thoughtful."

The elevator doors open, and I put my hand into my suit pockets and pause as I wait for her to step forward. Her eyes fly around in wonder. "Enrico!" she gasps. "What in the world…?"

I wince as I look around. Maybe I went a little too far.

There are bags and bags of designer clothes all around. Shoes boxes are stacked in two lots of ten. There's Christian Louboutin, Manolo Blahnik's, Valentino, Jimmy Choo, plus a few racks with evening dresses lined up. Six huge bunches of red roses sit in large crystal vases, and there's a sliver tray of chocolate covered strawberries beside a bottle of the best champagne money can buy.

Her eyes come to mine. "What did you do?" Her tone is clipped.

I shrug casually, trying to play it down. "I took the liberty of buying you a few things."

She frowns as she looks around. "This isn't a few things. This is an entire shop."

"You had nothing."

"I don't need all this," she scoffs. "And, I didn't have nothing. I had you. That's all I need." She gives a disgusted shake of her head and walks up the stairs.

"You're welcome!" I call as I survey the fruits of my shopping expedition.

"Yeah, thanks!" she calls out.

"Are you going to come and open them?"

"No, it's okay. You do it." She's upstairs now. "These things are your jam, not mine."

"You know, you could at least be a little excited," I call.

"Cook me dinner. That will excite me. You know… like a normal boyfriend."

I frown. What? "I don't cook, and I don't do fucking normal."

"Ha, funny that. I don't speak Italian but I'm learning because I know *you* like it."

I roll my eyes. Here we go. *Smartass.*

I hear the shower turn on, and I give the Louboutin box a subtle kick with my toe.

"Well, that fucking backfired, didn't it?" I mutter under my breath. "Cook her dinner. What next?"

It's just past 10:00 p.m. and I'm lying on the sofa behind Olivia. She's in her pyjamas, watching a movie on Netflix. She's makeup free, relaxed, and happy. Her blonde hair is splayed across my arm. The sound of her laughter makes me smile. I have no idea what she's watching—some Jennifer Aniston movie.

While she watches the movie, I'm watching her.

Her smile is like a drug to me. Her soft soul has carved its way under my skin, and her body... God... it's an addiction I have to feed.

I've never felt like this—never had any idea that I could be so intoxicated by a single person.

I'm drunk on the feeling she gives me. My heart is literally in her hands.

She told me tonight that she doesn't need anything money can buy, and for the first time in my life, I actually understood it.

Being here with her is the ultimate prize.

I tighten my arms around her and pull her close. She laughs out loud again.

"This is the most hilarious show ever," she tells me.

I smile into her hair. "I know, bella," I lie. "I know."

Olivia

We drive up the huge driveway through the rolling green hills and I look around in awe. Just when I think that I've become accustomed to Enrico's money, he brings me here to this next level mansion, his mother's house.

"She knows we're coming, right?" I ask nervously.

His eyes flick over as he concentrates on the road. "Of course, she does."

I glance behind us to see the cavalcade of cars trailing us up the majestic road that pretends to be a driveway.

"What did she say when you said you were bringing me here?" I ask.

He frowns at my stupid question and he holds his hand up as it rests on top of the steering wheel. "Good, see you then."

"Oh right." I nod. "She knows I'm Australian, right?"

"Yes."

I get a vision of her hurling abuse in Italian and chasing me away from her beloved boy with a rolling pin. "Because I just want to know what her reaction will be to me."

"Olivia." Enrico puts his hand on my thigh. "Stop worrying."

I nod as I peer out the window at all the white horses in the paddocks. I turn to him suddenly panicked. "She won't want to go horse riding, will she?" My face falls in horror. "Because I don't know how to ride horses, Enrico. It's just going to be awkward and she'll hate me forever."

He breaks into a deep chuckle and squeezes my thigh. "You ride very well."

"This isn't funny," I snap.

"Olivia." He looks over at me. "My mother just wants to see me happy."

My worried eyes hold his.

"And I am." He smiles broadly. "Stupidly happy."

I nod, mollified for the moment. "Okay." We pull up to the house and my heart begins to pump hard.

Please let her like me. Please let her like me.

I don't know much about Italy, and I don't know much about mother-in-law's. But I do know that Italian mothers are supposed to be crazy possessive over their children. Especially their sons.

I look down at myself and smooth my dress. "Are you sure I look alright?" I whisper. "Maybe I should have worn pants?"

He rolls his eyes and gets out of the car and I sit nervously as he comes around and opens my door. The property is huge and fancy, even the gates back at the road were gilded gold. There is security *everywhere* and this is next level fucking terrifying.

"I'm so nervous," I tell him.

"Really?" he says with a sexy wink as he helps me out of the car. "I would never have guessed."

"What if she doesn't like me?" I whisper as he takes my hand in his.

"She will, but it won't matter if she doesn't." He kisses me softly. "Because I like you."

"I thought you loved me." I frown.

"That, too." He smirks.

It's Saturday morning and we are at his mother's house. He's brought me here to meet them. His grandmother is away this weekend. I know he's been strategically waiting for a chance to introduce me to them when she's not here.

Hand in hand we walk up the front steps and as I hold my breath, he opens the door.

A beautiful woman comes into view. I remember her from the ball before Enrico and I got back together. She has long dark hair that's perfectly styled. She's wearing a black fitted dress with high heels. Not exactly what I would call Saturday loungewear.

She looks like some exotic Italian movie star, so glamourous and beautiful. Knowing her history, I was expecting a mousy woman of some sort, but this woman is a knockout.

"Hello, my son," she says, her voice is soft, hushed and her accent is beautiful.

She kisses Enrico on both cheeks.

Enrico's eyes come to me and he smiles proudly. "Mamma, please meet my Olivia and Olivia, may I present my mother, Bianca Ferrara."

She smiles and holds out her hand. "Hello, Olivia. It's lovely to meet you."

"Hello." I smile as I shake her hand, nerves tumble in my stomach, I feel like I'm about to swallow my tongue. "So, lovely to meet you, too."

Enrico turns to the girl who has just appeared beside his mother. "And this is my pride and joy, Francesca." He presents a young girl, his only sister. She's young, beautiful in a crème tracksuit, she has long thick dark hair and the most unusual colored eyes I've ever seen. She looks like a fashion model.

Bianca holds her arm out in a welcoming gesture. "Please, do come in." She turns and walks down the hall as if it's a catwalk and I widen my eyes at Enrico. He smiles playfully and squeezes my hand. I'm glad he thinks this is so amusing, I'm beyond terrified.

We walk through the grand palace and out into the back

area, the house is as big as Enrico's but it has more antiques in it. It feels more formal and less house like. "Just out to the terrace." She smiles as she gestures outside.

Enrico leads me through and past a beautiful white kitchen and out through concertina doors to a mosaic terrace that overlooks a huge pool. The house sits high and rolling green hills can be seen for miles, my mouth falls open in awe. "Oh my gosh, this is beautiful out here," I gasp.

Bianca smiles as she looks around. "It is." She takes a seat at the table and Enrico pulls out a chair for me. "We take it for granted sometimes."

A young woman appears from the house wearing a traditional white maids uniform. "Marcella, puoi portarmi un caffé, per favore?" *Translation: Marcella, can you bring some coffee and tea please?*

The young woman's eyes flick to Enrico and she nods her head nervously in a greeting. "Buongiorno, signor Ferrara." *Translation: hello Mr. Ferrara.*

Enrico gives her a slow smile as he leans back on his chair. "Ciao, Marcella! È bello vederti." *Translation: Hello Marcella, it's good to see you.*

Marcella blushes and tips her head bashfully, she can't hide her excitement that he addressed her, she rushes inside.

Ha...so his mother's staff think he's a bit of alright, do they? I look at him sitting there, legs wide and back straight, all confident and gorgeous...can't say I blame them to be honest.

My eyes float over to my flirty boyfriend and I raise an eyebrow.

He smirks with a wink in reply.

"Enrico behave, stop encouraging her," Bianca scolds.

He holds up his hands. "I said hello."

I bite my bottom lip to stop myself from smiling at his mother's comment.

Bianca turns her attention to me. "How are you liking Italy, Olivia?"

"It's beautiful." I smile nervously.

"Yes. It is." Her eyes hold mine for a moment. "Andrea tells me that you two met a few years ago."

"Yes." Oh shit, his brother has been talking about me.

"And how did you end up back here?" she asks.

"I brought her here," Enrico replies sharply.

My eyes flick to him in surprise, I didn't expect him to tell anyone that.

Bianca raises an eyebrow. "Really?"

Enrico's eyes hold hers and I get the feeling he doesn't like her tone. "Yes mamma.... really."

Marcella returns with a tray of coffee. She puts them down on the table with a shaking hand as we all watch on. Poor girl, I feel sorry for her.

Enrico must too, because he sits up and helps her put things onto the table. "Grazie Marcella." He smiles kindly.

She nods and disappears again as Enrico pours everyone a cup of coffee. He passes them to us.

"Where are you living?" Bianca asks.

"With me," Enrico says as he sips his coffee. "We have moved into my lake Como house."

Bianca's face falls as she looks between us, a frown crosses her brow.

"Yes, mamma," Enrico says flatly. "That's right."

What does yes, mamma mean? Did I miss part of the conversation? I look between them in confusion.

Bianca drops her head and clasps her hands on her lap. "I

see." Her back is ramrod straight and I don't know why, but I get the feeling she isn't happy about something.

"Olivia will be converting to Catholic this week," Enrico says. "I have everything lined up with Father Delpini already."

Huh?

This is news.

He seems to be putting out some kind of fire with her, one that I don't even know about.

I think back to the conditions he laid out for us to get back together and I vaguely remember something about being Catholic.

I begin to perspire.

"Francesca, portala dentro," *Translation: take her inside.* Enrico says with his eyes locked on his mother's. I get the feeling that if I wasn't here it would be all guns blazing.

"Do you want to come and see my bedroom Olivia?" Francesca asks softly.

I look over at her in surprise, I forgot she was even here. "Yes." Anything to get me out of here. "That would be lovely."

She stands, holds her hand out for me and I take it gratefully.

She leads me into the house with my heart pumping fast. Once through the doors I peer through the window to see the two of them still glaring at each other.

"Oh no," I whisper. "What's going on?" I ask Francesca.

"It's okay." Francesca smiles. "Mamma is about to freak out and Enrico didn't want you to see."

"What about?" I stammer with wide eyes.

"You." She takes my hand and leads me through the house.

"Me?" I gasp. "Did I do something wrong?"

"She'll be okay," she says as we start walking up the stairs.

"But what did I do?"

"It's not you."

"Then what?"

"Enrico."

"Oh." I exhale feeling a little mollified. I don't care if she hates him, just not me.

We walk down the luxurious corridor and she takes me into her room. It's cream and pinks with a chandelier and fireplace. It's huge. "Wow." I smile as I look around in wonder. "This is beautiful."

"Thanks." She hunches her shoulders as if excited. "We just had it redone."

There is artwork on the walls and the carpet is lush underfoot. The color pallet is so unusual but somehow it all works perfectly. The king bed is white and four posted with a white netting. "Did you pick the furnishings?"

She nods. "Everything."

"Wow." It really is incredible, in fact, the most beautiful room I have seen since I've been in Italy. "You have impeccable taste."

"I'm hoping to major in interior design." She shrugs bashfully. "That's if I get in."

"Incredible" I smile. "Wow, this is amazing." Finally, a Ferrara who wants to be something other than the mob. "Do you think you would be able to help me with the interior of the Lake Como house?"

Her eyes widen. "Really?"

"Yes, it's so stuffy and boring." I shrug, embarrassed that I just said that out loud. "Not that I'm ungrateful or anything."

"I would love to. I could come over tomorrow if that suits," she asks hopefully.

"That would be fantastic."

Francesca smiles and I feel hope bloom in my chest, I don't have a sister. It will be so great getting to know her.

"Do you want to see the rest of the house?"

"Sure." For half an hour Francesca shows me through her home and I'm utterly impressed. This place is something else. Grand like the Lake Como house but in a stuffier way.

It feels more like a museum than a house.

"Olivia," Enrico's deep voice calls from downstairs. "Are you ready, my love?"

I frown to Francesca. "Are we going already?"

She shrugs as if puzzled. "Maybe."

We walk down the stairs to find Bianca and Enrico standing at the bottom in the foyer.

Enrico holds his hand out for me. "Come, we have to go."

"Oh." I smile as my eyes flick to Bianca. "It was lovely meeting you."

"Likewise," she replies politely.

"Francesca is going to come to visit us tomorrow if that's okay?" I ask.

"Of course, it's okay." Enrico smiles to his sister seemingly happy that we have made arrangements to see each other.

"I will send a car in the morning to pick you up."

"Okay."

He takes my hand. "Goodbye, mother." He kisses her on both cheeks and I shake her hand and we walk out and he opens my door.

He gets in and without a word we drive down the driveway. "Well?" I ask.

He smiles and puts his hand on my thigh. "She loves you." He turns his attention back to the road.

God...something tells me that's a lie.

Francesca

"Can I get you anything?" Olivia asks as we stand in the kitchen. "Drink? Dinner will be a couple of hours away."

I twist my fingers in front of me nervously as I stand in the kitchen. "No, thank you, I'm fine."

Enrico smiles lovingly over at me and rubs my arm. "Thank you for coming and spending some time with us, Chesca. It means a lot."

I've been here at Lake Como all day. Olivia and I were supposed to be looking at their house, but we've mostly been chatting. Enrico took us out for lunch and we laid by the pool. I really want to get to know Olivia, it's important that I make an effort with her. I don't want to be cut out of his life and I know that once he sets his mind on someone, she will be it for him.

"Thanks for inviting me." I smile awkwardly.

"Spend as much time here as you want, Chesca." He smiles.

I watch him then lean down and kiss Olivia lovingly on the cheek as she cooks. I've never seen him like this before, he's different with her. Softer, like he is with me.

I'm nervous and I have to steel myself to make conversation. "Rico said you work for Valentino."

"Yes." She smiles broadly.

"What do you do there?" I ask.

Rico smiles, proud that I'm making such an effort. He knows how shy I am and how big of a deal this is for me.

"I'm a textiles consultant," she tells me.

I stare at her, wondering what that means.

"Basically, I couldn't get a position as a designer, so they gave me this job." She shrugs. "I do love it, though. Fashion design is my ultimate goal eventually."

"Oh." I smile. "I see."

"What year are you in at school?"

"Year Eleven."

"So, you're eighteen?" she asks.

"Seventeen."

"You seem much older—so pretty."

I really like her.

Rico smiles, happy that we're both making the effort to get to know each other.

The doorbell sounds. "Who's that?" Olivia asks.

"I'll get it," Rico says before he disappears. We hear him talking in the distance, and then he appears again with two people.

"Francesca and Olivia, this is Angelina and Giuliano." Rico frowns as he looks between us. "They are friends of Lorenzo."

Olivia's eyes widen. "Hello." She smiles, as if excited, and she shakes their hands. "Can I get you both a drink? Welcome, welcome."

I smile awkwardly as I twist my fingers in front of me.

Angelina is a blonde woman, pretty and middle aged. Giuliano, the boy, is around my age. His eyes come to me and I feel a flutter in my stomach.

He has dark hair, huge brown eyes, and olive skin. He's tall, lean, and he has big red lips.

Oh......

He frowns as his eyes hold mine.

My heart begins to beat faster—so fast, that I have to concentrate on breathing.

The adults talk for ten minutes and I sit nervously to the side. I can feel him staring at me. Every now and then I glance over, he doesn't look away but gives me a soft smile instead.

I can hear my heartbeat in my ears.

Oh...he makes me nervous.

"Francesca, why don't you show Giuliano around the property? I need to talk some business with his mother," Enrico says.

Giuliano stands immediately. "That would be nice."

Oh my God.

I force a smile and nod. "Okay." I gesture to the backyard. "This way." I walk out and he falls in line beside me. We walk in silence for ten minutes through the garden. I'm too nervous to speak. The air between us is electric.

"Hello," he eventually whispers.

His voice is deep and raspy. It does things to me.

"Hi."

"And to think that I didn't want to come today," he says.

I frown. "Why do you say that?"

"You are so beautiful," he whispers.

My heart completely stops as we stare at each other.

Not as beautiful as you.

"Do you have a boyfriend?" he asks as we walk around to the side door.

I shake my head. "No." I want to ask him if he has a girlfriend, but I can't push the words past my lips.

"Do you live here?" he asks.

"No. I live in Milan." We begin to go up the service steps at the back of the building. "I'll show you upstairs."

The close proximity of his body next to mine sends goosebumps up my arms.

"Enrico is your brother?" he asks.

"Yes," I reply as we get to the top of the stairs.

"Where is the guest room?"

My heart begins to thump hard in my chest and I nervously point down the hall. "This way." We walk down the hallway, and I show him the first guest room.

He looks around it and smiles. "Nice."

"How many rooms are there on this floor?"

"Oh, um." I frown. "I have no idea."

He goes out into the corridor and counts the rooms. "Is this the bathroom in here?" he asks.

I'm so damn nervous that I can hardly speak. "Yes."

"Show me."

We walk in and gesture around the room with my hand. "This is it."

"It's lovely," he whispers, his eyes drop to my lips.

The air leaves my lungs and he turns and closes the door behind us.

His eyes hold mine and my chest rises and falls as I fight the urge to run.

He steps toward me and picks up my hand. "I'm so sorry, but you are too beautiful. I have to kiss you."

My eyes widen in horror.

"I-I've never kissed anyone before," I stammer.

He smiles as he tucks a piece of hair behind my ear. "I'm a good teacher."

Oh my God...is this happening?

He leans in slowly, and his lips softly brush mine. My eyes close at the contact. His tongue gently sweeps through my lips and he smiles against me. It's a sweet kiss—one that's gentle and tender.

The air leaves my lungs.

"It's nice to meet you, Francesca." His hand slides down and takes mine in his. Our foreheads touch, and this feels special.

"It's nice to meet you, too, Giuliano."

26

Olivia

THREE WEEKS.

It's been three weeks of utter bliss.

Enrico and I stay in Milan from Monday to Thursday and on Fridays we go to Lake Como for the weekend.

The best of both worlds, privacy and luxury.

I'm so damn happy that I could explode.

"I was thinking we could maybe go out for some dinner and drinks tonight with Natalie." I pull my black pencil skirt up and raise the zipper. "I haven't seen her much, and I want to make an effort."

It's Wednesday morning, and we are at the Milan apartment getting ready for work. Enrico is in the bathroom with a white towel around his waist, shaving. "If you like," he says as he concentrates on his task.

I watch him in the mirror as he slowly slides the razor over his chiseled jaw. No matter how many times I watch him do this, it will never be enough. I've found that the best way to ensure that I make it to work on time is to keep my distance while he gets ready in the morning. Him wearing a sharp designer business suit, encasing all that man, is simply to gorgeous for words. I throw on my dusty pink, chiffon, ruffled shirt, and I fasten the buttons.

"Maybe I could invite Giorgio and his boyfriend, too. I would like Natalie to get to know them better."

"If you wish." He continues shaving.

"Can we go to my favorite restaurant? The seafood one?" I slip on my high heels.

"If you like." He finishes up shaving, and he puts his suit pants on along with a crisp white shirt. He begins to pull on his tie, and he loops it around as we talk.

Is he even listening to me? "What about your mother? Shall I ask your mother and Francesca?"

"No, Olivia," he replies. "My mother doesn't do drinks on a Wednesday, and Francesca is too young to drink."

I smile as I walk into the bathroom. "So, you *were* listening?"

His eyes drop down my body, and then rise back up to my face. He steps forward and fastens up the top buttons on my shirt. "Yes, I was listening."

"Will you book a table?" I kiss him softly and turn to the mirror to undo the two buttons again.

"Yes, I'll book." He turns me back toward him and does one of the buttons back up.

I go to undo it again, and he holds his hand up. "Leave it."

I instantly stop. My body won't disobey him, even if I wanted it to.

His eyes drop down me again, and he rearranges my skirt, tucking in my shirt.

"You look beautiful." He smirks at me. "I don't want anyone

looking at what is mine. Leave the buttons fastened." He runs his hand down my waist to my behind and gives it a hard squeeze before he goes back to working his tie. "We have to go to Roma this weekend," he says.

"Why?"

"I have a business meeting there."

I think for a moment. "I might stay here. It will be a good opportunity to see Natalie and catch up on a few things." And by things, I mean sleep. This man is wearing me out with all his nocturnal activities.

"No." He puts his suit jacket on.

"No?" I frown.

"You go where I go." He slips on his shoes. "And we go to Roma this weekend. We can go to the bar where we met. I will take you dancing, we can re-enact our first date."

I smile, knowing he's dangling carrots now. "Okay."

He lifts his briefcase. "Maso will take you to work this morning. Where are your keys?"

I begin to apply my makeup. "In my bag. Why?" I watch on as he slowly slides a key onto my keyring. "This key." He passes me another two of the same one. "This is a key to your safety deposit box in Milan." He passes me a business card. "Keep one of these keys at work, and another with Natalie or Giorgio."

I frown as I stare at the large silver key. "What do I need a safety deposit box for?"

"Just in case." He kisses me quickly.

"In case of what?"

"My death."

"What?"

"I've made arrangements for you in the event of my death. If I die, I will have been murdered, and you will be their next target."

My face falls.

What the actual fuck?

"In the safety deposit box, you have five passports of different nationalities, and instructions on how to access money that I've secured for you in offshore accounts."

I begin to hear my pulse in my ears. "I don't want to talk about this."

"Olivia. Listen to me. Lorenzo has all the instructions, but in the event that he goes with me, I need to tell you this. If I die, you get yourself to that deposit box without being followed, and you get out of Italy immediately. Tell nobody—and I mean absolutely nobody—where you are."

I stare at him, completely lost for words.

His face softens with empathy, and he cups my cheeks. "Bella, I have to be prepared, that's all. Don't worry."

"Do you think you're going to die?" I whisper. What the hell is going on here?

"No," he replies as he takes me into his arms. "But what kind of man would I be if I didn't have arrangements in place for you?"

"A normal one."

He smiles broadly, and then goes to his wardrobe. "I am not a normal man, Olivia, and we have had this conversation too many times this week." He glances in my wardrobe and looks at all the shopping bags that I haven't even opened yet that are sitting on the floor in there. "When are you going to look at the things I bought you?"

My heart drops. To be honest, I don't want to. I've been putting it off. I can't even begin to fathom the money he spent on me.

"I haven't had time. I'll do it tomorrow night." I shrug, disappointed in myself that I'm coming across ungrateful. "Thank you again. I'll wear one of the dresses tonight."

He raises a brow, clearly unimpressed.

I stare at him, rattled that he has just given me his death plan as casually as taking out the trash. And yet he stands here, annoyed that I haven't looked at the fruits of his shopping trip.

Priorities.

He glances at his watch. "I have to go."

"Who's taking you to work?" I ask, suddenly panicked that something may happen.

"Lorenzo is here. My normal crew."

"Oh." My eyes hold his. "Please... be careful."

"I will." He kisses me softly. "Ti amo." He pulls me in for a hug, and then turns and walks out of the room. I hear him walk down the stairs, and then out of the front door.

It closes with a sharp click as he turns the deadlock.

The room is silent. Heavy.

I walk into my wardrobe and stare at all the expensive things in bags, and I feel sick to my stomach.

What good is all the money in the world if I don't have him?

His love doesn't have a price tag.

I walk out of work just after 5:00 p.m., and my heart drops. Enrico isn't here to pick me up. Lorenzo is. I know he's busy running the world and all that, but his little death talk this morning has me feeling needy.

"Hello." I smile as I get into the car.

"Hello, Miss Olivia."

"Where are Maso and Marley?" I ask as we pull out into the traffic.

"In the cars behind us."

I turn and look out the back window to see two cars trailing us today, not one.

"Has something happened, Lorenzo?" I ask.

His eyes flicker up to mine in the rearview mirror. "Why do you ask?"

"Enrico gave me a plan this morning in case he dies."

"It's just a precaution," he says.

"Is it, though? Do you think Enrico in danger?" I pause for a moment. "Like, more danger than usual?"

His eyes meet mine in the mirror again. "You'll have to speak to him about that, Olivia. I'm not at liberty to discuss these things with you."

I stare out the window.

Maybe he really was just being cautious. Don't all couples have wills?

Stop freaking yourself out.

Go get gorgeous for your man. Enjoy the night out with your friends.

I go through the mental catalogue of dresses on the racks at home. Hmm... what will I wear?

I lift the wineglass to my lips and take a long sip.

I'm sexed up to the nines, wearing a cream evening dress that's fitted to my every curve. It has delicate spaghetti straps on the shoulders, and I've matched it with gold, sky-high stilettos. I've even worn super sexy creamy, lacy lingerie that he bought me. The set includes a matching bra and G-string with suspender belt. I smile as I imagine him buying it.

My blonde hair is out and set in big curls. My makeup is smoky, and my lips are Enrico's favorite shade of red.

It's 6:30 p.m. and he isn't home yet. *Where is he?*

I go to the window and peer down at the street below, hoping to see his procession of cars coming around the corner.

I'm trying not to worry, I really am, but it isn't working. I'm driving myself crazy here.

To top it off, I'm feeling as hormonal as fuck. My period is due, and I wish the bitch would just arrive so I wouldn't feel so fucking edgy. I pour myself another glass of wine and I hear the door click.

He's home. My heart skips a beat.

He turns the corner into the kitchen where I'm waiting, and his eyes find me across the room.

"Hello, Olivia."

"Hi." I smile and hold the bottle up. "Want some?"

"Hmm." He walks past me to the cupboard and takes out a bottle of blue label scotch. After he pours a glass, he immediately lifts it to his lips.

"Don't I get a kiss hello?" I frown, this is unlike him.

"Sorry, sweetheart." He sighs as he takes me into his arms and kisses me.

"Rough day?" I frown up at him as I run my fingers through his hair.

A trace of a smile crosses his lips. "You could say that." He steps back from me while holding my hand in the air. "You look breathtaking."

I perform a little curtsy on the spot. "Thanks. This hot guy bought it for me." I wiggle my hips.

He chuckles, and then tips his head back to drain the glass.

Jeez.

He pours another glass immediately.

He's going to be drunk before we even get there. "Everything all right?" I ask.

"Yeah, give me ten minutes to get ready." He picks up the scotch and drains the glass again.

"Okay, you'd better hurry. We are supposed to be there now." I pick up the scotch bottle, secure the lid back on it, and put it back in the cupboard. He takes the hint and disappears into the bathroom.

His phone beeps on the kitchen counter and I pick it up. It's a text from Sophia.

I'm going to need you to come to Sicily.
I can't calm the girls. They need to see you.

Huh?

What the hell does that mean?

What girls need to see him? My blood begins to boil. That fucking bitch, demanding he go to Sicily with her so she can try and get her hooks back into him. And who are the girls?

How many of them has he fucked?

I get a vision of him in the luxurious brothels, and the beautiful girls all lining up to try and get picked to have sex with him.

What a prize he would be among them all. Enrico Ferrara a badge of honor. Is that what Sophia was? His favorite girl? That one he always took home because she was just so good in bed?

How many times did they fuck? How many times did she please my man?

Because I know for sure that he would have pleased her.

An ugly vision of her on her knees, sucking his dick comes to me, and I pick up the wine bottle to pour another glass so fast that it sloshes over the side. I sip it with a shaky hand.

Anger pumps through my blood.

Stop it. Stop being a hormonal bitch.

I know what I'm doing. I can feel myself being moody and insecure. I know I need to turn it off. I inhale deeply as I try to not think about it. Bringing that shit up when I'm feeling this crazy will never end well.

Right now, I feel like taking his phone and flushing it down the toilet so Sophia can never call or message him again.

I breathe deeply to try and regain some composure. After a few moments, Rico comes back into the room wearing black jeans and a black button-up shirt.

"You ready?" he asks.

"Uh-huh." I snatch my handbag from the counter. I should really tell him he got a message from Sophia, but I can't push the words past my lips.

He takes my hand in his and we leave the apartment. We stand in the elevator and he stares straight ahead. He seems off tonight, too. Cold and detached.

"Are you okay?" I ask.

"Yes." He glances down at me. "Why?"

I widen my eyes. "No reason."

We ride the elevator in silence, and then walk out into the underground parking lot.

I glance up to see Sergio's hungry eyes drop down the length of my body. I can almost feel him mentally undressing me. The hairs on the back of my neck rise in disgust. I want to tell him off for being so disrespectful to both Enrico and me, but now is not the time. For some unknown reason, my man is angry today.

The car pulls up and Maso is in the driver's seat, with Marley in the passenger side. Enrico opens my door in a rush, obviously impatient.

I slink into the backseat, and he slams the door shut. He storms around to his side.

It seems everyone's hormonal tonight.

Two hours later, we're sitting at the table. The bar is bustling. Chilled dance music is being piped throughout the speakers, and the mood is loud, filled with laughter and chatter. Enrico is talking to Giorgio, and I to Natalie at the other end of the table. Giorgio's boyfriend is away for business, so it's just the four of us.

Giorgio is talking non-stop. Enrico is listening to him but he is quiet and pensive. Every now and then our eyes meet across the table and a trace of a smile crosses his lips.

A warm glow heats my blood every time he lights up. I'll never get sick of the way he looks at me.

I glance over and see Jennifer at the bar.

"Oh, look. It's my friend from the gym, Jennifer." I smile. Jen sees me at the same time and we wave. "Come and meet her. She's so nice. She's new here, like us."

"Okay," Nat replies.

I look over to Enrico and point toward the bar. "Just going to see my friend."

He looks to where I pointed and then frowns. His gaze comes back to me in question.

"Jennifer from the gym," I say.

He nods, and then goes back to his one-sided conversation with Giorgio who is now discussing politics in great detail.

I lead Natalie to the bar.

"Hi." I smile at Jennifer.

"Hello." She laughs and kisses me on both cheeks. "What are you doing here?"

"Drinking." I gesture to Natalie. "This is my friend Natalie; the Aussie girl I told you about at the gym."

"Oh, hi." Natalie smiles and shakes her hand. "You're the one who's looking for a job?"

"And failing spectacularly."

We all laugh.

"This is my partner, Diego." She introduces us to her boyfriend, and we shake his hand, too. He's tall and muscular. Good looking, too, actually. "Are you guys here alone?" she asks.

"No, we have my boyfriend and a friend with us," I tell her.

"Oh, which one is your boyfriend?"

I point to the table, and Enrico looks up at the same time. "That's him in the black shirt." I give him a wave, and he gives us a sexy smile in return.

Jenn smiles and widens her eyes, as if impressed.

"I know, right?" Natalie giggles.

I curl my finger at him, but he ignores me and stays put. Five minutes later, he glances over and I wave him again. Finally, he gets up and comes over.

"Enrico, this is my friend from the gym, Jennifer, and this is her boyfriend Diego," I introduce them.

"Hello." He shakes their hands and gives me the sideways look. I can read his mind as clear as day. He doesn't want to talk to these people.

"Nice to meet you." Diego smiles. "Can I get you a drink?"

"No, thank you," he replies politely.

I widen my eyes at him. *Don't be rude.*

He fakes a smile, and then his eyes go back to Diego. "Okay, just one." He calls Giorgio over, and I can feel his discomfort at being made to talk to strangers. I smile to myself, knowing he waved Giorgio over so that it will save him having to talk.

Giorgio is in all his glory when the center of attention. He loves to talk. I think he could do it underwater.

They make idle chitchat. Enrico puts his arm around me while I talk to Jennifer and Natalie.

Look at us, being all normal and shit.

Enrico chucks his chin toward the door asking if we can go, and I give him a subtle shake of my head before I carry on talking to the girls.

"Let's go and sit down," Giorgio says with on over exaggerated eye roll. "My feet are killing me."

Enrico exhales and I inwardly smile. He really hates this socializing business. It's kind of fun watching him squirm.

"Yes, okay," Diego replies. "I could do with a seat, too."

They walk back over to the table and Enrico puts his arm around me.

"We are leaving in half an hour," he whispers in my ear.

"Yes, dear," I tease as he kisses my temple.

He ambles over to the table with the boys. I watch him sit down, and I smile as he joins the conversation. Giorgio is talking and I don't think anyone can get a word in.

I don't want to go home yet. He can talk to my friends for once. It won't kill him to be friendly to someone outside of Ferrara. In fact, it might do him some good. He needs to realize that there are plenty of nice people in the world if he just gave them a chance.

We talk for another ten minutes, and then I feel an arm slip around my waist from behind. I lean back against him. I knew it wouldn't be long until he came back. "Hello, Olly," a strange voice purrs.

I spin around and the blood drains from my face.

Franco.

My Tinder date from hell.

"You look happy to see me," he slurs as he reaches for me again. He's visibly drunk, and he stumbles to the side, off balance.

Natalie must see the sheer terror on my face. "Go away, please," she says.

Jennifer winces at the smell of his breath when he laughs out loud.

He puts his hand around my waist and slams my body up against his.

I push him away. "Stop it."

I step back and out of his reach but he leans for me again.

I feel him before I see him. A large arm reaches past me and grabs Franco around the throat. "We meet again," Enrico's deep voice growls.

Franco instantly gags at the chokehold around his neck. His feet are now dangling off the floor.

"R-Rici," I stammer. "Just leave it. Let's go."

Franco struggles free. "I should have knocked you out last time, prick." Franco throws a punch and misses spectacularly as we all dive out of the way.

Enrico grabs him by the throat, once more. "I told you. Go near her again, and I'll kill you."

Natalie and Jennifer's eyes widen in horror as they watch on. Oh hell, this is appalling.

I glance over and see Maso and Marley standing to attention.

"Enrico," I whisper angrily. "Leave him. He's drunk, let's go."

"Oh, I'm so scared," Franco goads him. "I'll show Olly what a real man can do." He grabs his crotch for added affect. "She's going to fucking love it."

"Rici," I warn him. "Let's go." But it's too late, he's already lost his temper.

Enrico punches Franco hard on the jaw, and he crumples to the floor in a heap.

"Stop it!" I cry.

Not happy with the result, Enrico drags him back to his feet.

"Don't you dare hit him again!" I snap as I look around at the people all staring at us, oh this is mortifying. "Rici, I mean it," I whisper.

With total disregard for anything I've just said, he hits him once, twice, he hits him three times—the sound of his fist connecting with Franco's face hard and brutal.

My eyes fill with tears. I can't deal with this. I can't stand his detached aggression. I storm toward the door.

Infuriated.

"Olivia!" Enrico barks behind me.

I'm just going to make a scene if I stay. I need to get out of here, and away from him.

I begin to run. What the hell does he think he's fucking doing? You can't just hit people like that. It's unnatural. He could kill him.

"Stop her!" I hear Enrico yell across the bar.

Maso runs after me and grabs my elbow. "Get away from me." I push him hard in the chest and run out onto the street with Maso and Marley hot on my heels. I jump into the back of a cab.

"Drive!" I force out.

"Where to?" the driver says casually.

My eyes fill with tears. God, where do I go? He will come and get me wherever I am anyway. There's no point going anywhere. I just didn't want to fight with him in a crowded bar in front of everyone, that's all.

I give the driver the address of the apartment in Milan, and I rustle through my handbag to dig out my key and clutch it tightly in my hand. I turn and look out the back window to see Maso following in his car. No doubt Enrico won't be far behind.

"Power freak," I whisper to myself.

He could see Franco was drunk and yet he hit him anyway. Not once but, like, six times.

Fucking asshole.

I'm so mad with him that I can't even stand it. Who does he think he is?

His over the top reaction was just uncalled for.

The cab pulls up out the front of the apartment. I pay the driver and get out. Maso and Marley sit in their car as they watch me go in. I take the lift and arrive at the apartment.

I'm furious and looking for a fight, but I know he is, too, and it's not a good combination. I'm going to go to bed so that we don't get into an all-out war.

I take off my makeup, put my pyjamas on, and I get under the covers, just in time to hear the door open. He's home.

I scrunch my eyes shut tight and pretend to be asleep. The bedroom door bangs open.

"Do not ever fucking leave a club without me again. Do you hear me, Olivia?" he bellows.

"Get out," I snap. "Sleep in the spare room tonight."

"Cazzo, non osare dirmi cosa devo fare," he yells as he takes off his shoes.

"I can't understand you!" I yell into my pillow.

"Learn fucking Italian, then." He throws his shoe across the room. It hits the drawers with a bang. "Like you said you would."

Something inside me snaps, and I sit up in a rush. "Are you fucking serious, right now?"

"Oh, I am fucking serious." His dark eyes are crazy. He's just as furious as me, maybe even more so.

"That's it." I get out of bed, pick up my pillow and blanket, and I storm past him to make my way to the other room.

"Where are you going?"

"Away from you." I walk into the spare bedroom and slam the door behind me.

I get under the covers and I hear him coming up the hall again. The door bangs open and he throws shopping bags onto the bed.

I sit up in a rush. "What are you doing?"

"Your unopened presents are not staying in the room with me." He turns and disappears again.

I roll my eyes at his dramatics and lie back down.

He comes bursting through the door again with another armful of bags and throws them over me. "Give these away. It is obvious that you don't want them."

"That's right. I *don't* fucking want them."

His eyes look like they are about to pop out of his head. "Three-carat diamond fucking earrings are not good enough for you?" He hurls the small black box that he bought to my office as hard as he can at the wall above my head and it dents the plaster.

"I don't want your fucking presents, Enrico." I get out of bed and walk out of the room in a rush.

"What do you fucking want, Olivia?" he yells as he follows me.

I arrive in the kitchen. "I want you." I shake my head as I try to articulate my feelings. "I want you to be sentimental and to think about me and my feelings."

He screws up his face, and I think he's about to explode... literally.

"Pensi che non sia sentimentale?"

I narrow my eyes. He knows I can't fucking understand him.

"You think I'm not sentimental, Olivia," he sneers. "I remember every fucking word that leaves your lips. I know every curve on your body." He disappears up the hall and into his office. I peer after him. What's he doing now?

He reappears, carrying a wineglass and holding it up toward me. "What is this?" he yells in an outrage.

I frown in confusion.

"What is this?" He repeats.

"It's a glass," I say.

"Not just a glass." He holds it higher. "This is the glass that you drank out of on the first night in my apartment in Roma." He spins the glass so I can see the red lipstick marks on it. "I kept this for two years because it had your lips on it. I couldn't wash it because I knew if I did, I would have lost the only mark you left with me."

My eyes hold his.

"You think I'm not sentimental?" he yells like a madman. "Explain to me why the hell I couldn't orgasm for two years without imagining I was with you."

My heart drops.

"Two fucking years I lived a lie with every other woman, while my heart ached for only you!"

He turns and hurls the glass into the kitchen sink so hard that it smashes. He storms up the hall, and I hear the bedroom door slam.

I hear something hit the wall with force.

I stare at the broken glass in the sink, and my eyes fill with tears.

God, I'm a bitch.

I sit at the kitchen counter and exhale heavily. I knew we

were going to have a fight tonight. I knew before we even left home.

I walk into the spare bedroom and take a long, hot shower. Half an hour later, I make my way up to our bedroom to find Enrico in bed. The blankets are pooled around his waist, and his forearm is over his eyes.

"Can I sleep in here?" I whisper.

"No."

"I don't want to fight with you."

"Too late."

I get into bed beside him and snuggle up against his large, naked body. "I didn't open your presents because I want you to know that money doesn't mean anything to me. I don't care about gifts. I care about your safety."

He stays silent.

"I'm scared, Rici," I whisper.

More silence.

"What good are gifts if I have to live without you?"

"You're talking about the key?"

"Yes, I'm talking about the key. It freaked me out."

He closes his eyes. "I can't help this, Olivia. It is just a precaution."

"Yes, you can." I kiss his chest. "This business that you lead, this life that you live... it isn't your dream, Rici."

His eyes find mine.

"I'm scared you're going to be murdered for fighting someone else's battle."

He exhales heavily, puts his arm around me and pulls me close. We lie in silence together for a moment, and I look up at him. "Can you promise me something?"

"What's that?"

"Promise me that we will die on the same day."

He frowns. "Don't say that, bella," he whispers. "I couldn't bear it."

My eyes fill with tears. "I don't want to live in a world without you in it. Don't leave me behind."

He kisses my temple as he holds me close. "Nobody is going to die, my love."

"Promise me… we go together," I whisper through a lump in my throat.

"Shh, baby." He rolls me onto my back. His lips drop down my neck, and the emotion coming out of him tears my heart wide open.

I love this man.

With all of my heart I love this man.

We made it through our first fight.

Roma. What a beautiful place.

I'm reminded why it's so special to me.

It's Friday night, and Rici has bought me here for the weekend. We've just had dinner at the restaurant where we met. It feels so long ago now. So much has happened, and I've never felt closer to anyone in my life. Something about our fight on Wednesday cemented something. The energy has shifted between us. Him telling me that he couldn't orgasm with another woman has calmed my insecurities. I have completely given myself over to him.

I've been in Italy for three months now, and my time with him has been the happiest of my life.

And I was deadly serious; I don't want to live in a world without Rici Ferrara. He promised me that everything is all right and that he was just taking precautions.

"Where are we going?" I ask as he leads me through the crowds of people by the hand.

We come to an opening, and I see The Pantheon come into view. Its lit up with an aura around it.

"Oh, it's so magical," I whisper.

"Our special place." He smiles softly and takes me into his arms.

"Thank you." I kiss his lips. "This is the perfect date."

He takes my hand and leads me to the secret side door. Once there, he calls someone. The man in the suit comes and opens the door. "Enrico, my child. Welcome. We have been waiting."

We walk through and the man leaves us alone. I look around and my heart stops.

There is a small round table with candles, a bottle of champagne, and two crystal glasses on it. It's sitting right near the spot where we spoke our truths all that time ago.

"Rici," I whisper. "You are perfect." We kiss softly, our lips linger over each other's.

"Olivia, non posso vivere senza di te. Ti amo con tutto il cuore. Vuoi sposarmi, amore mio?" He goes straight into the translation. "Olivia," he whispers. "I cannot live without you. I love you with all of my heart. Will you marry me, my love?"

He drops to his knee and pulls a ring from his pocket.

My hands fly to mouth in shock. "Rici," I whisper.

He slides the ring on my finger and then presses my hand to his face. "Answer me, my love."

I smile through tears. "Si." I drop to my knee beside him and kiss him softly. "A million times, si."

27

Olivia

ENRICO'S EYES search mine making my heart constrict at the overwhelming love passing between us.

It's emotion overload, and my own eyes well with tears.

Marriage.

"Are you sure?" I whisper up at him. "We've only just found each other. It's so soon."

"Bella, I've never been surer of anything in my life." His lips brush mine. "Why should we wait? I know what I want."

This is insane, but somehow I know it's right, and I smile softly.

Marriage.

"We have to get up." I wince.

He pulls me up and takes me into his arms to kiss me once more. It's not hurried or sexual. This is a kiss from the heart, and a promise of a life together.

Our life.

"Ti amo," I whisper up at him.

"I love you, too." He takes my face in his hands, and I smile against his lips, unable to believe what's transpired here tonight.

We've developed this quirky habit of declaring our love for each other in our opposing languages. I always say it in Italian. He says it in English.

However it comes out, it's perfect every time, and it means so much.

"Do you like your ring?" Enrico asks.

I hold my hand out and look down at it. Is this really happening? The ring isn't fancy and showy. It's a gold band with a single solitaire diamond—a big diamond, but simple all the same.

"It's perfect."

It feels heavy on my finger and is going to take some time getting used to. I smile as I stare at it.

"I love it and I love you." He breaks out into a big, beautiful smile. "Finally, a present you like."

God. What must it be like to be with me? "It's the only present that matters."

I throw my arms around his neck, and he squeezes me so tight as he lifts me up. "Let's go home."

The bar is empty but our hearts are full.

Fairy lights hang over us in the garden's courtyard. It's drawing to the end of our perfect night.

I smile up at my handsome dance partner. He was determined to recreate our first date. We've been to the exact same bars and danced on the same dancefloors.

The songs are different now, though—not that I remember the originals, to be honest. My brain was high on Enrico Ferrara, and still is.

Although it's a different kind of high now. The kind that lasts a lifetime.

Out of all the woman in the world, he picked me to fall in love with, and I'm so incredibly grateful that things have worked out the way that they have between us.

He's sweet, sexy, dominant, caring, and he listens to every damn word that I say.

I smile as I listen to the lyrics of "Lover" by Taylor Swift, and we sway side to side.

"This song is better than the last song you liked," he tells me.

"What song?" I frown.

"The..." He frowns as he tries to remember the name of it. "The used to being loved song."

"Huh?" I try to think back.

"Something about used to being someone you loved."

"Oh." I smile. "'Someone You Love' by Lewis Capaldi."

"The sad song about a girl leaving her man."

"I remember. Although I think it's more about death."

His face falls. "Well, I hope you never get to play it."

I giggle and rise up on my toes to kiss him. "Thank you."

"What for?"

"For being my lover... and becoming my best friend."

He stops moving. "That's the nicest thing you've ever said to me."

"What?" I frown. "Why?"

"Anybody can fall in love." His eyes search mine. "But it takes a lot to be someone's best friend."

We begin to sway to the beat again, which, by the way, has

now gone down in the history books as my favorite song ever. "Take me home, lover."

"Maybe we should just get married tonight?"

"Find somewhere and we will."

He chuckles, steps back, and tugs on my hand. "Don't tempt me. Home time."

He lifts my dress over my head, tosses it aside, and his lips dust my neck. We are back at the apartment in Roma—the one where we spent our first weekend together in.

His wife. *Mrs Ferrara.*

Suddenly, I'm desperate. Desperate to have him naked. I tear his shirt over his shoulders and throw it to the side. He gives me a slow, sexy smile and holds his hands out wide. "I'm all yours, my love."

"Literally." I undo his jeans and slide them down his legs to reveal his perfectly thick cock that's hanging heavily between his legs. Thick veins run down the length of it.

He is one beautiful man.

Mine.

Unable to help it, and with a new sense of urgency, I drop to the floor in front of him and take him in my mouth.

This is it. This man and this body will be mine for life.

He hisses as he strokes my hair. "Yes, Bella," he whispers darkly.

I keep going and going, and then he drags me to my feet and throws me on the bed. He moves over me, and in one swift motion, he slides in deep.

"Ah," he hisses. "I love you, Olivia." His dark eyes are locked on mine, and his hands trace my face, as if he's memorizing every inch. His knees are wide to give him traction, and I lift my legs higher around his body, encasing his perfection.

"I want you deep," I moan. God, I don't think he can get deep enough today. I want every inch of him.

He inhales sharply and slams in hard, and I throw my head back with a laugh.

We can't make gentle love if our lives depended on it.

This man makes me bad to the bone... and I fucking love it.

It's been the most romantic night of our lives, and I can already see we are going to fuck like animals.

"Are you going to fuck me like this when we are married?" I tease.

He slams in hard. "Forever."

Rici is wrapped around me like a blanket. My head is on his chest, and his lips rest on my forehead. We've made sweet, tender love well into the morning. I'm on an all-time high. I think way back to the two occasions I have been hurt when he left me. It all seems so long ago now, but even with all that devastation and heartbreak, I would do it all again to get where we are today. This is a closeness that we've earned, and I think the hard times have only made us a stronger unit.

"Where do you want to get married?" he asks.

I look up at him, surprised at the question. "Here, in Italy." He frowns down at me. "Really?"

I shrug. "I'm not into big fancy things like your family are. If we got married in Australia, half of Italy would have to travel, whereas I have, like, twenty people I would want there."

"Thank you. It would kill my mother if I didn't marry here."

"What do you think she's going to say when you tell her?"

We decided not to call anyone tonight. We wanted to bask in the excitement alone for the weekend. Secretly, I think that Rici didn't want anyone spoiling our excitement with the '*you barely know each other*' talk.

We don't care what they think. We know what this is.

"I shall look into next month then," he says casually.

"Oh, you want the engagement party that soon?"

"No. I want the wedding that soon." "A month." I scoff. "We can't organize a wedding in a month, Enrico. I have so much to do. I need at least... I don't know... three months."

He rolls his eyes. "We'll have the engagement party in two weeks."

"Two weeks," I squeak. "Are you mad?"

"It will be easy to plan. My mother will do it all. This is her thing."

I get a vision of her taking over the entire day. "No, that's okay," I tell him. "I want to handle this."

He pulls me closer and inhales with a sleepy smile. "I am happy, my love."

I kiss his broad chest. "Me too, baby."

"Hi, Liv. How are you, lovely girl?"

"Hi, Mum."

"How was the weekend in Rome?"

"Perfect." I glance over to Enrico who is lying on the lounge listening, and I scrunch my face up. "Guess what happened?"

"What?"

"Enrico proposed."

There's silence for a while, until she eventually whispers, "What?"

"I'm getting married, Mum."

"Liv, you hardly know this man."

"I know him. He's the one. He got down on one knee and proposed to me in The Pantheon. Mum, I'm so happy."

Enrico's eyes twinkle with a certain something as he watches me.

"Honey," she sighs.

"Can't you just be happy for us?" I ask. "We know what we're doing. We're not kids, Mum. I'm twenty-nine. I'm pretty sure I know what I'm doing."

"I just worry."

"You don't need to worry. I've got this."

She stays silent for a moment before she speaks again. "What's your ring like?"

"Gorgeous." I smile. "It's a simple gold band with a stunning two-carat diamond."

"Wow!" She gasps.

I laugh at her reaction. "Will you come over for a holiday so we can pick my wedding dress?" I ask hopefully.

"Darling, yes, of course. I'll have to save for a while though. My car needed major repairs that cleaned out my bank account."

"Okay." I smile knowing she's coming around. This is really happening. "I can show you around Italy. It's so beautiful here. You'll love it."

"Olivia, I can't believe this. I'm so shocked."

I giggle. "I know. Me, too."

"I have to go to work. I'll call you tonight."

"Okay, I love you."

"Love you, too."

She hangs up, and I turn to the sexy man on the couch. He

taps his knee for me to go to him. When I do, he wraps me in his arms. "Was she okay?"

"A little worried about how quickly it's all happened. She'll come around as soon as she meets you." I run my fingers through his curls. "Are you going to call your mother?"

"I'm going to see her today. I'll tell her then."

"What do you think she's going to say?"

"She'll be fine. It's not up to her, anyway." He flips me over and lays me on the couch to hover over me. "It's up to us."

On Monday morning, I dance into the café like a rock star, while holding my hand in the air. I wiggle my fingers to make my ring sparkle.

Jennifer and Natalie bounce in their seats with excitement. "Oh my God!" Nat cries. "I can't fucking believe it."

"I know," I cry.

"Holy shit," Jennifer whispers as she holds my hand in hers. "That ring is something else."

With a laugh, I glance outside to see Lorenzo and Maso looking on through the window. They're smiling almost as much as I am. Rici and I have been on Cloud Nine all weekend. We can hardly wipe the smiles off our faces. I never knew I could be this happy.

"Your coffees, lovely ladies." The waiter arrives at the table with three cappuccinos.

"Thank you, Bosco," Nat and I say in unison. We've gotten to know our waiter well.

Bosco gives us a huge smile of appreciation. This isn't the nicest looking café in Milan, but the staff are so lovely, and it's the only place that makes coffee taste like it does back home. It's mostly filled with Australians all the time.

The other day, I made Rico come here with me before work. When Bosco saw him, he nearly swallowed his tongue at the sight of him.

"Ah." He notices the girls staring at my engagement ring. "Are we celebrating?"

"We are." I smile proudly and hold my hand up. "I'm engaged to be married."

"Enrico Ferrara?" he whispers with wide eyes.

"Uh-huh."

His mouth falls open and he claps his hands together. "Holy mother of God, we must celebrate."

He rushes behind the counter, digs out a bottle of champagne, and pops the cork. It spurts out in spectacular fashion as we all laugh out loud. The other customers are giggling—his excitement is contagious.

I glance outside again and see Lorenzo and Maso laughing, too.

This is a happy day.

Bosco pours us all a bottle of bubbly and hands us the glasses. He pours one for the other three people in the café, also, and he takes two glasses outside for the boys. "I propose a toast," he announces once back inside.

We hold our glasses up. "To Mrs. Ferrara to be."

"To Mrs. Ferrara to be," everyone says, I giggle in embarrassment. I feel famous.

Everyone goes back to their conversations and the girls' attention comes back to me. "Were you expecting this?" Jennifer asks.

"No. I mean, I thought we would get married one day. But this early? No way. This is all his doing. It bothers Enrico that

I'm not his wife. He wants it to be legal."

Jennifer leans on her hand and smiles dreamily. "He's so romantic."

"I know, right? So, tell us about the proposal," Nat says.

"He took me to our special place."

"Where's that?" Jennifer asks.

"The Pantheon." I smile as I stare lovingly at my ring.

"In Rome?

"Yes, he took me there two years ago when we first met."

"You've been together for two years?" Jennifer squeaks.

"No." I laugh. "It was terrible timing back then. His father and grandfather were killed in a car accident that weekend, and he was too upset to start anything."

"Murdered," Nat mutters into her wineglass. "Tell it as it is."

"Murdered?" Jennifer gasps as she looks between us.

"We don't know that." I widen my eyes at Natalie to tell her to shut up.

"He was totally murdered." Natalie scoffs. "Haven't you noticed how much security Olivia has around her."

Jennifer leans in toward the table. "I had noticed that," she whispers. "I wondered why."

"It's just because he's wealthy, that's all," I reply. "It doesn't mean anything." I frown over at Natalie. Thank God I didn't tell her anything. Imagine if she knew the truth. I need to change the subject. "Oh, there's a problem, though."

"What's that?" Nat asks.

"Enrico wants to have an engagement party in two weeks at the Lake Como house." I shrug, feeling totally overwhelmed. "I have no idea how to organize it in that time. He said he will get a party planner, but I hate the thought. It's so impersonal."

"Oh." Jennifer's eyes widen. "I can do it. I was an event

manager back home. I used to do this all the time. It's a piece of cake."

"Really?" I frown.

"Sure, and I'm not working right now. I could just work on it full-time."

"Oh, I don't want to impose."

"It wouldn't be an imposition. I would love to help out. I'd be happy to have something to do to be honest."

"That's a fantastic idea," Nat says. "Just pay her to do it."

"Of course, I would pay you," I say.

"If you like. I can invoice you when we're done. I won't charge much."

"Don't worry, she's loaded." Nat tips her head back and drains her glass.

"If you could send me the numbers and what you want, I can get started today."

"Really?" I smile in wonder. "That quick?"

"Yes. Thank God my day is looking up. I thought I was going to die of boredom." She thinks for a moment. "What's the house like so I can organize flowers and decorations? Would you be able to give me a key so I can go and check it out today while you work? That way, I can start straight away."

"Yeah, sure." I go to give her a key, and then hesitate. No, I can't do that. Enrico would have a fit. "I'll have someone there to meet you."

"Oh." Her eyes hold mine. "Okay, whatever is easiest. I don't want to bother anyone. I'm used to being in houses alone."

"It won't be a bother." I smile. "The house is guarded all the time so someone will be there."

"Why is the house guarded?" She frowns.

"That's the million-dollar question." Nat raises her eyebrow.

"I told you, his family is rich. It's just a precaution." I roll my eyes at her dramatics. "Stop with the conspiracy theories, Nat. You watch way too much Netflix." I stand. "I have to go. I'm going to be late for work." I kiss them both on the cheeks.

"Email me the party details and I'll get to it."

"Okay, thank you."

I leave the café filled with relief. Thank God I know someone who knows all about event management. The world is saved.

I'm not going to fuck this up.

Giorgio smiles as he holds my hand and inspects my ring. We are in my office, pretending to work.

"I knew you were the one for him. From the moment I saw you, I knew you were the one."

I giggle. "And how did you know that?"

"From the way that he looked at you."

"How does he look at me?"

"Like you're the only other person on earth."

My heart swells because that's how he makes me feel too.

"So?" He sits back on my desk. "When's the wedding?"

"I don't know. Enrico wants the engagement party in two weeks." Giorgio's eyes widen. "What are you going to wear?"

"Not sure yet." I smile nervously. "Something nice."

Giorgio stands and immediately looks me up and down. "You must wear Valentino." He taps his finger on his lips. "I'm going to go down to production and find something from next year's line."

I roll my eyes with a smile.

"Leave it with me, darling. You will look fabulous." With a

kiss on each cheek, he practically runs from my office, and I drop into my chair.

It is fun being Giorgio's hobby.

My eyes flutter open. "Bedtime, Bella," Rico whispers from behind me.

We are lying on the couch in the apartment in Milan. It's late now, and the last thing I remember, we were watching a movie. I'm tight in his arms and he kisses my temple.

"Did you fall asleep too?" I ask.

"Yes. This movie is very boring."

I giggle because I love his accent when he says certain things. *This movie is very boring* seems to be one of them.

Enrico's phone dances across the coffee table, and the name Sergio lights up the screen. What does he want? That guy gives me the creeps.

"Yes," Rico answers flatly, clearly annoyed at being called at this hour. He frowns and listens for a moment. "What?" he barks. "Are you fucking kidding me?"

"What is it?" I mouth.

He begins to yell in Italian, screaming at the top of his voice. I've no idea what he's saying but he's absolutely losing it. He slams his hand on the coffee table in fury, and I jump. Jeez.

Calm down already.

He points to the bedroom. "Get dressed, Olivia."

"What?" I frown. "Why?"

"Get dressed," he repeats. He goes back to his conversation and continues to yell in Italian.

"Prepare the jet. We leave in an hour," he instructs.

"Leave." I frown. "Where are we going?"

He points to the bedroom. "Get dressed." He's furious. The anger radiating out of him is thermonuclear.

"Tell Lorenzo to pick up Olivia and take her to my mother's. He can stay here with them. I want extra men on the Ferrara house while I'm gone." "What?" I whisper. "I don't want to go to your mother's. That's just awkward."

His eyes widen at me. "Do not even think about disobeying me tonight, Olivia. You *will* stay at my mother's. Get fucking dressed. Now!"

Oh my God. I storm up the hall and quickly throw some clothes on. He soon follows and marches into his wardrobe.

"What's happened?" I ask.

He rips his clothes off a coat hanger, and it flings across the room with force. "I have to go to Sicily."

"What, now? It's the middle of the night?" I frown. "What's happened?"

He kisses me quickly. "Nothing that you need to be worried about. I have something that I have to take care of. You will stay at my mother's house until my return."

"I'll just stay here."

"You will not stay here alone."

"Okay. Calm down."

It's obvious he's under a lot of stress about something, and I don't want to add to it.

"Pack a bag." "Well, how long will you be?"

"I don't know." He tears out an overnight bag and begins to throw clothes into it with force. He's completely losing his shit here.

Fear starts to run through me. "Is something wrong?"

He opens the safe in his wardrobe and removes two guns. He puts one under his jacket.

"Just trouble at one of the brothels. Nothing for you to worry about."

"Why do you need a gun then?"

He brushes past me and goes into the bathroom to pack his toiletries.

I storm in after him. "Is Sophia there?"

"Olivia," he bellows. "Do not fight with me tonight. This has nothing to do with Sophia. Pack your fucking clothes."

"You don't have to be an asshole about it!" I snap.

I walk back into the bedroom and begin to throw some clothes into the overnight bag he has gotten out for me. I go into the bathroom and grab my toiletries. I stare at the closed bottom drawer for a moment, and then I snatch the pharmacy bag that I picked up today.

"How long are you going to be?" I ask.

"Not long."

"Not long, as in one night, or not long, as in eight?" He glares at me. "Bella."

I purse my lips. "What kind of trouble is it?"

"Just one of the patrons."

"Can't someone else handle it? It's midnight, Enrico."

"No." He picks up his packed bag and storms from the room. I run after him. "Is this dangerous?"

"No."

"Are you sure?"

He closes his eyes and pinches the bridge of his nose, his frustration obvious. "God, give me strength, Olivia." He inhales sharply. "I have to go. Lorenzo is coming for you."

"This is all very dramatic for something that isn't dangerous."

The doorbell sounds, and Enrico looks at the security screen. Lorenzo is waiting in the hall. Enrico buzzes him in.

"Hello," Rico greets him. "Take Olivia to Ferrara House and don't leave her side."

"Yes, sir."

Enrico picks up his bag, throws it over his shoulder, and lifts my face to his. "I'll be home soon, my love." He kisses me softly. "I'll call you as soon as I can."

"Okay." I force a smile. "Please, be careful."

"Always." With one last kiss, he walks out of the apartment without looking back. The door clicks quietly behind him.

I drop my shoulders, deflated. "It's midnight, Lorenzo. It's rude to go to Bianca's at this hour. She'll be fast asleep. Enrico is being dramatic. Why can't I just stay here?"

"Olivia," he warns in his best Italian accent. "You *will* follow his orders."

The car pulls into the circular driveway of Bianca's home.

Ferrara House.

This place is like something from a magazine. It's over the top luxury like nothing I've ever experienced before. More guards are here than anywhere else, and I wonder who assigns them. Is it Enrico's doing or was it his father's? My mind goes off on a tangent, and I idly wonder if Angelina has this many guards at her house, too. Which partner gets better protection? More importantly, from what?

Nerves dance in my stomach as I think of Enrico on his way to Sicily.

Please, be safe.

Lorenzo opens my door and takes my overnight bag from the trunk. "I don't want to wake anyone up," I whisper.

"Bianca knows you're coming." Just as he says that, the front door opens, and Bianca comes into view. She's wearing a cream satin nightdress and gown—as glamorous as ever.

"Hello, Olivia," she says with a forced smile.

I clutch my handbag with white knuckle force. "Hi." I look around nervously. "I'm sorry about this, I hate to trouble you. I really could have stayed at Enrico's."

"It's fine." She holds her hand out for me. "Come, come." She leads me into the house. "It will make Enrico feel better if he knows you're safe."

I clutch my bag harder. Gah, this is awkward. "Thanks."

"Can I get you a drink or anything?" she asks.

"No." My eyes flick nervously to Lorenzo. "I think I will just go to bed, if that's okay?"

"Yes, yes, of course." She leads me up the stairs and down a huge corridor. "This used to be Enrico's room as a child," she says as she opens the door. "I thought you might want to stay in here."

I look around the luxurious furnishings. The walls are navy blue, and the furnishings are all white. To the left is a beautiful white marble bathroom.

Wow.

Who has a bedroom like this as a child? "It's perfect, thank you."

"Do you need anything else?" I shake my head. "No, thank you. Goodnight."

"Goodnight." With one last look and another forced smile, she leaves and closes the door behind her. I drop down on the bed before I flop onto my back. I lie for a moment and stare at the ceiling. I know there's something I really have to do.

I've been putting it off for a week, but now I need to know. I dig out the pharmacy paper bag from my luggage and I read the box.

First Response Pregnancy Test

I'm on the pill. I know it can't be positive, but for some reason I have this weird gut feeling that I am.

I mean, I did miss a pill or two a few weeks back, but I took double the next day, and I've always done that before with no consequences.

I study the instructions and then go and pee on the stick. I sit on the bathroom counter while I wait.

I wait.

And I wait...

And I wait.

Before my very eyes, one line appears... and then a second faint line appears not so long after.

Hmm, that's interesting.

I frown. What does that mean? I snatch the instructions up and read them again.

Two lines indicates a positive result.

My mouth falls open in shock.

What the fuck? I'm pregnant.

Enrico

I'm livid.

Never in my life have I ever been so angry.

One of our girls has been found in a back ally in Sicily, dead.

Beaten, and then strangled—the name Lucky Lombardi carved into her face.

How fucking dare he?

She did not deserve to die like this. His fight is with me, not her. His name carved in her face is for my benefit. He wants a war, and he just got one.

"You find where he is?" I growl as I get off the plane.

"We have a location," Sergio replies. "He's in a bar on the South Side."

I clench my jaw as I imagine what the girl's family are about to go through. A new wave of anger ravages through me. "Take me to him." I pat my suit pocket and feel the heavy weight of my gun.

"We can't go there unmanned."

Nobody touches a Ferrara girl... *nobody.*

"Then get the men," I reply flatly.

Twenty minutes later, the car pulls to a halt in a parking lot outside a bar, and I get out of the car on autopilot.

We are in a seedy part of Sicily. The bar is loud, but the rest of the streets are quiet.

What kind of man does that to an innocent woman?

I walk across the cobblestone street to the bar. It's been raining and the ground shimmers with the afterglow. The sound of my feet crunches on the hard surface.

I have ten men with me now, and I'm here for blood.

His blood.

I open the door and walk into the bar. The musicians instantly stop playing, and everyone falls quiet. They stop and stare. I walk in, and my shoes creak on the wooden floorboards.

I look around at the patrons. It's filled with men of many ages. They know who I am, and it tells me a lot.

"Where is Lucky Lombardi?" I ask loudly—calmly.

Silence.

"Give him to me... or write your own death certificate."

They all stay deathly still.

I grab the closest man to me. “Where is he?” I ask as I give him a shake. “I speak the truth. Anyone who hides him from me will meet their maker today.”

One weaker man points to the backdoor of the bar. “He left,” he says softly, his eyes darting the door.

“Check the bathrooms,” I tell Sergio.

I hope to fuck he’s in there so I can kill the fucker with my bare hands.

We walk back out the front door and into the parking lot. I look around, my ten men beside me.

The parking lot is dark and eerily. I can see no movement.

He’s hiding…

“Mr. Lombardi!” I call. “Show your cowardly face.”

Silence.

My men and I exchange looks.

“Get out here!” I yell.

I hear a phone ringing in the distance and we all glance at one another. The phone keeps ringing and we look over to see it’s coming from a payphone on the corner of the street.

Sergio goes and answers it. “Hello.”

His eyes glance up and over to me before he holds the phone out. “It’s for you.”

My eyes scan the roads and buildings around us. Is this a set up?

I take the phone from Sergio.

“Hello, Enrico,” a husky male voice sneers. “Looking for me?”

“Show your face.”

He laughs out loud. I narrow my eyes as I look around at the buildings surrounding us. He’s here somewhere. I can feel him watching us.

"You will get out of Sicily and hand me possession of all the brothels, or *you* will face the consequences."

I smile at his stupidity. "Or, what?"

"Or I'm making a visit to House of Valentino."

What?

My blood runs cold.

"And your blonde... Olivia Reynolds...will pay for your stupidity on the end of my knife." He laughs out loud. "I'm going to chop her up into tiny pieces and fry her bones." He laughs again, a sick and twisted sound. It echoes through my brain causing a shock wave through my system.

Then... the phone goes dead.

28

Enrico

ANGER SURGES throughout my body and I turn to my men.

"Kill him." I squeeze the phone in my hand so hard, I'm certain it will break. "Kill anyone who stands in your way. I want him dead. I want them all fucking dead!" I growl, I turn and storm to the cars. I jump into the driver's seat, and the men scramble behind me to keep up.

Getting home to Olivia just became my only priority.

He threatened her. He's already killed an innocent woman.

He knows where she works.

I start the car as men are still jumping in. I don't have time for their delays. "Hurry up!" I yell as they scramble around me. I dial Lorenzo's number on hands free. My stress levels are at an all-time high.

"Hello."

"Where's Olivia?" I snap.

"Asleep in bed."

"You stand outside her door all night, and you double the security outside the house."

"W-what's wrong?" he stammers, sensing the urgency in my voice.

"Lucky Lombardi just demanded I hand over all the brothels or he'll kill her."

He pauses for a moment. "He brought your family into this?" This is unheard of, this isn't how we operate. Women and children have always been safe on both sides in every Ferrara war. This time, we're dealing with a new level of low life. "You have my word, Enrico. I'll guard her with my life."

"We're headed to the airport now. See you soon."

Olivia

It's late and I'm at Bianca's house, staring at the ceiling from my bed, in complete shock. There's no chance of me going to sleep anytime soon.

I'm on the pill. How can I be pregnant? Maybe it's all a big mistake. I should be mortified. I should be freaking out. What I am, is trying to contain my excitement.

A baby.

A part of Rici and a part of me, together in the form of a child.

The most precious gift.

I slowly slide my hand down and rest it over my stomach. A slow burning excitement begins to chase away the initial shock. This is so unexpected. The timing could be a lot better, but we're getting married already so it's not like it wouldn't have happened at some stage in the future.

I wonder what Enrico is going to say. I imagine myself

telling him, and him losing his temper… but I already know that's not going to happen. He wants children.

He talks about having children often. I smile to myself as excitement begins to bubble from deep inside. I pick up my phone and scroll through to his number.

It's 4:00 a.m.

I wonder if he's in bed or at work handling the situation. A nagging little voice from deep inside taunts me.

He's in a brothel… surrounded by beautiful women who all want to sleep with him. I close my eyes as I try to chase away the destructive thoughts. It's not good for me to let my mind go there. It's toxic and will only bring jealousy and hurt between us.

When I said yes to marrying him, I said yes to trusting him, too. I have to stand by that decision, no matter how much insecurity his line of work brings.

Should I text him to make sure he's okay and say goodnight?

No, I'll probably wake him. I'll have to wait now.

I put my hand over my stomach again and smile into the darkness as I imagine his face when he finds out.

I can't wait to tell him.

I wake to my phone dancing on the side table, and I pick it up.

Rici

"Good morning." I smile sleepily.

"Good morning, my bella. How did you sleep?" he purrs, his voice deep.

I rub my eyes as I try to focus. He has the sexiest fucking voice on earth. "I missed you. I don't like sleeping alone."

"I'm just about to get on a plane to come home to you."

"Good." I smile.

"Don't go to work today."

"What?"

"I want to see you when I get home. Call in sick."

"I can't do that."

"You can." His voice is commanding. "In fact, why don't you just resign. You don't need to work for someone else. You can start your own company now."

Ugh, not this again.

"I'm not doing that, we already discussed this. And besides, I have meetings all day." What does he think this is? I can't just have a day off or resign every time he snaps his fingers.

"I don't want you going to work until I get home." "That's ridiculous. I'll see you tonight." "Olivia," he warns.

He's beginning to annoy me now. "I have to go, Enrico. I'm going to be late. Have a safe flight. I love you." I hang up.

The phone rings immediately again and his name lights up the screen.

I exhale heavily. "Yes?"

"Don't hang up on me." The phone goes dead as he returns the favor.

I roll my eyes at his dramatics. God, somebody got out of the wrong side of the bed. What's up his ass? I drag myself out of bed and make my way into the bathroom to pick up the pregnancy test stick that sits on the counter. I stare at it again.

Two lines.

Two perfect lines—the ones that will perhaps change our lives.

I need to book in to see a doctor this afternoon. I don't want to get all excited for nothing. It may be a false alarm. After all, I am on the pill. I think back to the last few months and how regular I've been taking them. I missed a few, but I took them the very next day. I've accidently done this every once and a while, and never fallen pregnant before.

Excitement bubbles in my stomach and Enrico's request to have a day off doesn't seem so ridiculous. How am I supposed to concentrate on fabric when I am possibly making a baby?

I walk back into the bathroom and text Lorenzo.

Good Morning.
Are you awake?

A text bounces straight back.

Outside your door.

I frown. That's odd. I text back.

Can we go back to the apartment so I can get ready for work?

He replies.

Yes, of course.
See you soon.

I stare at my phone and bite my bottom lip as I contemplate asking the next question. Oh, stuff it, I want to know. I text back.

Is Bianca Awake?

A reply comes in.

Yes, she's in the kitchen.
I'll meet you there.

I cringe. Fuck.

I was hoping not to see her. She seems nice but she's very vague with me. I know she is only being polite. I can feel an underlying edginess coming from her. She didn't mention our engagement at all last night, and I know she knows. Enrico told me that he called her on Sunday. He said she was happy, but now that she didn't say anything to me, I'm not so sure. It was late when arrived last night, though. Maybe we'll get a chance to chat now.

Damn Enrico for putting me into this position. Bianca and I have said like five words to each other and now he makes me sleep here without him. What was he thinking? Hopefully Francesca is awake. She's lovely and may help me break the ice.

I puff air into my cheeks as I stare at my reflection in the mirror. I do have to get to know them better at some stage, I suppose.

Here goes nothing.

I quickly dress and make my bed. I throw on my clothes, and with one last look around the beautiful room, I open the bedroom door.

I'm greeted by the sight of three men, each sitting on chairs in the hall. There's Marly, Pedro, and Alexander.

What the hell?

"Hi." I look between them. "What are you guys doing?"

Marly stands. "Just a nightshift. Are you okay? Ready to leave?"

"Have you been out here all night?"

Marly takes my overnight bag from me and holds his hand out to lead me downstairs. "Just doing our job."

"Oh." I walk down the grand staircase and can hear people talking in the kitchen. Francesca's laugh echoes, and relief fills me. Thank God she's awake.

I twist my fingers nervously in front of me and walk into the kitchen. I find Bianca and Lorenzo sitting at the kitchen counter drinking coffee. Francesca is at the table eating her breakfast in her school uniform. Her face lights up when she sees me, and she jumps to her feet.

"Olivia." She smiles happily as she hugs me.

"Hi." I smile back. "It's so lovely to see you again." I look up to Bianca who forces a smile and sips her coffee.

"Hello," she says.

"Hello." Oh God, she hates me. I can tell. "Thank you for having me last night."

"That's okay, dear." Her eyes hold mine, and I just want the earth to swallow me up.

"Mamma, don't forget I'm going to the library this afternoon after school," Francesca says.

"What is this sudden interest in going to the library every day lately? Can't your friends come here to study?'

"No, Mamma, it's easier for my study group to meet there. It's central for all of us."

"Antonio has to wait around there for you every day," Bianca replies.

"It's okay, that's what he gets paid for," Lorenzo interrupts. He looks over at Francesca and gives her a warm smile with a wink, and she smiles back. It's obvious these two get along well.

I'm assuming that Antonio is Francesca's bodyguard.

"Would you like a cup of coffee?" Bianca asks me.

My eyes flick to Lorenzo. "Do we have time?"

"Yes, of course." He stands. "Come, Francesca, I'll walk you out."

Don't leave me alone with her.

"It was great seeing you again." Francesca kisses me on the cheek and skips out of the room. I watch her and Lorenzo as they walk side by side.

Hmm... still no mention of the engagement. Does she even know? My eyes come back to Bianca, and hers are fixed firmly on me. "How do you like your coffee?"

Damn, Enrico is getting an earful when I see him. Why would he put me in this position?

I slide onto the stool beside her. "Just with milk, please."

I watch her as she makes my coffee. My heart is beating fast. I don't know what to say to her. She makes me nervous as fuck.

She puts the coffee back down in front of me, and I look down at it. "Thank you."

It's so strong, it could start a car.

I smile as I take a sip, and I clench my jaw to stop myself from gagging. It wouldn't just start a car, it could fuel a fucking rocket ship.

She sips her coffee as her eyes assess me, and we sit in uncomfortable silence for a while. I feel like she has something to say but is holding her tongue.

I look around nervously. "It's a beautiful home you have."

"Thank you."

She's still wearing her cream silk robe with a matching nightdress. Her long, dark hair is styled like she's in Hollywood. She looks beautiful. There's not a hair out of place.

Who looks this good when they wake up?

I nervously drag my hand through my knotted ponytail. God, what must I look like?

I take another sip of my rocket fuel. Jesus Christ. Who drinks this shit for fun?

"I might just put some sugar in it, if that's okay?" I say nervously.

"Too strong for you?"

"Yes." I force a smile. "A little." Too strong for human consumption, actually. This stuff would kill a dog.

Her eyes drop to my engagement ring.

I wait for her to say something. Please say something.

"So, you're engaged?"

Oh shit. Not what I was hoping to hear. "Yes."

Her eyes rise and hold mine for an extended time.

I twist my fingers in my lap as I wait for her to elaborate, which she doesn't.

"You're unhappy about it?" I ask.

She rolls her lips and looks away from me.

I swallow the nervous lump in my throat.

"As long as Enrico is happy, I am happy." She eventually sighs.

"But you would rather he was marrying someone else..." Her eyes drop to the kitchen counter. "You want him to marry an Italian?"

"Yes," she replies with no emotion.

"Me, too."

She frowns up at me.

"I wish we didn't fall in love," I reply sadly. "Because then I wouldn't have to choose between my family, my country, and the man that I love."

Her eyes search mine.

"It's not ideal." I sip the caffeinated poison. "I know that I have to give everything up to live here if I want to be with Enrico. He's made it very clear that he will never leave Italy."

"And you're okay with that?"

I shrug. "I don't have a choice."

We sit in silence for a while before she eventually speaks. "I just wanted my grandchildren to be ..."

"Italian?" I answer for her.

She nods sadly.

"Bianca, I know I'm not Italian, and I know I'm not your choice of a daughter-in-law, but, I need you."

Her eyes hold mine.

"You and Francesca will be the only family I will have. I have to leave mine to become a Ferrara." Emotion suddenly overwhelms me at the prospect of leaving my family forever, and my eyes fill with tears. "Believe me, I would not choose to leave my country for love, but love chose me, and I have to make the most of it. We can't live without each other. We tried, and it didn't work."

Her shoulders slump. "It's nothing personal, Olivia."

"I know. I wouldn't want my Italian son to marry an Australian who can't cook either."

Her mouth falls open in surprise. "You can't even cook?"

The look of sheer horror on her face makes me smile. "Nope. Not really."

She pinches the bridge of her nose, and I bite my bottom lip to stop myself from laughing out loud.

"Dear God, Olivia, you will be the very death of me." She huffs.

"It's not all bad. I'm willing to learn. I'm learning your language and doing all I can..." I search for the right words. "I'll do anything to make Enrico happy. I'm trying really hard, but you need to try too. This isn't ideal, I know that, but we have to make it work between us... for him."

Her eyes hold mine. "You're going to be late for work."

She's dismissing me. "Oh." I drag myself off the chair and go to the sink to wash my cup. "Thanks for the coffee."

"You're welcome."

"See you later then." I sigh sadly.

She stays silent.

I turn and slowly walk toward the door.

"Olivia," she calls.

I turn back to her.

"Food is the Italian language of love. You will be cooking well for Enrico. My son deserves the best."

I frown. What's that supposed to mean?

"Your first cooking lesson is on Sunday with Enrico's grandmother."

Hope blooms in my chest, and I smile softly.

"She does not mince her words. Prepare yourself." She lifts her chin defiantly, her eyes are hard, but I see a glimmer of softness behind them. Something tells me Grandma is going to be a hard cookie to crack, though.

"Thank you, I'll look forward to it." I turn and walk out of the kitchen feeling very proud of myself. I feel like jumping and punching the air.

I think I actually did okay.

It's 4:45 p.m. when my phone rings and I see Rici's name on the screen.

"Well, hello there," I answer playfully.

"Hello, Olivia." His commanding voice echoes down the line.

.I smile broadly, I missed him last night and I can't wait to see him. "And to what do I owe this pleasure, Mr. Ferrara?" He never calls me this close to home time.

"I'm picking you up today. Catch the lift straight down to the basement parking lot. I'm parked just outside the elevator."

"How come?" I frown.

"Just do it."

"All right." I sigh. "Still in your bad mood, I see." "Olivia," he warns. "Do not give me your attitude today. You are right, I am not in the mood."

I smile. I love stirring him up. I think back to not so long ago when that tone in his voice would have had me running scared. How times have changed.

"I'll be down in ten."

"See you soon."

"Goodbye."

Fifteen minutes later, I bounce out of the elevator and see the procession of cars waiting for me. Not only is Enrico here, but there are an extra three cars today. Every day it seems like more and more guards are added to the procession. I give the cars behind a wave, and I make my way to the front car. Enrico gets out and opens the door for me.

"Olivia," he says as I approach him.

"Mr. Ferrara." I smirk as I get into the car. He shuts the door and makes his way around to the driver's seat. He gets in and starts the car, leaving me to smile over at him.

I don't even try to kiss him in public anymore. I know better. He keeps that part of himself locked up safely for when we're in private. At first it used to bother me that we couldn't be affectionate around other people, but now I get it. He has twenty sets of eyes on him at all times. He's much more comfortable with his cold persona. It's easier this way. He keeps his feelings insanely private, and I like that I get a part of him that nobody else does.

The car pulls out of the parking lot, and I reach over to put my hand on his thigh. He takes it in his hand.

"How was your day?" I smile.

"Fine." He keeps his eyes on the road.

"You know, I had the best day."

"Why?"

"Well, I had a talk with your mother this morning."

"About what?"

"How I'm not Italian and how I'm not her choice for you."

"She said that?" he barks.

"Not in a mean way," I add. "In a being honest way." I pick up his hand and kiss it to try and calm him. "And it's not like I wasn't expecting it, you know? I mean, at least she was honest, and she wasn't being nasty." I frown as I think back to what she said. "She talked to me at least. Last time I met her she didn't address me once."

He clenches his jaw and glares through the windscreen.

"What's that look for?" I ask.

"She had better want to fucking talk to you," he snaps.

I roll my eyes. "I'm not saying we're besties or anything." I shrug. "But it's a starting point."

His eyes rise to the rearview mirror.

"I start cooking lessons with your grandmother on Sunday."

"Olivia, my grandmother will eat you alive. This woman makes grown men cry. Stay away from my grandmother."

"That's okay. I can hack it."

He frowns and mouths the words *hack it* as he tries to process its meaning. "What is hack it?"

"It means I can take it. I'm willing to put up with it until she comes around to liking me."

He rolls his eyes.

I reach over and run my fingers through his hair, pushing it behind his ear. "I'll do anything for you."

"We are moving back to Lake Como tonight. Your things are already there."

"What? Why?" I frown.

"Because I said so."

"Well, I don't want to."

"You will do as you are told. And when I tell you to stay home from work, you will fucking stay home from work."

I screw up my face. "What the hell? What's wrong with you today?"

He clenches his jaw as he glares out at the road.

"Don't give me your attitude, Enrico. I'm not putting up with your bossy bullshit."

"I have a lot on my plate at the moment and I don't want to be dealing with your disobedience."

"Disobedience?" I snap. "I'm not a dog, you know?"

He rolls his eyes as we take the turn off to Lake Como.

"I said I want to stay in Milan at the apartment." He is really beginning to piss me off now.

He punches the steering wheel hard, causing me to jump. "And I said *we are staying at Lake Como*. I can't keep you safe in the apartment in Milan. Do not push for a fight with me tonight, Olivia. I am not in the fucking mood."

I sit back in my seat, affronted.

Safe.

He thinks I'm not safe. Why would he think that?

What happened in Sicily? I've been so preoccupied with all of my news that I didn't even bother asking what the emergency was last night. His eyes flick to the rearview mirror again. That's like the tenth time he has done that. I turn in my seat and look through the back window. There are two cars behind us and one in front. It's more security than ever.

Something's going on.

I watch him as he drives. He's deep in thought—miles away. Anger is radiating out of his every pore.

Jeez.

I exhale heavily. He doesn't need me adding to his stress levels and to be fighting about crap. I snuggle back into my seat and close my eyes. I'm going to ignore him. We can't fight if I'm not awake. I let happy thoughts fill my mind. I dream of our baby... and I wonder if it's a boy or a girl.

Francesca

Antonio opens the door, his smile broad. "You're really trying this term, Francesca. No doubt your marks will represent all your hard work this year. Your father would be so proud of you."

I smile at my trusty bodyguard. If only he knew.

Every day for the last fortnight, I have come to the library for one reason only.

Giuliano Linden.

He's like a drug I can't quit, and we meet here in secret. I'm not allowed to date, and even if I were, I wouldn't be allowed to date him. He's nineteen. My mother would see him as too old for me. He's not too old for me. He's just right—perfect in every way.

I walk into the library with Antonio behind me. I'm holding my breath as I take a seat at the communal table next to a group of girls.

"Hi." I smile as I pretend to know them.

"Hi," they all reply politely.

I open my book as Antonio does his usual walk around of the library, checking to see that everything and everyone is in order. Once satisfied, he gives me a nod and goes to wait outside near the front doors. I breath out a sigh of relief.

Every afternoon, I live in fear that he's going to spot Giuliano in the corner, pretending to study. I can't imagine what would happen if he did.

Giuliano wears a cap to shield his face. From a distance he looks a lot younger than he is. Antonio hasn't noticed him yet. Giuliano blends in with the young crowd. I'm hoping Antonio never will discover what's going on.

My mother would hit the roof if she knew I'd been lying to her.

Right on cue, Giuliano lifts his head, and our eyes meet across the library. He gives me a broad smile. My heart somersaults in my chest and I feel myself light up. I never knew that a smile could make me feel ten feet tall.

But his does.

When I'm with him, I feel invincible.

I make my way over to where he sits. "Hello."

His eyes search mine as I take a seat beside him. "Hi."

We stare at each other for a moment. There's this swirling chemistry in the air between us, and it's like nothing I've ever felt before. A palpable energy.

I know he feels the same as me because he tells me often.

We meet every afternoon and talk for two hours. Then we go home and talk to each other all night long on Snapchat. We never run out of things to say. We discuss our hopes and our dreams and everything in between.

He's sweet and funny—so different to anyone I've ever met. He makes me feel like I'm the only girl in the world, and to him... I am.

From our first kiss, we have been inseparable. Our chance meeting at my brother's house was meant to be. We were meant to be.

It's serendipity in its finest form.

I just wish we could be alone, but for now, stolen time in the library is all we have.

He takes my hand under the table. "You look beautiful," he whispers.

I tuck a piece of my hair behind my ear, and I feel myself blush under his gaze. "You say that every day."

His eyes twinkle as he watches me. "That's because it's true."

I squeeze his hand and he squeezes it back. It's like we have a secret language only the two of us can understand. "How was your day?" I whisper.

He looks out over all the people in the library. "It's better now."

I smile softly.

His eyes drop to my lips. "I just want to kiss you."

I squeeze his hand again. Me too.

My heart beats faster in my chest.

Giuliano Linden is everything and more.

Olivia

"Olivia, we are home."

Enrico's deep voice wakes me from my slumber. I'm tired. I must have gotten all of two hours sleep last night. He leans into the car and helps me out. The first person I see is Sergio. His hungry eyes drop down my body, and the hairs on the back of my neck stand to attention.

Enrico stops still and glares at him.

My heart stops. Fuck, he saw it.

"What was that look?" He frowns.

Sergio swallows the lump in his throat.

Enrico walks up to him and leans in only an inch from his face. "I asked you... what was that fucking look?"

Shit.

Sergio shakes his head. "I-I didn't... I wasn't... I mean."

Enrico reaches up and grabs him around the throat, and he squeezes hard. The men and I all take a collective gasp as our eyes widen.

"If I see you look at Olivia like that again," he sneers in a whisper. "I'm going to hang you by your feet." He tightens his grip around his neck. "I'm going to cut your fucking throat and watch you bleed out. Do you understand?"

29

Olivia

"ENRICO." I gasp. "Calm down."

He doesn't calm. He keeps his grip around Sergio's neck and tightens it even more.

"Let's go inside," I urge.

Enrico glares at Sergio. I'm not sure if he's about to completely lose it and actually strangle him for real.

"Enrico," I repeat. "Let's go... *now*." I rub his back as a silent reminder that I'm here. He pushes Sergio back, releasing him from his vise-like grip. "Get out of my sight. Go downtown and look after the club. You're not to come to my home or be near Olivia again."

Sergio drops his head, his face filled with shame.

"Do you understand me?" Enrico barks.

"Yes, sir."

Enrico glares at him, and I know he isn't finished with this conversation, but right now, I need to diffuse this situation. I grab his hand and pull him away.

"Come on."

Enrico walks inside, and I close the door behind us. His jaw is clenched and he's raging mad. I look around at the Lake Como house. It's familiar, grand, and beautiful. It feels like a long time since we've been here.

He takes his suit jacket off, and then jerks his tie hard as he removes it. He throws them both to the side. I watch him knowing this isn't about Sergio. There is something else going on, I can feel it.

"Don't worry about Sergio. Don't let him get to you," I say softly.

He storms past me to the bar, and with a shaky hand, he pours himself a drink. He tips his head back and drains his glass only to refill it straight away.

"What's wrong?" I ask.

He drags his hand down his face.

"Baby, talk to me," I urge him.

He takes me into his arms and holds me tight—so tight, I may snap. He doesn't speak. He doesn't have to. He needs my comfort. I can feel that need pouring out of him.

"Just work things. It's nothing for you to worry about," he eventually murmurs.

I slowly slide my hand down over his broad chest as I kiss him slowly. His eyes close at the contact. "You're home now, Rici," I whisper against his lips. "It's okay, baby. Forget work." I slide my hand down lower and cup his penis through his pants. I feel it slowly begin to grow. "Let's get you relaxed, shall we?"

His face softens as he returns my kiss.

I undo his suit pants and slide my hand down to cup his balls. They're heavy, hard, and engorged. "Look how full you are," I whisper up at him as I give him a long stroke. "No wonder you're stressed."

His lips take mine and I can feel his stress begin to evaporate.

I stroke him slowly as we kiss. His breath is quivering, and I know he's already close to the edge.

His hands move to my shoulders and he pushes me down to my knees. I smile as he slides his pants down a little. His large cock hangs heavily between his legs.

Begging… no, *demanding* my attention.

With my eyes locked on his, I slowly lick the pre-ejaculate that drips from his end. Hmm. Tastes good.

He hisses in appreciation. "Yes, Olivia." His hand moves to the back of my head to hold me in place as his instincts take over. He wants in my mouth.

He wants it all in my mouth.

He grabs his dick at the base and brushes his end over my parted lips. He's taunting himself, watching his cock with dark eyes as it brushes over me.

I smile up at him. He motions to push himself into my mouth and I tighten my lips. "Not yet," I whisper.

I begin to fist him hard and fast, and he inhales sharply as he watches on. He pushes on the back of my head. He wants in.

I lick up his thick shaft, and his eyes roll back in his head. This is the best part about giving head: the anticipation.

Putting him through hell until I decide when he can have it.

"What do you want, baby?" I whisper.

"Suck me."

I run my lips over his end, and he grabs the back of my head. I push back and resist.

"Ol-iv-i-a," he purrs.

I take just his tip in my mouth, and I flick my tongue back and forth. His head tips back and he moans.

I smile around him. God, I love this. I love bringing him undone.

Never have I felt more powerful than when I am on my knees in front of Enrico Ferrara. The world stops. There is nothing else but his cock and my mouth.

I own him when I'm here and he knows it.

I take him deep into my mouth and I feel his legs nearly buckle beneath him. He instinctively pushes on the back of my head and I gag around him as his cock closes over my throat. I give him a subtle shake of my head.

"Too deep," I moan.

His hands tighten in my hair as he struggles to regain control over himself. His chest rises and falls as he gasps for breath.

I continue to suck and lick to the sounds of his soft moans. He loves this.

This is his thing. Just five minutes ago he was ready to kill someone. I smile at the thought.

My mouth is Enrico Ferrara's form of Xanax.

I suck harder and harder as I begin to fist him. He clenches and hisses, and then drags me to my feet before he throws me on the sofa. He flips me over so that I am on my knees, and he drags me to the edge of the seat. He lifts my skirt, pulls my panties to the side, and in one motion, he slides in deep.

I moan out in appreciation.

With his hands griped firmly on my hips, he pulls out slowly to let me get used to him. No matter how aroused he is, he never forgets his size and the real possibility that he could hurt me.

His hand roams over my back, and he grabs a handful of my

hair to pull me back onto him. My neck stretches back toward his vice-like grip.

My eyes roll. God, I love it when he dominates me like this. He pulls out slowly and pushes in again.

And then he slams home hard.

The air is pushed from my lunges, and I cry out. His hand drifts to my shoulders as he pushes them down. He wants my ass in the air.

Total domination.

With my face pushed down into the sofa, he begins to ride me hard.

Our skin slapping together echoes around the room, and my eyes dart to the front door. Good God. At least ten men stand just on the other side of it.

Can they hear us?

He begins to pant, and I close my eyes and clench in a rhythm around him.

A move that I know drives him to the point of no return.

"Fuck. Fuck. Fuck!" he growls. "Come." He pumps me hard. "I can't stop. You need to come."

I smile against the cushion. He can't stand the thought of coming first. It's his worst nightmare.

God, I love this man.

"Olivia!" he cries as he completely loses control. "Now. Fucking now."

I clench and spiral hard as his deep guttural moan fills the room. He pumps me full of his semen. I can feel the heat as it leaves his body and enters mine. He moves me slowly to completely empty himself, and then he lifts me and falls onto the sofa in a seated position. He pulls me over him to straddle his lap. He slides his cock deep back into my body and kisses me softly.

This is the time that I love.

No matter how hard we fuck, no matter how animalistic we get with each other,

after we're finished, he always puts himself back into me in a missionary position so he can kiss me.

Just him, me, and the love that we share. A perfect moment of clarity between us.

A tenderness that we only get from each other.

"I love you," he whispers against my lips. My heart constricts.

Now... it's time.

I pull back from our embrace. "Rici," I whisper. "Ti amo."

He smiles softly.

"I'm pregnant."

His face falls.

"I don't know how it happened, or if the timing is right."

His eyes search mine.

"Is this okay?" I whisper, suddenly nervous.

He grabs me, pulls me to him, and he buries my head into his neck. "Of course, it's okay, my love." He pulls me back so he can see my face. "Are you sure?"

"I did a pregnancy test and it came back positive."

His face breaks into a breathtaking smile. His eyes are filled with tears. "I love you so much, Olivia." He kisses me. "Thank you, thank you, thank you. A child... your child," he whispers in awe.

"Our child." I smile softly.

His face falls, as if he's suddenly remembering something. "Oh dear God."

"What?"

"I was so rough just now." His hand goes to my stomach. "Are you all right? Did I hurt you?"

I smile to myself. Never would I have imagined he would be worried about having rough sex.

"You were perfect. *We* are perfect."

His hand spreads over my stomach and we both stare down at it.

A baby. Our baby.

So, so precious.

Jennifer

I put the earpiece into my ear and stare at the computer screen in front of me. "Are we on?" I ask.

The screen rolls and then flips open. I can see the six people on the other end of the conference call. The Carabinieri—the ones who assigned me to this mission—is made up of five men and one woman. They are the team who are determined to bring the Ferrara reign over Italy to an end.

"Hello, Jessica," Alexander says.

It's nice to be addressed by my real name for a change. I've never worked undercover before. It's felt weird being called Jennifer all the time.

"Hello." I smile. We have these phone conferences every two to three days. Today I'm excited. I have new information.

"How's everything going?" Smithson asks.

"Great. I've made some progress since we last spoke."

"How so?"

"Enrico and Olivia just became engaged. I pretended that I'm an event planner, which led to Olivia asking me to help her with the engagement party."

"That's fantastic." Alexander smiles. "Great work. We need to plant bugs throughout the house as soon as possible. Did you manage to plant one in Olivia's handbag yet?"

"No, unfortunately I haven't been left alone with it long enough. Her friend Natalie was at the table when we had a coffee. It's ready and waiting, though, so as soon as I get her alone, I'll activate it. I've started wearing a body wire in case she slips up in general conversation. She knows everything. She's no dummy."

"Good, more than ever we need intel. We are so close to bringing him down—closer than ever before."

"Has something new happened?"

"Yes." They flick up the screen in front of them and a series of images. "Have you seen this man before?"

I study the images of two men having coffee in what looks like a café. "One looks familiar. The one with the lighter hair."

"Yes, you would have seen him at times with Olivia. His name is Sergio Morelli. In the past, he's been the kingpin in the narcotics arm of Ferrara. Ten years ago, he started out as the hitman for Stephano, but his business brain soon got him a promotion. He ran the Sicily and Roma cocaine circuit for years. We haven't had any new intel on the drug situation for over eighteen months—not since Enrico took over. Not until this week."

I keep looking over the images as I listen to their story. "What happened?"

"See this man he is having coffee with?"

I look at the images of an older man in a suit. Distinguished, he doesn't appear to be Italian. "Yes."

"This is Adolfo Rodriguez."

My mouth falls open in surprise. "*The* Adolfo Rodriguez?" I gasp.

Alexander smiles smugly. "Yes, and you know what this means?"

Adolfo Rodriguez is the biggest cocaine supplier in the world. "Holy shit," I whisper.

"Up until now, Adolfo has been untouchable. Nobody has seen him in public for years. It's no coincidence that he's in Milan now."

Nerves swirl in my stomach. This case just became super important. I can't fuck this up. "You think Ferrara is going back into drugs?" I ask.

"Sergio and Adolfo had this meeting, and three days later a large shipment of something arrived by water, which was unloaded directly onto Enrico Ferrara's yacht in Monte Carlo."

My eyes widen. "You think it was cocaine?"

"We're sure of it, and by the size of the shipment, we're talking a large multi-million-euro deal. It's enough to put Ferrara away for a very long time. Thirty years, minimum"

"Wow," I whisper.

"The yacht is being watched around the clock. Hopefully, you will get those wires in place before they try and move it and we are forced to close in. The more solid evidence we have, the cleaner the court case will be."

I nod with renewed determination.

"Jessica, I can't stress enough how important it is that you get some wires into their properties. We need this case to be watertight. Forty years of Ferrara's crime hold over Italy will come to an end if you can come through on this. More than ever, this case is crucial."

I force a smile, a fission of guilt running through me. I wish I didn't like Olivia. It would be so much easier to ruin her life if she was a bitch.

But I knew what I was doing before I took this job, and Enrico is a low life criminal. In the long run, she's better off without him. I'm actually doing her a favor by locking him up for life.

"What if they try and move the drugs before we get any evidence?" I ask.

"Then we have to close in, and we can charge him based on possession alone. But if we have extra incriminating information, it will only help us further."

"Okay."

"When is this engagement party?" Alexander asks.

"It's next weekend. I'm going to need some help organizing it. I have no idea what I'm doing."

"Let us handle everything. All of the catering staff will be undercover police. You will be well covered and completely safe. This is the perfect scenario. Good work, Jessica."

I smile proudly. "Thank you." I hunch my shoulders together. "I'll report back tonight when I have some of the party details."

"Have a nice day." The screen goes black, and I stare at it for a moment.

Wow, shit just got real.

Enrico

I lie in the darkness and listen to Olivia's regulated breathing.

My angel is sleeping peacefully.

What must that feel like?

She's curled up on her side, facing away from me. Her head is on my arm and my other arm is around her, tucked up in between her breasts. I couldn't be any closer.

But it's never close enough.

Every time I close my eyes, I see the zipper of the body bag in the morgue slowly sliding down.

The pale blue face with the name Lucky Lombardi carved into it.

Her lifeless body kept in the freezer, as if she was insignificant—as if she didn't matter.

I close my eyes, the horror too real to handle.

I inhale as I try to calm myself, to chase away this fear, the sheer terror that my Olivia is on his radar.

Our baby.

I get a vision of Olivia's body floating in sea water, her pale blue face with the same sadistic carvings there, and her blonde hair floating on the surface.

She's dead.

I scrunch my eyes shut to try and block it out.

Why do I keep seeing it? Why do I keep seeing visions of my Olivia in the sea? Is it just a product of my fear or a premonition? Either way, the vision is haunting me.

I've never been scared of the consequences of who I am. Not until now.

What if he gets to her? What if he tortures her?

What if she dies?

I roll onto my back and stare up at the ceiling.

We will kill Lucky Lombardi. The war has only just begun. Ten of his men have already lost their lives today, but until I see Lombardi's lifeless body with my own eyes, I won't relax.

I need a plan—something to keep Olivia safe.

I glance over at the clock and see that it's 2:00 a.m. It will be 8:00 p.m. in New York. I slowly slide out of bed, throw on some boxer shorts, and walk downstairs to my office.

I scroll through my phone until I get to the name I'm searching for.

Gabriel Ferrara

My cousin.

Our grandfathers were brothers. As the second in line, his grandfather Emilio wasn't committed to Italy. His passion was very different. He moved to New York City and opened Ferrara Media, which is now one of the most successful media empires in the world. Gabriel is the CEO.

We have the same blood, yet the life he lives is so very different to mine. We grew up on opposite sides of the world —my family in Italy and his family in New York—but we understand each other. A strange comradery has built between us over recent years.

We have both struggled with being Ferraras. Both struggled being the CEO of a family business we didn't choose of our own accord.

Different ends of the spectrum.

Different businesses that are worlds apart.

The same goddamn battles.

Nobody gets it like we do.

We live with it every day. Like an insidious monster that sits on our shoulder, the pressures of expectation are heavy burdens to bear.

I dial his number and listen as it rings.

"Enrico." His voice is filled with happiness. "Tell me someone died."

I chuckle. We always say that we only get to see each other at funerals. "Not today. Hello, my friend."

"It's good to hear your voice. How are you?"

"Good. Engaged to be married." I smile at the sound of those three words. Who knew it would ever feel so good to say out loud?

"What?" He gasps. "Engaged? Poor woman. Who is she?"

I laugh. "Her name is Olivia Reynolds, and she's the most beautiful woman on the planet. Listen, I need a favor."

"Name it."

I exhale heavily. "I have some things going down here. A threat has been made on Olivia. A madman has threatened her life if I don't do as he asks. He knows where she works. He knows everything about her. We are handling it, but not as fast as I would like."

"Okay." He listens.

"If I need to, can I send Olivia to you in the states? I may have to get her out of Italy in a hurry, but I need somewhere that I know she will be well guarded."

"Of course. Send her. You know I have impeccable security."

"Thank you." I smile sadly. "How are you?"

"All right." He pauses. "I have a lot to tell you when we catch up next."

"And your family?"

"Are all well. Yours?"

"Good, everything is great, except for this madman murdering my working girls."

"Jesus, Enrico."

"I know." I sigh. "Look, I'll let you know if I'm sending her. Maybe this week for a few days."

"I will guard her with my life, Enrico. You have my word."

"Thank you." I close my eyes. We both linger on the line, not wanting to hang up the call.

"Are you really all right?" he finally asks.

"As long as Olivia's safe, I will be fine."

"Take the threat out."

"I will. He's gone into hiding." I get a vision of the name

carved into her face, and contempt fills my every pore. "Once I find him, there'll be hell to pay."

"I look forward to hearing his screams." He chuckles.

I smile. Gabriel is the only civilian I know who can deal with my lifestyle.

He gets it.

Nothing comes as a shock to him. He is a Ferrara, after all. "Thank you. I'll let you know if I'm sending Olivia. If she does come, I may send her friend or her mother with her so that she's not alone."

"Send whoever you want. Speak soon."

I hang up and sit in the silence of my office for a while. I go over the last forty-eight hours in my mind.

A whirlwind of emotions rush through me.

I'm marrying the love of my life. We've been blessed with a child. There's so much love and light in my life, and yet all I can feel is an overwhelming fear that I'm about to lose everything.

An eerie sense of calm hangs in the air. I can feel it—like a storm brewing on a mountain ready to fall. Something is coming.

I close my eyes. Please... don't let it be that.

Olivia. My darling Olivia.

"Rici?" I hear her call from the stairs. "Where are you, baby?"

"Here, my love." I jump to my feet and rush out into the living area. I find her coming down the steps in her nightgown.

Her face lights up when she sees me. "I didn't know where you were."

"I had to take a call." I put my arm around her and lead her back up the stairs. "Come... back to bed." I kiss her

temple. "We have a doctor's appointment in the morning, remember?"

She looks up at me with a beautiful smile. "How could I forget?"

Olivia

I roll over in the darkness. It's late... or should I say early? With the shutters down I have no idea. I hear a creak and I frown.

I know that creak.

That's the creak of the bottom step.

I sit up in bed.

Someone's in the house.

30

Olivia

I SIT STILL in the darkness and listen. I glance over to Enrico who is fast asleep beside me. He's been restless all night and has only just drifted off.

Silence.

I slowly get up and tiptoe over to the door. I quietly close it and flick the lock.

My heart is hammering hard in my chest. I stand and listen.

I hear another creak and I know that creak is near the top step.

I run to Enrico. "Wake up."

"Huh?"

"Someone's in the house."

"Huh?"

"I heard the step creak."

He launches out of bed and grabs a gun from his top drawer. "Get dressed." He quickly dials a number on his phone.

I look down to see I'm naked.

Shit.

I'm running into my wardrobe when I hear him whisper, "C'è qualcuno in casa." *Translation: Someone's in the house.*

He walks up behind me. "Go into the bathroom and lock the door. Do *not* come out," he whispers.

"Yes, let's go." I grab my nightgown and run to the bathroom. He hands me a gun.

"Keep the door locked, and if anyone comes in here, don't ask questions. You shoot to kill."

"What? Where are you going?" I look down at the gun in my hand with wide eyes. It's heavy, made of cold, black metal. It's designed to take a life.

"I'll be back in a minute."

"What? No, you stay here, too," I whisper. I grab his arm, suddenly frantic. "Stay here. Don't you go out there. Please don't go out there."

He pushes me into the bathroom and closes the door. "Lock it," he snaps angrily through the heavy wood.

My face scrunches up and tears fill my eyes as I flick the lock. I begin to pace. Oh my God, what is happening. I hear our bedroom door open and I hold my breath as I listen. My heart is hammering hard in my chest.

I wait... and I wait... and I wait.

Eventually, I hear voices I recognize.

Marley and Maso.

I hear Enrico say something from up the hall. I open the bathroom door and peer around the side of it. What's happening out there?

"Libero," someone yells. *Translation: Clear.*

The house is a hive of activity. There must be ten men

inside searching it. I can hear them walking through and banging around.

Enrico comes into the bedroom.

"Why do you have the door unlocked?" he barks.

My face crumbles, and his falls as he sees my tears and my shaking hand holding the heavy guy. I'm a nervous wreck.

"Olivia," he says softly as he takes the gun from me and wraps me in his arms. "It's okay, it's okay." He holds me against his chest. "What did you hear?"

"I heard the step creak."

"Are you sure?"

"Yes, and I heard the top one creak a few moments later."

He frowns as he holds me tight.

"What's going on?" Sergio asks as he comes into the room. "I was in the boathouse and heard the commotion."

We both turn toward him, surprised. "What are you doing here?" Enrico snaps.

"I was covering a shift for someone who called in sick."

"Olivia heard something."

Sergio's eyes flick to me. "Did you see anyone?"

I shake my head. "No."

"It's impossible. Nobody could get in here. We have the place surrounded."

"Just search the fucking house," Enrico growls impatiently.

He storms out of the room on a mission.

The hairs on the back of my neck rise to attention.

For some sick reason, my gut instinct sets off an alarm bell.

It was him. Sergio was in the fucking house. I can feel it.

"Why do I think it was him who was in the house?" I whisper.

Enrico frowns down at me, as if surprised by my accusation. "Why would he be in the house?"

"You tell me," I whisper angrily. "Why is he even here? Didn't you tell him to leave last night? I don't trust him at all."

Enrico glares out the door after him, his jaw clenched, and I know that he's suspicious, too.

The house is now abuzz with people. Every light is on as they go through and search the rooms one by one. Every now and then I hear someone call to give the all clear in the distance.

I wrap my dressing gown around me tightly. If someone did happen to get in here, they would never be found. This house is as big as a state library.

"I hate this fucking house, Rici," I whisper. "It's too big and I don't feel safe here." I swipe the terrified tears from my eyes. "There could be fifty people hiding in this house and we wouldn't even know it."

Enrico drags his hand down his face, his frustration clear.

"Let's go to the Milan apartment," I plead. "Let's just get in the car and go now."

"It's not safe to transfer us both in the middle of the night."

"Why isn't safe? Who the fuck is waiting out there?"

"Will you stop fucking cursing?"

"No, I will not! There won't even be a fucking baby if we're all dead!" I cry.

"We can't leave now, Olivia." He passes the gun back over and walks me to the bed. "Get into bed."

"With a gun?" I hold it up.

"The house is clear."

"Then why do I need a fucking gun?" I snap.

"Olivia," he growls. "Do not fall apart on me now. Tomorrow we can move. For now, we stay here."

I get into bed, pull the covers over my head, completely

furious to be in this position. I can hear men speaking in Italian in the distance and doors being open and shut.

The tears take over.

I just want to be normal.

"Congratulations, you're nine weeks pregnant, Olivia," the doctor says across the desk. "The heartbeat is strong, and everything looks to be in perfect order. Your baby is fit and healthy."

Enrico's broad smile beams over at me and he grips my hand tightly in his.

We are at the obstetrician, and it's been a rough morning.

Enrico and I have hardly spoken. I'm stressed out after last night's activities, while he's been avoiding the subject. He thinks it was a false alarm—that I'm imagining things. They searched the entire house and found nothing.

But I know what I heard.

"You will have your baby by Christmas. Your due date is on the 15th of December."

Enrico leans over and kisses me softly. He's this big important man with all the money in the world, but when it comes down to it, nothing is more important to him than becoming a father.

"Congratulations, baby," he whispers.

I smile proudly. My heart is so full that it feels like it's about to explode.

"Your next appointment will be scheduled in four weeks." The doctor looks between us. "Do you have any questions?"

Enrico's eyes flick to me, and I know he has a million. "Is there anything particular that we..." He pauses as he searches for the right wording. "Shouldn't be doing?"

I can think of a few. Not being killed as I sleep is number one.

The doctor smiles, understanding the true meaning of his question. "No, carry as normal. Sexual activity is natural and completely fine. It won't hurt the baby at all."

"Oh." Enrico's shoulders drop in relief. "Can she eat everything?"

"I would avoid raw seafood and soft cheeses, and of course alcohol and recreational drugs."

"Of course." Something tells me he is going to micromanage this pregnancy with strategic precision. "Okay then." Enrico stands and shakes the doctor's hand. "Thank you. We'll see you in a month."

He takes my hand and we walk out through the swanky surgery. When we make our way to the car, I try my hardest to not notice the bodyguards. I'm still on edge.

Enrico opens my door and I get in. He walks around to the driver's side and slides in beside me.

"We're going to be parents?" He smirks as he starts the car.

I hunch my shoulders up. He looks over and we smile goofily at each other.

No matter what else is going on in our lives at the moment, this right here is all that matters.

I can't believe this is happening.

"I love you." He kisses me softly and I melt into him. I can whine all I want about things that go bump in the night, but I could never whine about him.

He is perfect.

"Can we go out to lunch to officially celebrate?" I ask.

"I'd rather go home and celebrate." He kisses me again.

I know this kiss, it's an emotion overload kiss. The type he gives me when we have to be close.

"Lunch first." I smile.

He exhales heavily.

"Everyone's looking at us."

"Who cares? I'm having a baby. I'll do whatever I fucking like." He forces himself to refocus. "Lunch… then the afternoon in bed."

"I'm not quite sure that pregnant women spend the afternoon in bed doing rude things, Mr. Ferrara."

He gives me the best *come fuck me* look of all time. "Mine does."

He pulls out into the traffic and we drive for a while.

"We will have to bring the wedding forward."

My eyes flick over to him in question.

"I don't want anyone to know until we are married. I don't want them to think this is a shotgun wedding."

"Okay." I think for a moment. "I wish it happened a little later. I know the timing isn't that great."

He gives me a heart-stopping smile. "A child is a gift whenever it arrives."

I smile over at my gorgeous man; how did I get so lucky? "Thank you for being amazing."

"Thank you for being mine."

Enrico raises his wineglass with mine. "To us."

"To us." I smile. "Although a toast with mineral water doesn't seem to pull the same punch."

He chuckles. "Get used to it."

My phone buzzes on the table. "Hello," I answer.

"Hello, darling," Giorgio sings.

"Oh, hi." I cringe. "I'm so sorry I had today off. I… I had to go to the doctors."

"That's okay, darling. I was calling to tell you that they have found asbestos in the building. You will have to work from home for a week or two."

"What?" I frown. "Really?"

"It wasn't in the building, just in a wall structure that had been added over the years. It's being removed this week."

"Oh."

"It will be completely safe to return."

"So, I'll just work from home tomorrow?" I ask.

"Yes, unless you would rather have some time off. I can arrange that, too."

I frown over at Enrico. He frowns back in question. "Did you tell him?" I whisper.

He shakes his head. "No," he mouths back.

"Okay, that's great. I'll call you tomorrow, Giorgio."

"Goodbye, sweetheart. Have a nice day." He hangs up.

"Jeez."

"What?"

"They've found asbestos in the building. I have to work from home for a few weeks."

"Oh." He picks his drink up and sips it, not saying anything else.

I stare at him. He can't lie for shit. "Did you organize this?"

"No." He rearranges his napkin on his lap.

"Enrico." I gasp. "I have to work."

"And you can… from home." He takes my hands over the table. "My guards are super busy at the moment and it's easier if you work from home for security reasons. Giorgio didn't mind at all and, well, I just thought that now might be a nice time to bring your mother over."

I frown. “What?”

“I haven’t met her yet. She can come to the engagement party next weekend, and you can tell her about the baby in person. You don’t want to do it over the phone, do you? As soon as she knows, we can tell everyone else.”

I sit back in my chair in shock. “Really?”

“Yes, I want to get to know her, and who knows?” He shrugs. “We may convince her to move to Lake Como for a while. I can get her a house of her own on the lake so she will be close while you’re pregnant.”

I put my hands over my mouth. “That would be so amazing,” I whisper. “You are so thoughtful. Thank you. I’ll call her tonight.” I take out my pad and paper and write the words.

To do

“My friend is going to help me organize this party,” I say as I begin my list.

“What friend?”

“Jenn.”

“Who’s she?”

“My friend from the gym. Remember? You met her the night you carried on like a pork chop and punched Franco.”

He rolls his eyes, unimpressed by the memory. “He deserved it.”

“She used to be a party planner in Australia.”

“No.” He sips his drink.

“What?”

“I am not having a stranger involved.”

“She’s not a stranger.”

“She is. You don’t know her. Who knows who she is?” He sits back, annoyed. “She can’t even attend the party,” he adds.

My face falls. "What? Why not?"

"We don't know her." He widens his eyes, as if I should already know this.

"I know her."

"You really don't. Lorenzo will have to check her out. She isn't to come to the house at all until we get it through security."

I roll my eyes. "You're so dramatic. She's just a girl from the gym."

"No," he replies sharply. "I'm a realist. Nobody has access to you unless they are security checked first."

I look over and frown in surprise. "Speak of the devil. Look." I wave at Jennifer and her boyfriend Diego who have just walked into the restaurant. They smile, wave back, and make their way over to the table.

"Hi." I stand and kiss them both.

Enrico politely shakes their hands. "Hello." He looks them up and down.

Oh shit, he's going to be snarky.

"Will you join us for a drink?" I ask, a little uncomfortably.

"Yes." Jennifer smiles and sits down beside me.

Enrico glares at me and sips his wine.

Shit.

Diego orders a bottle of wine. "I'll have four new glasses, too, please," he says.

"What brings you here?" Enrico asks.

"We were in the area and thought we'd have lunch." Jenn smiles. "It's great that we ran into you. What a coincidence."

Enrico's calculating eyes hold Jennifer's, and he raises an eyebrow. "Yes, it is."

Oh God, what is he thinking? He can be such an arrogant ass when he wants to be.

Just be nice.

"Did you go to the gym this morning?" I try to break the ice.

"Yes, where were you?"

"I slept in." I glance over to Enrico who is staring at Diego.

"We need to get working on this party planning." Jennifer smiles as the wine arrives.

"That won't be necessary," Enrico interrupts. "We have it covered."

"Oh, it's no bother. I want to." Jennifer smiles. "I really need something to do."

"I said that won't be necessary," he asserts.

Diego fills three wineglasses, and then when he goes to fill the fourth, Enrico puts his hand over the glass. "No." He glares at him.

Shit, why is he being so rude?

I begin to perspire.

"The party is already organized." He sits back in his chair. "I never did catch your surnames, though?"

I swallow the lump in my throat. Earth, please swallow me up.

Jenn and Diego look at each other. Diego laughs. "Are you going to do a security check on us?"

Enrico smiles and raises his glass sarcastically. "Naturally."

"Enrico, ha-ha, such a joker." I fake a smile across the table and open my menu in a rush. "Let's just order our food, shall we?"

Fuck.

"My surname is Rogers and Diego's is Romano," Jennifer tells him. "What are you wearing to the party?" she asks me, clearly trying to change the subject.

"Where are you from?" Enrico asks.

Oh hell, what is this? The Spanish inquisition?

I eye the bottle of wine on the table, and I wish to God I could just drain it.

"Sicily," Diego replies.

Enrico's eyes hold his. "What do you do in Australia, Jennifer?"

"Ah… um… oh."

She hesitates, as if she's being put on the spot. Hang on. Her delay did sound a little suspicious, I do have to admit.

"I told you, I was an events manager."

Enrico pushes his chair out. "Unfortunately, Olivia and I have to get going."

My face falls. "What?"

"Now." He stands in a rush.

"But…" I frown.

He holds his hand out and glares at me. "Let's go."

I turn to Jennifer, embarrassed. "Sorry. Something has come up."

With one last death stare to my friends, Enrico dips his head. "Goodbye."

"Bye." I force a smile.

Enrico leads me out of the restaurant, and I have to practically run to keep up with him.

"Why are you being so damn rude?" I whisper.

"They're up to something."

"What? That's ridiculous."

"Mark my words, I'll call it in tomorrow." He looks back up the street toward the restaurant. "Something is off with those two. I can sense it."

I roll my eyes as we arrive at the car. "I am allowed to have friends."

"Get in the car."

I get into the car and slam the door. Damn control freak.

It turns out that finding an engagement party dress isn't all that easy.

We've been at this for hours.

"Okay," Giorgio says. "Let me see."

I peek my head out through the dressing room curtain. "Is anyone around?"

"Just me. Get out here."

I walk out and smirk as I put my hands on my hips. "This dress is ridiculous. I look like a stripper."

Giorgio's eyes drop down my body, and he frowns and holds his chin. "Well, that's not going to work." He begins to try and tuck my boobs back in as he wrestles with the fabric.

"You think?" I giggle as he tries to stretch the fabric over my exposed breasts. "It was definitely designed for a more petite woman."

"One without boobs." He looks me up and down. "Next one."

I go back into the changing room to try on my tenth dress.

"Giorgio, you need to prepare yourself for the fact that I might not be able to wear Valentino," I call. "I have a lot of beautiful dresses at home. I can just wear one of those."

"Nonsense." He huffs. "If there's nothing here you like, we'll be making you something. This is the biggest event in Milan."

I flick the curtain open and poke my head out. "What is?"

"The engagement party, of course."

"There's only fifty people coming." I frown.

Giorgio laughs at my horrified face. "Darling, have you seen the front page of the paper today?"

"No, why?"

"I'll find a copy for you." He closes the curtain in my face. "Try the next dress on. You are quite the celebrity now."

I flick the curtain open again in surprise. "Who? Me?" I scoff.

"Darling, you are marrying Enrico Ferrara, the king of Italy. What did you expect?"

I roll my eyes and flick the curtain closed.

"He's kept you relatively well hidden up until now. But from here on in, you are officially the property of Italy. Everything you do and wear will be splashed across every magazine in the country. Look at Bianca. She's the envy of every woman—the queen of fashion."

My anxiety begins to grow. "We need to find a fucking dress."

"Okay then. Next," he says, his urgency growing along with mine.

I begin to try on the next dress, and I hear him talking to someone. "Do you have a copy of today's newspaper?" He listens for a moment. "Can you chase one up for me, please?"

I pull up the dress and look in the mirror. It's a deep red fabric, and it's strapless with a rouged kind of look to it. I turn and look at my behind. This one is better.

I flick open the curtain and Giorgio's eyes light up.

"Oh, Olivia." He gasps as he spins me away from him and inspects my behind. "Oh, yes, I like this. I like this a lot."

I wiggle my hips in the mirror with a cheeky smile. "Me, too."

"Here you are." Someone hands Giorgio a newspaper, and he smiles as he studies it.

He holds it up, and on the front page is a picture of me. I can't understand what it says. It's written in Italian.

"What does it say?" I ask.

"Enrico Ferrara chooses his queen."

"That's the headline?"

He kisses my cheek. "It takes a brave woman to love a Ferrara man."

I smile, but my heart drops. "Why do you say that?"

He takes my hand in his. "Nothing really, just not everyone is cut out for the life of a Ferrara man, that's all." He flicks the curtain shut and I stare at my reflection in the mirror.

An insidious festering fear begins to swirl in my stomach, like the calm before the storm. *It takes a brave woman to love a Ferrara man.*

Bravery has never been my strong point.

"What about this?" I come out of the closet in a pink dress. I hold my hands out to give him the full effect. "Is this better?" I do a twirl.

Enrico rolls his eyes. "You look gorgeous, like you have in the last five dresses. Just pick one because we need to go."

God, all this fucking picking outfits lately has me going crazy. I wish Giorgio never showed me that damn newspaper. Now I'm second-guessing every damn outfit I wear.

How the fuck am I supposed to compete with Bianca?

"Pick one," he repeats.

I look at him, deadpan. He doesn't need to worry because he looks amazing in anything he wears, and how wrong can you go in an Armani suit?

I turn and look at my behind in the mirror. "I'm getting a fat ass already."

He smirks.

"Your baby is making me fat." I huff as I walk into the

wardrobe. "What do you wear to fucking church, anyway?" I call as I flick through all the coat hangers.

"The word fucking doesn't go in that sentence, Olivia!" he calls back.

"Stop telling me not to swear."

"I never knew a mother who swore so much."

"The baby isn't here yet so I'm saying all the fucks I can."

God, so many dresses and none that look good.

I'm nervous as all hell. I'm going to church with the Ferraras.

The whole damn family is coming. Enrico's brothers are home, and after church we are going back to Nona's. It's Sunday, and I was supposed to be having a cooking lesson, but I hope she's forgotten.

I know I want to.

At this stage, I don't care if Enrico eats toast for the rest of his life.

I put on a cream pantsuit. It has fitted trousers and a matching blazer jacket. I study myself in the mirror.

"Okay, we can work with this." I take the jacket off and put on a bronze silk blouse before draping the jacket over the top. I undo the top button of my blouse and walk out of the wardrobe. "Do I look like I'm going to work?"

Enrico looks up. His eyes drop down my body and he gives me a slow, sexy smile. "If being on your knees and sucking my cock is the work you want to be doing, then yes."

I put my hands on my hips and give him a wiggle. "Yes?"

He nods once. "Yes."

I walk back into the wardrobe and put a high heel sandal on one foot and a closed in pointy pump on the other. I clomp out. "What shoes say that I am a sensible, church-going Italian."

Enrico chuckles. "Nobody is listening to your shoes because your outfit screams *bend me over the pew and fuck me hard*."

"This suit is such a slut. I had no idea."

"Filthy. In fact, get out here now."

I go back into the wardrobe to continue getting ready. I apply sensible makeup and style my hair in big waves. I clip it back on one side. Twenty minutes later, I walk out into my bedroom. "Are you ready to go?"

"Have been for half an hour now," he replies flatly. He walks over to me and does up my top button. I let him because he will make me do it up anyway.

"It's not easy being this beautiful." I smile up at him.

He chuckles and rubs his hand down my behind. "I can only imagine."

The car pulls up at Milan Cathedral, and I dip my head to peer through the window. "Wow," I whisper. The church is majestic. It seems like everything in Italy is that way. Italians definitely don't do things in halves.

The stone detail is incredible, and a gold statue sits perched way up above, as if looking down from the Heavens.

Enrico smiles and holds my hand in his lap as he, too, peers up. "Beautiful, isn't it? It took over six centuries to build."

Nerves flutter in my stomach as Marly opens my door. "Miss Olivia." He nods with a smile.

"Thank you, Marly."

I get out of the car and Enrico takes my hand.

We walk up the gray stone steps and into the foyer of the church. Century old artwork lines the walls. There's tapestry and huge paintings, and holy cow, this place is on another level.

Enrico leads me farther into the church where the floors are mainly white with a large black and apricot pattern on it. I look up at the ceiling. It's hundreds of feet high and lined with exotic, stained-glass windows. This place is simply breathtaking. It reminds me a lot of Notre Dame Cathedral in Paris, filled with huge, gray stone columns and so many beautiful things, you don't know where to look first.

Enrico leads me to the side of the second entry doors and over to a white marble dish. He dips his fingertips in and crosses his chest.

"Now you do it," he whispers.

Oh, shit. I dip my fingers into the holy water and copy what he just did. He gives me a soft smile and leads me down toward the front of the church. He kneels toward the alter, bows his head, and crosses his chest again as he mutters something quietly before walking to sit down. He turns and gestures for to me to the do the same.

What do I say?

He bows, as if to prompt me, and I quickly bow and do the cross thing on my chest. Then I scurry into the church pew behind him. Oh man, I'm terrible at being a Catholic already. I need a full lesson on church etiquette when we get home.

The church is silent—sacred.

Hushed voices can be heard but nobody dares speak aloud.

We sit down behind his mother and Francesca. An older woman is with them, who I am assuming is Enrico's grandmother, and his two brothers sit to the left of them.

The priest appears and the worshipers all watch on with love.

They adore him, I can feel it.

He addresses the parish. His voice echoes through the

majestic church as if a rock star singing the crowd's favorite song.

He seems kind and knowledgeable, although I can't understand anything he is saying. It's all in Italian.

For the next hour, I sit silently through the service, as everyone seems to know a secret protocol—one I don't. They stand and sit in perfect unison. They know all the songs and they sing proudly.

Enrico doesn't look my way. His focus is completely on his priest, and it becomes clear very quickly why he wants me to be catholic.

Religion is important to him.

His family are all focused as they watch on. My eyes roam between them, and I wonder what was it like growing up in this family.

A heritage based on tradition.

Rules and regulations that cannot be broken.

I watch Bianca from behind, her back ramrod straight. She's wearing a black pencil skirt, a blouse, sheer stockings, and sky-high stilettos. She looks like a super model.

She fascinates me, to have lived the life she has lived. I can't wait until I get to know her better. His grandmother is in black, too, Enrico explained that they are in mourning and will wear black for three years after their husbands died.

It seems so bizarre, and is yet another tradition I don't understand.

The service ends and people begin to leave the church. Bianca turns and smiles. "Hello."

"Hi," I reply nervously. I grip my bag tightly.

The priest walks down to us and shakes Enrico's hand. "Hello, my child."

"Father, this is Olivia. The one I told you about."

"Ah, yes." He smiles as he shakes my hand. "You are right, Enrico, she looks like an angel."

I fake a smile. What the hell? He has his priest on speed dial?

"Friday night?" Enrico asks.

"Yes." The priest bows his head. "Our first meeting will be on Friday night." He looks over at me. "We will start your communion then, Olivia."

"Okay."

"Lovely meeting you." He disappears from the church, and I look up into Enrico's proud eyes. He gives me a sexy wink, and I bite my bottom lip to hide my smile.

I think I passed.

Enrico pulls into the parking space and turns the car off. His eyes come to me.

"You're quiet."

I clench my hands together on my lap. "I'm okay." I shrug casually, as if going to Nonna Ferrara's house with the entire family on a Sunday afternoon is an everyday occurrence. "A little nervous, perhaps."

He leans over and kisses me. "You'll be fine."

"I know." I drag my hands though my hair. "But, just to warn you, your grandma is probably going to hate me. I'm not much of a cook."

He gives me a slow, sexy smile.

"What?" I ask, confused by his amusement.

"I beg to differ. You cook very well… just not necessarily food."

"What have I cooked that isn't food?"

"My balls. My brain." He leans in to kiss me again, and his tongue sweeps through my open lips. "My heart."

I smirk. "Stop being cute."

"I can't help it." His hands rise to fasten the top button of my shirt.

I roll my eyes. Control freak.

He gets out of the car, opens my door, and takes my hand before he leads me up the stairs. The house is a huge mansion, made of marble and sandstone. Guards dressed in black suits are scattered everywhere.

It screams Mafiosi

Hell. I lied before. I'm not a little nervous. I'm fucking terrified.

We walk in through the front door, and Andrea and Matteo are the first people we see.

Andrea's eyes light up. "Olivia," he coos as he kisses me on the cheek.

"Hi."

"You remember Matteo?" Enrico asks.

"Hello." He smiles as he kisses me, also.

"Hi."

Their eyes are fixed on me, and then they glance at each other.

What are they thinking?

Francesca walks around the corner. "Olivia." She smiles and kisses my cheek.

"Hi."

"Come and meet Nonna," Enrico says.

I swallow the lump in my throat. "Great." I fake a smile as he leads me through to the back of the house.

Bianca is sitting at the counter with a glass of wine in her hand. She smiles warmly when she sees me. "Ciao, Olivia."

"Hello." I smile in return. Good God, this woman freaks me out.

There is a little old lady in the kitchen cooking, and the food smells amazing. The lady turns to look at me.

Enrico presents me to her. "Nonna, this is Olivia."

She stares at me for what feels like eternity before she finally says, "Ciao, Olivia."

I shake her hand, and she eyes me suspiciously again.

My nervous gaze travels to Enrico.

"Sii gentile, Nonna," he says.

Translation: be nice, Grandma.

She rolls her eyes and flicks her tea towel at him. "You come!" she snaps at me.

Huh?

"You come help me." She gestures to the pot of food.

"Oh." I nod. "Of course."

Bianca gives me a sympathetic smile. She takes an apron from the drawer and passes it to me. "Here, Olivia."

"Thanks."

She spins me around and helps me put it on.

"I'll leave you to it," Enrico says.

I widen my eyes at him. *Don't leave me with them.*

He smiles and gives me a wink.

"Sii gentile, Nonna," he says again before he disappears out to his brothers.

"Today, we make Sunday gravy with sausage and spaghetti," Nonna announces.

I stare at her for a moment. Did I hear that right?

Huh? *Gravy?*

Gravy and pasta? The gravy I make is brown and goes with chicken.

Oh, fucking hell.

What next?

Nonna begins to explain what is in the pot in great detail, while I try my hardest to take in her instructions.

She's firing orders at me, and I'm beginning to realize that this isn't just a kitchen. This is the army, and Nonna is the drill sergeant.

Francesca comes and stands beside me, and I take her hand in mine. "Don't leave me here alone with her," I mouth behind Nonna's back.

Francesca giggles in response. I glance over to see that Bianca is smirking into her wineglass, too.

I'm glad I'm keeping everyone amused.

"Olivia... concentrate!" Nonna snaps. I step forward and take the spoon.

"Yes, Nonna," I whisper.

Fuck me, he owes me some good sex for this.

It's just after 8:00 p.m. when we walk out to the car, hand-in-hand.

We've said our goodbyes and are finally alone in the dark

Dinner was a success, and I didn't poison anyone. Bianca made dessert, and we sat around the table and talked. There was laughter and fun.

It was actually pretty good. I survived.

Enrico opens my door and stares at me. It's like he has something on his mind.

"What?"

He kisses me softly. "I was just wondering how many times you can fall in love with the same person." I smile. "Because just when I think I can't love you anymore, my heart grows so I can love you harder." He kisses me softly. "Thank you."

"For what?"

"For teaching me how to be happy."

"Hello, Mum." I smile down the phone.

"Hi, darling. How is the fiancé today?"

I giggle. "Good. Great, actually."

"You wouldn't believe it, but Henry has had a fall."

"What? Is he okay?" Henry is my elderly uncle. He's gay, never been married, and has no family of his own. He's like a second father to my mum at eighteen years her senior.

"No, love, he's not. He broke his hip. I'm on my way to the hospital now but I wanted to let you know."

"Oh no." My heart drops. "I was going to see if you wanted to come over for the engagement party."

"When is it?"

I wince, knowing how ridiculous this sounds. "Next weekend."

"Oh, love, I just don't think I can swing it. I haven't saved enough money."

"We will pay. It won't cost you anything."

"Honey, I can't leave Henry at the moment."

My heart drops again. Great, I'm going to have none of my own family at my own engagement party.

"I'll come over for the wedding and stay a few months. How does that sound?"

I smile sadly. "That would be great, thank you."

"Did you ask your father?"

"No." I exhale heavily. I don't want Dad here ruining my mood. "It's okay. You go to the hospital and send Henry my love, okay?"

"Okay, love. Sorry, but it is really short notice."

"I know."

Enrico

"What are we doing here?" Lorenzo asks from the passenger seat.

I watch the front doors of the Milan Library from our parked car across the street. "Just checking something out."

"Like what?"

"You don't think it's weird that Francesca has been frequenting here?"

Lorenzo frowns. "What do you mean?"

"Francesca has been here every day for weeks."

"So? She's studying."

I watch Francesca's car arrive and pull into the parking lot. She gets out of her car with her driver and walks up the front steps. "I smell a rat."

"You're being ridiculous." He scoffs.

I smile and sit back in my seat. "We shall soon see, won't we?"

Twenty minutes later, Francesca's guard is sitting on the front steps of the library having a cigarette. He did his job, went in, and searched the premises with her. I get out of the car and cross the street. He stumbles to his feet as he sees me.

"Mr. Ferrara." He throws his cigarette to the side. "I just checked on her."

"It's fine. Stay where you are. I'm just here to talk to her." I brush past him and walk into the library to take a look around.

Where is she?'

My eyes scan the room until finally I find her. She's sitting in the back corner with a boy. I can't see his face. He's wearing a cap. I walk over to behind a bookcase and watch them. For five minutes, they talk, and then eventually, he picks up her hand and kisses the back of it.

They're obviously more than friends.

I clench my jaw. I knew it. I march over there at once, and they both look up.

My heart stops.

Giuliano.

What the...?

"What are you doing?" I growl.

His eyes widen in horror.

"Enrico," Francesca whispers in a panic. "We're just talking."

Before I can help myself, I grab him by the arm and I'm marching him toward the door. We burst out the front doors, and I throw him across the garden. He rolls spectacularly across the lawn.

"Rico!" Francesca cries from behind me.

"She is underage," I shout.

He scrambles to his feet and steps forward. "You can't stop me seeing her."

Lorenzo comes running across the street. "Rico. Rico, no!" he cries, waving his hands in the air. "Stop it. Stop it now."

For the second time tonight, I lose control. I grab Giuliano by the throat. "She is too young for you."

"Stop it!" Francesca cries. "I love him. Stop it, Rico. Don't hurt him."

I turn to her, my eyes wide. What the fuck?

He's her brother.

Lorenzo's horrified eyes meet mine, and he shakes his head in disbelief.

I squeeze Giuliano's throat so hard that his eyes nearly pop out of his skull.

"You go near her again and you will be dealing with me." I throw him across the garden, once more, and he falls to the ground.

Francesca runs to him but I grab her arm and tear her from his side. She fights to try and get back to him. I drag her to the car and throw her inside, slamming the door shut behind me.

I turn back to Giuliano as he watches on. He glares at me as he pushes himself to his feet. His fists are clenched by his sides, and anger is radiating out of him.

"I'm not leaving her alone," he states, as if daring me to come at him again.

I step forward, dangerously close to losing control.

"Rico, don't," Lorenzo whispers. "Leave it."

"I love her, and you can't keep her from me."

Contempt drips from my every pore. I don't think I've ever despised someone as much as I despise him.

"Watch me," I whisper.

He steps forward.

The kids got guts; I'll give him that.

"Over my dead body will you ever see Francesca again," I sneer.

He growls at me through gritted teeth, and I turn to get into the car. Once inside, I slam the door.

"Drive!" I yell to Antonio. I turn to Francesca who is crying in the backseat.

"I hate you, Enrico," she cries.

I turn back to the road and drag my hands through my hair.

I can't even speak to her, I'm too angry. This situation is completely out of control.

What the actual fuck just happened?

He's her brother.

"Enrico, can I see you for a moment?" Marly asks as he pokes his head around my office door.

"Yes, please come in."

Lorenzo stands to leave, and Marly looks between us. "Can you stay, Lorenzo?"

Lorenzo's eyes meet mine. "Sure." He falls back into his seat.

Marly falls into the seat. He seems nervous. "I had a phone call today from a private number."

"And?"

"Someone offered me ten million euros to kill you."

"What?"

He swallows nervously. "Lucky Lombardi is trying to recruit someone from your own team to kill you."

I stare at him, lost for words.

"What?" Lorenzo explodes as he jumps from his chair. "Are you serious?"

"Yes." He twists his hands nervously in front of him. "I told him I would do it, because I didn't want him to contact anyone else. It will buy us some time. If I said no, he would have offered it to someone else. This way, he thinks I am going to do it."

"Good thinking, Marly. Well done," Lorenzo tells him.

I begin to hear my heartbeat in my ears, and I go to the window and stare out the city.

My inside team? Who can I trust now?

"He's gone too far!" Lorenzo barks. "I'm going to kill him with my bare hands."

"Who else has he contacted?" I ask. What if he bribes one of Olivia's guards?

"Nobody would ever take a deal, Enrico. Our men are family."

She's in danger.

I stare out over the city as my mind begins to race. "Ten million euros is a lot of money, Lorenzo. It's only a matter of time before someone accepts it."

"Put a bounty on his head for fifteen million. His own men won't be so loyal," Lorenzo fires back.

I go to the bar and pour myself a drink where I quickly drain the glass. "We're losing control," I say quietly.

"We aren't."

"Lombardi has contacted my private security guard and offered him ten million fucking euros to kill me. What control do you think I have left?" I cry.

Lorenzo puts his head into his hands, and I turn to Marly. "Thank you, my friend. Your loyalty is greatly appreciated and will be well rewarded. Please, put your ear to the ground and try to find out if anyone else has been contacted."

"Yes, boss." He dips his head and rushes from the room.

I pour another glass of scotch as a heaviness hangs in the air. There has been a lot of bad things happening lately, but this is a low blow.

"Who can we trust?" I whisper. "I have no choice. I'm sending Olivia to New York."

Lorenzo drops his head in defeat.

"It's the only way I can guarantee her safety."

"Go with her," he pleads. "Run, hide... just until I find him. We will flush him out."

"No." I sip my drink. "I'm staying. He doesn't even want the brothels. His war is with me. He wants my Ferrara skin for bragging rights."

Lorenzo drags his shaky hand down his face. He knows I'm right.

My phone vibrates on my desk and an unidentified number comes up. Lorenzo's eyes meet mine.

"Keep him on the line for three minutes," he says.

I nod. "Hello," I answer.

"Hand them over or pay consequences."

"Go to Hell," I whisper. "What do you think you are doing?"

"You were warned."

The phone clicks as he hangs up.

Another threat from Lucky Lombardi. It's the third this week.

I stare straight ahead, and anger rages inside of me like a wildfire.

This time in my life is supposed to be exciting. Announcing my marriage. Planning for a baby.

What I am is stressed beyond belief.

"We'll find him. You have my word," Lorenzo says from his seat beside me.

"He's in hiding." He shakes his head in frustration. "But he can't hide forever. When he shows his face, he's a dead man."

My buzzer sounds. "Mr. Ferrara, I have Sophia here to see you."

I roll my eyes. Fuck, this is the last thing I need now. "Give me five minutes," I say to Lorenzo. I push the intercom. "Send her in."

The door opens and the beautiful Sophia comes into view.

"Hello." I stand, smile, and I kiss her cheek.

Lorenzo kisses her in a greeting, also.

"What do I owe this pleasure?" I ask, trying to act calm.

She clutches her handbag nervously. "I'm being followed."

I frown. "By who?"

"There's a man. He's been following me for three days now."

"What man?"

She looks around nervously. "I don't know who he is. I saw him the other day when I came out of my apartment, and now I keep seeing him."

"Are you sure he's following you?"

"Positive."

"Lorenzo, organize some guards for Sophia, please."

"Of course." He stands. "Can you describe him for me?"

"He's outside right now. He's... he's downstairs," she stammers. "Blue suit. White shirt."

Lorenzo's eyes meet mine. "Get Sergio and take care of it," I order.

Lorenzo rushes from the room as Sophia runs her fingers through her hair. She's visibly upset. "I don't know what to do. What if I'm next?"

"You're not." I take her into my arms and hold her. "It's all right," I whisper into her hair. "You're safe now."

"I haven't felt safe since you left me," she whispers against my neck. I feel her breath on my skin.

She lifts her hand, and the gold bangles that she always wears rattle together.

It's a familiar sound—one that evokes memories. I feel an unwelcome wave of arousal seep into my body. I instantly release her from my grip and take a step back.

When Sophia fucks, the sound of her bangles hitting together echoes throughout the room. The harder she fucks, the louder the sound.

Fucking her is like a game a child would play to hear the sound—to make it louder. It's the ultimate aphrodisiac. A goal that drives a man wild. Anytime I hear bangles clang together, I have a physical reaction. I clench my jaw as I try to chase away the memory.

"I miss you," she whispers.

"Don't."

She steps forward and takes my hand to place it over her heart. "How can you push me aside so easily?" Her eyes fill with tears.

"Sophia." I don't like seeing her like this.

"I love you, Enrico."

"Sophia," I whisper. "You need to understand that I'm with Olivia now."

"Why do you think it has to be me or her?" Her eyes search mine. "You can have me, too, my darling."

Our eyes are locked as the air swirls between us.

"You can be married to her and you can love me, too."

We stare at each other.

"We need each other, Enrico. We need each other's bodies." She smiles softly despite her tears. "I can't come without you. Nobody fucks me like you do." She lowers my hand to her breast. "Nobody can get the job done. I need your body. No other will do. How could I go back to another man after having you?"

Memories pass between us. Nothing is off the table with Sophia. There's no denying the woman is on fire in bed.

No.

I take a step back from her. "Stop it."

She reaches for me. "I know you want me."

"You're wrong. I want Olivia."

"No. You *love* Olivia. You *want* me. Your body wants me. You can have it. You don't have to choose between us, Enrico. Why would you choose when you can have the best of both worlds?"

I glare at her, my anger beginning to escalate. A vision of my pathetic father and grandfather with their mistresses comes to mind. "Just stop it."

"Give me two hours a week to please you. I'll do anything you want, my darling," she whispers seductively. "We could meet on your lunch breaks. I can satisfy you, keep you sated and happy. You can go home to her every night, and nobody will ever know. You have needs that I only I can meet. She won't get hurt because she will never find out." She takes my hand in hers again. "Enrico," she whispers. "Baby, come back to me."

I get a vision of my Olivia at home with our child. "Sophia!" I snap.

She rises up onto her toes and kisses me. I pull my face away as I lose control of my anger. "Get out."

Her face falls. "What?"

"Get the fuck out," I growl. "If you ask me for sex ever again, you're fired. In fact, just get out now." I grab her arm and drag her to the door. "Do you fucking understand me?" I open the door, push her out, and I slam it shut. My heart is racing, I'm so angry.

Red is all I see.

I go to the bar, and with a shaking hand, I pour myself a glass of scotch.

I'm rattled that the sound of her bangles affected me physically.

Weak.

I take out my phone and text Olivia to try and calm myself—to remind me of who I am.

How are you feeling, my love?

A reply bounces back.

Better now. Hurry home.
I miss you.
xo

A gun shot rings out outside on the street.

Another one, and then another.

What the fuck?

I run to the window and look down. I can see a commotion and people running out from the building, but I can't see what's happened.

"Attack!" I hear Lorenzo's voice cry out. "Downstairs. Go!"

I run out to see our men running toward the stairwell on high alert.

I grab my gun and follow them. I take the steps two at a time.

Hurry, hurry.

The door opens in the foyer, and my heart drops at the sheer horror before me.

I see Sergio lying in a crumpled heap—a bullet hole in his head. His brains are scattered across the marble floor.

Next to him lies Sophia, her lifeless eyes staring up at the ceiling. She's still clutching her designer bag.

I drop to the floor beside her. "Sophia," I whisper as I pick up her hand. "Sophia, Sophia!" I cry.

A puddle of dark blood pools around her, and I see that she's been shot through the chest.

I shake her. "Wake up, wake up." I look up at the surrounding buildings around us.

My blood runs cold. Dear God.

I look back down as I watch the life slip away from her.

She's dead.

31

Enrico

"THIS WAY, MR. FERRARA."

I'm led into the police station by an officer for routine questioning over Sophia and Sergio's deaths.

I'm shaken to my very core.

Devastated.

They died because of me.

Once in the interview room, I take a seat. "The chief will be here in a moment, sir."

I force a smile. "Thank you."

I sit for five minutes in the silence, my mind going over and over the last hour.

I keep hearing the gunshots—seeing their crumpled bodies. I hear the ambulance sirens in the distance as they arrived.

I watch them being put onto stretchers as paparazzi cameras click and click and click without remorse.

This is a dark day.

I think back to how hard and cold I was to Sophia only moments before she died. *Because of me.*

My chest constricts, and I inhale through a shaky breath.

The door opens and Renaldo, my old friend, comes into view. He's the Chief of Police here in Milan now. He walks in and immediately turns the tape recording off.

"Enrico, my friend." He smiles.

I stand, relieved to see his face. We hug.

"Are you okay?" He frowns as he holds me at arm's length.

"I can't believe this," I whisper.

"My God, we need to talk. I have so much to tell you." I fall into the seat opposite him at the interview desk.

"We've just had a call from the Carabinieri with strict instructions on what I am to say to you." "What?"

"Apparently they are working undercover to try and bring you down. They sent in a young Australian woman as a mole to befriend your fiancée."

I frown and drop my head. Jennifer.

I knew it.

"There's nothing to get me on. I'm completely clean now. You know that."

"Why the hell would you have cocaine delivered to your yacht in Monte Carlo?" He shakes his head in disgust. "You're getting sloppy, Enrico."

"What?" I snap in confusion. "I haven't had cocaine delivered to my yacht."

"They watched Sergio meet with the dealer last week, and then they saw it arrive by ship at your yacht. They know."

I sit back, shocked. *Fucking Sergio.*

"Sergio must have gone rogue." I drag my head down my face. "What are they going to do?"

"They are sitting and waiting for you to move it." I close my eyes as horror dawns on me. "It's not mine."

"Sergio's dead, Enrico. Who do you think they are going to blame?"

"Fuck." I put my head into my hands. "How long until they move in?"

"I don't know, but I can't contact you. I think your phones are bugged. Has this woman had access to your fiancée's phone?"

I stare at him as I think. "Maybe."

Fuck… I warned Olivia. Time and time again, I warned her.

"I have to do the formal interview now." He gestures to the tape recorder. "You good?"

"Thank you for the warning." I shake his hand.

He turns the tape recorder on. "Mr. Ferrara, I'm Chief Inspector Paella. I'll be interviewing you today."

"Hello," I reply flatly, my mind anywhere but on this interview.

"What happened today, sir?"

"I'm not sure." I get a vision of Sophia on the hard, cold concrete.

Sophia.

I walk through the front door of our Milan apartment just after 8:00 p.m.

It's been a long, horrendous day—one that I never want to repeat.

"Hi." Olivia smiles as she rushes to greet me. "Are you okay?"

I wrap her in my arms and hold her tight. "I am now."

I get a vision of Sophia and Sergio on the concrete, and I bury my head into her neck.

We stand in each other's arms for an extended time. Olivia doesn't move and she doesn't speak. She just lets me hold her, which is what I need right now.

I know that Lorenzo had called her to tell her what happened and where I was.

"What did the police say?" she asks as she takes my hand and leads me into the kitchen.

"They just wanted to know what happened." I take my tie off and throw it to the side. "I made a witness statement."

She pours me a glass of wine as she listens.

"Something else came to light at the police station."

"Oh?" She hands over my glass.

"Your friend from the gym, Jennifer and her guy, are undercover federal police."

She frowns. "Huh?"

"They've been sent in to try and get me on something." "Who told you that?" "The Chief of Police, Olivia." I sip my wine, unimpressed that she would doubt me, even for a second.

"Oh my God," she whispers.

"It gets better," I continue. "Sergio bought drugs under my name on credit. He was obviously going to sell them without me knowing. He had them delivered to our yacht in Monte Carlo. The police know all about it."

Her face falls. "What does that mean?"

"It means they are waiting for me to pick them up so they can arrest me for drug possession."

Her eyes widen. "Fuck."

My phone rings. It's Lorenzo. "I have to take this, Bella."

"Sure."

"Hello," I answer as I walk up the hall to my office.

Olivia

After turning the faucet off, I lie back and squeeze the hot water from my sponge, watching as it falls over my chest. The bath is deep and hot, causing the room to fill with steam.

Sophia. Poor Sophia.

My mind is ticking over at a million miles per minute, taunting me of how naïve I really am. I keep going over and over the conversations I had with Jennifer over the last few weeks while at the gym, and the casual questions she'd been asking.

How much did I unknowingly tell her?

The fact that she pretended to be someone else has shaken me to my very core.

A planned operation?

How long were they watching me *before* they sent her in?

Enrico warned me, too. He's warned me on several occasions not to trust anyone, but like a fool, I thought he was being over the top.

There's a reason he is the way he is. Trust; it's one of the purest forms of emotion.

The bathroom door opens and Enrico strides in.

"Hey." He smiles softly.

I fake a smile back. "Hi."

He carefully sits on the side of the bath, as if unsure what to say.

"You getting in with me?" I ask.

He stands, takes his clothes off, and he climbs in at the opposite end of the tub. We sit in silence for a while.

I squeeze the water onto my chest again. There are so many emotions between us, but the one that's clogging up my throat is fear.

"What's going to happen?" I ask him quietly.

He stares at the water, unable to answer my question.

"Sergio had these drugs delivered to your boat, which technically makes them yours now that he's dead."

"I know."

"What's the jail term for this much cocaine possession?"

He inhales deeply, steeling himself. "Thirty years to life."

My eyes fill with tears as I watch him. "You can't go to jail, Rici," I whisper.

He slides down farther and puts his head back against the edge of the bathtub.

I try to get a grasp of what Sergio was planning.

"What was he doing? Why?" I shake my head, words escaping me. "Why did he have those drugs delivered to your boat?"

"Because he knew the dealers wouldn't give him that much credit. I'm guessing his plan was to sell the drugs on his own and then pay the dealers back immediately. He was using my name as a line of credit. The dealers thought they were selling to me, and because they always have sold to Ferrara, there was no hesitation at all."

"But... but they aren't yours," I splutter. "You need to explain the whole thing. Make them understand that you knew nothing about this."

His eyes hold mine. "Possession is nine tenths of the law, Olivia. I have no proof that they aren't my drugs. Do you think a drug dealer is going to come and testify on my behalf?"

"So... what?" I shrug. "Are they just sitting there on the dock waiting for you to go to the boat so they can arrest you?"

"Yes." He nods slowly. "That's exactly what they're doing."

"Then don't go to the boat. Simple."

"They'll only wait a few more days before they move in. If I go to the boat to remove the drugs, I'll be arrested. If I don't go to the boat, they will arrest me anyway."

I put my head into my hands as tears fill my eyes. "This is too much, Enrico," I whisper. "This isn't even your fight. This is Stefano's fight. He wanted this, and then he died and left you in this big fucking mess. And poor Sophia and Sergio." I angrily wipe the tears from my eyes. "If you don't get murdered by that madman, you're going to jail for a crime that you didn't commit." He doesn't try and comfort me. I don't think he can.

Because he knows I'm right.

I stare into space as I search for options. Everything seems so dark and dismal. What are we supposed to do? Rico's eyes are focused on the water, hardened by sadness and anger. "What we need to do is disappear for a while," I say

"And how do we do that? It's a lot easier said than done," he replies.

I think for a moment. "It's not actually a bad idea, to be honest. Why don't we go off the grid for a while? Hide until everything is over with." I smile to myself as I imagine a life on the run.

"I'm not taking the cowards way out and running. I'll handle Lombardi myself." He watches me for a moment. I can see his brain ticking over before he raises an eyebrow.

"What? What are you thinking?" I ask.

"If I were dead..." His voice trails off.

"What?"

"He wouldn't be expecting me."

My eyes widen as I stare at him. "Stop, Enrico. Whatever the hell you are thinking? Just stop it."

He stares into space; his mind miles away.

"This is one big nightmare. I don't know what to do. I don't know what to say, I don't know who to trust. I mean, what in the hell are we supposed to do now? Just wait here until you get arrested?" I huff.

"What we do is we go to bed. We'll get up tomorrow, and then *you* try not to worry. Let me handle this. I'll do the worrying for us both."

My brave man, always taking the load from me.

"We'll fight it in court," he eventually says.

"And winning in court... what will that do?"

He frowns at me, not answering.

"You're okay with the fact that our children will be perceived as criminals? That they'll spend their lives not being able to make new friends? That we will live in this fucking bubble of protection from the outside world?"

"It is what it is."

"What it *is* is fucked up." I stand in a rush, and water sloshes out of the bath onto the floor.

"Olivia," he sighs.

I snatch the towel from the rack, my anger exploding like a volcano.

"Don't you *Olivia* me. I'm going to bed to dream about a life where I'm not in this mess—where the friends I make are there because they actually like me." I flick the towel around my shoulders. "I know why you're not scared about going to prison, Enrico." I dry my back with vigor. "It's because you already live in one."

"Do you think I like this?" he yells.

My eyes well with tears anew at his anger. I'm fragile enough already. I don't need him yelling at me, and I know this isn't his fault, but I have nobody else to blame.

I storm into the bedroom and throw myself onto the bed.

I knew who he was. I knew the life that he led, but I never realized how hard living day-to-day without trusting a single soul was going to be. This isn't who I am. I trust everybody I meet. It's my nature. I like people. I want new people in my life. I'll never make a new friend again after this.

I screw up my face to fight the tears. It's all so overwhelming. I feel like my head is about to explode.

I get under the blankets, bury my face into my pillow, and I let myself cry.

I wake to the feel of a lead ball on my shoulders. It's like I'm carrying the weight of the world. Enrico came to bed late last night but he didn't touch me. He got into bed and turned his back.

I get up and go to the bathroom. Once I'm done, I climb back under the covers.

I'm more hopeful today.

We can fight this.

Good always wins over evil.

Enrico Ferrara is a good man. He's the best.

I snuggle into his back. Eventually he rolls over, and we lie face to face on our sides.

"Hi." I smile softly.

"Hey."

He looks so sad.

"I'm sorry I blamed you," I whisper.

"Don't be. It is my fault." He eyes hold mine and we lie in silence for a while, both deep in thought. He reaches up and trails his finger down my bare arm. "Having second thoughts about a life with me?"

"No." His face is solemn. "Why would you even say that?" I pull him into an embrace. "I love you. I would never have second thoughts about us. This isn't your fault, Rico. You can't help the things that your family have done before you. Tell me about this madman."

He sighs. "About six months ago, this guy started recruiting men." He pauses, as if searching for the right words. "He's burned down five of our brothels. He murdered one of the working girls in Sicily. He even carved his name into her face as a warning to me."

My face falls. "What does he want?"

"The brothels."

"Give them to him."

"It doesn't work like that." He sighs sadly. "He'll beat the girls, get them addicted to drugs, and eventually kill them if they ever try and leave. If I hand him the brothels, I hand over their lives, too." He fiddles with the sheets between us. "And then he'll come after us, anyway. It's a power thing now, and he wants control. The ultimate trophy would be a Ferrara skull."

Fear runs through me. "Did you tell the police this?"

"Yes, they know what he is: the worst of the worst. He's killed about fifteen people so far, and those are only the ones the police know about. They want him, too."

"God, this is one big mess."

His eyes find mine. "This is why I can't let you go to work anymore, Olivia. We can't guard you properly while you're there. Too many people come and go from your building every day. I know this is overwhelming but I promise you, it will pass. These uprises happen from time to time, and we always win. It's just taking a little longer than usual to find this guy."

“Do you think he’s going to try and kill you? And be honest with me… please.”

“I’m not worried about my life.”

My eyes search his as the real reason for his fear presents itself. “You think he’s going to try and kill me next, don’t you?”

He swallows the lump in his throat and tucks a piece of my hair behind my ear. “If anyone wanted to hurt me, that’s the only way they could.”

My eyes fill with tears.

“I’m sorry, baby.” He sighs sadly. “I’m sorry that I dragged you into this life.”

Empathy fills me. “Rici,” I whisper. I pick up his hand and put it over my stomach. “Do you feel this?” I ask.

His hand spreads over my stomach as if it’s magical. Maybe it is.

“We’re having a baby.” I kiss him softly. “And we’re starting our life together—the three of us together. I’ll be fine. You have men everywhere. Nobody can get to us. I’m not going to leave the house until the police find this man, and then we can fight this bogus drug charge. You have the best lawyers who will get you off this. Of course they will because you’re innocent.”

He buries his head into my shoulder and holds me tight in his arms. I can feel his fear in his vise-like grip.

“Promise me you won’t die,” he mutters against my neck.

My vision clouds with tears. What a promise to ask to ask of me. “I promise you.”

He takes my face into his hands and kisses me. His tongue slowly slides against mine, the emotion between us too much to bear.

I love this man. I love how he loves me. I would walk through heaven and hell to feel the way he makes me feel. I hate that he’s scared he’s going to lose me. I hate that he has to go through this. I want to protect him from everything and everyone.

"Now, you promise me something," I say to try and lighten the mood.

"Anything." He rolls over the top of me and lies between my legs. I wrap them around his waist. He begins to slowly slide his dick through my sex as we stare at each other.

"Promise me that when this is all over, we can take a vacation to a secluded beach somewhere." He smiles against my lips. "And we can just be normal and pregnant for a while."

He chuckles, and he slides into my body. "I promise." He pulls out and slides back in deeper. "Sunbathing with you never sounded so good. I can't wait."

32

Enrico

OLIVIA STRAIGHTENS my tie as she sits on the bathroom vanity. She's wearing her white robe, and her hair is in my favorite style of just fucked.

My nerves are at an all-time high. "You're not leaving the house today, are you?"

"No, Rici." She smiles at me. "I'm going to read my book, *What to Expect When You're Expecting*." She wiggles her eyebrows.

I tighten the sash around her waist as my stomach churns. I can't even look her in the eye.

"Hey." She grabs my face and drags it back up to hers. "You okay?"

I nod, although I'm far from okay. I don't want to leave her alone for even a second. "I just have to go into the office for a few hours and then I'll be home. We can watch a movie or something this afternoon."

"Okay."

"If you need anything, call Marly. Nobody else is to come into the house."

She rolls her eyes. "Yes, you've told me already. Trust nobody."

I grab the lapels of her robe and stare down at her. She's so beautiful that my heart constricts. The mere thought of having to live without her terrifies me.

She's going to be okay.

"You need to get going. The sooner you go, the sooner you can get back." She smiles.

I take her into my arms and hold her tight. My eyes close to enjoy the comfort she brings me.

"Ti amo," she whispers into my neck.

"I love you, too." I squeeze her tighter. I don't want to let go.

But I know I have to. I have to go try and clean up this cocaine mess.

I bend, pull her robe apart, and I kiss her stomach tenderly. Our baby is the light in my life—the only thing that matters.

"This is your father speaking," I whisper to it. Olivia giggles as she runs her hand through my hair. "Behave in there today." I kiss her stomach again, and with renewed purpose, I stand and cup Olivia's face. I dust my thumb over her bottom lip as I stare into her big blue eyes. "See you later."

"Bye, baby."

I grab my briefcase, and with a heavy heart, I leave my love.

It's 11:00 a.m.

Lorenzo and I are sitting at my desk, contemplating life. We've been talking for two hours.

A lot has happened in the last seven days. I'm engaged to be married. There's impending fatherhood. Not to forget Sophia's tragic death.

I'm overwhelmed and overwrought, and I had to talk to someone, so I told him everything. Lorenzo knows about the baby, and he knows my deepest fears. He knows I despise my father and grandfather for passing their dark life onto me.

He knows how badly I want Lombardi dead.

He will not get away with this. I will avenge Sophia's death if it's the last thing I do.

My phone rings, and the name Davidoff lights up the screen. It's the police commissioner.

"Hello."

"Enrico, I'm sorry. I couldn't stop it."

"What?"

"A warrant has just been issued for your arrest." I close my eyes and exhale heavily.

Great.

"They're on their way to your office right now. Get the hell out of there."

I hold the phone to my ear for a moment, numb and dumbstruck. In all of my family's history, a Ferrara has never been arrested.

"Thank you." I hang up and stand. "The Carabinieri are on their way. We need to go."

"What are we going to do?" Lorenzo frowns.

My eyes meet his, and I know that everything we just spent the last two hours debating is about to come into fruition.

This isn't a choice anymore. It has to happen.

At least this will give me some time and allow me to come back to Italy unannounced. Then I can kill Lombardi and take him out of action for good.

For Sophia.

Being dead is the perfect alibi.

Diabolical.

But first, we have to get out.

Adrenaline begins to surge through my system, and I know the odds are against us. I dial Olivia's number.

"Hello," she answers.

"It's go time."

"What is?"

"Get your belongings. You have five minutes until you leave. Throw a few things into a bag. "What? Where are we going?"

"Away. Your plan from last night is about to happen. Right now, Olivia. A warrant has been issued for my arrest."

"Enrico," she whispers. "Are you serious?"

"Deadly."

"What... w-what will I pack?" she stammers, her voice rising.

"Whatever the fuck you want. Marly will be waiting outside for you. Hurry."

"Okay."

"Olivia, stay calm, and whatever you do, don't tell anyone anything about this."

"Oh my God, Enrico, are you sure about this? It seems so very drastic."

"We have no choice. We've been backed into a corner. This will just give us some time to prove the drugs aren't mine."

"Yes, yes, okay," she whispers. "You're right." She sighs. "See you soon."

Olivia

I sit in the back of the car and wait. We're parked on the tarmac at the airport.

We were whisked through the security gates and allowed to drive straight through to the Ferrara jet as it was being refueled.

About ten minutes ago, the pilot and a stewardess boarded. They weren't Italian.

Who *were* they? And if Enrico got them at such short notice, how much did he fucking pay?

My heart is in my throat. What if this plan backfires?

What if we don't get away in time?

Will we both be thrown in jail for obstructing justice? God, I feel sick.

"What's taking them so long?" I ask Marly.

He peers up into the rearview mirror. "They'll be here soon."

I close my eyes. Fear has infiltrated every cell of my body. Just getting here without other security was tough enough. I'm being watched for every moment of the day now. Marly lied and said he had to take me to a beauty appointment around the corner in Lake Como. With a few grumbles from the other guards, they finally agreed to let him take me on his own.

Now, we're here at the airport, planning an escape. It's a plan we are being forced into taking. We're lying to everyone. We have no idea who we can trust anymore.

I put my hand over my stomach. Fuck. Imagine if I'm pregnant and in jail. I'll be one of those women you see on cable with no teeth and two black eyes.

My eyes widen. What if I get deported?

"Oh my God, Marly," I gasp. "What in the hell is taking them so long? Call someone."

"Here they are," he says.

I turn and see the black Mercedes pulling in through the gates. My eyes roam to behind their car. Is anyone following?

The car pulls up beside us, and Enrico gets out. He's wearing his customary navy suit and tie. He offers me a calm and sexy smile as he opens my car door.

"Hello, my love."

"Hi." I climb out carefully. How the hell does this man look so in control when this is an out of control fucking situation?

He takes my hand. "Where is your bag?"

"In the trunk."

Marly retrieves it for us and passes it over.

Enrico shakes his hand. "Thank you, Marly... for everything. You will be well promoted within Ferrara for your loyalty." He turns to Lorenzo. "See to it that this happens this week."

"Yes, sir," Lorenzo replies with a nod. "Of course."

Enrico leads me up the stairs of the plane, and I take one last look around.

"Olivia, time is of the essence," Enrico reminds me.

"Hello, Mr. and Mrs. Smith." The captain smiles.

"Hello." I'm quite sure that there is an unwritten rule somewhere to never lie to the pilot who is flying your plane.

Bad Karma or some shit.

I fake a smile as we pass him.

Don't be alarmed. You're just smuggling the mafia boss of Italy out of the country so that he can fake his own death. You won't go to prison or anything if we all get caught.

This is safe, safe, completely safe.

Fuck...

I feel sick.

I make my way up the aisle. The plane is filled with white leather recliner chairs. I've been in it before, although it didn't seem to have the same importance then.

Lorenzo takes a seat near the front, while Enrico and I sit in the middle.

Enrico leans over, straps me in, and then sits back, waiting for take-off.

Meanwhile, I'm perspiring.

The stewardess walks up the aisle. "Can I get you anything, Mr. Smith?" she asks.

"An amaretto and a mineral water with ice, please."

"Of course, sir."

I pinch the bridge of my nose. "Jesus, don't get drunk now," I whisper under my breath.

Enrico smirks over at me and winks.

I'm so envious of his ability to keep his cool during stressful situations. How the hell is he so calm?

The stewardess brings us our drinks, and before long, the plane slowly travels down the runway.

I crane my neck to peer through the window. "I don't see anyone."

Enrico sits back and rests his head on the headrest. "They think I'm in Sicily."

"Why would they think that?"

"Because when they get to my office, that's what they will be told." His sips the amber fluid in the glass.

"Oh." I nod. "Right." I swallow the lump in my throat. "Good idea."

Enrico takes my hand and kisses it. "Go to sleep, bella. You will need your energy later."

Energy later?

I stare at him as my brain fires a million horrible scenarios my way. Running from police. Being tackled to the ground. Being beaten to a pulp. Being thrown in jail.

"Olivia," he says firmly.

I put my head into my hands.

"Would you have preferred I faked my death and left you alone in Italy to grieve?"

"No." I frown at the horrible thought of thinking he was dead. "God, no."

"Then relax. We will be in Roma in eighty minutes, and then we are out. It's under control."

"If you say so."

I peer back out through the window and put my head back into the headrest as the plane launches down the runway at high speed.

Life of crime, here I come.

We're standing on the boat ramp by the ocean, just outside of Roma.

Just Lorenzo, Enrico, and me.

"You have the details?" Lorenzo asks.

"Yes," Enrico replies. "We get this boat to Ponza. Once there, we pick up a car from this address." He takes out a folded piece of paper and opens it. There's an address written down. "It will be rigged with explosives to which I will detonate once we get on a deserted road, leaving us dead... apparently."

Lorenzo passes over two syringes. "Don't forget to take blood and put it in the car. We need DNA evidence you were both in it."

"Of course." Enrico takes the syringes and puts them into

his suit pocket. "Then," Enrico continues, "I will pick up the car from the second location and drive to the runway on the other side of the island, where a plane with an American pilot will be waiting to pick us up."

My eyes widen as I listen to the upcoming events.

Dear God.

I feel the blood drain from my face. This cannot be happening.

Lorenzo leans down and kisses my cheek. "Goodbye, Miss Olivia. I shall see you on your return."

I put my arms around his neck and squeeze him tight. "I'm so grateful that you're helping us."

"It's what family does." He turns and takes Enrico into his arms. "I love you, my son. Be careful."

"I love you, too. Thank you," Enrico says into his shoulder.

We climb into a small boat that has a canopy over it. It's nothing like what Enrico usually travels in, but of course, we're trying to go unnoticed.

I sit down on the bench chair, while Enrico starts the little engine.

Lorenzo gives us a sad smile, and before we can decide against it, we head off into the ocean.

33

Olivia

THE DRONE of the airplane is the only background noise.

I'm exhausted but I can't sleep. Not after what we have been through for the last four days.

We blew up a car and faked our own deaths.

Enrico's cousin from New York, Gabriel, has organized a string of strategic plane hopping all across the world as a way for us to escape being found. We are apparently now off the grid and on the last flight before we arrive at our final destination.

This is the ninth plane we have flown on.

I can't even call Mum because we had to leave our phones in the car. Lorenzo assured me he would let her know that I'm okay. I just hope he didn't forget. He wouldn't. I'm sure he wouldn't.

"Olivia," Enrico says softly. "You must be exhausted."

"I'm okay." I smile softly. I'm really *not*, though. I just can't get my head around the fact that we are now officially criminals.

I'm pregnant and on the run, while my fiancé is wanted for cocaine dealing. He's also in the mafia and, oh my God, this can't be happening.

What is this life?

I mean, I know I wanted adventure, but this is totally out of control now.

Enrico puts his strong arm around me. "Shh," he whispers against my temple. "Ol-i-vi-a. It's going to be okay."

I smile as I close my eyes. His voice is like a Xanax. It's calming, deep, and exactly what I need to hear.

"Go to sleep, bella, our baby needs you to rest."

I snuggle into his shoulder and close my eyes. With Enrico's lips resting against my forehead, I will myself to sleep.

I wake with a start as the engine stops, and I look around.

Enrico is standing and gathering my things.

I rub my eyes. "Are we there?"

He smiles down at me. "Yes, my love. We are here."

"Oh." I peer out the window and see unfamiliar landscape. "Where exactly is… here?"

"The Caribbean."

I frown in surprise. Jeez.

The stewardess opens the door, and we make our way out onto the stairs. A black car sits on the tarmac waiting for us. The driver is standing beside it.

He's wearing a dark suit, and he's tall, handsome, with dark skin.

He smiles and waves us over. "Hello, there," he calls.

Enrico bows his head.

I look between them and try to hide my smile. Enrico is used to his staff being super formal around him.

The man rushes to greet us. "My name is Bobby." He shakes Enrico's hand and then mine.

"Hello."

"This is Bella, and I'm Rici."

"Yes, yes, I know who you are." He laughs as he opens the car door.

No, actually, you don't.

Once we're all in the car, Bobby chats away happily as he drives. Enrico's eyes float over to me and I smile. This is such a weird experience for us—having a chatty driver.

After half an hour, Bobby pulls up at a dock by the ocean. "This way." He smiles as he grabs my things. "The boat is waiting."

"Boat?" I frown over to Rici.

"Last one." He taps me on the ass. "I promise." We board the flashy looking speedboat, and Enrico puts a life jacket on me before he carefully sits me down.

I'm sure he thinks I'm three years old. Either that or that I'm just too exhausted to function. He could be onto something there.

I'm damn right delirious.

Bobby takes off fast. He crosses the waves at record speed, and I hold on for dear life. The boat bounces around, and my hair is flying loose everywhere.

Enrico smirks, and I look around in wonder with a goofy grin plastered on my face.

This is actually pretty cool.

The sun is low over the water now, casting a beautiful shade of pink in the sky. I know there's not long left of daylight.

Eventually, Bobby begins to slow down, and I look up ahead to see white beaches, palm trees, and a huge white mansion that sits along on a small island. It has its own jetty and everything. Bobby slowly pulls up to it, settles the engine, and ties the boat in place.

"Here we are. Your new home." He looks up at the island in awe. "Perfect, isn't she?"

Hope blooms in my chest. *This* is our new home?

Enrico stands and takes my hand. "Come, bella."

He leads me off the boat and down the ramp. The closer we get to the house, the more in awe I become.

It's like a plantation mansion, straight out of a movie set. It's made of white weatherboards with a big balcony around the perimeter, and there is wicker furniture scattered everywhere.

The pool is huge, and the gardens are manicured to perfection.

Enrico leads me into the grand house, and I look around in awe again. The tiles on the floor are black and white. The trimmings are all timber, with huge potted palm trees all around. "Wow."

Enrico turns to Bobby. "Thank you."

Bobby nods with a huge smile. "The kitchen is stocked. The supplies you asked for are in the safe. I will be about two hundred meters away if you need me." He passes over a card. "Here's my number. Do you need anything else, sir?"

"No," Enrico replies.

Bobby gives a polite nod before he leaves us alone.

"This will do," Enrico says.

"You haven't been here before?" I ask.

"No. I bought it sight unseen when I took over two years ago. Just in case..."

"Just in case you needed to hide."

He smirks as his eyes roam over the interior, and he turns his attention back to me. "You. Dinner. Shower. Bed. You're exhausted."

I smile as the hot water streams over my face.

I'm relaxed—so relaxed that I'm bordering on falling asleep. We've been here for three heavenly days, and I am officially in love with island life.

I turn off the shower, get out, and wrap myself in a towel when I feel lips kiss my shoulder from behind.

Hmm.

Enrico pulls my hair around my neck and kisses me with an open mouth, and then he trails his tongue up to my jawline.

My eyes close at the contact.

We haven't had sex for a week. It's the longest we've gone without in our time together. With the worry and the travelling, I was so exhausted that I slept for two days straight when we got here. Time has gotten away from us.

Enrico licks up my neck, and then he bites me sharply.

His breathe quivers on the inhale, and I know what he wants.

Me.

His hands float up to my bare breasts, and he cups them in his hands. His open mouth rests on my neck, sending goosebumps scattering down my spine. He puts his lips to my ear. "I need to taste you."

My eyes close when he bites me again, this time with a little suction. My legs weaken beneath me.

Oh, this man and the way he commands my body to obey him. His touch is like nothing I've ever felt.

No matter how many times we fuck, no matter how many ways he has me, it's never enough. It's never deep enough. He's like a thirst I just can't quench.

He leads me out of the bathroom and lies me on the bed. He spreads my legs.

He loves to look at me like this—laid out and wide open for him.

His.

He takes his cock in his hand as his gaze drops to my sex. He slowly begins to stroke himself as I smile up at him.

"Hmm," he moans. He reaches down to spread my lips open, revealing the soft pink flesh there. His strokes get harder; more urgent.

One of the things Enrico loves about my body is my coloring. With pale skin and fair blonde hair, I'm so very different to him. His jerks take on an almost violent motion.

I smile as I watch him in wonder. I know what he's doing.

He's going to make himself come before we have sex so that he isn't too rough with me.

He leans down and holds my legs wide, and his thick tongue sweeps through my flesh. His eyes close and, unable to help it, he begins to stroke himself again. He really lets me have it. His tongue is lapping and sucking, and the more into it he gets, the harder he strokes himself.

He's eating me with all of his face as he loses control, and his whiskers are burning me.

Oh God, this is Heaven.

This man is Heaven.

He bites my clitoris, and I jump.

He rises over me with dark eyes and jerks himself over my face.

"Ol-i-vi-a... open your mouth," he commands.

My back arches off the bed, and I open my mouth and cup his balls.

He slides in deep, and with one deep suck, I feel his hot seed roll down my throat.

He tips his head back and moans. He's so fucking hot, I can't stand it.

His lip curls, his eyes darken, and I know for certain that only the very tip of his arousal has been tamed.

I'm going to get it tonight, and I'm going to get it good.

He continues to slowly pump me, and I smile around him. "What now?" I whisper.

He bends and takes my face in his hands, dragging me closer to his.

"You've been a very bad girl and you need to be punished." He bites my bottom lip and stretches it out.

"Yes," I whimper.

He picks me up and throws me onto my hands and knees. He slaps me hard on the ass. "Prepare to be fucked… *hard.*"

I laugh out loud.

I love this man.

Enrico

Olivia slowly climbs out of bed.

"Where are you going?" I ask, my eyes flickering to the clock. It's 2:44 a.m.

"I'm just getting a drink. Be back soon."

"Do you want me to get it?"

"No, I'm already up. Go back to sleep." She walks away, and I lie for a moment before I get up and go to the bathroom.

The moon is shining through the side of the curtain. I go

over to readjust it, and I look out over the ocean. It's a full moon tonight, and the blazing white light dances off the water.

It's breathtaking.

I stare at it for a while, and then I see something moving in the back corner of the yard.

I look down and see Maverick the property dog. He's lying in a funny position on the grass. I stare at him and as my eyes adjust to the moonlight. I can see that he's covered in blood. I think he's been shot.

Fuck.

They've found us.

34

Enrico

ADRENALINE SURGES THROUGH MY BODY. I rush to my bedside drawers to put a pair of jeans on. I take out two guns, and I tuck one in the back of my waistband.

I walk over to the bedroom door and listen. I can't hear Olivia. She should be coming back up the stairs by now. I hold the gun in front of me and make my way up the hall before I tiptoe down the stairs.

The lights are off. It's completely dark.

I know for a fact that Olivia would have turned them on. She hates the dark.

He's got her already.

My heart hammers hard inside my chest as I creep down the stairs.

I hold the gun up to my chest, and I slink around the corner. The room is dark. I can't see anything.

What the fuck is going on?

I walk out into the kitchen where the light is on and a glass of water sits on the bench.

She's been interrupted.

I carefully go to the kitchen drawer and take out the sharpest carving knife I can find. I eye it, watching as the blade glistens in the moonlight.

Adrenaline surges through me, and I look around. "Olivia?" I call. "Where are you, baby?"

Silence...

I continue to creep into the living room.

"Olivia!" I call.

Where the fuck are they?

I clutch my gun with white-knuckle force. I move around another corner, and that's when I see them in the dark.

My eyes can't focus properly, so I flick the light on.

Olivia's scared eyes hold mine. A gun is wedged against her neck. Lombardi is holding it tightly in his grip.

I raise my gun and point it at his head. "Leave her out of this," I growl. "Your gripe is with me."

Lombardi gives me a slow, sarcastic smile. "It is." He jams the gun hard into Olivia's neck, and she cries out.

"Let her go!" I demand, clutching the gun.

"I don't think so." He sneers. It makes me take a step forward. "You're in my way." He pulls Olivia's hair and she screams out in pain. It only makes him smile darkly. "I need you gone, Enrico."

I readjust the grip on my gun. "Let her go." I snarl. "Mark my words. You will die tonight, fucker."

"*You're* the one who's going to die."

Olivia's eyes widen as she looks at something to the side of us.

I glance over and see Jennifer and Diego standing behind the wall in the kitchen.

They have their guns drawn. Jennifer points to outside and holds up three fingers.

There are three more of them outside.

Fuck.

I take a step forward, and I take off the safety as I take aim. "What kind of coward kills a woman?"

Lombardi lets out a low, evil laugh. "One that's bringing a Ferrara out of hiding. It's called bait, pretty boy."

"Sophia?" I sneer. "Why did you have to kill her? She had nothing to do with me."

"Oh, your whore? How sad." He tsks. "Maybe if you'd done what I said she'd still be alive. You only have yourself to blame." He presses the gun harder into Olivia's neck, and she cries out again. "Put the gun down, Ferrara."

"And Sergio?"

"Ah, my boy Sergio. I didn't mean to kill him." He shrugs. "Pity, that."

Contempt drips from me as I connect the dots. The puzzles finally fall into place. "Why are your drugs on my fucking yacht, Lombardi?" I snarl.

He laughs out loud like a madman. "You don't think I'm stupid enough to get them delivered to mine, do you?"

I grip the gun impossibly tighter.

"Perfect plan." He smiles darkly. "Set you up, wait for you to fake your death, and then kill you both for real. The world already thinks you're dead, Ferrara." He presses the gun harder and Olivia whimpers. "How can I kill a dead man?"

"Let her go," I demand.

"Put the gun down and I'll think about it."

I know that if I don't do as he asks, he's going to shoot her. I also know that he's got back up outside.

Fuck.

I can't win this fight while standing here like this. I need to move it along.

I bend and slowly put the gun down in front of me on the floor.

"Get your hands up and kick it over to me," he orders.

I lift my hands and kick it toward him.

A click sounds from the side as someone else takes aim.

A gunshot rings out.

One of Lombardi's men falls.

I take this momentary distraction as a cue, and I rush them. I grab Lombardi's gun and we struggle over it. It fires in the air. I hit him in the head hard, and his grip loosens. I push Olivia out of the way, and she falls to the floor.

"*Move*!" I yell at her.

The gun is held above his head as we fight over it.

I punch him hard in the face again and again.

I have never hated anyone as much as I hate this man.

I hear another five rounds of gunfire from Jennifer and Diego as Lombardi and I struggle on the floor.

I'm hit across the head with a vase from behind as another man attacks me. Olivia screams, and I momentarily lose focus at the sound of her pained voice.

Lombardi gets up and runs.

I roll onto my stomach and take aim at Lombardi. I fire off a single shot that hits him in the leg just as he disappears out of the door. Then I turn and shoot his other man who is moving over me. Once clear, I jump to my feet, pick Olivia up, and I look in the direction after Lombardi.

Did I hit him? Did I get him?

"Watch her," I order Jennifer.

Without another thought, I take chase and run out after Lombardi. I can see the trail of blood guiding me closer.

Yes! I got him.

The trail of blood disappears into the nearby forest. I reach around to the back of my pants to find the other gun is gone.

Fuck.

I only have the knife now.

I take it out and clutch it tightly as I follow the trail of blood into the darkness.

And then, without the moonlight to guide me, I lose his trail.

I stand at the edge of the forest for a moment and I slowly walk in.

I have no idea if he's still armed. I know I took one gun from his grip, but I don't know if he had anything else on him.

The echoing of crickets and the noise of the waterfall in the distance are the only sounds.

I step slowly through the dense foliage.

I don't have shoes on, and it's difficult to walk on the uneven and sharp ground.

My eyes scan the dense landscape. Tall trees block the moonlight. Out here, it's nearly pitch-black.

Where are you?

He would have seen me walk in with the moonlight behind me. I duck down into the foliage and crawl out of sight.

I sit still for ten minutes and slowly allow my eyes to

adjust. I can soon see a lot more than I could before. I pick up a small rock and hurl it as far away as I can. It hits a tree a fair distance away with a bang.

I slowly climb to my feet and scan the forest as I grip the knife in my hand.

I see a shadow on the hill, and I creep toward it.

It's him. I can see his chest sucking in air as he gasps for breath. He's losing a lot of blood.

Does he have a weapon?

I hunch down and make my way toward him.

"Ferrara!" he cries.

I stay silent.

"Ferrara! Let's make a deal!" he calls, his voice echoing over the valley.

He's bleeding out and he knows it.

I throw a rock and it lands next to him. He jumps back in fear.

He's unarmed.

I stand up and show myself, knife in hand as I slowly walk toward him.

His eyes hold mine. "We can be great together. We can join forces—be the strongest syndicate the world has ever seen." He's wet with perspiration, and he's desperate.

I hunch down beside him. "You're dying, Lombardi."

He pants.

"I guess you're not so lucky after all."

"Enrico," he whispers. "I've always admired you."

My skin prickles. I know he would say anything to try and gain my sympathy. I glare at the lying bastard sitting propped up against the tree.

Die.

"We could run the biggest crime syndicate in the world.

With your connections…and my…" He coughs, and blood splutters from his mouth.

His face falls as he realizes what's happening, and he reaches out for me. "Help me."

I kneel down and watch the life slowly drain out of him.

Eye to eye.

I want to see the moment he passes. I want to taste the victory of retribution.

"Enri…" He coughs, and a large amount of blood comes from his mouth.

His face falls and he grabs for me again. He lets out a pained gargling sound.

I watch on in fascination.

I've never watched someone die before.

I've seen people pass, but I've always fought to save them.

I've been frantic with words of encouragement and prayer.

I envision myself dragging his head back by the hair and slicing his throat.

I would have loved to have taken his life myself, but that would have been too kind.

He deserves to suffer.

His eyes still… and I smile.

His head drops, and I know he's gone.

I stare at him and take a moment to reflect on Sophia.

I get a vision of her with her curves and her long dark hair. Perhaps in another life she could have made me happy.

"Enrico!" Jennifer calls.

I stand, and with a heavy heart, I turn to her. She has her gun drawn.

"He's dead."

I walk past her and back to the house where two local

police cars have arrived. Their siren lights are flashing, lighting up the sky.

I find Olivia crying and wrapped up in a blanket. Her face lights up when she sees me, and she stands.

"Oh, thank God!" she cries.

"It's okay," I whisper as I take her into my arms. "He's gone now."

She puts her head onto my shoulder and cries as Jennifer walks back into the room.

"What are you doing here?" I ask.

"I believe *thank you* is the word you're looking for," she says sarcastically.

I roll my eyes. I hate this woman with a passion.

"I was following Lombardi. I had no idea he was coming for you." She shakes her head as she looks at the smashed-up room. "We have enough evidence to clear your name, Enrico. I'll organize a transfer back to Italy for you both first thing in the morning."

I look down at the beautiful woman in my arms. "No."

"No?" She frowns.

"I think I might like to stay dead for a little while longer." I smile down at Olivia. "I promised my girl a holiday."

EPILOGUE

Olivia

Four months later

The sea breeze blows through my hair, and I look into the big brown eyes opposite me.

Enrico and I are standing on the sandy beach outside our house. We're as happy as happy can be.

It's our wedding day.

I'm in a tight, crochet white dress with my baby bump proudly on display. My hair is down, and I have a yellow flower tucked behind one ear. Enrico is wearing white hippy clothes and is completely barefoot. It's so unlike Enrico Ferrara.

But so Australian.

We had to change locations after Lombardi found us.

After the ordeal I went through, Enrico decided that he wanted to have more time alone before we went back to Italy.

He wanted my pregnancy to be as stress-free as possible. At first, it was going to be for just one month. That then turned into two, two turned into three, and now here we are, living on an island just off the Australian North Coast.

Of course, our mothers know we are safe... but nobody else just yet. We're flying completely under the radar.

Giuliano is in training, while Lorenzo is currently running Ferrara.

For now, we can stay where we are in our stress-free little bubble.

Alone and happy.

Without enemies, bodyguards, or family.

We have never had this in our relationship: time alone.

It's so precious, and we are savoring every second together.

We talk, laugh, and lie in the sun. We make love endlessly. This time alone in our pregnancy is his gift to me, and we are so looking forward to our baby coming along in eight weeks.

Life is surprisingly... normal.

That is, until you see the mansion we live in. Enrico couldn't live in any other type of home.

Luxury is who he is. He's a Ferrara to the bone.

The priest continues, "Do you, Enrico Ferrara, take Olivia Reynolds to be your lawful wife?"

Enrico blinks back his tears, and I smile softly. He's the most sentimental man I have ever known, and most definitely a far cry from the hardened mafia boss that everybody else knows.

I get the best of him.

His undying love and everything we have been through together has all been worth it to get to where we are right now.

To where we are supposed to be.

This isn't how we planned to do things, but we've learnt that no matter what happens in the world, us being together is all that matters.

It's important to him that we be married before the baby arrives. Today is our beach wedding. We will have a Catholic ceremony in The Pantheon when we get home to Italy.

Our sacred place.

"To have and to hold, in sickness and in health, for as long as you both shall live?"

Enrico gives me a broad, beautiful smile, and I melt. "I will." He slowly slides the gold band onto my finger, and it's my turn to blink back the tears.

"And do you, Olivia Reynolds, take Enrico Ferrara to be your lawful wedded husband?"

Enrico gives me a sexy wink, and I giggle despite my tears.

"To have and to hold, in sickness and in health, for as long as you both shall live?"

"I will." I slide the thick gold band onto Enrico's finger, and he smiles proudly.

"You may kiss your bride."

We both laugh. Enrico leans in and softly kisses me. It's full of emotion, love, and hope.

It's perfect.

Just like him.

My love, my life, *my Italian.*

Two years later

The sound of the music floats through the air. I look around for my family. We are at a local fête. Or as we call it here... a carnival.

People are dancing in colorful costumes, and there are food

stalls everywhere. The air is filled with laughter; so much laughter.

I see a little head bopping around up ahead, and I smile.

Enrico is standing and talking to three of his friends. Our son is high on his shoulders.

Romeo is two now, and he's the spitting image of his father with big brown eyes, and dark hair full of curls. He's also as smart as a whip and as cheeky as hell.

I stand and watch them for a while. Enrico has a hold of Romeo's legs, and Romeo is laughing and dancing with another little boy who sits on his father's shoulders while the men talk.

The other man says something, and Enrico throws his head back and laughs out loud. Romeo reaches down and pulls his hair.

Enrico winces in pain.

I laugh. This child is mischievous. He's also the absolute apple of his father's eye.

Enrico adores him.

I'm pregnant again—six months now—and healthy and happy.

Life's good. It's better than good. Amazing.

We'll go back to Italy one day, but not yet.

Enrico wants all of his children to have this childhood. He misses Italy desperately, but not at the cost of his children's safety and freedom.

He gets it now. He understands his father and why he did what he did. It took a long time, and he's read that letter his father left for him many times over. But I know that, on many levels, he's grateful that he didn't know the finer details back then. He's grateful that his father stayed with his mother for the sake of his children, and to be there for her.

We're both grateful that we survived what we did.

Enrico's eyes meet mine across the park and he says goodbye to his friends before he walks over to me. He bends and kisses me softly, and then takes my hand in his.

I look up to the little boy on his father's shoulders.

"Ciao, amori miei! Sei pronto per tornare a casa, Romeo?" I ask. *Translation: Hello, my loves. Are you ready to go home, Romeo?*

"Si, mamma." He nods.

Enrico reaches down and puts his hand over my stomach.

"Ti ho detto che sei bellissima oggi?" he asks. *Translation: Did I tell you that you look beautiful today?*

I giggle as I kiss his big beautiful lips.

"Una o due volte." *Translation: Once or twice.*

We speak Italian at home now. It's Romeo's first language.

We make our way to the car.

"Dobbiamo fermarci all'ufficio postale andando verso casa. Il mio pacco è arrivato," Enrico says. *Translation: We have to stop off at the post office on the way home. My parcel has arrived.*

I smirk. "Cosa hai comprato?" *Translation: What did you buy now?*

He gives me a sexy wink as he loads Romeo into the SUV.

Enrico still buys designer everything, he just does it online now.

I'm the best dressed woman in Australia.

You can take the man out of Italy.

You can't take the Italy out of the man.

The End.

FERRARA - COMING SOON

Giuliano

I sit at the desk in Enrico Ferrara's office.

He was murdered last week, and I don't know why I've been brought here. I'm nervous that my mother made me come.

Does this have something to do with our fight last week at the library?

An elderly man sits down at the desk beside me, while two other men are sitting at the desk, also.

"My name is Lorenzo, and this is Andrea and Matteo."

I nod. "Hello."

Lorenzo exhales heavily. "There are some things that you don't know, son. You have been protected up until now, but with the passing of Enrico Ferrara, you must be told of your heritage."

I frown.

"Your father—"

"Leave my father out of this," I snap.

He glares at me, unimpressed that I interrupted him. "Your father's name wasn't Lindon."

I frown harder now.

"Your father was Giuliano Ferrara."

"What?"

Lorenzo and the other men exchange worried looks.

"It's a very complicated story." He pauses as he searches for the right wording. "Giuliano, your father lived a double life—one with your mother and you, and one with his wife and their three children." "What? That's ridiculous!" I scoff. "He wasn't married to someone else. You have the wrong man."

"We don't. These are your two brothers, Giuliano." He gestures to the two men and they smile sadly. "Andrea and Matteo."

My eyes flicker between the three of them. "You're lying." I stand abruptly.

Lorenzo stands, too, and he pushes me back into the chair. "Your other brother was murdered last week. His name was Enrico Ferrara."

My eyes widen as I begin to hear my heartbeat in my ears.

The floor moves beneath me.

"You have been left in your father's will to take over management of the Ferrara family empire."

My face falls. "It's okay," Andrea says softly. "You won't be alone, Giuliano."

"We will be here every step of the way to train you and to help you with the transition," Lorenzo says.

I stare at him as the walls close in.

That means...

She's my sister.

AFTERWORD

Thank you so much for reading.
You are making my dreams come true.

Find me at tlswanauthor.com

ACKNOWLEDGMENTS

There are no words meaningful enough to thank my wonderful team.

I don't write my books alone. I have an army.

The best army in the world.

Kellie, the most wonderful PA on Earth.

You are amazing. Thank you for all that you do for me.

Keeley, not only are you an amazing daughter, but you're now a wonderful employee. Thank you for wanting to work alongside me. It means a lot.

To my wonderful beta readers: Mum, Vicki, Am, Rachel, Nicole, Lisa K Lisa D, Nadia, and Charlotte. Thank you. You put up with a lot and never whine, even when I make you wait for the next chapter. How I got so lucky to have you come into my life, and to be able to call you my friends, I will never know.

To Rena, you came into my life like a breath of fresh air and somehow adopted me.
Thank you for believing in me. You're the Ying to my Yang, or the Ting to my Tang.

Vic, you make me better, and your friendship is so valued.

Virginia, thank you for everything you do for me. It is so appreciated.

To my motivated mofos. I love you to bits. You know who you are.

To Linda and my PR Team at Forward. You have been with me since the beginning
and you will be with me until the end. Thank you for everything.

To my home girls in the Swan Squad. I feel like I can do anything with you girls in my corner. Thanks for making me laugh every single day.

This year I'm adding someone new to my list.
Amazon.
Thank you for providing me with an amazing platform to bring my books to life. I am my own boss. Without you, I wouldn't have the job of my dreams.
Your belief and support of my work this last year has been nothing short of amazing.

And to my four reasons for living, my beautiful husband and three children.

Your love is my drug, my motivation and my calling.
Without you, I have nothing.
Everything I do is for you.

ALSO BY T L SWAN

Stanton Adore #Stanton book 1

Stanton Unconditional #Stanton book 2

Stanton Completely #Stanton book 3

Stanton Bliss – The epilogue #Stanton book 4

Marx Girl

Gym Junkie #Men of Marx book 1

Dr Stanton #Dr Stanton book 1

Dr Stanton the Epilogue #Dr Stanton book 2

Mr Masters #Mr book 1

Mr Spencer #Mr book 2

Find Me Alastar #Alastar book 1

Play Along

The Stopover

STANTON ADORE EXCERPT

AVAILABLE NOW - FULL SERIES COMPLETED

"Yes I'll have a tall latte, double shot" Joshua smiles.

"I'll have a skim cap please." The waitress scribbles on her pad and leaves us alone.

He rests his elbows on the table and links his hands together under his chin, waiting for me to speak first. His eyes have a mischievous glow to them.

"So Josh, tell me about your life?"

He shrugs his shoulders. "What do you want to know?"

"I hear you're wealthy."

He smiles. "In some things."

I tilt my head on the side. "What do you mean?"

"Well, I have money. It depends on your definition of wealthy."

"Oh, I suppose. What's your definition?" I ask, surprised.

He shrugs again. "Happily married, healthy kids."

The waitress returns with our order.

Smiling, I rest my chin on one hand while I find myself swooning at his feet. "Are you dating?" I ask.

He scrunches up his nose, "Hell no." Our drinks arrive and the waitress' eyes linger a little long on Mr. Orgasmic here. I narrow my eyes at her. Ok, enough, buzz off.

"You." I frown.

"Huh?"

"Are you dating?" I ask.

"No, nothing like that. Mum told me you had a boyfriend."

I nod a little embarrassed. "Um, ex-boyfriend," I murmur.

"What happened? Why did you break up?"

I smile. He smiles. "I see you're still a shit liar."

"I hoped you hadn't heard about that," I wince.

"What? Heard that some poor bastard asked you to marry him and you knocked him back and dumped his sorry ass?"

I put my hand over my face in embarrassment. "It sounds cold when you put it like that." I peek out from behind my hands to see him smirking at me.

"What happened?" he asks.

"We were never going to work out. I've never been so shocked in my life as the day he proposed. It was awful." His thumb is under his chin and he is wiping the side of his pointer across his lips as he listens, his gaze locked on mine.

"Why wouldn't you have worked out?"

"We weren't ...compatible."

He raises his eyebrows. "Compatible," he repeats.

Why did I say that?

"You mean sexually?" His eyes darken with an emotion I'm familiar with. Arousal.

"Among other things," I quickly add. I suddenly feel very uncomfortable.

"Why aren't you married?" I blurt out.

He smiles a slow sexy smile. "I haven't found anyone who fits the job description."

"What's the job description?" I breathe.

His eyes bore into mine with an intensity that heats my blood. "Someone who fucks like a slut, with the morals of a nun."

I choke on my coffee. Of all the things I thought he would say, that was definitely not it. I feel a frisson of uneasiness creeping up on me. "You can't be serious?" I gasp.

"Absolutely." He nods as he takes a sip of his latte, his eyes not leaving mine.

"You want to marry a slut?"

He nods again. "It depends what your definition of a slut is. What do you think a slut is?" he asks.

"Someone who will sleep with anyone," I reply.

He nods and takes another sip of his latte. "You see I think a slut is a woman who loves to fuck."

I swallow the large lump in my throat. His voice has dropped to a low husky sound, one that is screaming to my subconscious. He continues, "I couldn't be with a mousy woman who doesn't love to fuck as much as I do. I have an insatiable appetite for sex." He licks his lips. "High maintenance so to speak." His eyes burn into me once again, silently daring me to say something. His eyes drop to my lips and want pools in my stomach. "The woman I marry will have to endure hours and hours of being tied to our bed, legs spread wide while I pleasure her with my tongue and fuck her with my hands. Then put up with me continually driving into her tight cunt with my

cock so hard that she won't know where I end and she begins. Constantly. She would have to love taking me orally, vaginally and anally.... repeatedly." He gazes at me again and steeples his hands under his chin.

For the love of God, my mouth has gone dry.

"Can I take your order, love?" I jump, oh shit did she just hear that?

"Um, bacon and eggs please, and an orange juice." I'm embarrassed and put my head down to hide my blush.

"I'll have the same." He smirks a sexy smile at me.

Bloody hell.

Ok, my brain has fried. I can't even speak as I visualize exactly what he has explained to me. Orally, vaginally and anally......shit.

That sounds exactly what I want to do today. Is he trying to drive me out of my frigging head? He's not playing fair.